AT MAUNSTON QUAY

Other Works by Ian Gouge

Novels and Novellas

The Opposite of Remembering - Ian Gouge, Coverstory books, 2020
At Maunston Quay - Ian Gouge, Coverstory books, 2019
An Infinity of Mirrors - Ian Gouge, Coverstory books, 2018 (2nd ed.)
Losing Moby Dick and Other Stories - Ian Gouge, Coverstory books, 2017
The Big Frog Theory - Ian Gouge, Coverstory books, 2018 (2nd ed.)

Short Stories

Degrees of Separation - Ian Gouge, Coverstory books, 2018
Secrets & Wisdom - Ian Gouge, Paperback, 2017

Poetry

The Myths of Native Trees - Ian Gouge, Coverstory books, 2020
First-time Visions of Earth from Space - Ian Gouge, Coverstory books, 2019
After the Rehearsals - Ian Gouge, Coverstory books, 2018
Punctuations from History - Ian Gouge, Coverstory books, 2018
Human Archaeology - Ian Gouge, KDP, 2017
Collected Poems (1979-2016) - Ian Gouge, KDP, 2017

Anthologies

Triple Measures - Ian Gouge, K.M.Miller, Tom Furniss, Coverstory books, 2020
Oak Tree Alchemy - Ian Gouge and Others, Coverstory books, 2019
Play for Three Hands - Tom Furniss, Ian Gouge, K.M.Miller, 1981

IAN GOUGE

AT MAUNSTON QUAY

First published in paperback format by
Coverstory books, 2019 (this edition 2022)

ISBN 978-1-9997840-8-9

ebook 978-1-9993027-5-7

www.iangouge.com

www.coverstorybooks.com

Chapter 1

The sea is the only constant. Grey waves indulge a brief white collar when they curl and fold inwards, foaming as they stretch up the shallow incline of the beach, striving to reclaim the land. Accompanied by the rhythmic pummelling of the shore, theirs is an onslaught that fears nothing in its perpetual motion. The bay waits, then surrenders just a little to each wave. One might stand and watch the cycle forever, every breaker unique, every moulding of the beach and its contours imperceptibly different. And because the threshold here is made of sand and not shingle, the transformation is almost invisible, indescribably subtle.

From both the top of the modest dunes that partly frame the beach and a similarly modest headland to your right, a promontory perhaps no more than fifty feet high, the gentle arc of the shoreline stretches towards you. Dressed in rough scrub and bushes made hardy by the wind and the fret, the cape is a darker green than one might have anticipated. The headland - known locally as Simon's Crag, though for what reason even the locals cannot seem to say - turns slightly away from you and inland a little where its profile falls. There you see the first of the few trees which lead to a small copse near its base. From here, only their canopy is visible, the bulk of their trunks hidden beyond a false horizon, one bookend to the next parcel of land. There are rocks at the seaward base of Simon's Crag, but these soon give way to the sand which eventually peters out further to your left in an untidy accumulation of more rocks and less significant, unnamed outcrops. End-to-end, the bay is perhaps little more than a quarter of a mile long.

Halfway between its two extremes and just to your right where the beach is at its narrowest - perhaps a hundred and seventy or eighty yards deep at most - the finger of a jetty points itself towards the sea. Although the tide has begun to recede now, two thirds of the jetty still has its feet in the water. Even at low tide it is rare that more than half the jetty's foundations might be considered dry. The wooden steps up to it from the landward end are never quite submerged; the tide, even at its fullest, being unable to get that far. Visitors to the bay - were there ever any of great number - might stand here and watch the sea for hours and remark how little the tide moves. They might compare this phenomenon with other places - such as Weston-Super-Mare or Morecambe - where the distance between high- and low-water can be measured in the hundreds of yards if not in the significant fractions of miles. But precisely here, on a completely different coast, that traverse is perhaps thirty or forty yards at most. It is as if the sea and the land have agreed a truce and are simply going through the motions, expending as little effort as possible. Such an accord could only exist through the benevolence of the water, for there is yet a sense that in this small, quiet engagement, the sea could yet be all-consuming should it wish to be.

From where you are standing at the top of the dunes, you can make out vague paths down to the beach - as much as sand will allow the definition of anything as specific as a path. The rough tracks downwards from the top of the headland are, however, more clearly visible, as if the land has been roughly gouged by some narrow implement, a palette knife taken to the green. The path from the top forks about a third of the way down. The left-hand track zig-zags towards the beach and the rocks behind which it seems to disappear, though that is just a trick of perspective. The other seems to fall almost arrow straight until it is met by the concrete plinth upon which a short terrace of three cottages sits. This structure, guarded by low railings, is punctuated with steps down to the sand. You could be forgiven for imagining the dwellings were located there in some Canute-like challenge to the elements, and that, by remaining there still, were proof of successful defiance. They are small, unremarkable whitewashed cottages you might easily lift and transpose to a myriad of other locations on almost any coast; and yet they seem to be perfectly set just here, facing the small bay, overseeing the empty jetty, waiting for something to happen.

The cottage at this end of the terrace is extended to its side with a large outbuilding whose wooden doors, closed at this moment, not only face the sea but a small slabbed ramp which leads down to the beach. This rough slipway, which immediately gives the impression of being inadequate or under-used or both, also serves to delimit the extent of the dunes, and if you were to walk across them from where you stand, perhaps traversing twenty yards to your right, you could easily find your way onto it. That an old green Land Rover is parked immediately outside this sombre panelled extension offers a counterpoint which suggests the structure on which the cottages stand is less shallow than first appears from the level at which you are viewing it, perspective again playing tricks with your eyes. If anything, when you pause to take all these clues into consideration, they only serve to embellish a notion that the cottages represent an end point, the full extent of the tentacles of something else.

Having part-way turned from the sea to examine the cottages, if you continue to rotate clockwise you can make out two small flat roofs which, though indistinct from here, are in fact the tops of the waiting rooms at Maunston Quay station. The dunes being where they are, it is easy to reconcile how the beach and the railway feel mutually exclusive, neither one visible from the other. Of course, wherever you stand, the sea betrays its presence through the sound of the waves upon the shore, and making your way along the path towards the station (a path of increasingly clear definition as you head away from the beach), you can still hear the tug of the tide; a sound which is only trumped by the passing of a train every hour or so. After very little distance, the dunes' elevation falls and the sand gives way to a roughly made tarmac path.

Having now dropped to a companionable altitude, you can see the composition of the station more clearly. There are two platforms, each housing a small open shelter made from the same white-painted wood panelling as that which goes to make up the fencing at the rear of each platform. Other than these constructions, the station is bare, the only ornament being a mechanical signal at either end, one of which is currently in the 'off' position suggesting that a train is due to pass through soon. You may be surprised that these have not yet been converted to modern electric signals, but perhaps on reflection you sense this may be fitting and in-keeping with the general ambience of the place. It feels something of a backwater, a station the rest of the network has forgotten about, or even worse, one that should have fallen under Beeching's terrible axe in the sixties.

But that would be to jump to an erroneous conclusion. Ten years prior to the day on which you are observing Maunston Quay station, trains would have been stopping here regularly throughout the day; at least hourly in each direction, sometimes every thirty minutes. As time passed, however, the railway company recognised that fewer and fewer people were embarking and disembarking here, and so the frequency of the trains' stopping was reduced to once every two hours, and then perhaps three times daily. For the last two years, Maunston Quay has been a request stop, its few regular users (regarded as 'commuters' only in the very loosest sense) being a handful of people from the village who work part-time in the towns both up and down the line. In the summer, when the weather is good, small handfuls of holiday makers occasionally take the train to be able to access the beach (as there is no convenient parking nearby), but such people seldom return as the absence of facilities almost always sees them cutting their day short and returning from whence they came not a little frustrated by the whole experience.

Arriving at street level where the path from the beach meets a narrow pavement, you are within just a few yards of the nearest platform. And it is here that you notice three things. The first is that the platform signs which announce "Maunston Quay" are immaculately painted in burgundy and cream, and are spotlessly clean. The second is that, to your left, there are a pair of level-crossing gates. Being of the wood-and-mesh variety, these are perfectly in keeping with the era of the station's signalling. They are also - as if to support the validity of the 'off' signal already noted - closed, though whether to protect passers-by from the train or vice versa you are suddenly not quite sure. The third thing you notice is that there is a car waiting at the gates, and as the car is pointing away from the sea it can only have originated from outside one of the cottages. Perhaps at this point you might instinctively look over your shoulder and back toward where you now know the narrow road ends. If you did, you would see part of the first cottage's extension, and part of the frontage and most of the roofs of all three. That you cannot now see the entirety of the terrace surprises you a little, as you did not realise that the dunes intruded inland quite so far. Nor did you realise that they were quite so high, that the road from the station curved subtly to the right, nor that the distance to the cottages from the station is as far as it now appears.

These are easy mistakes to make when taking in a place for the first time. But you are oriented now, and so the scene is set.

Chapter 2

Lewis Airy has turned off the car's engine. Any annoyance he felt finding himself approaching the crossing gates just as they were closing has largely left him, primarily because he knows the train should have already passed; he could not have anticipated its being late, and so that has exonerated him. Not that he is in any hurry. He had phoned Shirley earlier in the day to place his grocery order and is confident that, having had plenty of time to select and pack his goods, there will be two or three filled carrier bags waiting for him at the shop. It is an arrangement that had come about by accident, primarily as a result of a conversation with Oscar in the pub one evening when they found themselves discussing the various services offered by major supermarket chains. "We could do that for you, now and again," he had said, without consulting his sister. Perhaps he had been scared Lewis might experiment with a delivery from one of the retail giants and end up loving it; they could ill afford to lose any custom. Hence the lack of urgency and Lewis's acceptance of his situation. In any event, he knows the train will rattle through without stopping and the gates open soon enough.

For no particular reason, he glances in his rear view mirror and catches sight of the cottages' frontage. For a second he wonders whether or not he has locked his door, and then laughs silently at himself. It is something he always worries about these days, even though he has never left it unlocked. And if he had, who would there be to burgle him? He looks back at the gates and then up toward the platforms. He checks his watch; an automatic gesture. Hearing an unexpected squeal, his attention is drawn back to the station only to see a train slowing to a halt. He is not surprised by the train itself, of course. It is one of the ancient two-car diesel units that they now almost exclusively use on the line; had it been otherwise, then that might have been sufficient to pique his interest. But it is the fact it has stopped at all which is the conundrum. He checks his watch again to confirm he hasn't lost a couple of hours somewhere and that it is not what might loosely be called 'going home time', the small window of each day where the village's two or three commuters would actually be returning from work. He sees no-one waiting on the platform which, he surmises, can only mean that someone is about to get off. Perhaps, he thinks, it may be Maisie who has for some reason cut short her day in the library. If so, he will give her a lift to where she lives on the other side of the village. It is not far for her to walk, but making the offer is the least he can do for a friend. With someone to look out for, Lewis gives the train a little more attention than he might otherwise.

After a few moments of inactivity, a door opens at the far end and a figure, a woman, steps down onto the platform. Lewis sees instantly that it is not Maisie. The woman is dressed in a shortish red outdoor jacket - the all-purpose kind that is both water- and wind-proof. Over one shoulder is slung a large bag, something akin to a rucksack. Once she is on the platform, she turns and pulls a dark blue suitcase from the train, sets it down beside her, says something to someone who is clearly remaining on the train, then slams the door shut. Lewis watches her as she establishes her bearings, then pulls up the handle of the case and starts walking towards the platform exit. He can tell by the way she is scanning the scene that she has never been to Maunston Quay before; her head turns one way and then the other, eyes trying to assimilate as much information as possible. By the time the train has started moving and has cleared the level crossing, she has reached the steps down from the platform. His attention momentarily distracted by the opening of the gates, Lewis realises that he has been staring at her from the moment she emerged from the train, and so returns his own gaze to the barrier swinging clear in front of him, his hand automatically reaching for the ignition and turning the key.

If she looked at the car as it started, he does not know as he keeps his eyes firmly fixed on the road ahead as it gradually appears beyond the crossing. Part of him wants to open the window and to ask her if she needs help, but just as this thought comes to him he glances in his side mirror and sees her heading along the rough path towards the dunes. It isn't any of his business anyway, he tells himself. He waits for a moment before moving off, just to see if she is going to take the road to the cottages; but no, she goes left onto the dune path. It is as if seeing the sea is the first and most important thing she must do. He eases the car into gear and bumps slowly over the tracks, keeping one eye on the red-coated figure as it begins to ascend the dunes. As soon as the road bears to the left he has lost her, and returns his attention to the road and the familiar four hundred or so yards that separates him from the first building in the village.

The woman is a mystery. If she is going towards the cottages - and where else can she be going, he wonders - she cannot be coming to see him. That only leaves two other possibilities. The first is that she is a friend of Bradley's - which is something he immediately, if uncharitably, questions - and the second is that she is heading to the middle cottage which is ostensibly a 'holiday let', though it remains resolutely unoccupied for most of the year. In fact, in his relatively limited experience, it seems un-let for the majority of the time. Or perhaps the woman's motivation is neither of those things. As he enters the village, he turns right by 'The Anchor' and then pulls to a halt just beyond the Ryles' store. He knows he should be able to resolve the question soon enough. Turning off the engine, he gets out of the car, pausing to look back beyond the pub as if he might be able to see as far as the station and beyond - which he obviously cannot.

As he enters the shop, Lewis notes with some reassurance it appears as it always has: bakery rack to the fore, vegetables to the left, leading on to the tinned and dried goods. It seems important. He finds himself wondering if the background smell and general ambience of Oscar and Shirley's place is common to all such convenience stores. Not seeing anyone about, Lewis waits at the counter knowing that whoever is on duty will be out the back either packing or sorting or unpacking. They take turns when it is quiet, which it mostly is. Behind the small counter, the shelves containing all the tobacco products are clearly visible. Oscar, a once committed if now loosely reformed smoker, seldom closes the sliding doors to hide them from view, and Shirley always leaves them as she finds them.

"There you are," says a woman's voice, the tone suggesting he had been expected all along and was actually at fault for being a little late.

"Here I am," says Lewis, smiling at Shirley as she approaches him. She is wearing a bright blue and white stripped apron, one of a considerable range of aprons in her possession. It is, in effect, her 'uniform'. She has confessed on more than one occasion not to need to wear anything approximating to clothing protection, but regards the putting on and taking off of an apron as signifying the transition into and out off work mode.

"You've come for your shopping then?" she says unnecessarily, and then checks a list she has secured just under the corner of the till. "Seventeen pounds forty."

"And how are you today, Shirley?" he asks playfully, teasing her at the lack of polite greeting and the immediate demand for money.

"The same as you would expect me to be," she replies. "I'd be better if I didn't have to work with that idiot brother of mine - but then you know that anyway."

When he doesn't reply, busy with his wallet, she carries on.

"Is there anything else, otherwise I'll just go and get your bags."

Lewis looks back at her.

"One thing. Has the holiday cottage been let?"

Shirley's left eyebrow lifts a little.

"Why do you ask?"

"Because I just saw someone getting off the train. I think they were heading that way. Either that or Bradley has a secret woman!"

"Secret woman, indeed!" She laughs a little too guardedly Lewis thinks, but he has only known her for a small number of years, and Shirley - as with so many people who have spent their lives in relatively rural settings - can take a while to unravel.

"Yes, that's what I thought too."

At this she laughs a little more heartily. Lewis feels he has re-proven himself as a 'local'. It is a little game he has to play with them all from time to time.

"Well, yes, it has been let as a matter of fact." She weighs up how much she should tell him. "The lady - assuming you saw the right person - is called Anna Woolley. Booked the cottage early last week, actually."

"Oh? For how long?"

"Well, that's the strange thing; indefinitely, I suppose."

"Indefinitely?"

"She's paid for three weeks up front and asked for first refusal on the time after that. Of course, I told the Johnsons that was a little unusual, but they said considering they were hardly able to let it anyway, any money was better than none, so I should just go ahead."

"They were right there," Lewis concurs.

"Where?"

"About some money being better than none."

Shirley extends her hand.

"Talking of money…"

Lewis hands over twenty pounds which Shirley takes, rings up the seventeen forty in the till, then fishes out his change.

"Are you going straight home?" she asks.

"Yes. Why?"

"Well, you can do me a favour." She begins to walk away from the counter, speaking to him over her shoulder. "You can deliver some groceries to our Ms. Woolley for me. It's only a couple of bags. Staples, mainly. She ordered and paid for those in advance too."

Before Lewis can object, she has disappeared out the back of the shop. As he waits, he wonders whether he would really have wanted to object anyway. If this new woman is going to be a neighbour - even for a short while - it would make sense to start out on the right kind of footing with her.

Shirley returns with three carrier bags which she hands to him.

"These are yours," she says. "I'll get the other two."

"I'll put these in the car," he says.

Outside he opens the boot of his unlocked car, and places his shopping to one side. Having done so, he pushes his walking boots and waterproof jacket slightly further to the back to ensure he has sufficient space for the additional two bags.

Inside, Shirley waits for him, extra bags at her feet.

"What's she like?" she asks.

"The new woman?"

Shirley nods.

"I don't know. I didn't see her very clearly. Or at all, really. All I know is that she has a red coat and a blue suitcase."

"Not much to go on," Shirley confirms. "Anyway, she sounded nice enough on the phone. Said she'd been looking for some peace and quiet - and, of course, I told her she'd get nothing but that here!"

Lewis picks up the two remaining bags. As he turns, he says "I'll keep you posted, shall I?"

"You'd better!" she replies.

With the shopping secure, Lewis gets in and re-starts the car. Not bothering to check his mirrors, he pulls away and then makes a clockwise circuit of the green. Facing towards home, he glances out of the side window to see if Shirley is standing on the pavement. He has known her do so in the past, and once or twice she has later admonished him for not waving as he departed. Satisfied she is not there, he drives past 'The Anchor' once again, then down to the station where the crossing gates remain open. He slows to allow for the bump across the tracks, and hears a dull thump from his boot; the tell-tale sound of groceries falling over. Beyond the station, he eases the car to the right and coasts down to the terrace. Bradley's Land Rover is still in situ; the shed doors still shut. Knowing the cottage between his and Bradley's has been let, he is nevertheless surprised there is no car outside its front door, even though he knows the woman arrived on the train. Since he has been in the village, whenever the cottage has been taken there has always been a car that came with the tenants. Perhaps one will appear later, he thinks, and so finds himself parking more deliberately outside of his own cottage. When he gets out of the car, the space between his and Bradley's vehicle seems strangely large and vacant; it is the absence of a presence he feels - though he is immediately unable to rationalise exactly what that means.

Lewis unlocks his front door and then returns to his car where he opens the boot. It was one of his bags that had toppled over, though nothing material has spilled out. No damage done, he gathers the escapee items and returns them to their bag, then lifts all three and takes them into his kitchen where he deposits them on the floor near the refrigerator. Scanning the room, he confirms nothing has changed during his brief trip, something which is always both a surprise and reassurance in equal measure. As he leaves the kitchen and walks through the small hall, he notices the unopened mail resting on the small telephone shelf. When he gets back inside, he thinks.

The boot of his car still open, he pauses, deciding whether to carry the other two bags to her door or to knock first. He decides on the latter, so leaves them and walks the dozen or so paces to the front door of the middle cottage. He raps three times with his knuckles and waits.

After a few seconds the door opens surprisingly quickly, as if there is no need for caution. Although he has obviously not been this close to her before, Lewis can tell it is the woman from the train; the colour and style of her hair - nut brown and shoulder length - along with her height and general demeanour give her away. He is unconsciously amazed at how much information one can assimilate from a quick glance or a slightly longer stare.

"Hello," she says. "Can I help you?"

She has a face that is more oval than round, lips fuller than not; her eyes, although brown, are leaning a little towards hazel, and are attractively spaced; not too close together, nor too far apart. It is, Lewis thinks, an open kind of a face, though just at this moment a little reserved, and - if he is perceptive - a little careworn too.

"Actually I think I can help you," Lewis replies, smiling.

"Sorry?"

"Anna, is it? My name's Lewis; I live next door. I've just been into the village and Shirley - at the shop - asked me to deliver your groceries."

He half turns to indicate his open boot, then offers his hand, repeating his name.

"Yes, Anna," she says, shaking it briefly. "That's very kind of you. I was planning to go a little later."

"Well, saved you the journey then."

He walks back to the car and lifts out the two remaining bags. He can see tea bags, milk, bread. As Shirley had said, staples. For a moment he wonders what else might be in the bag; what she has decided to cook for her first meal there. When he gets back to her door, she holds out her hands.

"Thank you," she says.

He finds himself half hoping that she would invite him in, so passes the bags over a little reluctantly.

"If ever you're stuck for anything," he offers, "don't be afraid to knock. I'm just there." He nods towards where she could not fail to find him. "Don't try Bradley - he's the other side. Never has any decent food in his house."

She smiles a little in reaction to his quick laugh.

"And if you're really stuck, Tommy and Jenny up at 'The Anchor' can usually rustle up some food; that is, if you don't feel like cooking."

"Thank you," she says, "I'll remember that."

There is an awkward pause as they both wait, she for him to leave, he for her to further the conversation.

"Well," he says, filling the vacuum, "better get on. Remember" - this as he moves back to his car - "if you need anything..."

Her 'thank you' arrives over his shoulder as he places his hand on the boot lid; the closing of her cottage door sounds in sync with the shutting of the boot. As Lewis walks towards his own front door, he remembers he has his own shopping to unpack, then thinks "Anna Woolley" apropos of nothing.

Chapter 3

When the day dawns, based on what greets him, Lewis likes to think he can predict the weather for its remainder. One of the first things that had struck him about Maunston Quay was the way it seemed to possess its own micro climate, often proving the lie to generic forecasts he would hear on the television and radio. During his first few months, he had become accustomed to falling foul of the climate as a result of misjudgement, of believing what he had been told, almost invariably ending the day too something: too warm, too cold, too wet.

Having become, almost imperceptibly, a creature of habit, he rises this morning and works his way through his breakfast routine as usual. Always starting with the opening of his bedroom curtains and an assessment of the sky, it is an input he processes as he sits at the small breakfast bar in his inevitably small kitchen. In front of him and slightly to the side is an empty cereal bowl and a half-finished cup of tea. He is leaning in, elbows on the slightly tired wooden work-surface, contemplating the small tablet computer that rests between them. He allows his right index finger to occasionally tap and swipe, scrolling through the world. As he does so now, he thinks - and not for the first time - how comparatively remote Maunston Quay is; how it is divorced from the outside world, and how occasionally it can feel impenetrable.

And then he suddenly thinks of Anna Woolley, and wonders why he should do so.

He is, this morning - as he is most mornings - grateful to Maunston Quay for the life it has allowed him to lead. Even as he lifts his cup, drains his tea, then stands and takes the short walk to the sink, he knows it has given him what he needed when he needed it. Because of his gratitude, Lewis has never judged the place, and though, as he rinses out his mug and empty cereal bowl, it may not have registered, he has rarely questioned his existence there; never truly contemplated any notion of 'moving on', nor seen the need to do so. Making his way to the hall, he begins to climb the stairs and heads for the bathroom. By the time he has finished his ablutions he will have decided which route he will take for his morning walk, already knowing that today he will go up to Simon's Crag then back down to the beach before coming home. It will be a short walk; the weather appearing settled is, of course, a dissemblance, and Lewis is confident that it can no longer fool him.

He stares at himself in the bathroom mirror as he works the brush methodically around his teeth. Having gauged the need for a shave or not (and this morning is a 'not' morning), he focusses on his eyes. They regard him as if they belong to someone else; he examines their colour and depth, then tries to see beyond their surface as if there are secrets to be revealed. His soul perhaps. If he senses anything, it passes him by. Bending, he spits, rinses his brush and heads downstairs. In the small hallway, he removes his slippers and eases his feet into his walking boots. He wonders how many miles the boots have served him - and how many of those have been from this cottage. Sometimes - like this morning - the boots feel more comfortable than his slippers. Pulling his coat from its peg, he opens the door and steps outside. As he dons the jacket, he shivers and looks at the sky. It is still cold even though the sky is mainly blue. Contrary to current appearances, he knows there will be rain later, it is just a question of when.

He glances to the left as if to check everything is in order, and seeing the space between his car and Bradley's Land Rover, is reminded again that this morning he has a new neighbour.

As he walks towards the headland, the gradient slowly beginning to increase, Lewis measures his progress by familiar landmarks - not that the small rowan sapling or the remains of a somewhat ancient wooden bench by the path would qualify as 'landmarks' for most people. Being effectively little more than one boot-width wide and suffering the encroachment here and there of stinging nettles, it is a track which betrays the infrequency it is taken.

Lewis knows he must be its prime user; no-one else walks it as often as he. Reaching the point where the path up from the beach joins on the left, he pauses and glances down to the jetty. This morning - as with most mornings when he takes this route - he checks for occupancy, of the beach, the quay itself. Mentally, if not physically, he shakes his head and resumes his journey upwards. One day he would like to see a boat moored at the pier. It would justify its existence. Bradley's occasional use of the jetty is driven by whim and good weather - and just occasionally, tourists' requests. But when he does venture out, usually he will have his boat reversed from the shed straight into the sea and then back undercover again all within the space of a few hours. Oddly for a boatman, he has little need of the quay itself.

Lewis reaches the summit of the crag and pauses, checking the surface of the rocks exposed there for fresh gull deposits before half-sitting, half-leaning against them. Three-parts of the way to the horizon he can make out four container ships, two heading in each direction. If he were to turn his head to the right, away from the bay and towards the south, he knows he would see the off-shore wind farm erected further down the coast. He recalls the added interest generated when they were installing the blades two years previously, and for a short while Simon's Crag became more popular. But today - on a typically chilly, if bright morning - it is what it has always been for him since he arrived; a place of solitude and reflection.

That he has much to reflect on he never questions, even if the events concerned now lack the immediacy they once possessed. He tells himself this morning - as he has almost every morning since he took up residence in Maunston Quay - that it is surely time to let go, after all there is more fog to be found clouding his memories these days than the frequent fret which envelops the beach, and perhaps that is sign enough. Yet such thoughts, especially with respect to Emma, feel like a betrayal. He has imagined for a long time now that she would have wanted him to 'move on'. He thinks of her cracking a joke at his expense, pulling his leg about him not being Queen Victoria and suggesting that a little over three years is long enough mourning for anyone. As he traces the flight of a solitary gull, Lewis knows she is right. These days he thinks she was always right; it is a little indulgence he allows himself. And maybe he *will* move on. He watches two of the distant vessels pass each other on their respective journeys and conjures up a particularly apposite aphorism relating to 'ships in the night', trying to replay it to himself in Emma's voice. That he is unable to do so bothers him. He knows he has lost her voice and its slightly lilting timbre, as much as he has lost her. At least the photographs help keep her image alive.

He stands, then turns and retraces his steps back to the fork in the path, heading to the right now and more sharply downwards to where the path will peter out by the rocks at the southern end of the beach. As usual he takes care at the tight dog-leg where once he almost fell, then resumes his walk at a more appropriate pace. The sudden cry of a gull startles him to a standstill, and he looks up to try and locate it in the sky. He is reminded of other daemons and knows he would feel guilty if he let Emma go before he had been able to wrestle those into submission.

❁ ❁ ❁

When he reaches the level of the sand, nearly twenty minutes have passed. There is a small enclave where the path emerges from the foot of the headland and is surrounded by the crag, the sea, and a ring of large rocks. Lewis knows from experience if you are on the beach or dunes watching people descend, they momentarily seem to disappear, as if they have been swallowed up - though by sea or sand it is impossible to say. He pauses here as he always does and, knowing he is invisible, looks out to sea again, his view restricted by the encroaching geology. He knows the ships are still there, but from this vantage point the sea appears empty. This is often the case - as is the sense he now gets of being totally isolated, as if he were the last man standing, staring out into an emptiness at the conclusion of some kind of apocalypse. This is a fanciful notion more at home in the cinema than on the North Sea coast, but it is an image to which he can relate, born from different circumstances where he was surrounded by another kind of sand altogether.

He shivers - a reaction to suddenly fining himself enveloped in shade - and weaves across the largest rocks to emerge onto the sand and back into view. Looking around as he always does at this point, Lewis is surprised to find that he is no longer alone. At the far end of the jetty a figure in a bright red coat stands motionless, its owner staring out across the water. Brought to a standstill by this discovery, he sees the figure turn and look his way. Although there is no acknowledgement, he knows Anna Woolley has seen him, something which obviously limits his options. As she does not move, simply returning her gaze to the sea, he feels bound to join her. It would be rude, he analyses, not to go and say hello; and if she is going to be his neighbour for an indeterminate period of time, he is fearful of the damage that could do. He was planning to walk to the far end of the beach anyway, so the most minor of diversions - up onto the pier for a few minutes - is little hardship.

Although he doesn't travel any faster than he believes he had intended, Lewis reaches the steps surprisingly quickly and, before he knows it, is walking along the wooden boards, his boots sounding reassuringly robust. It is the reverberation of his footfall that prompts Anna to turn towards him again, this time her gaze settling on him for a few seconds. When he reaches her, she is looking away from the land again. He stops beside her, seeking out the horizon and the ships he had seen earlier. One of them has vanished.

"Good morning," he offers, "making the most of the bright morning?"

"I miss the sea," she says, as if skipping into the middle of the conversation, bypassing the pleasantries.

"Miss it?"

"When I was a child," she glances at him briefly as she speaks, but for no more than an instant, "we used to live by the sea. Not this close, of course, but near enough. We used to go for walks along the beach - even in winter."

"Where was that?"

"Where?" To Lewis she seems to pause just a fraction as if pre-processing her answer to check it for something before actually uttering the words. She carries on. "Somewhere nondescript on the south coast. A horrible place really. I didn't like it much as a child - apart from the beach, of course - and then liked it even less when I moved away."

"Isn't that the wrong way round," he suggests, trying to apply his own experience. "Most often aren't distance and time more likely to generate fondness than anything else?"

"Wrong? I don't think so." Her reply, delivered in a balanced way, seems definitive and - to Lewis, at least - somewhat out of keeping with the figure she now cuts on the end of the jetty.

"I just thought..." Lewis is immediately unsure of exactly what he thought, examples coming to mind where he too felt worse about a place after he had left it.

She rescues him.

"Not like here at all."

"Here?" He is forced to look about to validate where they are, as if they may have been transported to another location without his realising it.

She half turns towards him.

"Isn't it perfect in its own small way? The little headland, the bay, the beach." She taps one of her feet. "Even this old pier."

Lewis feels a little lost, as if they are having a conversation from either side of slightly off-kilter realities. He needs to jump back to where she is.

"Perfect?"

She laughs brightly, as if at the notion - or at her turn of phrase.

"When I saw the photographs - of the cottage, the bay, this - then I knew that it was what I needed. Not that it's perfect, not really. But maybe it's somehow 'right'; for me, for now. It's just what I was looking for. Does that make sense, Lewis?"

If he is taken a little aback at her using his name for the first time, it is a sensation that is trumped by the relief that he has made it onto her wavelength.

"That," he says, "is something I can completely understand. It was how I felt when I came across the place - though in my case it was more by accident than anything else."

He allows a pause, expecting her to ask what was 'accidental' about his being there. He is ready to share the story of his getting lost in the dark, coming across the pub, being put up for the night; then, in the morning, walking down to the bay and feeling suddenly at home.

But she says nothing.

Sensing it is not his story in which she is interested, that perhaps her own situation supersedes everything just at the moment, he realises his only choices are to let the subject fade away or to see how much she is willing to share.

"And why is it right for you, Anna? If you don't mind me asking..." He adds the appendix primarily to give her a way out, to allow privacy should she need it. It is also added - quickly, with a little too much haste - to cover up the fact that now *he* has spoken *her* name, to mitigate the strange sense Lewis has that he may have just crossed a line.

"Oh, I don't know," she says, looking at him slightly quizzically. And then she laughs a little, a sound that seems to him to echo from somewhere in her past. She snuggles down into her coat. "That's ridiculous, of course. I do know why it's right for me. Because it's small, quiet, anonymous. From the description and photos I mean, it seemed to offer me a place where I could lose myself for a while. Does that make sense?"

Knowing she is seeking validation, Lewis nods. It would be easy for him to tell her how much he can understand her motivation - and then to tell her exactly why - but he has already discovered that it is not yet his turn. And he suddenly finds himself, bizarrely and for no reason that he can immediately articulate, hoping that at some point it will be.

If she has noticed any underlying turmoil in him, Anna keeps it to herself.

"Not that I'm running away," she says, facing the sea again, "not really. Not in the sense that I've done anything wrong."

"You're not a criminal or an escaped convict," he suggests, consciously not picking up on the image of fleeing, instead striving for a laugh which does not come.

She shakes her head.

"It sounds a little odd when you say it to yourself," she carries on, "but I just need some time to myself, for me."

"And that's odd because…?"

"Because that's actually all I have now."

When she leaves the statement simply hanging, incomplete, demanding to be followed by explanation or qualification, Lewis is momentarily confused. He wonders if he has inadvertently gone too far. He tries to recall how the conversation made it to this point, wanting to assure himself that he has not been nosy, prying. And when the silence - a silence that is filled with the rolling of the sea, the rhythm of the waves, and so is not silence at all - when the silence seems to have gone on for too long, he wonders if he has missed his cue. Just as he tries to decide if he has been dismissed, if their conversation has reached a natural conclusion, she speaks.

"Would you like some tea?"

Twenty minutes later they are sitting on small canvass chairs outside Anna's cottage, staring at the beach and cradling mugs. She had insisted she make it; the offer had been hers after all. Lewis, keen to try and ensure a contribution of his own, had suggested sitting outside in spite of the chill, he providing the chairs. As they had walked back from the jetty Anna said nothing further that was material, but rather made small talk, apologising at one point for deflecting Lewis from his walk. It was, he assured her, no hardship and therefore required no apology.

"So, where were we?" she asks, looking back towards the pier.

It seems to Lewis as if she is winding-in the invisible thread she had laid out across the sand in their wake, and in doing so, in re-connecting them to the starting point of the conversation, collapsing those twenty minutes until they simply vanished. It feels like time travel. He knows exactly where they had been in terms of what they were discussing - Anna's requirement for some time to herself - but cannot recall the exact words, unsure if it matters.

She rescues him.

"For the last few months I have been a little at sea - if that isn't somehow an inappropriate description, considering where we are." She pauses to allow Lewis space to make an observation, but he remains silent. "In October last year I lost my husband, you see. It was unexpected, but in a way not surprising. In any event, it was a little like having the rug pulled from underneath me. It was strange. It coincided with the weekend the clocks went back, so the days were suddenly darker for two very different reasons."

"I'm so sorry," Lewis offers, "I had no idea." It is a lame and hollow thing to say, but he has never found a way of expressing condolence that has ever rung true, that has ever been able to express exactly what he means - and he has had more experience than most.

"That's all right," she glances at him, the slightest of smiles showing. It is a smile to reassure him as best she can. "Of course it isn't all right - that he's gone, I mean. But anyway..."

"You said it was not surprising. Had he been ill?"

"Oh no," and she laughs, which surprises him. "Quite the opposite! It was nothing like that. He was as fit as a flea. Fitter, if anything. He was a soldier - in Afghanistan. One day the jeep he was in got caught by an IED as he and two colleagues went to investigate some shooting or other."

Lewis feels his chest tense. He is aware that his grip on the mug has tightened considerably, and is suddenly concerned that he might simply shatter it. He takes two deep breaths and tries to force his hands to relax. 'It all starts in the mind' he was once told, and for a second that's where his concentration is fixed. When he looks back at her, Anna is staring at him.

"I'm sorry," she says, "I didn't mean to startle you. Shall we talk about something else? I know I'm being terribly selfish, and you don't know me from Adam."

"Or Eve," Lewis suggests, trying to lighten the tone for both of them.

"Or Eve," she echoes, and takes his comment as permission to carry on. "So anyway, that was suddenly that. Which left me a little bit alone; cast adrift, if we wanted to carry on using a nautical theme. I rattled around the house, tried to be enthusiastic at work. You can imagine."

"It must have been hard for you," he offers, wincing internally that he has resorted to another cliche.

Slowly she shakes her head, then takes a sip of tea.

"That's what people always assume, isn't it? I mean, it's perfectly natural of course, especially when you've lost someone you were close to. The default, the only possible logical response, is that it was hard." She pauses for a moment, looking back towards the pier. "And it was. But not in the way that people think. It wasn't hard because I'd lost him; it was hard because I was suddenly on my own. That was the hard part. You see, we'd had a son - Tom - just two years before. He had been born prematurely. There were complications. He died before his first birthday."

As she looks back at Lewis expecting a response, she can instantly tell he is refraining from saying anything.

"*That* was really difficult. That's when I wanted to lean on Ryan. But I found he wasn't there for me, just when I needed him the most. In the end I realised he'd taken it harder than I had; in fact, I'd been more prepared to lose our little boy than he had. I think he blamed me in a way. And his response was to throw himself more into his work. He was away so much of the time anyway, but I'd expected him to take some time off; to be around to help me. But the opposite was true. He started to volunteer for things. Things that put him more in harm's way than he needed to be."

"He wasn't a 'regular soldier'?" Lewis suggests.

Anna nods.

"Something like that. Do you know what I mean?"

"I have," Lewis pauses as he looks for the words, "experience. I know some people."

She ignores the connotation.

"So in many ways I started to lose Ryan almost as soon as I'd lost Tommy. We weren't quite strangers when he was killed, but almost. The thing was, I suppose, his not being there - his never going to be there - opened it all up, made my situation all the more real. Whatever words you want to use. But the fact was that I found myself suddenly alone in some new and profound kind of way. That's what was different and that's what was hard. The 'me' being me part, not the 'me' no longer being half of a couple. Does that make sense, Lewis?"

It does make sense - and more sense than Anna could possibly realise. But Lewis knows that now is not the time to be talking about his own experience, to be drawing parallels. He feels as if it would be cheapening what she has told him. He knows there is a remarkable amount of trust being shown in him here considering that he is, after all, just a stranger. But he also knows how powerful and unstoppable the urge can be to share, especially if things have been bottled up inside.

"Yes, it does," he says. He takes a sip from his tea, but it is suddenly cold. She sees him recoil.

"Oh, I'm sorry. Your tea's gone cold. Can I get you another one?"

He finds his hand on her arm before he knows it; a gesture that stops her just as she is about to get out of her chair. His tea is the least important thing in the world.

"It's fine. Really." He pauses, just a moment, allowing them both to settle again. He tries to retrieve the moment. "So Maunston Quay, then? I'm guessing this is all about getting away from things, from the familiar, the past. Reorienting yourself, in a way. Answering a few questions - once you've found the ones you need answers to."

She laughs a little.

"Have you been reading my mind?!" When he shakes his head, she carries on. "That's funny, though; it's almost exactly like that. A spring clean, perhaps - from the inside, out. Everything has become so cluttered and jumbled up." A pause. "How do you know?"

"Know?"

"That that's what it feels like. The reason I'm here."

Lewis knows this is a chance to relate his story, but he remains disciplined, steadfast. If there is one thing the Army taught him which he has retained, it is that.

"Because that's why I ended up here, I suppose. Not why I came. My being here in the first place was nothing more than a happy accident. I hadn't planned anything really. I suppose I was looking for something. Looking for somewhere. I woke up one morning - in 'The Anchor', the pub in the village - and then walked down to here, the beach. It suddenly felt 'right'. It's a good place to get your bearings."

"I think that's what I need. Don't you?"

He is surprised she has asked him, but can see that at this precise moment validation is important. Lewis knows what it means to have nothing to hold on to. Everyone needs a fixed point.

"Just resting somewhere for a while, only having to think about mundane practicalities? Yes. And Maunston Quay's as good a place as any. Better than most, I'd say."

"How long have you been here?"

"Me? Three years or so."

"Three years!" Her surprise is evident.

"I know." He laughs. "I arrived by mistake, and now look at me!"

There is a slight pause. Overhead a gull caws, and they are suddenly aware of the sea rolling in and out. A cloud momentarily blocks the sun and the winds bites. Lewis knows the moment has passed.

"But you need something to keep you busy."

"Busy?"

"There's nothing here. Nothing apart from the beach and the pier. It can be both blessing and curse. The village has a shop, a pub, and a church. That's it. You can walk a little way along the coast in either direction, and there's a kind of circuit you can do inland to the next village. After that, you'll need to take the train to anywhere interesting."

"What do you do?" she asks, "To keep busy, I mean."

"Apart from walk and learning to cook? I sketch and paint a little."
Seeing her face brighten, he rushes on. "Oh, I'm no good, no good
at all! Really rubbish! Honestly."

"I don't believe you," she says. "You protest too much."

"But it's a good way to lose yourself, to get absorbed in something
else. Works for me, anyway."

"I bet you're like Picasso," she suggests.

"Picasso?" He laughs.

"Didn't he used to paint the same thing over and over, trying to get
it right? I bet you've got dozens of drawings and paintings of the
beach and the pier."

"Hundreds. Hundreds!"

❀ ❀ ❀

"Years ago I used to write," she says, her words now edging out
slowly, more nervously. It seems to Lewis as if this is a more
significant confession for her than revealing the deaths of her
husband and son. "I thought I might try again. You know, start
something."

"Well there's no better place," he suggests. "Maybe you could write
hundreds of poems about the sea to go with my miserable
paintings!"

She laughs.

"And we could have an exhibition in the village hall."

"If there was one, yes."

"We'd be like Ted Hughes and Fay Godwin."

He frowns.

"OK, you've got me there. Ted Hughes I've heard of, but Fay…?"

"Godwin. There's a book called 'Remains of Elmet'; Hughes wrote
the poetry and Godwin took the photos that went with them."

"You like poetry?"

"I used to" she says, then immediately corrects herself. "I mean, I do. I used to read a lot, but not so much lately."

"I'm afraid I don't get much further than 'I wandered lonely as a cloud'..." he confesses.

"But that's something," she says, trying to be encouraging. "It's what I studied at college, literature. I used to try and write. Badly of course."

"Like my paintings?"

"If you say so," she smiles just as the sun breaks through again. "I began to prefer prose. Short stories were always manageable because they didn't go on for too long. The beginning, middle and end all come close enough together not to get fatigue somewhere half-way through. And you didn't need to be too clever. I think clever's a bit beyond me at the moment, so I might try that again."

Out at sea the ships he had seen earlier have now disappeared, and Lewis views an unblemished horizon held in place to his right by Simon's Crag.

"And you should try poetry again too."

"Oh," her interest is piqued. "Why?"

"I don't know. It's always felt to me as if Maunston Quay is a poetic kind of place - even if there's not much here and the beach is too small."

"I think everyone needs a little poetry in their lives," she says after a pause. She looks at him then away to the sky, shielding her eyes with a hand as she traces the path of a gull. "Sounds a bit naff, I know, but... Well, there it is."

Lewis looks up. From not so very far away, the sound of a diesel train as it rattles through the station. His reflex to check his watch is an automatic one.

"On time?" she asks, testing out her assumption that he would know.

"Pretty much," he replies, "or as close as they'll ever be."

He feels her eyes on him and looks back from where his gaze had taken him, to the corner of the sand dunes beyond which the invisible station - and the rest of the world - awaits.

"It's funny," she says, incongruously not smiling.

"What is?"

"Well, you didn't instantly strike me as a poetic kind of person; I mean, not the sort of person who paints and draws. You probably read sensible books too."

"What's a sensible book?"

"Oh, I don't know. Not all Grisham and Dan Brown. My guess is that you've got some proper books hidden away somewhere."

"Maybe. But then my definition of 'proper' could be wildly different from yours. Almost certainly is." He pauses for a moment. "You'll have to check out my bookcase at some point - and I do have a bookcase! - to see if I pass muster."

She is suddenly quiet. Lewis looks at her as she glances towards the front door of her cottage - which has remained open throughout their exchange - and then on through the sitting-room window to where the somewhat awkward green curtains have been pulled hard back.

"Sorry," she says, "that was a bit clumsy of me. I know we've only just met and everything, so I've no right to make judgements. One of my weaknesses I'm afraid."

Over her shoulder, Lewis sees the front door of the far cottage open and a heavy set man step out into the sunshine.

"Well," he says, lowering his voice, "this should test you then."

Milton Bradley pauses on the threshold of his cottage and absorbs the day. One breath, a scan of the horizon, the feeling of the air on his skin, these tell him all he needs to know. Hearing their voices, he turns his head towards Lewis and Anna, and then, without any change of expression starts walking towards them. He is a compact individual, though more by impression than degree. When Lewis stands up to greet him, Anna can immediately see that the two men are the same height, but the other, walking ramrod straight, gives the impression of being twice as solid.

"Anna", says Lewis, a fresh and slightly playful tone in his voice, "this is Milton. Shall I get you a chair?"

The second comment is addressed to the newcomer who is already pausing before them.

"Don't bother, thanks. I'm just going into the village." Having answered Lewis's question, he turns to Anna, hand extended. She has also risen. "Milton Bradley. Please call me Bradley. Almost no-one calls me Milton, as Mr. Airy well knows."

Lewis laughs as he sits down. It is very clear to Anna that he is at home in the other man's company; introducing him as 'Milton' was clearly a joke, and one to which the response would be known. She suspects the offer of the chair was probably made in the same vein.

Having shaken hands, Bradley motions for Anna to resume her seat. He stands equidistant from them, leaning his back against her cottage wall between door and window. In most people it is a pose that could look too casual, even slovenly; Anna thinks Bradley makes it look like formal relaxation; relaxation to order.

"Anna's taken the cottage for a little while," Lewis says unnecessarily, knowing that Bradley will resist the temptation to look at the cottage as if to draw for himself the link between her and the building.

"It will be good to have someone in there," Bradley says. "When were the last lot? Five months ago?"

"Longer, probably." Lewis pauses momentarily. "September, I think. And then July before that."

"I didn't take to the last lot," Bradley admits.

"Why was that?" Anna asks, not missing a certain undertone in his voice.

"They used to smoke like chimneys, and because they couldn't light up in the house, would sit outside until all hours chatting and smoking."

"It was like being constantly fumigated," Lewis suggests with a laugh.

"You don't smoke?" Bradley asks, though whether with a note of concern or admonition Anna is unsure.

"No, I'm pleased to say I don't."

"I've nothing against smoking, mind," Bradley says, seeming to double back, "Lewis and I very occasionally partake of the odd cigar of a summer evening" - Anna looks at Lewis who has his eyes fixed on the other man; she finds something there that is suddenly appealing - "but we won't be doing so at all hours, prattling on about nothing."

She laughs.

"That's very reassuring, though I have to say that I'm already finding it hard to imagine you and Lewis 'prattling'."

As Lewis now takes his turn to laugh, Bradley inclines his head slightly in recognition of the compliment. Anna finds herself liking him immediately.

"Bradley's our resident boatman. In that dark monstrosity of a shed at the end there he keeps the village's fleet."

"A fleet?"

"I don't know about that," Bradley shoots him a look. "You mustn't believe everything Lewis tells you; at least not as far as I'm concerned."

"Oh?"

"Bradley knows I'm only joking," Lewis protests.

"So," she continues, "if not a fleet, then what?"

"Just a smallish dinghy and a row boat. The dinghy's large enough to take me and maybe four others - when there's others to take, that is."

"The last lot wanted to go out, didn't they?" Lewis interjects, "but Bradley refused. Point of principle."

The other man inclines his head as if to concur, and knowing nothing further needs to be said, shifts his posture slightly without diminishing the overall impression of controlled restraint.

"But why are there so few people who rent out the cottage?" she asks. The two men exchange glances, but say nothing. "I mean, it's a lovely little place - I assume you've both been inside - and there's this little beach. What's not to like if people want to get away from it all?"

"I have to say that I agree with you," says Lewis, looking from Anna to Bradley, out to sea, then back to her, "but then you've probably already worked that out."

"What's not to like," Bradley picks up on her phrase, "are all the things that aren't here, the things that people want or think they need."

"Such as?"

Bradley detaches himself from the wall, freeing his fingers from behind his back to use as a counting device.

"There's no car park for a start. Not that the beach is large enough to accommodate that many people. The trains aren't frequent enough. There are no toilets, no ice cream hut, no changing facilities. There's no restaurant - I don't think we can count 'The Anchor' - and the village shop is hardly convenient nor well enough stocked to cater for picnics and the like. And when you're tired of the beach? You can't walk very far in either direction along the coast - at least not easily. And there's nothing much in the village or beyond to do."

"But most of all..." Lewis prompts, as if part of a well-rehearsed double act.

"But most of all," Bradley picks up his introduction, "there's indifferent mobile telephone signal. Cable hasn't reached all the properties yet, so unless you've a satellite dish, there's no reliable wi-fi and internet."

"You make it sound positively dreadful!" Anna admits with a laugh.

"And so," Lewis intercedes now, "as you say, it is a great place to get away from it all, which - nowadays - is actually the last thing that people want to do."

"But *you* stay," she observes, focusing more on Lewis than Bradley, "in spite of all those failings."

"Or because of them," Lewis suggests, at which Bradley laughs in agreement. It is a rich, deep laugh that Anna believes is probably something rarely heard. Smiling, she looks back at Lewis who offers a conspiratorial wink.

They are silent for a few moments, each of them looking out beyond the beach, scanning for unnamed somethings. Anna breaks the silence.

"But it needn't be like that."

"Like what?" says Lewis.

"The village. Here. All of those things you've mentioned; there's no reason why you couldn't have them all, is there? Build a car park, a cafe; put up a telephone mast. This is a wonderful little place. A secret place, almost. It could be thriving. You could..."

"Make a fortune?" Lewis finishes her sentence for her. They both look towards Bradley, somehow recognising that his should be the next word.

"I've been here over twenty years," he begins, "and just about every year - around about this time, actually - a few of us get together to discuss what we are going to do about 'the season', kidding ourselves that such a thing exists, or that we're capable of having one. And almost every year we have the same discussions about a car park or toilets or some such. And why do we do that? Because we feel we have to. Because that's what most other places do. Because Maunston doesn't conform to how 'the seaside' is supposed to be. This year's meeting will be coming up soon. You should come along, Anna; it will be 'instructive'."

"But why don't you do something?"

"We do," Lewis says, then quickly qualifies his statement, "Oh, I know I've only been here a short while, but people do try - a little. If you want to know what stops them..."

He allows his sentence to trail away, then looks up at Bradley who inclines his head a little, as if giving permission for him to carry on, as if Bradley knows what Lewis is going to say and that he is cleared to do so. It is an exchange that is not lost on Anna.

"Tell me."

"It doesn't change because people don't want it to change. They are happy with their lives. They don't want hoards of tourists, or ice cream, or non-stop internet. They don't want traffic jams and drunks. And so the efforts they make - we make -" at this he glances at Bradley again, "are just tokens. Little things that allow people to feel as if they are doing something, but which - deep down - they know can never make a real difference."

"You have to understand that's why we're here," Bradley adds, "because of all those absences. Because it *is* a backwater; a place to get away from it all. In the end, that's what makes it special - to us, at least. And because it's what we need, for one reason or another.

So if what you want is that - to truly have some time to yourself - then you'll do just fine here. If not..."

"If not," Lewis intercepts, "you'll be gone by the end of the week."

She smiles as they look at her, knowing it is her turn.

"Oh, I think I'll still be here next week."

She gestures towards Lewis's mug.

"More tea?"

Lewis shakes his head, as does Bradley when she looks at him. She places her own mug - which she has been cradling all this time - down beside the chair.

"So if we've established what isn't here, what is?" She asks. "A pub - 'The Anchor' - and a shop where my groceries came from." She smiles at Lewis as she says this. "There's a little beach and a pier no-one ever seems to use. But what else?"

"Well," says Bradley, "the village is about five hundred yards that way. Across the train tracks. You can't go wrong. You should go and have a look."

"I intend to, in a little while actually. But before I go, whet my appetite!"

"Where shall we start?" Lewis replies with an air of mock enthusiasm. "We've mentioned the pub - which will be closed now until probably twelve, depending on how Tommy's feeling. And we've mentioned the shop - which conversely will be open now - but which may close around twelve, depending on how Oscar's feeling." Bradley laughs, though more softly this time. "What have I forgotten, Bradley?"

Anna senses that Bradley's present pause is as far as he's prepared to go in terms of play-acting. She wonders if the term 'straight bat' might have been coined with him in mind.

"No," says Lewis, following up his own question. "I think that's just about it."

"Except," Bradley interrupts Lewis's burgeoning laugh.

"Except?" Lewis wonders what he has forgotten. He takes a quick mental tour of the village green and all he sees are small cottages, the entrance to the cul-de-sac where Maisie lives.

"Double Diamond," Bradley suggests.

"Richard!" Lewis's own exclamation seems to take him back just a little.

"Okay, okay," says Anna, endeavouring to insert herself into the conversation again. "Double Diamond?"

"Richard Dyson. The Reverend Richard Dyson," Bradley explains. "Lewis here forgot the church - which probably tells you something, eh?"

"Unfair, Bradley," Lewis protests.

"But Double Diamond?" Anna is still striving to catch up.

"Richard, occasionally known as Dick or Dickie," Bradley explains. "His initials; D.D. Which is short form for a rather awful brew that is thankfully no longer in existence: Double Diamond."

"You probably needed to be there," Lewis admits, seeing the joke fall flat. "But there is, as Bradley says, the church. Small but beautifully formed, presided over by Richard; the proverbial pillar of the community. Nice enough chap, but he has his detractors."

"It's not him so much," Bradley throws in, almost under his breath.

Lewis carries on.

"Whether the church will be open now, I can't say. Unlikely. Or whether it will be open when you eventually wander into the village. Sunday mornings is more often than not a certainty, but other than that… Richard keeps irregular hours."

Anna frowns, then looks back to Bradley feeling she needs his straight bat.

"Is he not - 'reliable'?" She pauses before delivering the final word, evidently unsure if it is appropriate, or indeed what she meant at all.

Bradley sees his hand has been forced.

"Reliable? Surely. And if you also mean, is he a solid, devout, God-fearing kind of Vicar, then he'd plead guilty as charged. Does he minister to his flock? Again guilty. In fact, multiple flocks. Lewis's reference to irregular hours is actually a compliment; Richard stretches himself quite thinly over a number of parishes, though Maunston is his 'home base', as it were. What Lewis really means to say is that Richard is there if and when you need him. He is," Bradley pauses in his own search for a word, "driven. I think you could say that."

"Or enthusiastic, possibly."

Anna looks back to Lewis.

"But that's a good thing surely? All those things - especially the part about being so attentive to the needs of the village when he has a whole benefice to run."

Her use of the ecclesiastical terms causes Lewis to pause for a fraction of a second.

"Indeed. And we mustn't mock, even though we do." He looks at Bradley who displays tell-tale signs of being publicly chastised. "We're not - how should we say, Bradley? - 'regulars' as far as Richard is concerned. But lost sheep though we may be, that doesn't stop us from sharing a drink with the man. As I say, he's a decent chap. The sort of man you'd want to have on your side rather than not. Is that fair?"

The question is directed towards Bradley, who nods affirmatively.

"It is."

Anna takes those final comments as a ringing endorsement. She can see how Bradley would not be the kind of man to suffer fools gladly, and his support of Lewis's proposition is enough for her.

There is a brief silence during which it dawns on Lewis that, because she has not responded further, they may have offended their newest visitor.

"Look, Bradley and I are just joshing. Richard's a good bloke. We don't mean to cause offence, if you know..." He doesn't even attempt to find the word, relying on Anna's ability to interpret.

She places her hand on his arm very briefly.

"Don't worry, no offence taken. And he actually sounds exactly how a vicar should be in many ways. I daresay that I might, in the normal course of events, see more of someone like Richard than you gentlemen - which is fine isn't it? Each to his own. But right now," and here she shoots Lewis a look that he cannot fail to see is meant as a link back to their earlier conversation, "under present circumstances, I'm not entirely sure."

"Well," says Lewis, looking up to Bradley for a moment, making it plain that he is just about to close this particular door, "if you did want to talk to anyone, then there's probably no-one better - or better qualified - than Richard."

"On the other hand," Bradley says, his voice suddenly a little more upbeat as if he has taken his lead from Lewis, "the person you would least want to seek advice or counsel or anything else from is Oscar."

"Oscar?"

"Oscar runs the shop," Lewis explains. "You may have spoken to him when you booked the cottage."

"No. I spoke to a lady. She sounded nice."

"That was Shirley, Oscar's sister." Lewis glances up to Bradley and then back to Anna. "And she is nice. Of course. Pretty much everyone you are likely to meet here is nice. Friendly. Harmless."

"Except Lewis," Bradley suggests, his deadpan delivery bringing a smile to Anna's face. "Don't be fooled by that naive bumbling quality he seems to present. Underneath, he's lethal; a cold-blooded killer!"

Anna means to laugh but it escapes more as a squeal, which only makes her laugh even more. Lewis waits for her laughter to subside, shaking his head and glancing warningly at Bradley as he does so.

"Yes, obviously. Goes without saying really."

"But what's wrong with Oscar, Bradley?"

"What's right with him, more like." Bradley has a small smile playing about his lips while he speaks; a sign that there is a pinch of salt to be had somewhere. "Let's just say that Shirley's the brains behind the outfit. Good job you spoke to her otherwise Oscar would have booked you into a hotel in Filey!"

"Bradley! That's a trifle harsh, don't you think?" Lewis steps into the breach. "As I say, he's a perfectly nice bloke. And if the shop's open when you go in to the village, you'll probably meet him."

"Well, you're probably right, Lewis. I may be being a little harsh. But here's a thing Shirley told me. Oscar has recently put in his monthly order from the cash-and-carry. Should be delivered in the next day or two."

Lewis can tell when there is a punchline in the offing.

"So?"

"So, Shirley also tells me that Oscar's put in his standard order for a typical month's staple; you know, dried and tinned goods that can't go off. Washing powder, soap, bleach…"

"And?"

"Well they normally sell about thirty or forty packs of toilet rolls. You know, the ones that come in four to a packet. Anyway, Shirley says they were getting low - something about eating into their backup stock - so Oscar says he'll order a few more."

"Surely there's nothing wrong there?' Anna suggests.

"Indeed. But Shirley's pretty sure that Oscar managed to put the decimal point in the wrong place on the order, so instead of getting sixty packets, she's expecting six hundred!"

Anna puts her hand over her mouth to suppress a laugh. Lewis makes no such effort.

"She says that if she gets enough notice of when they'll be delivering she'll let me know. I think she's keen that Oscar has an audience!"

"But that's dreadful!" says Anna, her intermittent laughter demonstrating that it is, in fact, anything but.

"Priceless!" suggests Lewis. "Typical Oscar."

"And typical Shirley, if I may say - just to make sure we're balanced here," Bradley concludes.

"Don't they get on?" Anna asks.

"As well as any brother and sister, I suppose," Bradley offers. "In any case, that's why you shouldn't ask Oscar for advice or counsel!"

A large dark cloud suddenly appears from behind the cottages and robs them of the sun's warmth. In unison they all look up to the skies.

"Rain later?" Lewis proposes.

"I should think so. About an hour maybe."

"Well," says Anna rising, holding out her hand for Lewis's mug which he retrieves from beside his chair and gives to her, "in that case I think I should be going for my little constitutional. See if I manage to bump into any of these weird and wonderful characters. After all, I've already met two, haven't I?"

❖ ❖ ❖

When the front door of Anna's cottage closes behind her, Bradley eases himself away from the wall and takes his place in the seat opposite Lewis. Neither men speak. Lewis's focus is on the sea when Bradley breaks the silence.

"I think she'll do, don't you Lewis?"

"You mean she'll stick around, and not run away prematurely?"

Bradley nods.

"How long has she got the placed booked for?"

"From what I can gather from Shirley, indefinitely."

"Interesting." If Bradley were the kind of individual who rocked on just the hind legs of a chair when thinking, he would be doing so now. After a moment he resumes. "You know why?"

"Why she's here?"

"Yes."

"I do."

Lewis is unsure exactly how much he should tell Bradley. Indeed, for a moment he isn't completely certain how much he knows himself. He glances towards the cottage to satisfy himself that the door and windows are indeed closed.

"She lost her husband last year. And just before that, her son."

"I had no idea," Bradley lowers his voice. "That's tragic."

"Undoubtedly incredibly painful and difficult - even if she and her husband were growing apart."

"She told you that?"

Lewis nods.

"Well that makes it even clearer that she's taken a shine to you."

"Don't be daft!"

"All I'm saying is that you can relate to her; that's all. And that maybe she's picked up on that. You know me and women, never been able to understand them. But I know what I see." He pauses to allow Lewis the opportunity to object, then carries on. "In a way she's found herself here for the very same reason you did." Seeing the objection about to arise, Bradley hurries on. "Or similar. Oh, I know the backgrounds and circumstances are different, but you can't deny there is a chord there."

Lewis smiles, a little weakly.

"I cannot."

"What did he die of?"

Checking the door and windows of the middle cottage one more time, Lewis leans forwards a little towards Bradley. When he speaks, his voice is softer, lower; it is a tone he reserves for when he needs to convey seriousness and calm.

"Afghanistan. IED."

Bradley lets out a low whistle.

"More in common than I thought then."

Lewis lets the comment pass, knowing there is no need to reply. Bradley's next word makes him jump.

"Bugger!"

"What is it?"

"That crack I made about you being lethal and a cold-blooded killer."

"What of it?"

"It might have fallen terribly flat, under the circumstances," Bradley suggests.

"I think it was fine, Bradley; though from what she's said, I think her Ex would have put us both in the shade. Some kind of special forces. Anyway, she seemed to take it in the spirit it was meant." Lewis pauses. "I, on the other hand, thought it was sailing a little close to the wind…"

Bradley smiles.

"One has to push the boundaries from time to time… In any case, I don't think it makes any difference."

"Difference?"

"That she likes you."

When Bradley falls silent they both look out towards the sea, Lewis focused on the rocks at the northern end of the beach. Bradley's eyes are fixed on the pier and do not move when he next speaks.

"Does she know - about you, your past?"

Lewis shakes his head.

"No. Not yet. It didn't seem right to say too much, having only just met her - and she seeming so keen to unburden herself."

"But it's another connection, don't you think?"

"Stop making connections, Bradley. It's a coincidence, nothing more. I might as well say the same thing to you; I wasn't the only one in the army."

"Fair point. But to state the obvious, I'm old; you're her age. You can relate to her - through her husband, and through Emma. That's all I'm saying."

Lewis shakes his head then stands up with the air of a man who is going nowhere.

"Which means nothing - or at least nothing more than I may be able to empathise with her, to offer her someone to talk to if that's what she needs. And she clearly believes she does."

"Well then. And - if I might be so bold, my friend - vice versa."

Staring again at the beach, Lewis thinks about sand, and how different the sand is here to the Middle East; how it feels moist, variable; how it doesn't go on interminably, a vista without interruption for as far as you can see. He knows that's why he likes this beach; it is small, compact, and has defined limits. The rocks at either end are important because they contain it, they have features. And the headland offers height and perspective, from the top the chance to see something else, somewhere else. For a while all he was used to were dunes offering views of other dunes - or rocks that framed more rocks. Or inaccessible mountains. He remembers never-ending roads that cut through vast barren wastes like arteries just beneath the skin; arteries that, in the end, were always vulnerable. Blood spilled from them too often - and, on one occasion, from too close a proximity.

Lewis also knows Bradley is right, that there is a link fostered by that same infertile desert; a link compiled of sudden noise, sudden light, sudden pain. And although his losing Emma may have been nothing like Anna's experience, that they have both lost half of themselves is undeniable. At least he and Emma had never had children. Was that a blessing? He has never been sure.

"Don't worry about me," he says once his thoughts have reorganised themselves, "I'm managing just fine. Haven't I got you to talk to?"

"You have," says Bradley, his voice betraying a gentleness that would surprise any who did not know him well. "Of course you have. But I'm only good for half of you."

He leaves the implication hanging, knowing that it will not be lost; knowing Lewis will pick it up, mentally feel the weight of it, brushing his fingers across its surface for barbs. Bradley knows his friend has been rubbing away at his grief ever since his arrival; if it had been a stone it would now be smooth and polished and round. But it would still be a stone. If Bradley were a man of words rather than a man of action - or an ex-man of action - then he would find a way of telling Lewis that he needs to rid himself of it, to find a way of launching it elsewhere, almost as if he were throwing a pebble into the sea. But he cannot. All he can do is observe, and he sees in Anna the possibility of something; that perhaps they can find a way of helping each other. That is about as far as his sophistication can take him.

He stands.

"Well, I need to be getting on."

"Still varnishing the dinghy?"

"You can never have enough protection. I hate being attacked by something you can't see, and the salt in the sea does just that."

Before he can move, Lewis speaks.

"Was that one of the worst things for you?"

"Was what?"

"Not being able to see who was attacking you. Not being able to see danger - and because of that, seeing danger everywhere. Never able to relax, just in case..."

A couple of seconds pass before Bradley replies.

"When I was a young soldier, Northern Ireland could be like that. Belfast or out in the country, you never knew. And even when you could see people, you didn't know, you couldn't be certain about them. You can't see a religion; you can't see beliefs. I suppose it's the same in the Middle East, but I was only there for a short time at the beginning of Desert Storm. I didn't get to see as much of the place as you."

"You didn't miss much," Lewis smiles, looking back at him. "Now go and polish your bloody boat!"

Bradley places a paw-like hand on Lewis shoulder, then turns and walks to the boat house where he opens the door and then disappears within.

Once he has returned his two outdoor chairs to their rightful place in the small lean-to conservatory at the rear of his cottage, Lewis finds himself standing in the middle of his kitchen somewhat confused and off balance. His day, as he had originally envisaged it, has been strangely compromised. Once he had finished his walk - out beyond the northern rocks and a little way towards the next bay on the hunt for a new perspective for a drawing or painting - he had intended to return to the cottage and, working through his linen basket, sort out some washing and perhaps undertake a little cleaning. He likes to assign specific chores to specific days, finding that by doing so it both gets those things done with reasonable frequency and helps him navigate his week.

His present situation - standing stock still beside his kitchen table - brings back memories of those first few difficult months in the cottage when, unable to get himself organised, he would lurch from activity to activity in a haphazard and incoherent way. Often this would mean that he would do no washing for perhaps two weeks or more, or that his floor would remain un-hoovered for too long, or the dust accumulate to unacceptable levels in the bathroom. A flurry of activity would then remedy the situation, only for his general disquiet to eventually translate itself into the same unsatisfactory state of affairs.

He had given himself a good talking to one unheralded birthday and, apart from the very occasional minor lapse, has stuck to a strict regimen that addressed pretty much all his domestic shortcomings in one fell swoop. Giving himself orders to follow was reassuring. But standing as he does now, his eyes scanning the kitchen work surfaces as if they might hold the clue to an unarticulated dilemma, he feels an echo of that prior time. It is not comfortable, and from somewhere he shivers. Luckily, he thinks - and not for the first time! - he is not the kind of person who is prone to talking to themselves. Had he been, he knows the present circumstance would almost certainly have resulted in a fierce internal dialogue being spoken aloud.

He immediately rules out undertaking an as yet undefined domestic endeavour, partly because he is not in the mood, and partly because it will put his overall routine out of kilter. If he is unsettled at this moment, he has no wish to prolong the agony into tomorrow or the day after. He knows that he could revert back to his original plan and head out to the northern end of the beach - directly this time, rather than via Simon's Crag. He checks his watch. It is not the losing of an hour or so that permits him to rule this option out, but rather his certainty that it will rain soon - and given the time, that rain will be closer than before.

As he ruminates he suddenly hears a door slam. It is, he knows, Anna leaving her cottage and making her way into the village. He realises her doing so simultaneously removes another of his options, namely that of going into the village himself. He knows this is partly a defensive mechanism, but mainly because he does not wish to create the wrong impression. He had wanted to ensure that his relationship with his new neighbour started out in the right kind of way, and considering how the previous hour had been spent, he is satisfied that it is mission accomplished on that front. Were he to then appear to follow her into the village… Well, he knows how that might be construed and their positive beginning might prove all for nothing.

Recognising this, Lewis decides on the default action for any such situation and walks over to the sink where he fills the kettle and then switches it on. He is in no desperate need for anything else to drink, but at least settling down with a coffee will buy him some time. As he organises a mug, the coffee and milk, he finds himself reflecting on his conversation with Bradley, who, he decides, has clearly read a little too much into his exchange with Anna. Perhaps he was only trying to be helpful. In one way it would, of course, be totally in keeping with the unstated motivation of the man he now considers to be his closest friend. Lewis knows their shared - if somewhat divergent - army backgrounds provide the most solid of links. There are things they can talk to each other about which he - and he is certain Bradley - would find difficult to share with most other people. He also knows that Bradley has only his welfare at heart, having taken him under his wing when he first arrived. Bradley's being perceptive enough to see that he was a kind of kindred soul who was somewhat lost, is something for which Lewis can only be grateful. But Bradley's assertion that there had been a connection as far as Anna was concerned is fanciful in the extreme.

The kettle having boiled, he pours the hot water into his mug and stirs the coffee. This has now given him the impetus for the next sequence of actions which is to take the coffee into the front room and to plant himself into his favourite chair by the fireplace. He places the mug down on a coaster on the side table and looks towards the window. Seeing the bookcase in his peripheral vision, Lewis turns his attention to it and finds himself wondering how 'proper' his books might be should they come under Anna's scrutiny. He lifts the coffee and blows the steam away, then replaces the mug on its mat without having attempted to drink any. He is as certain as he can be that she will find her way into his cottage, and that can only mean that she will stand just there, perhaps five feet from where he is sitting right now, and cast her eyes over his shelves. Will they past muster?

Lewis stands and moves to the position which will approximate to where she might one day be standing. Never very good at thinking outside of himself, he tries to assume the attitude of a disinterested observer, and runs his eyes over the shelves, left to right, starting at the top. The first two shelves are perfectly acceptable: mostly maps, a few books on local history and flora and fauna. Two books on birdlife have been particularly well used since he has been in the cottage. He feels he can give these two shelves a 'tick' - even if most of the books had actually been left behind by the cottage's previous owner. The next shelf - and possibly the one upon which Anna's eyes might most naturally fall first - is more problematical. Grisham, Pattison, Clancy, Brown. Lewis suspects that these would not qualify, and what is worse, none of these are leftovers, all having either been brought here in the beginning or subsequently purchased by him. He shakes his head - which is as close as he comes to talking to himself.

There is redemption on the next two shelves he feels. Although the books are old and have been unread for a considerable period of time, there is a good blend of more classic material. Not only the odd Dickens and Hardy, but a copy of 'The Odyssey' that is perhaps Lewis's most treasured book. He first read it at school and it is a story that has stayed with him since then. He picks the volume from the shelf and flicks through its pages in a vague but satisfied way. As he weighs it in his hands, he reconsiders the shelf from which it came. Another tick, he feels, but by the time Anna's eyes will reach it the damage from the shelf above might already have been done.

Lewis walks back to his armchair, drops the Homer onto it, then lifts his mug and takes a sip. Now certain of what he needs to do - and thankful that he has, by accident, suddenly the time - he walks back to the bookcase and starts to remove everything from the third shelf.

Chapter 4

It is telling that they have never truly settled on a term for the somewhat insubstantial structure that juts out apologetically into the sea. Whoever originally named the place, mapped out their vision in a single word - 'Quay' - as if by doing so they might set in motion an unavoidable chain of events that would define both the nature and the fabric of it. The original plinth on which the cottages stand may well have been the vanguard for what was to follow, the unspoken intent being to extend it in breadth and depth so that it would eventually mimic other picturesque harbours; probably not so much those on the east coast, but most likely their more romantic and photogenic brethren further south complete with cob or harbour wall. If that were the case, then the present wooden pier would have been constructed in some haste, the placeholder for a grander vision. That it remains pretty much as built - except for the occasional running repair funded by the village and, most often, executed by Bradley - speaks volumes in terms of both the quality of that original construction and Maunston's failure to meet those initial aspirations.

Some may argue had the railway line been built further inland and on the other side of the village, then the general expansion of the place could only have been towards the sea, conjoining the quay with an early hamlet centred around the green and church. Traffic - in all senses of the word - would have fused both the land- and sea-ward. Under such circumstances, it would surely have been easier to find both drivers and locations for all those facilities which, in being missing, contribute to contemporary folk choosing not to visit Maunston Quay. But instead, the railway acts not as an artery pumping lifeblood into the place, but as something that severs the village from that which was supposed to be its raison d'être.

Ultimately the pier more closely resembles a jetty. It reaches out far enough to accommodate two or three small shallow vessels when the tide is reasonably high, and perhaps just one when not. The wooden planks which form the structure upon which people walk are uniformly spaced, and where Bradley has been at work, his efforts are only noticeable by the age of the decking rather than any misfitting or misalignment. The upright spars - also wooden - stand reasonably straight and true, though the odd one or two have clearly slipped a little over the years and list at imperceptibly modest angles. The lattice of stanchions that hold them together are the sole use of metal in the structure (other than the bolts through the planks and the supports for the steps' treads). There is no guard rail. Although installing one has been discussed, there has never been anything that might be classed as an accident attributable to its absence.

But jetty is something of a derogatory term, and so the villagers will often talk of 'the pier' in preference to anything else. Few harbour any notion that it will be one day replaced by a structure to match the original ambition, and some of those will - if caught off-guard - be the same people who inadvertently drop the 'Quay' from the place name. If asked where they live, 'Maunston' is becoming an increasingly prevalent and popular answer. Not everyone sees things this way, of course. Many guard 'Quay' fervently. The railway station signs are deliberately kept in pristine condition, through pride rather than functional necessity. Bradley again, of course.

Across the last few decades people have sporadically tried to revitalise the dream; to generate momentum which would allow the initial vision to move on again. Fishing seemed an obvious lure, but the bay proved too shallow to accommodate most vessels of even a modest draught, and the jetty too small. And when they did find a suitable ship for a trial period, its catches were too insignificant to be commercially viable. Occasionally Bradley will take people out for recreational fishing. There used to be a small cohort who, annually, would rent the middle cottage for a week and go out almost every day, but it is five years since they were last there. Probably three or four times a year the cottage is let to holiday makers, usually small families whose children enjoy the bliss of having a whole beach to themselves for building sand castles. But there is always something not quite right as far as the parents are concerned, and so these families also fail to return. For the Johnsons, who own the cottage but live in London, it is an investment that was undertaken with ambitions of being their 'holiday pad by the sea' - but it remains an investment almost forgotten. One day they know they will sell it, but only when the price is right.

Yet all this inadequacy does not make Maunston Quay a failure; it simply makes it something other than it was once envisaged becoming. The people who live there tend to have either been born there or have - like Lewis, Bradley and others - found themselves washed up there and never left. Either they have accommodated their lifestyle to suit the place, or the place suits their ambitions impeccably. Ask Oscar and Shirley if they would like to run a larger shop elsewhere and they will say yes; ask them if they would leave the village… Well, that's another matter entirely.

And so it goes on with the small band of people who drape their lives over and around the place, who go about their business - and occasionally each other's business too! - in a generally calm and contented way. There is a surprising degree of solidity and permanence about Maunston Quay. It was one of the things that attracted Lewis, and one Anna is beginning to discover after only a few days. The certainty of the sea, the beach, the cry of the gulls; the rhythm and routine the village forces upon her; the space - in what, paradoxically, is actually a very small slice of geography - to do what she needs to do. One might say 'to be who she needs to be', but it is a little too early for that, though in people like Lewis and Bradley she has examples par excellence.

❋ ❋ ❋

True to her word - and as if to demonstrate the collective nature of an individual's business in Maunston Quay - when Shirley Ryle has confirmation of the delivery slot for Oscar's monthly order, she rings Bradley to let him know. And Bradley - also being true to his word - passes that information on to Lewis, leaving it to him to decide if it is worth informing Anna. When he does mention it in passing, Anna observes that it would probably be better if she wasn't seen laughing at Oscar's expense. Souring a relationship before it had begun is, she suggests, the kind of thing from which one struggles to recover.

Lewis, however, finds himself loitering around the village green just before ten-thirty on the day in question. Knowing that neither Bradley nor Anna will be there to witness events as they unfold, he somehow feels as if the cottages should be represented, especially as Shirley is keen to share the ignominy to be heaped on her brother - and because it is always of value to remain in Shirley's good books. As the real power and influence in the shop, hers is a unique position as far as the village is concerned; so much of their everyday need passes through her hands.

Consequently, he has walked inland this morning and taken the short route through the churchyard and part way to the next village before doubling back and emerging onto the lane near 'The Anchor'. He is sitting on one of the two benches that overlook the green, eyes alternately fixed on the shop and the landward road into Maunston Quay. The day is grey but still; the kind of English spring day that could go either way.

"So Shirley's got you to act as witness too?"

A voice from his left forces him to turn.

"I thought I saw you as you went past the pub, and guessed you might be heading here."

Jenny Christie takes a seat next to Lewis and looks not at him but towards the shop.

"Well, you know how it is. Of course, I don't condone public humiliation, but if this ends up being part of village folklore - even for a short while - then, sadly, it might be good to be able to say 'I was there'."

"Sure. And you don't want to cross Shirley."

"There is that," he confesses with a smile.

Ignoring Bradley's recent theories, if anyone has taken a shine to him it is Jenny. Lewis can recollect no specific incident which gave rise to such interest, nor identify anything that he may or may not have done which would have given her cause to pursue him. Even now, in a minuscule example of proximity, she sits just a little too close to him on the bench as if she is gradually wearing away at him like a drip from a tap onto a not entirely granite surface.

That Lewis genuinely likes Jenny makes the situation both bearable and awkward by degrees; likewise that she is Landlady of 'The Anchor'. But the fact she is married renders consequence - even if that were on Lewis's mind - impossible. By her own admission, Jenny had more than once confessed to others that her marriage to Tommy was on the rocks, and that she is sinking, fearing she will be lost without trace. And then Lewis arrived, an arrival that brought with it promise, opportunity. Although flattered, Lewis has never seen himself as anyone's knight in shining armour, least of all Jenny's. Had her domestic circumstances been different, had she and Tommy been siblings like Oscar and Shirley, would that have made any difference? It is a question he doesn't like to contemplate too much, in part because he thinks he knows the answer; and knowing the answer, he is certain that one simple movement to take Jenny's hand could be all that is needed to divert destinies, and not just theirs. The slim distance that exists between them now as they sit - perhaps observed by Tommy, who knows? - remains charged. Jenny brings that charge with her wherever she goes, and he is always the recipient. And it is not as if it is unobserved by others. Bradley, whilst affirming that it is none of his business, has more than once urged caution. Lewis's assertion that "nothing has happened, nothing will happen" has quite obviously been taken with a pinch of salt. "People are not stupid" has been Bradley's stock reply.

Tommy, to his credit, has not allowed his wife's evident leanings towards Lewis get in the way. He strives to run the pub according to a series of unwritten rules, and tries to treat all his customers as friends rather than clientele. He knows his service - like Oscar and Shirley's - is a monopoly as far as the village is concerned, but he is not so naive as to think 'The Anchor' will continue to enjoy their patronage no matter what. Lewis knows a little of Tom and Jerry's life before Maunston Quay - 'Tom and Jerry' being the affectionate sobriquet used for them by their fellow villagers, largely behind their backs. They have been in charge of the pub for nearly five years; before that they were further south, somewhere in London. Lewis has more than once wondered what brought them here. What were they looking for something or running from? For him, these are the only two options. And perhaps uncharitably, he has found himself asking the question as to whether Jenny 'has form', and if he is perhaps the latest in a line of conquests, either failed or not. It is not a chivalrous line of enquiry, but one which constantly badgers him whenever he is in Jenny's presence.

At the edge of his vision, the arrival of a blue van belonging to one of the shop's regular suppliers intrudes on his thoughts.

"Show time!" says Jenny, seeing it at the same time as he, yet rising first.

As he stands, he sees Shirley appear out of the shop. She glances their way. Lewis thinks he can see the trace of a smile, but he is a little too far away to be sure.

It takes them just a few moments to cross the green. As they reach the shop, Oscar emerges from it and follows the driver to the back of the van.

"Morning," says Shirley, standing sentinel at the same location as before.

"Morning," says Jenny as Lewis nods. "Morning Oscar."

Oscar, staring into the back of the van, fails to respond. Either he has not heard her or his present preoccupation is taking all his concentration.

Hearing an expletive escape from the shopkeeper, Jenny and Lewis wander to the rear of the van and peer in. On the left hand side of the van is a small palette containing a varied array of boxes of different shapes and sizes. Lewis can make out packs of baked beans, boxes of biscuits and chocolate bars. Opposite it on the other side is a second palette comprising entirely of packs of toilet rolls.

"You can check it," the driver says as he hands Oscar his copy of the documentation, "but this is what you've ordered and what you'll have been charged for. So where do you want them?"

There is something in his voice that betrays amusement, though he is doing well to refrain from laughing.

"How many are there?" Oscar pleads.

"Six hundred. Packs that is. Individual rolls? Well, nearly two and a half thousand."

Shirley joins them.

"Problem?"

"Are you expecting some kind of epidemic?" Jenny asks, trying to add a note of fear to her voice.

The notion of an uncontrollable explosion of bottoms proves too much for the van driver who bursts out laughing.

"Bloody hell," says Oscar, realising his mistake.

The driver pulls the first few packets from the pile.

"So, where do you want them?"

"Bloody hell," repeats Oscar.

Lewis takes a step forwards.

"Can we give you a hand with these, Oscar?"

For the next few minutes there is a relay from the back of the van, through the shop, and into the store room. Shirley insists they first find a location for everything except what she calls "Oscar's insurance against global incontinence", and she remains out the back directing the putting away as Oscar, the driver, Jenny and Lewis unload. Once the first pallet is emptied, they start on the second, taking between four and six packs of toilet rolls at a time. As he passes him in the shop, Lewis notices Oscar's face getting redder.

"He'll explode once we've gone," he says to Shirley once he has divested himself of his fourth load.

"He may well do," she agrees, "but it's his own stupid fault. Anyway, there's no harm done is there? It's not as if they'll go off or anything. We just won't have to buy any more for a little while."

"Good job they're white," he suggests.

"Oh, don't worry. If I'd seen he was about to order thousands of pink rolls or rolls with flowers on I'd have stopped him."

Jenny arrives with another few packs, attempting to squeeze past Lewis to get into the stock room.

"I'll get some more," Lewis says, excusing himself.

"Put your next lot in the shed out in the yard," Shirley calls after him, "I've already unlocked it. Thought we might be needing the extra space."

Lewis ends up taking the final few rolls into the shop where he places them halfway up the back stairs, the small available space in the shed having filled up a few minutes previously.

"Don't worry," Shirley says, "we'll sort things out in a bit; they won't stay there for very long."

When they get outside again, they are just in time to see the van making a circuit of the green. As it heads away, the driver toots his horn. Oscar is watching it disappear, the receipt for the order in his hands. Lewis sees Jenny walking back towards the pub.

"Thanks for helping out, Lewis," Oscar says.

Lewis notices his colour has almost returned to normal.

"No problem. It was handy I happened to be about." Lewis shoots Shirley a glance.

"I can see the issue," Oscar says, missing the inference and staring down at the paperwork. "Put the decimal point in the wrong place. You'd think their computer would know that wasn't what I wanted, wouldn't you?"

"I guess they're just not that clever," Lewis suggests.

"Maybe they figure you know what you're doing."

If Shirley's comment is intended to be a little incendiary, Oscar lets it pass.

"Anyway, now you're here; has anyone mentioned the meeting in the pub on Thursday evening?"

"Meeting?"

"You know, the annual village meeting. About what we're going to do this year."

"Ideas for summer events, things like that?" says Lewis, knowing exactly what Oscar is talking about.

"That's the one. Anyway, seven thirty. Is that okay?"

"Fine by me. I assume the usual crew will be there."

"As many as can make it, I daresay," Shirley chips in. "Most will just turn up to witness Tommy putting his hand in his pocket for the sandwiches."

Lewis acknowledges the joke.

"I'll be there. How about Anna coming along to?"

"Anna?" asks Oscar, out of step with events.

"The lady who's renting from the Johnson's. You may not have met her yet. She seems sensible enough, and as an outsider she might have a different perspective. What do you think, Shirley?"

In the process of turning to go back into the shop, Shirley pauses, her hands already moving to unfasten her apron straps.

"Why not? More the merrier. Might even be able to lend the proceedings a little badly needed common sense."

Oscar watches his sister go indoors, then sighs.

"Yes, of course," Oscar says, Lewis failing to understand the link he is making. He pauses for a moment. "Shirley's always so bloody sceptical about things. We're only trying to see if we can make the best of the place, that's all. I sometimes wonder where her heart lies."

Whether Oscar intended it or not, Lewis knows his words are open to multiple interpretations. Indeed, in one very specific direction there is no wonder involved at all. But he leaves it be; Oscar has had enough agitation for one morning.

"Well, better get on," he says, placing a hand briefly on Oscar's shoulder. "See you later."

He is half way across the green when he hears Oscar calling after him.

"Did you get what you came for, by the way?"

Lewis waves his hand in the air without turning, hoping to convey the message that he did.

When Oscar finds Shirley out at the back of the shop she has already hung up her apron and is looking in the mirror as she combs her hair. He loiters by the door waiting, knowing she has either seen or sensed his presence.

"You might have told me," he says after a while, it becoming evident that Shirley is not going to break the silence.

She stops fussing with her hair and turns towards him. Being an elder sister, Shirley grew up with an inevitable sense of superiority over her brother. It is something that suits her personality, though she is probably unable to say if her bossiness is natural or whether she just grew into it. Either the years have been kind to her or hard on Oscar, but the casual eye would be unable to tell that there is four years' difference between them. They have even - or rare occasions - been mistaken for twins; something that only further feeds Shirley's innate need to establish an air of superiority.

"Told you what?"

"About the order." Oscar is still holding his copy of the paperwork, and he flutters it in the space between them. "You might have told me I'd got it wrong."

"How was I to know?" she asks, pushing past him. "I don't check the orders, do I? I assume you know what you're doing."

"You say that," he says, following her, "but I know you've spotted things in the past."

"Maybe I have," she says, fussing with the chocolate display, ensuring that the various bars are neatly aligned.

"So why not this time?"

"Because I didn't see it? Maybe that was the reason, Oscar. Or do you want me to check all your homework?"

To the outsider, Shirley's comment is simply flippant, but for Oscar it brings back distant and painful memories when she *did* check his homework, when as a bossy teenager she was often given license by their parents to force her brother to re-write a story or repeat a series of maths questions. At the time Oscar was too young to protest, and even though it cost him time, his reward - and the justification Shirley used time and again in support of her actions - was that marks for his homework were consistently among the highest in his class. "Imagine if Shirley hadn't helped you" had been one of their mother's favourite sayings when suitably prompted by her daughter. Since then the word 'homework' had, for Oscar, been code for an entire childhood.

"Anyway," Shirley goes on, trying to be conciliatory, "no harm done really. It's not as if they'll spoil, is it? No worry that people are going to suddenly stop shitting. The back room will be a bit cramped for a while, but that's not a big issue. And if it were - *and* if I'd seen your mistake - I'd have stopped you, wouldn't I?"

Oscar doesn't trust the logic, simply because there is a large part of him that doesn't trust her. He glances back at the documentation, then walks behind the counter and slides it into a drawer. As he looks up, he realises that Shirley is at the door and just about to leave.

"Where are you going?"

"Out. I've done my shift. Your turn - if you think you'll be able to handle the lunchtime rush." She makes the comment knowing that no such thing exists, and because she feels the need to continually remind him of the smallness of their endeavour.

Many years previously, before they had come to Maunston Quay, they'd had the opportunity to open a store in Lowestoft. It would have been a step up from the corner shop the family ran on the outskirts of King's Lynn. There had been significant family debate. It would have been their first endeavour away from their parents, as well as a significant increase in terms of business size and complexity. The arguments in favour of making the move had been considerable. But Oscar had not felt ready for the responsibility; he'd argued that Lowestoft was too far away, and that their parents - who weren't getting any younger - would soon be relying on them more and more. Shirley had never forgiven them - the three of them - for outvoting her. And so the opportunity had slipped away almost as quickly as their parents seemed to a few years later. They'd been left with the old shop and a bagful of not great memories. When the idea was floated - this time by Oscar - that they needed a fresh start, Shirley had been only too willing to agree. Maunston Quay hadn't been her idea of where they'd end up, but it had it's compensations. And now, at fifty-three, it was almost too late for much else.

"So where are you going? Just so I know."

"A walk, Oscar. A walk. I might go down to see how Anna's settling in. Or I might go to the next village. Or, if I'm feeling really bold, I might just get a train to somewhere and never come back."

At that, Shirley turns and leaves the shop. She knows full well that her destination is no secret to Oscar. Aubrey Rees is a delicate subject between them, not because there is inherently anything wrong with Aubrey - like everyone else in the village, he is a perfectly acceptable individual - it is what he represents that causes the friction. Whether she realises it or not (and Oscar suspects she does), Aubrey is Shirley's last chance to change her life; and because of that, Shirley knows Oscar fears Aubrey more than anyone else.

"While you're there, ask him if he's going to the meeting on Thursday," he calls after her.

The walk from the shop to the forge takes Shirley less than two minutes. On one side of the green, near the bench from which Lewis and Jenny had awaited the commencement of Oscar's recent drama, is a row of four cottages bisected by a rough track wide enough to accommodate a small van. It is to this she immediately heads. To the uninformed observer, the track gives the impression it will lead to private parking at the back of the cottages, but it does not. Extending beyond the boundary of their rear gardens, the track bears slightly left and then, after a further thirty yards or so, back to the right. It is only at this point - and once the trees that sit at the corner of the dog-leg have been passed - that the forge comes into view.

Once upon a time it would have been central to the village, a focal point because of the indispensable services it provided to Maunston Quay's residents. But as the village expanded, it did so away from the forge, preferring the other side of the green and a greater proximity to the church. When the row of four dwellings through which the track passes were built towards the end of the nineteenth century, they effectively cut it off for good. It was a dissection repeated later by the railway between the village and the quay, the line running not that far behind the forge. By that point in time the forge was already in decline as a commercial concern. Over the next few years, the arrival of the car, the reduction in the number of farms in the area, along with the failure of the village to generate any meaningful trade from the sea, were triple body blows. Demand for hand-crafted, wrought metal work simply fell off a cliff.

Aubrey Rees is only too aware of the forge's history. It has been in his family for over one hundred and fifty years. When he was taught the trade by his father, they were skills passed on as heritage rather than as a talent upon which to base a business. Arthur Rees had attempted to diversify as much as he could, but lacked the imagination and flair to be proficient in anything beyond maintaining old farm equipment and the occasional fence or five-bar gate. The day he handed the metaphorical keys to his son was not one of celebration; Arthur was convinced the place would be in ruins before he died. "Give me two years," Aubrey had said to him; if it did not work out they would sell up and allow the forge to be remodelled as a pair of up-market cottages. From the proceeds, Arthur would be installed in a retirement home as close to the village as possible, and the son would seek his fortune elsewhere. It was the outcome everyone expected.

Aubrey's discovery of the flair and imagination his father lacked came as something of a surprise to both of them, possibly Aubrey most of all. He found he was able to turn his hand to more decorative iron work, and started to experiment with an output that was smaller in scale and more delicate in nature. His portfolio grew to include latches and locks, mountings and housings for external lights and lamps. He took an old Littlewoods' catalogue and went through it to find things that he might be able to make in the forge. In consequence, his output extended to hat stands and coat racks, frames for pictures and mirrors, chandeliers, even the odd barbecue. And then one day, almost by accident, he crafted his first sculpture - the form of a bird. It was never going to be a roaring success as a business, but by the end of that second year, Aubrey had satisfied himself that he could make an adequate living from the place, his only regret being that his father had never lived to see him do so.

Shirley knows all this too. As she takes that slight right turn and emerges from beneath the trees, she can hear the tell-tale hammering of Aubrey at work. She has always found it incongruous - and just a little amazing - that he can produce such delicate and beautiful things using hands that are rough and worn, scarred from years of accident and incident, and that boast fingers the size of prime farmhouse sausages. Almost every time she makes this short journey - which is almost daily now - she recalls her first sighting of him, bent over his anvil, goggles on, his right arm hammering at metal, back-lit by the glow from the forge. It remains something of a clichéd image she knows, but that first day it had simply taken her breath away.

The forge itself is housed in an open stone-built adjunct to the side of the house. The extractor above the fire tapers into a tall chimney which releases the gathered heat into the air. Most days the prevailing wind disperses what little smoke there is away from the village, but on contrary days when Aubrey is working, she can stand on the threshold of the shop and smell the place. She walks towards him slowly now, in part because she does not wish to disturb him, but also to make the moment last as long as possible. For those who do not know her well, the notion of Shirley as a romantic seems preposterous, completely at odds with the brusque, slightly harsh woman who rules over Oscar and the shop. Indeed, she had never considered herself romantic or weak in that way - at least not until she met Aubrey. If you were to ask Oscar what he felt about the whole thing - ask him in an unguarded moment, that is - and if he were capable of articulating exactly what he felt, then it would be described as fear, because he is afraid that Aubrey will take Shirley away from him, and away from the shop. Deep down, Oscar knows he is nothing without her.

Aubrey, sensing her presence, looks up from his anvil, then releases his grip on his hammer and raises his goggles. His left hand, still gripping the tongs that have been holding the heated metal he has been beating, now moves forward to plunge the iron into the water bath. It is a fluid action undertaken almost without looking and with simple and complete confidence.

"The delivery's been then?" he says.

"How do you know?"

"You wouldn't be here if it hadn't; wouldn't want to miss the show."

Shirley walks forward again, sitting herself on the low wall that frames part of his working space.

"How did he take it?"

"Pretty well, considering. Mind you, he could hardly explode, not with witnesses on hand."

"Who?"

"Jenny and Lewis." She sees Aubrey raise an eyebrow then try and disguise that he has done so by wiping the back of his hand across his forehead. "Coincidentally. Really."

Still holding the tongs, he pulls the object they are holding from the water. She stands up and walks towards him.

"What are you making?"

He releases his grip and allows the object - a swift - to drop into his free hand. It is perhaps eight inches across, yet looks smaller, more delicate. He holds it out to her.

"It isn't hot." As she takes it from him, he continues. "A request from that craft centre place up at the country park. They took a few on trial a couple of weeks ago and have managed to sell nearly all of them. So they've asked for some more."

She is mesmerised by the way he has been able to capture the grace and fluidity of the bird in his dark crude metal. She knows how brilliant it will look once he has treated it, burnished it.

"Swifts mainly - apparently the shape sells. But they've said they'll take one or two other things, to try out, like."

She opens her hand and offers it back to him.

"Tea?" she asks as he takes it from her.

"Aye."

As she walks past him towards the house, she plants a kiss on his cheek.

"You're filthy and you smell," she says approvingly.

❋ ❋ ❋

Lewis is almost away from the village, walking down the road towards the station and home, when he hears the first shout. Pausing, he turns and sees Shirley part-way across the green with Oscar standing in the doorway of their shop, shouting after her. Unable to make out what her brother says, whatever it is proves insufficient to stop Shirley as she marches onwards. She is, Lewis knows, heading to the forge to see Aubrey. As he resumes his progress, the thought of their relationship forces him to smile. The general consensus is that they make an odd couple - though no-one seems entirely confident of the exact depth of their liaison. Both are rough sorts in their own, distinct ways, but whenever Lewis has observed them together he has never been able to deny their proximity seems to uncover some softer trait buried within each of them. If he is honest with himself, initially he was not particularly fond of Shirley, and always took Aubrey to be the archetypal village artisan; almost a caricature of himself. But seeing them together changed both perceptions. He instantly warmed to Shirley after that, and, as if to compensate, also became more tolerant and understanding of Oscar. And as far as Aubrey was concerned, once he had revealed himself - and his indisputable metalworking talents had risen to the surface - Lewis was happy to add him to a very limited list of people with whom he would be happy to share a pint. One of Aubrey's swifts adorns the wall by the front door of his cottage.

Coincidentally, it is as he is having this precise thought he finds himself passing 'The Anchor' and hears the second shout. Certain of its origin, Lewis slows his pace but does not stop. He knows Jenny will be with him in a few moments and is certain that she will not wish to stand around in plain sight talking to him. It is a strange affectation, this apparent desire for some kind of superficial secrecy when everyone and his dog knows how she appears to feel about him - even her long-suffering husband. Perhaps that is part of the thrill for her.

"Hello again stranger," she says as he reaches him.

"Stranger?" he questions, glad she has not attempted to place her arm through his. "Hardly."

"You haven't been in the pub for days. Maybe nearly a week."

"Oh, has Tommy missed me?"

She falls into step, her countenance dropping just a little at the mention of her husband's name.

"Tommy misses everyone. Sometimes I think he has a secret list somewhere, like a register, where he keeps track of people, when they come in, when they don't."

"Doesn't he?" Lewis asks, the idea striking him as exactly the sort of thing Tommy *would* do - but solely for professional reasons. "If he did, he'd only be doing it for the sake of the business, not to keep tabs on people."

He is unsure why he has made that final remark. Perhaps it was a reference - unconsciously made - to Jenny's observation that he hadn't been in 'The Anchor' recently. Was that some kind of 'keeping tabs' on her part? When Jenny fails to reply, Lewis reverts to the conventional.

"How is business?"

She laughs and looks up at him for the first time since falling into step.

"The same as it always is. You know that! How can it be any different? Apart from maybe getting worse. Where would all our new custom come from to make it better?"

Jenny, who is just a year younger than Lewis, is the kind of woman who looks precisely her age. Lewis is convinced that if you were to ask a group of random strangers how old she was, they would all guess late thirties or early forties with the average coming out at precisely forty-one. You could be forgiven, therefore, for describing her face as 'honest', at least in that sense. Considering she has made no secret of the crush she has on him and the contempt in which she holds her husband, Lewis knows he should also trust Jenny's honesty to extend beyond her looks; yet there is something upon which he cannot put his finger and in consequence suspends that particular belief.

Having endured various stages of fear and flattery as far as Jenny's overtures to him have been concerned, Lewis has arrived at a point where he simply tolerates them. If he now occupies a position where they just bounce off him, perhaps it is because he cannot believe anyone who is so overt could possibly be serious about him. Perhaps it is also because he does not hold himself in sufficient regard that he fails to perceive himself as desirable material. His relatively open indifference has stood him in good stead with the rest of the village, at least - and perhaps most noticeably with Tommy. Lewis seems to have been able to tread an undefined line in such as way as to permit him to balance what might reside on either side of it, a skill that he has recognised if not openly acknowledged. The fact that it is a narrow line, however, is plain - something which both his own and Bradley's consciences are only too happy to frequently remind him. As he has already felt that very morning, it might only take one movement, one gesture, one unguarded word, for the apple cart to be well and truly toppled over. But he has no intention of doing so; no desire to call Jenny's bluff. And it is perhaps this - the notion that she is bluffing, that it is all just a game - that allows him to play along.

"He's hoping - as ever - that someone comes up with a brilliant idea on Thursday that gets the punters flooding in. That's why he's prepared to make the investment."

"Investment?"

"The sandwiches."

"Oh, yes."

"And," she says, pausing for effect, "the first round on the house!"

"That is serious!" says Lewis, picking up her tone. "We'd better bring our 'A' game."

"At the very least."

They have reached that point in the road where the level crossing is just ahead and the cottages are beginning to edge into view. The railway representing a boundary, Lewis wonders how far Jenny is intending to accompany him. When they are together he feels safe enough on the village-side of the line, but once they have crossed, vulnerability creeps up on him. It is an emotion that surprised him the first time he felt it; surprised him sufficiently for him to try and avoid a repetition if at all possible.

As they get to within the faded yellow warning boxes painted on the road, Jenny stops, looking straight ahead. Following her gaze,

Lewis sees a figure descending from Simon's Crag towards the cottages. In her red coat, it can only be Anna.

"How's the new neighbour?" Jenny asks a little flatly.

"Anna?" Lewis stops too, some ten feet or so ahead of her. "She seems very nice. Have you met her yet?"

"Should I have?"

"I just wondered if she'd been in the pub at all; or maybe you'd bumped into her in the village."

Jenny shakes her head.

"I've seen her once or twice, but not to speak to." Jenny's eyes are glued to the figure. "She's young."

"Not really," Lewis finds her observation slightly surprising. "She's younger than us I think, but only a little. I wouldn't say she was 'young' per se."

When Jenny says nothing, Lewis feels strangely defensive.

"She's had a hard time of late," he offers, "and just needs some peace and quiet. Great place to come for that, eh?"

"Nothing ever happens here," Jenny says, a little cryptically. "But maybe it will soon, who knows?"

Lewis laughs a little.

"Somehow I doubt that, don't you?"

"Well, it's not for the want of trying."

There is an edge in Jenny's voice that surprises him; a tone that seems to encompass all his knowledge about her and more. For a split second it is as if she has pulled back a curtain and permitted him a glimpse beyond; as if somewhere there is a truth hidden of which he is currently unaware, and which would upset all his preconceptions if it became known.

"I need to get back," she says suddenly, "floors to sweep and bars to polish."

He expects more, but after the most minute of pauses, she simply turns and starts to walk away.

"See you Thursday," he calls after her.

Lewis watches for a moment, half expecting a turn to glance back or a wave. But there is nothing. He breathes out deeply. It is almost a sigh; almost as if he has been holding his breath. He registers his surprise then begins to head for home.

The red coat is nowhere to be seen.

❉ ❉ ❉

"The brewery have just phoned to say the delivery will be a couple of hours late." Tommy is behind the bar restocking the mixers when Jenny walks in.

From the outside, 'The Anchor' appears to be more red brick than timber framed, though hints at the latter - and a nod to the pub's history - can still be found both in the porch where the main entrance is located and, incongruously, in a conservatory-style extension to the 'Lounge' bar that was added perhaps twenty years ago. The faux beams suggest leanings towards an historical legacy of which the pub may not be worthy. A new visitor, whether or not confused by the jarring blend of external styles, will almost certainly be thrown by the interior. Judging the book by its cover, one would be forgiven for expecting to be met by somewhat dark and sombre decor, the bar and the shelving behind it clad in a dark wood, stained or otherwise, and surely around the periphery of what can only be the common area, waist high panelling against which deep but dated in-built sofas and padded benches are ranged.

In fact, the interior of 'The Anchor' is much more welcoming than that. At some point in its history it has been opened out and the division between the traditional 'Public' and 'Lounge' bars removed to present a surprisingly cavernous space. That there is light too is probably the second thing to hit a new visitor. Any dark wood that may have existed has been replaced by a much friendlier veneer, and the walls against which free-standing chairs and sofas are arranged have been painted a cream colour; a magnolia with just a trace of pink. Set out as a dining area, the conservatory extension admits great swathes of light into its space, too; light that is enhanced by the mirrors which run the full length of the bar. Two light wells - strategically placed near the pool table and darts board - drag brightness in from the sky. Having taken it all in, the visitor - pleasantly surprised or not - can only conclude it is a good pub in the wrong place; that it probably belongs in a city, or perhaps as a bijou watering hole by the side of a canal basin. Such was certainly Lewis's first impression.

For Jenny, as she now walks towards the bar, weaving between the pale blue and light orange armchairs, slipping around one of the dining tables that has found itself located outside of the conservatory, it is a landscape invisible to her. When she and Tommy had first viewed the place they too had been surprised at what they had found. Coming from a small, inner-city pub, here was somewhere which cried out for bustling weekend clientele and a menu that would rapidly gain a reputation. It had been easy for the agent to sell them the dream, and in buying it they had ignored the practicalities and implications of location.

During their first few months, they had tried hard to create an image and build a profile. They had experimented with menus, spent money on advertising, distributed posters and fliers in the nearby towns - all with little effect. After six months they were talking about leaving. But Tommy had already come to like the quiet routine Maunston Quay offered him; he didn't miss the city at all, and was beginning to relish being a known member of a small community, rather than an anonymous fish in a very large pond. When it became clear he was not for retreating, Jenny threatened him. He ignored her, and she stayed. A political historian might chart that episode as the beginnings of civil disobedience.

"Did they say why?" she asks.

"Something about a driver strike somewhere. I'm not sure."

It wasn't that she was particularly unhappy; it was rather that her dream, the belief as to what she would 'get' from their move, had failed to match expectations. She had been let down. For that she blamed the only person she could, outside of herself.

"Did you ask Shirley about the salmon?" Tommy's disembodied voice comes to her from behind the counter where he is now busy emptying the glass washer.

She moves to one of the bar stools and sits down, her eyes running along the mirrors, trying to seek out dirt or smudge marks Tommy might have missed.

"Salmon?"

"I thought you were going to check with Shirley that she'd been able to order that extra salmon for Thursday."

"Yes, of course."

"'Yes, of course' you were going to ask, or 'yes, of course' she's ordered it?" Tommy's head appears in front of her as he stands up.

She looks at him and for a moment tries to remember what it was that first attracted her to him. He is only slightly taller than her, but solidly built; when they had first met, use of the term 'athletic' would not have been out of place. The memories she has of watching him play tennis have been blurred by both time and the disappointment that the man at whom she now looks gives the impression of never having lifted a racquet in his life. She can't recall when she started comparing him with other men in an overtly critical way; at least she now knows that she does, even if she also knows she shouldn't. Just at this minute, Tommy is running a distant second to Lewis. She tries not to think what it means when she feels he might be trailing behind Bradley.

"So we're sorted then." Tommy says more to himself, not expecting a reply.

"Yes," she says, her thoughts clearly elsewhere.

"How's your friend?"

It is all he can muster, but whenever Lewis comes up in conversation between them, he always refers to him as "your friend". He actually quite likes the man and is free enough with his name either face-to-face or in other company. Although he knows he may appear not to know what is going on all the time, Tommy is confident he is sharper than most people give him credit for, and certainly more on the ball than Jenny thinks.

She looks at him properly, but says nothing.

"Did he say anything about his new neighbour?"

"Why should he?" Jenny asks, dismissing the impulse to let on that she has seen Anna, if only from a distance. Although she was too far away to make any kind of judgement, she would not be averse to concocting something if the need arose.

"No reason," Tommy says casually, turning his attention to an examination of the spirit optics. He can see Jenny in the mirror, her eyes following him. "I met her - Anna - in the shop yesterday."

"You didn't say."

"Didn't I? Didn't think it was important, I suppose. Nice looking woman, though, I'll say that. Slim. Looks a little tired, if I'm honest, but I suppose some rest or whatever here will do her the world of good."

Jenny, knowing she can add nothing legitimately or otherwise, has no choice but to let it go. She looks along the bar then stands up.

"Funny he didn't mention her though," Tommy smiles to himself, "considering."

Chapter 5

It is seldom a good thing when the kettle seems to take longer than usual to boil; it nearly always opens up a sliver of time useful for little else other than thinking. It is the same now as Lewis stands in his kitchen, eyes fixed on the kettle's spout, awaiting the tell-tale steam, Jenny front-and-centre in his mind. He doesn't like being on his guard when she is around - nor having to double the guard when they are isolated from anyone else. Being on his guard is no longer a natural state for him.

There had been a time, of course, when he had needed to be aware of every sound, every movement - and every subtle nuance hidden in those sounds and movements. But that related to a time when he had been striving to preserve his life and there could be no other focus. He doesn't kid himself that there is any real comparison. Finding yourself in a situation where you were about to enter a building through a darkened doorway with no idea what might lay on the other side, has no parallel with his entanglements with Jenny. Back then, for a few seconds everything in the background was instinctively eliminated; all sounds vanished apart from those of your boots on the rubble; all feelings are expunged other than that of the tactile attachment of finger to trigger. Stepping out of the light and into the dark, you know it can go either way.

Lewis knows he was lucky. He knows too intimately people who went through similar doorways never to come out, never to have their senses - sound, touch, sight - returned to normal because they had them all stolen away. Of course his experience with Jenny is nothing like that. Nothing can be. Yet it is the one thing - her presence and her potential unpredictability - that still puts him on edge.

As the steam starts to rise from the kettle, he walks to the fridge to retrieve the milk. He would like to be able to resolve the situation with Jenny, convinced that there is something which requires resolution. He would like to be able to relax in her presence, to discuss mundane things with her in the same way he does with Shirley or Maisie. There is nothing intrusive there; no spectre sitting on anyone's shoulder; no destabilising genii threatening to run amok once outside of its bottle. He makes his coffee then returns the milk to the fridge. Cradling the mug, he walks into the front room and looks out through the window. It is slightly greyer now, both the sea and the sky. He watches the distant waves as they roll in to the beach, then retreat to build up their strength. They, of course, are oblivious to his predicament; oblivious and unconcerned.

He has considered trying to bring the situation with Jenny to a head. Soft and subtle rejection does not seem to be having any effect at all, but to take irretrievable and drastic action is to risk so much more. In spite of the indifference of the natural elements, the human dimension of Maunston Quay has some interest in him. His dilemma - if it might be considered that - is not a private one. Occasionally, he feels as if he is an actor in a play - a three-hander probably - with the bulk of the villagers paying spectators. If he has given himself lines to act out, then he tries to stick to them as best he can; but he knows there is no written script, and that each cast member is entirely at the mercy of the improvisation of the others. He sips his coffee and wonders 'what if?'. What if Jenny suddenly declares herself more openly or forcefully? What if Tommy, having suffered subtle humiliation long enough, decides to take the bull by the horns? What if, one day, he weakens? He needs to trust himself. He knows how much self-control he has. He has demonstrated - by walking towards a darkened doorway - just how disciplined he can be.

There are times - and he is not sure if these are real or the fantasies of a confused mind - when he thinks that Jenny is just playing a game too, that she has no designs on him at all. Hers is a masquerade, a charade designed to achieve some other, unspecified end; a scenario where he is nothing more than a puppet, a bit-part player in her plot. He wonders - hopes more than wonders, probably - if she is not really pursuing him at all. But even here, Lewis feels he is letting himself down; he feels as if he is not sophisticated enough to know exactly what is going on, never mind being able to handle it. At least with the threatening darkness of a rectangle in the wall of a building you really knew where you stood - it was black and white.

If this struggle for certainty in the clouded present day is in part a consequence of his past, then he knows he must accept it. As he stands, drinks his coffee, watches, he catches sight of a small boat as it rounds the headland. Bradley, rowing, returning home. Out fishing perhaps, or simply taking exercise. Lewis watches the stroke which, even from this distance, he can clearly see is smooth, measured. It is the stroke of a man who is in control. If he envies anything in Bradley it is this control; the fact that he understands how to live with himself, that he has reconciled both his past and future. Lewis knows that such reconciliation is what he too needs above all else. He is grateful for Bradley's help, their conversations about the past. Bradley helps him wrap context around his life; helps him to see where he is - even if he is yet to get to where he is going. But as he stands, sipping his coffee, Lewis is beginning at last to have a view on that. It may be slightly hazy and out of focus, but he is comforted that there is something there. And it is a something that does not include Jenny, of that he is sure. Does it include Maunston Quay? Lewis thinks so, for now at least.

❀❀❀

Anna had seen Bradley setting out in his rowing boat from the top of Simon's Crag. She had waved, a sign he acknowledged without seeming to break stroke. She had loitered at the top of the promontory for a few moments watching him, then looked out to sea before descending, her mind made up.

Had she not returned to her cottage for the sole purpose of changing into a lighter jumper, she would have left the quay a few minutes earlier and encountered Lewis as he came back from the village. But as it is, she emerges into the fresh air for a second time just as he is waiting for the kettle, and by the time he is at his window observing their small slice of the world, she is already across the railway tracks and heading for the village.

She has no appointment as such and, as she approaches the church, finds herself unsure whether she would prefer it to be open or closed. She had made the decision to introduce herself to the vicar as she stood on top of the headland, and, having done so, to be forced to postpone the introduction would be less than ideal; firstly, because there would then be a possibility they would meet when she was unprepared, and secondly, because that coming together might occur publicly. Unsure of herself, the one thing she knows she wants is privacy. In spite of all that, even as she places her hand on the church door's latch, she finds herself hoping it is locked.

The latch lifts easily, and she hears the resounding echo of its movement as the trapped sound ricochets within the confines of the building. Pushing the door open, it feels strange that she should hear the space before she sees it, and wonders what kind of omen that may be. Once across the threshold, she pauses to absorb the place.

The church is entirely the opposite to 'The Anchor', not only in the nature of its ministrations but because what greets you on the inside is exactly what you would expect to see. At the far end, there is a small and not particularly elegant or elaborate stained glass window above a chancel which boasts a simple altar decked in white cloth and supporting a relatively small gold cross. There are two single benches on either side, set against the wall, to form the choir. Standing slightly to the left of the nave, the pulpit is similarly simple and modestly adorned, the single step up to it plainly visible from where she stands. There is one central aisle on either side of which are narrow rows of almost rustic pews. She estimates that the church can perhaps hold no more than two hundred people. Towards the rear of the building where she has paused, the font stands in splendid isolation. The only other furnishings are immediately to her left; two small tables covered in a dark green baize upon which various leaflets lie.

She moves further in, pauses at the end central aisle and faces the altar. Rather than go any further, she looks up to the ceiling. The exposed solid wooden trusses look, in the main, as if they have been there for hundreds of years, though the plastering between them appears more modern and recently painted. Running around the edge, where wall and roof abut, there is a wooden lintel adorned at regular intervals by exquisitely detailed carvings.

"Seventeenth century," says a voice behind her, and she turns to see a relatively small but neatly dressed man walking towards her from the very rear of the building, "in case you were wondering."

"They're beautiful," she says, slightly thrown by his sudden appearance - thrown, that is, until she notices his somewhat unobtrusive ecclesiastical collar.

He comes to a halt by her side.

"That one," he says, pointing to a figure high above the pulpit, "had to be replaced three years ago. We were lucky we found someone who possessed the skills and talent to recreate it for us."

"Who are they?"

"Well," he says, smiling, "there are twelve of them, if that gives you any clue."

"Who needed to be replaced?" she asks.

"The tax collector," he replies looking away from her and back to the figurine, "though whether that is of any significance or not I leave up to you!"

She smiles and looks back to the newest figure, spotting the tell-take book held in his right hand.

"Are you just visiting?"

Anna turns back.

"Yes - and no," she says, almost blushing before explaining. "I've just taken the Johnson's cottage for a short while, so I suppose that's a bit of both."

"You must be Anna then," he says, extending his own book-free right hand.

"How do you know?"

He laughs.

"It's a small village."

"Ah, of course," she says unsurprised. "And that makes you Richard."

"Touché," he says as she takes his hand.

There is a short moment as she returns her gaze to the wooden Apostles, trying half-heartedly to decipher which is which. She is unsure if her action should be a prompt for him to move off and leave her alone, or whether she is actually inviting him to name the carvings for him. Not knowing which she would prefer, she finds herself grateful when he offers a third option.

"Is there," he pauses just a fraction, long enough for her to know that he isn't going to refer to the figurines, "anything I can do for you?"

If her smile is somewhat uncertain, it betrays enough for him to pick up on it and motion for her to sit. Anna lowers herself onto the very end of of the first pew; Richard takes a similar position on the other side, the aisle defining the space between them.

"I'm not sure," she says hesitantly, "it's a little difficult to say."

"And awkward too, I suppose," he offers, to try and help her along, sensing there is something needing to be said, "after all, I'm a stranger you've never met before, and the only thing I've got going for me, the only qualification I have, is this." He motions to his collar. "It may be small, but more often than not it's powerful enough to turn most people mute."

"No, it's not that," she says, offering a slight smile in response to his joke, "I have no issue with you being a stranger, or trust, or anything like that. I grew up around churches. You might say it was in the family."

"Really?"

"My mother was quite devout, and so was my Aunt Polly - her name was Delores, but we called her Polly for some reason I never quite knew. She was always around our house. Her husband, my Uncle, was a Vicar."

"Ah, I see. So you grew up not being one of those children who only went to church when forced to by the school for services at Christmas and Easter?"

"Exactly." Anna pauses, relaxed a little more now. "And I used to like it; Church, I mean. And Sunday School. I loved the stories, I suppose."

"They are classics, aren't they?" he asks rhetorically.

Anna is impressed by Richard's manner. He seems calm, reassuring. She was afraid that he might prove to be ancient and old fashioned. She tries to recall Bradley's description: 'solid', 'devout', 'there when you need him'. She thinks she can see why Bradley might say such things, even if they come from a perspective obviously not akin to her own.

"Of course, things changed when I grew up. I suppose they always do. Teenage years happen to everybody."

"They do," Richard says, "and thankfully most of us come out the other side. Even I was a rebel - what? - all the way from fourteen to thirty-four, I suppose. I don't think I ever lost my faith, but it's fair to say that it took something of a back seat for a while. There are some things I did... If anyone in the village ever found out they'd run me out of the place!"

"But something made a difference," she observes, "made you what you are today."

"Yes, indeed. We each of us have our moments along the way, whether we're Christian, or Jew, or Muslim - or none of the above. It's how we deal with those moments, those challenges, that define who we are. Don't you think that's true, Anna?"

"I do," she says, slightly unnerved that he seems to have been able to read her so readily.

"And - if I may be just a little presumptuous - I'm guessing perhaps that's where you are…"

Richard allows the silence of the place to fill the space after his words have died. He has always felt that silence has a tremendous part to play in faith, especially his own. He loves the way silence - here in his church more than anywhere else - is his boon companion; the friend who is always there when needed, who helps to guide and instruct, who answers questions - and poses those that need answering.

"Things have been - hard," Anna begins, slowly, almost as if she is hearing her voice for the first time. "Two years ago my little boy died." She pauses to allow Richard the condolence that normally follows such a statement. He says nothing, allowing the silence to do the work for him. "He had been born prematurely. We'd been trying for ages and then suddenly I was pregnant. It felt as if all my prayers were being answered. And then he came early, and was very poorly. I think we knew from early on that he wasn't going to survive."

"What was his name?"

The question surprises her. And it surprises her the way in which Richard asks it. He might have been enquiring about a loved one you had lived an entire life with - which in a way she had, of course.

"Tom. Thomas. We'd liked the name because it gave us choices - would have given him choices - as to what kind of boy he was going to be. Tom and Thomas and Tommy are all so different, don't you think?"

"I do, I do indeed. But a blessing and a curse, if my own experience is to go by."

"Should I call you Richard? Is there something else?"

He shakes his head and says nothing.

"Anyway, Tom died very quickly really, and we were left - my husband and I - alone. I felt cheated, I suppose. Prayers answered and all that, and then to have him taken away... I couldn't imagine the future at that point. But Ryan - my husband - suffered much more. I couldn't see that at the time, of course. I suppose we get so wrapped up in ourselves."

"What does he do, Ryan?"

"Did," Anna says, simply.

"Ah," says Richard before he gives way to silence again.

"Ryan was in the army. Some kind of Special Forces. He didn't talk about it much. He'd been all over, usually short notice stuff to wherever. I never really knew. But he was home a fair amount of the time too. And then he started not to be. He started being away more and more. I found out later that he'd been volunteering for things; dangerous things. Maybe it was his way of trying to cope; his way of trying to work the heartbreak of Tom out of his system."

"I suppose that was how he chose to deal with that moment, that challenge." Richard allows the thought to hang there before following on. "You said that's what he did?"

"He went to Iraq, I discovered. Later, when they told me. He was caught by an IED, he and his colleagues. They said it was 'swift', that he wouldn't have known anything about it."

Richard leans forward a little and places a hand on Anna's arm which she allows to rest there. After a few seconds he withdraws it almost as if, having transmitting his message, she has permission to carry on.

"It's a horrible thing to say, but in a way it was a blessing. I could see that he was being eaten away from the inside. And it had affected us, as a couple. Well, we weren't really a couple any more, not by the time he went out to Iraq."

Anna looks up at the Apostles again and knows she should be crying, but her eyes are dry. She wonders, suddenly, when it was that she had actually cried. For Tom she cried, for days it seemed. But for Ryan?

"And so now it's just me."

"Which is perhaps the biggest challenge of them all," Richard suggests.

"You see I had nothing to lean on. Before Tom died, the future was right there. And then - it wasn't. I was confused, angry, cross. I felt cheated. I asked questions. What kind of a God would do that to me? And why? What had I done?"

"And you had no answers?" Richard suggested.

Anna shook her head.

"So when it came to Ryan… Well, I'd already stopped going to church. It felt as if I'd stopped believing. I had no evidence, no feeling or sense of compassion or caring to keep me going. I fell abandoned. Totally. I tried to carry on - with my life, I mean. My job and such. But it didn't seem to work, didn't seem to be the same. So I just stopped. Financially I didn't need to work - not for a while anyway. I decided to just go away, to somewhere. To see if I could - I don't know - 'find myself', I suppose." She pauses, and looks back at Richard who has not taken his eyes from her. "And there you have it."

"And you came here."

"Here?"

"To Maunston Quay."

"Yes."

"Why? I mean, why here? Why not - I don't know - Penzance or Scarborough or Perth or Cork?"

She laughs

"If only I'd thought of Cork!"

It is a small joke and they both laugh a little. Then Richard waits.

"It seemed - empty. From what I could see, there was nothing here - and I don't mean to be rude - but no distractions, no noise, no crowds. And the cottage looked lovely, and I've always liked the sea. And I just thought, why not? Even though I was on my own at home, not working, I felt as if I really needed to be on my own in a much more tangible way. I thought if I had nothing to distract me then I might be able to find myself again."

"And find God?"

His suggestion surprises her a little.

"Perhaps - though we're not exactly on speaking terms at the moment."

At this Richard throws back his head and laughs loudly. It is a rich and deep laugh that surprises her - in part by its quality, but mainly because it is there at all, almost as if it belongs to someone else.

"That's wonderful!" He smiles, then sees her confusion. "I'm sorry, but that's such a wonderful way of putting it. I may have to steal it for one of my sermons."

"I don't follow."

"For me, God is a relationship. A deeply personal relationship. You have every right to be - how shall I say - 'pissed off' with Him. If we were talking about a friend or relative who'd upset you, of course you'd not be on speaking terms with them. And the big question would be whether or not you wanted to be on speaking terms with them again. Or have they gone just too far this time? I perfectly understand, Anna. And I suspect that's one of the questions you need to find an answer to. Indeed," he was was warming to his theme, "it must be, because you came here. If you were adamant it was all over then why bother? Good riddance, eh? God riddance, even. But you're here because you're giving God a second chance. And actually, you're giving yourself a second chance too." He pauses because he sees Anna is smiling. "You're smiling," he says a little uncertainly. "You're laughing at me."

Now it is Anna's turn to put a hand on his arm.

"Not at all," she says, a lighter tone in her voice. She withdraws her hand. "I just think that you're very perceptive, and very clever, and very enthusiastic."

"And hopefully a little bit right?" he prompts.

"Probably a lot right!"

"How shall I put it?" He pauses. "There's some good news, and some good news. Which do you want first? No, let me guess. The good news?"

"Please."

"The first bit of good news is that you know where you are, Anna, and you know your problem, your situation, challenge - call it what you will. But you know it. And you know *you*; where you are. And, from my point of view, you know where you are with God. Which is very important. And more good news is that you've come to Maunston Quay. Oh, it's not a magical place. In many ways it's something of a tired, drab, failure of a place. But in other ways it's quite wonderful. It *will* give you space and time. Space and time to think. Walk; talk to people; come here and talk to me - and maybe God, who knows. But listen to the sea, the wind in the trees, the waves on the beach. Listen to the silence. You will find questions, and you will find answers. I promise you."

Anna leans forward to get up, and places a hand on Richard's arm as she does so.

"Thank you," she says.

Slightly thrown, he stands too.

"Others have come here to find themselves; a small number, perhaps myself included. Their circumstances have been different from yours of course. Some left, but some have stayed. Some have found what they were seeking - or settled on something else, an equilibrium that has worked for them. Or maybe they are very close to completing their puzzle, perhaps seeking the last piece or two of the jigsaw. So you are in good company, Anna, believe me. And I know. Have faith - first in yourself, and then... Well, one step at at time."

He offers her his hand again.

"And if you need me, my house has the biggest door in the village." He pauses. "Of course, the second biggest door belongs to 'The Anchor'. You'll tend to find more parishioners in there than here most days, but I recommend it. In fact, there's a meeting on Thursday evening."

"Yes, Lewis mentioned it in passing," she says.

"Lewis? That's good. Anyway, we get together every year, like clockwork, to discuss what we're going to do for 'the season'; to see if we can make Maunston more like the place lots of people think it ought to be. You should come along. It will be a good way to meet people."

"And what kind of place does Maunston Quay need to be, Richard?"

"Ah," he smiles, "I'm a little biased, I'm afraid. From my perspective it's already the place it needs to be. But there are always other points of view, other drivers. I suspect I know the outcome, based on experience; but we'll see."

He watches her as she walks to the door, hearing the echo of the latch from the inside this time.

"Will we see you there on Thursday evening?" he asks.

"I may get Lewis to chaperone me," she says with a laugh, and opens the door. For a moment there is a break in the clouds, the sun has come out and the light floods in.

❋ ❋ ❋

When Lewis, Bradley and Anna walk through the door, they find Jenny busying herself in the conservatory, some of the tables there having been rearranged to form a large square, one laid with plates, cutlery and napkins. Apart from Jenny, there is only one other person visible, a man sitting at the bar on a stool. Based on an initial glance, Anna guesses he is about seventy.

"Now then Jack," says Bradley, immediately going over to him, "come here for the meeting?"

There is a slight grunt of dismissal.

"Don't mess with me, Milton. You know I'm not one for your bloody meetings. As soon as I've finished me pint, I'm off."

Bradley glances back towards Lewis and Anna, smiling knowingly.

"Let me introduce you," Lewis says, walking towards the big table, Anna following.

Jenny straightens from her work arranging the table.

"Well, this will have to do. I don't know what his Lordship had in mind, but he'll have to settle for this."

"Where is he?" Lewis asks.

"Out the back probably. Just got back from Shirley's. Said he'd forgotten something. Typical, of course."

Although she was talking to Lewis, Jenny has been more intent on Anna, who feels herself being taken in and measured by Jenny's gaze.

"I'm Anna," she says, taking the initiative and holding out her hand. "You must be Jenny."

"I suppose I must be," she says, taking the hand briefly and then glancing at Lewis. "Well I hope you're not hungry. If you didn't eat before you came out, more fool you."

"I'm sure it won't be that bad," Lewis offers.

"Drink we can do much more readily. Usual?" Jenny directs this to Lewis as she moves back towards the bar.

"Thanks. Anna?"

"A small cider, please," she sends the request after Jenny who offers no indication it has registered. "Apple, not pear or any of those new-fangled ones."

Lewis feels embarrassed but not surprised by the lack of warmth in Jenny's welcome.

"She'll defrost in a bit," he suggests to Anna, quietly.

As Anna is about to reply, the door opens and Richard and Aubrey enter. There is a general shout of "Hello" from Richard which is accompanied almost immediately by Jack getting up from his stool which scrapes against the floor.

"Now the Reverend is here, I'd better be off," he says, and without any further interaction, shuffles across to the door and then out.

"What shall we say, Lewis," says Richard as he joins them, looking back to where Jack had been sitting, "one of our more 'traditional' villagers?"

"Perhaps, Richard - if you were being kind."

"My fault then," he replies smiling. Then he turns to Anna. "So you made it? Couldn't keep away?"

"How could I resist the opportunity to see what really goes on here," she says.

"Well, we already know not to expect too much from the food," says Lewis, "so keep your sights nice and low."

Twenty minutes later, Tommy is tapping a fork against his half pint of bitter, trying to bring the meeting to order.

"Come on then," he says, a note of defeat already in his voice, "let's get started."

As the volume of chatter begins to subside, Anna looks around the table at the assortment there. She is a little surprised by the physical distance between the host and hostess, and has not yet been able to determine whether Jenny's greeting was especially frosty or whether she is like that with everyone, including her husband. She is aware of some of the dynamics of the village thanks to an irreverent briefing she was given by Lewis and Bradley on the walk up from the cottages. Bizarrely, it is these two who - in addition to Tommy and Jenny, and Shirley and Oscar - appear to make up the third 'couple' around the table; and certainly the one whose constituent halves seem the most comfortable in each other's company. Including herself, there are nine around the table, the last two attendees being Richard and Aubrey.

Of all the new people she has met, she senses that Aubrey is likely to prove more affable than he first appears. She wonders if he is a little shy, in spite of being probably the most imposing figure there. She marvels at how small a pint glass looks in his hands. Lewis has sung Aubrey's praises in terms of his creativity - which is another thing she will need to reconcile - and she has mentally added a visit to the forge onto her list of things to do. "And there is something else about Aubrey you'll need to work out for yourself," Lewis had said, then, in response to her protests, "I'm not going to tell you everything you need to know!". At this, she had punched his arm playfully. In spite of this assault on the way up, Lewis is happy to sit next to her at the table, with Richard on her other side, his greeting offered without ceremony or fuss, as if she were already an old friend.

"Alright," Oscar says, once he feels there is sufficient order, "we know how this works. I'm assuming we'll just do what we've done in previous years; go round the table, get a few ideas, that sort of thing."

"Two things," says Richard. "Firstly, I'll take a note of anything we want recorded, shall I, just as I did last year?" He pauses and looks round the table at the general murmur of approval. "And secondly, I think we should welcome Anna to our little congregation." All eyes - or nearly all eyes - turn her way at this point, at which she finds herself beginning to blush. "I know Anna is new and may not be here that long, but you never know what a fresh outside perspective might bring."

Anna waits a few seconds - long enough for Tommy, Lewis and Shirley to publicly welcome her - before speaking.

"Thanks Richard. I doubt I'll be much use, but you never know."

"You'll fit in just fine," says Shirley with a wink.

"So," says Tommy, regaining control, "I suggest we see what ideas people might have, if that's OK."

"Before we do that," Shirley jumps in, "can we just agree what we're *not* going to bother discussing. You know, the things which come up year after year we never do anything about either because actually we don't want to or we can't be bothered or they're too difficult."

"Like a car park?" suggests Bradley.

"Exactly!" Shirley is immediately vindicated.

So for the next few minutes of what Anna can only regard as verbal chaos, people try to agree the topics that are effectively disqualified. Richard, in trying to make sense of it all, very occasionally adds something to the sheet of paper in front of him. As the momentum begins to wane on this preliminary topic, Anna glances across at what he has written. There is a '1' in the margin, and then a list comprising: new car park; new toilets; new pier; beach-front shop/cafe.

"You can see why we never get very far," Lewis whispers to Anna, having seen her examining Richard's list.

"But those are all such very big things," Anna says, a little surprise in her voice. "Not the sort of things you would be able to get done on your own anyway. And where would the money come from?"

Her last words carry a little further than she has intended, coinciding as they do with a general lull around the table.

"That," says Bradley, picking up her thread, "is exactly the problem. Or one of the major problems. We talk about grand things, many of which may - I say *may* - be good ideas, but without significant funding are just pipe dreams."

"Well, what about beach huts?" Anna says, slightly concerned that she is breaking into what little structure the meeting has.

"Discussed those two years ago," says Oscar.

"And the year before that," Shirley confirms.

"Permanent ones?" Anna asks.

"Yes," says Shirley.

"Have you ever looked into hiring them? I mean, can you get temporary ones? A bit like portaloos. That sort of thing. Not permanent. You'd only have to worry about covering the rental, and then charge them out with a margin."

"Did we discuss temporary?" Tommy asks round the table, "I can only recollect us talking about building permanent ones."

"We talked about portable loos," Shirley says, "I'm pretty sure we did. But I don't think we saw the point of them on their own."

"But if there were beach huts…" Richard allows the idea to settle.

"And you could do the same thing with your beach cafe," Anna suggests. "Don't think about permanent, but hire out concessions - if you can get permissions from the council. That way the people who operate the mobile vans or trailers will be bearing the risk, not you."

"I would have thought we must have discussed options like these in the past," Lewis ventures, "even since I've been here - but why do they sound like new ideas?"

"Because they are," Richard whispers, loud enough for both Lewis and Anna to hear him.

The discussion takes on a life of its own, powered by the fresh notion that they need not necessarily commit to permanence. Anna, having unintentionally lit the fuse, takes a back seat to observe the main players as they are drawn into the battle. She watches Lewis with particular interest. Having instinctively felt he was someone likely to be aloof and disinterested, a recent enough resident to retain some detachment from the inherent culture of Maunston Quay, she smiles to herself as he becomes one of the most vocal there - and one of the most positive. She sees Richard making the odd note again, though this time connected to the number '2', a firm line having been drawn beneath the simple list attached to '1'.

Time passes quickly, their flow not particularly interrupted when the odd stray drinker enters from outside, or when Jenny is needed to help at the bar. When a break is called for - primarily driven by the need to refill glasses, and bolstered by Tommy's offer to bring out the sandwiches - it is nearly eight-forty-five. As the bulk of the participants gather at the bar, Jenny serving, Lewis stands a little way off with Anna, Richard having volunteered to supervise the replenishments.

"So what do you think?" he asks, open-endedly.

"About the meeting?"

He nods.

"Interesting," she offers, at which he laughs. "What's wrong?"

"'Interesting' isn't allowed, I'm afraid. Typical British non-committal get-out-of-jail card."

She smiles.

"Just testing. Anyway, the meeting? A bit 'haphazard', I suppose. Not really like any meeting I've ever been in, but it lives up to what I was expecting."

"In what way?"

"Well, the lack of discipline, I suppose. And then watching the enthusiasm for an idea growing and people getting excited about it."

"The beach huts, for example," he interjects.

"Exactly. Getting excited and then starting to become less so once reality dawns and vested interests begin to surface. Like the food concessions and the ice cream vans - and then Oscar and Shirley realising what they might imply."

"You mean Shirley."

She smiles.

"Yes, I suppose I do." Then in a softer voice. "She does seem to wear the trousers there doesn't she?"

"Oh, very much so. I suppose you can tell a lot about people by how they behave in a situation such as this."

Richard arrives with their refreshed drinks as Lewis is finishing his sentence.

"There you go," he says. "I think I caught the end of that. Telling a lot about people by observing them?" Lewis nods. Richard turns to Anna. "So what have you learned?"

"I couldn't!" she says a little shocked.

"Why not?" Lewis asks. "Richard and I know them all well enough - he more than I, of course. And we like them all; they're our friends. I doubt you'd be saying anything that we haven't thought or said before. Isn't that right, Richard?"

"Fire away," he encourages, inviting them to sit down at a separate table even further away from the bar.

"Okay," Anna pauses. "Bradley, then."

"Safe ground, straight away," Richard laughs.

"A mix of practical, realistic and cynical - depending on your point of view," Anna suggests.

"Fair enough," says Lewis, happy to comment on his friend. "Some people say that a cynic is what an idealist calls a realist. I don't know about you, Richard, but I think he's a realist."

"Largely," Richard concurs, "but there are some topics about which he's quite the cynic."

"But I get the impression," Anna jumps back in, not wishing for things to get too deep, "that he really likes the place the way it is."

"Spot on," says Lewis, approvingly. "Now what about Aubrey?"

Anna glances up to the area away to the right of the bar where he and Bradley are engaged in an impromptu game of darts.

"A bit like Bradley, I think," she says, "but very hard to read. He doesn't say much. You'd think he'd welcome more visitors considering what he does; it might boost his income. But then I think he probably also likes it just as it is."

"And he has another master to serve too," Richard prompts.

"Or mistress," corrects Lewis.

Anna's confusion is plainly evident and the two men laugh in unison. She tries to locate the second half of this particular equation, scanning the bar as she does so. There are only two candidates. And then she realises there is actually just one.

"Shirley?!"

"We're saying nothing, Anna," Richard admonishes her, "but as you've mentioned her, what about Shirley and Oscar?"

"That's easy. She's the boss, the one who runs things. Big sister syndrome all over. Maybe she'll occasionally let Oscar have his way, but that's purely tactical." Both men are smiling. "What?" she asks, fearing she may have overstepped some kind of mark.

"Just spot-on again," Lewis says. "We're just agreeing with you."

"Though," says Anna, in the mode of an interruption, "I do think Oscar may, from time to time, be able to pull out a gem from somewhere. And I suspect Shirley doesn't give him enough credit for it."

Richard nods. Lewis, his smile fading, picks up his beer.

"And our hosts," Richard asks. "Be kind, now…"

Although she doesn't look at him, Anna can feel Lewis's eyes fixed on her.

"Difficult," she says, more slowly, suddenly conscious that there may be other forces at work here. "Tommy is clearly the organiser as far as the pub's concerned. Jenny hardly said anything - probably because she had to keep one eye on the bar - but when she did it seemed primarily negative. I got a sense of friction, though maybe that's just the stress of setting this up and having you lot here."

"*Us* lot," Richard corrects, still smiling. He glances at Lewis. "I don't think they've been particularly happy for some time. Which is a shame. But maybe all couples go through that, eh? Not quite on speaking terms, you might say." He checks to see if Anna has picked up on the reference. She has. "But they've both worked really hard to make a go of this place. I think it's better now than it was before they came - if it's quiet tonight, that'll be because we're here. But if there's an issue underlying it all, then I think it's that they want different things. You can see that in the way they've contributed this evening." He pauses. "Lewis?"

Lewis puts down his glass and nods, offering Anna a smile.

"Richard's right, of course. Different ambitions, expectations. Always makes things difficult, hard."

There is a slight pause in the conversation, driven by the direction it has suddenly taken. Richard strives to rescue them.

"So what about Lewis?" he asks Anna.

"Hey!" says Lewis, taken by surprise. "What about Richard?"

And suddenly all three of them are laughing just as Tommy raps something metallic onto an empty glass and calls them to order for the second time that evening.

When they resume their seats at the table, Richard draws another line on the sheet of paper in front of him, and then writes '3' beneath it.

"I assume," he says, taking advantage of the minor hiatus as they gird their respective loins for another skirmish, "that we'll now be discussing what we are actually going to *do*. A list of things is all very well…"

"Quite right, Richard," says Tommy, attempting to reassert himself as the chairman.

"Good. And then later I'll type up my notes and give you all copies; that way we all have the same hymn sheet."

"Very droll, Father," says Bradley.

The inaccurate appellation is noted by Anna but evidently ignored by everyone else, including Richard.

It is after ten thirty when they finally call a halt. The few casual drinkers who have popped in during the evening have all left. Having seen a little sporadic activity, the area that houses the darts board and pool table are now in darkness. As people stand up from the table, variously draining their glasses and putting their more-or-less empty plates into a pile in the centre of the table, there is a general sigh and expulsion of air as if they have emerged from something of a trial.

Seeing Anna glance down at his notes once more, Richard lifts them from the table.

"It's a small list, I suppose," he says, vaguely running his finger across the paper beneath the large '3' he wrote an hour and a half ago, "but it's something. We have done our duty."

"What happens now?" Anna asks, feeling a little deflated all of a sudden.

"Oh, I'll type these up tomorrow morning and then shuffle around with a copy for everyone. Then we'll meet up in maybe two or three weeks' time to see where we've got to."

"Which most likely," says Lewis, insinuating himself into the conversation, "will not be very far."

"You cynic!" she says playfully.

"Can I walk you back?" he asks.

She nods.

"What about Bradley?"

"I have a strange feeling," Richard says, looking to where Bradley is standing slightly conspicuously by the door, "that he may want a quick word with me. Better you two go on."

There is suddenly a round of unenthusiastic leave-taking, and moments later all except Tommy and Jenny are outside, drifting away from 'The Anchor', Lewis and Anna stepping out with the most purpose.

"Well. What did you think?" Lewis breaks the silence when they have nearly reached the crossing gates.

"Where do I start?" she replies, trying to strike the right note, a blend of genuine interest and the more negative 'I knew it would be like that'.

"Was it what you expected?"

"Pretty much I suppose; though overall I was probably disappointed."

"With the people?" he asks.

"No; not with the people. After all, it's a good thing that you get together to discuss this stuff. Most places don't have any sense of community from what I've seen. It shows a commitment to the place."

"I sense a 'but' coming."

"But - I don't know - it also felt a bit futile, in a way. I mean, I didn't really get any sense of belief. Maybe that's because people want different things, and maybe they don't share that - what they want, I mean."

"They don't need to," says Lewis. He pulls a small torch from his jacket pocket to help illuminate the way as they head down the now unlit road, beyond the station to the cottages. After the brightly lit crossing, the way seems especially dark all of a sudden. "Because we all know. Experience, I suppose. We know that what Shirley wants is not exactly the same as Oscar - though they have enough alignment in terms of their business to express a reasonably consistent view."

"What about Aubrey? He a bit of a strange one."

"Still waters," says Lewis, cryptically. "Aubrey's very 'flexible'. Most of the time he's quite happy wanting what everyone else wants. He doesn't like to rock the boat. He's fallen on his feet, in a manner of speaking. He could probably be so much more, if he chose to be. I mean with his metalwork. He's really quite talented. But he has no ambition, no drive."

"Is that a problem?" she asks.

"I don't think so, do you?"

She lets the question slide.

"And Bradley?"

"What about him?"

"I don't know. In some ways what you've said about Aubrey could equally apply to Bradley," she suggests.

"And Richard, and Tommy," he pauses for a fraction, "and me."

"You? I don't see that. In what way?"

They have now reached the cottages and have come to a halt outside Anna's front door.

"Because we all quite like our lives here I suppose - in a general, non-specific kind of way. We know having more tourists in the summer, more people coming here to spend money, the village having something of an identity - we know all those things are logical enough, but deep down we probably don't actually want them." He lets the thought hang in the moonlight as he looks briefly out to sea. "I think a few people are scared of taking the risk - in case we're successful. Which is why nothing much will happen, I suspect."

"That's a shame."

"Is it? I'm not so sure."

"But if that's how people feel, how they are somehow, why go through the motions?"

"Because I guess the motions are important. You said it yourself; a sense of community. Doing things like that keeps us together. Doesn't that make it worthwhile, even if there's no real end product?"

Anna doesn't reply.

"Well," he says, sensing the conversation has run its course, and begins to make a move for his own front door.

"Why does Bradley want to talk to Richard?" Her question stops him.

"That? Oh, they have a long-running battle of sorts - all good natured, of course. One of the few things that gets Bradley hot under the collar is religion, and almost whenever he's in the same vicinity as Richard he manages to manufacture something to debate with him." Lewis explains.

"He doesn't seem the type," Anna says.

"Bradley? I guess not. They like each other really - even if Bradley doesn't show it much."

"Richard seems to like everybody," she observes.

"Which is just as well, isn't it?" Lewis starts away from her again. "After all, that's pretty much part of his job description."

Anna watches Lewis as he unlocks his front door, then waves briefly just as he disappears. It is a still evening. She can hear the water against the shore, but from the sound it is making she imagines the waves caressing the sand rather than attempting to drag it back into the sea. Towards her right she can make out Simon's Crag which seems to loom closer and higher in the darkness. She shivers unexpectedly, then turns, unlocks her own door, and disappears into the cottage.

✾✾✾

"What do you reckon?" Bradley asks as he watches the others drift away.

"About what?" Richard says, his own eyes fixed more specifically on the backs of Shirley and Aubrey as they meander together onto the green.

"Will we do anything?"

"Oh, that," says Richard, returning his gaze to Bradley who is dimly lit by the moon and the single street lamp strategically placed between 'The Anchor' and its car park. "The usual, I suppose - if experience is anything to go by. Don't you agree?"

Bradley inclines his head which, if Richard takes it to be an agreement, turns out to be a qualified one.

"But sometimes I think we should do more."

"In what way?"

"Be more proactive, pushy," Bradley's voice displays an air of uncertainty in spite of the words he utters.

"Assuming that people actually want things to change - which I'm pretty sure is a moot point anyway - who do you mean by 'us', Milton?"

"I suppose the seniors; the people who've been here the longest." He pauses. "You."

"Me!" Richard cannot fail to contain his surprise. "Why me?"

"In your professional capacity as our local leader, if you like."

"That's an interesting thought," says Richard, unable to suppress a tone of amusement. "I've never thought of myself in that way. And somehow, even though you've said it, I still can't. It isn't my job to lead people - at least not in any non-spiritual sense."

Bradley shifts a little uneasily, his feet crunching on the gravel entrance to the car park.

"But who else is there? Tommy's all chocolate teapot when it comes to leading things. He was only in the chair tonight because it's his pub. You're always the one to take the notes, to chase people up, to see how they're getting on."

"I'm tempted to say that 'someone has to' - but I still don't see it's my responsibility. You or Lewis or Shirley are equally capable of taking notes and following-up on people's actions."

There is a slightly awkward silence. Richard senses Bradley hasn't actually made his point yet, and Bradley is uncertain how to do so. Richard tries to short-circuit things.

"What do you want, Milton? What's on your mind - because I don't think it's anything about the meeting at all." Bradley says nothing. "I think you're a bit like me; there's a huge part of you that doesn't want things to change. That's what it boils down to. And that dilemma - what we feel is logical, right, practical versus what we actually want - is at the crux of things."

"Is it?"

"Don't you think so? Would you really want to see your life turned upside-down? The beach filled with holiday-makers and screaming children with buckets and spades? Isn't that really why nothing happens - because we each of us like the balance we've found here?"

"But you do try, though, don't you; in your formal capacity?" Bradley asks somewhat obliquely.

"I'm not sure I'm with you, old friend. And it's getting late." Richard makes a move away.

"What about Anna?"

The question stops him dead.

"Anna? What's she got to do with any of this - other than make one or two telling observations this evening, that is? I don't think she really counts, do you? She's probably not going to be here very long. A week? A month? Who knows? She hardly has any vested interest in whether or not we get a car park or new loos, surely."

"But that doesn't stop you."

Richard turns so that he is facing Bradley square on and sets his hands on his hips.

"Stop me from doing what, exactly?"

There is a pause that Bradley is in no hurry to fill. He knows he has let his prejudice and emotions get the better of him again. But he has come too far, made too much of a statement to try and sweep it away. There was something in they way she and Richard spoke, the interaction he observed from the other side of the table, that seemed to prove they had not just met for the first time. He had become convinced, quickly and illogically, that Richard had latched on to her somehow.

"Convert her - or whatever the right word is."

"Convert her!"

"To add her to your flock; to persuade her of - I don't know what. To have her see the error of her ways." His complaint peters out.

"You think I've been drumming up business?" Richard laughs, then quickly reins himself back in. "Oh, Milton. I know how you feel about me - well, not about me, I hope, but rather the church. But you mustn't assume that I always have some kind of hidden agenda. Or even one that isn't hidden. Had I met Anna before this evening? Yes. She came to the church actually. Did we talk? Of course. Did I try and seduce her into becoming some kind of disciple?" He shakes his head. "I'm sorry to disappoint you - once again. Now, it's late and I'm tired. Please just go home, Milton, and try to stop thinking of me as some kind of pariah or cancer; the stealer of people's souls. I'll see you later."

Richard places a hand on Bradley's shoulder just for a moment, then turns and walks away. Part of him expects to be called back, but hears nothing. As he walks across the now deserted village green, he resists the temptation to look back, fearing if he does so, that he will see Bradley still standing motionless at the entrance to the car park.

Half way towards his little vicarage tucked away to the side of the church, he suddenly feels sad. It is a sadness primarily for Bradley and his past, the torture he has faced, and the disappointments that have led him to his extreme distrust of the church. But then Richard corrects himself. It is not distrust of the church per se, but more a broader suspicion of religion and what it stands for - and what it, or faith, can and cannot do. He knows Bradley's history well enough to be able to understand, and understanding, to forgive. He only wishes Bradley were in a position to do the same.

✼ ✼ ✼

Nothing is said until they are half way across the green, at a point approximately equidistant from the church, the shop and the forge. It is only here Aubrey is happy to speak, as if he has arrived on neutral territory. He slows and then stops, as if speaking and walking are mutually exclusive. Shirley has moved on a stride or two before she realises. He sees her silhouetted against the church.

"Well that's another year gone then," he says, as if he had just flipped December over to January on a calendar.

"Another year?"

"Since the last time we had one of those," he explains. "Don't you see it as a kind of marker, a bit like a birthday or Easter? We get together to discuss the village and what the summer will entail, then forget all about it and go on as before."

"Is that how you see it?" Shirley's voice is flat. It is not that she does not feel any passion for Maunston Quay and what they might or might not do, but rather her loyalties are somehow split. It is, she knows, a common enough complaint, but she realises it and articulates it better than most.

"Isn't that how it is?"

"That's how it always ends up, I'll grant you that. But it needn't be that way. We could take a step forward, in one direction or another. We could take a chance to make things a little different. Who knows, they could be changes for the better."

"They could," Aubrey concedes, "or not."

They both know it is this uncertainty that nurtures their indecision. If they could be shown the outcome in advance then they might jump one way or the other. As it is they remain, collectively, static.

"Don't you want things to be better?" she asks, a softer more personal tone in her voice.

"Better? Define better. Different isn't necessarily better, is it? You could double your takings in the shop if we did some of those things we talked about - or you could halve them. Same for Tommy."

"I don't think it would ever be that bad - or that good," she says. "Maybe we're just worrying over nothing."

"Because nothing's going to happen, or because whatever we do it's going to make no difference?"

Shirley looks back towards 'The Anchor' where she can see Bradley and Richard in conversation. Oscar is already back in the shop; no-one else is visible. She knows that, as a community, this is a conundrum; that because there is no unified view, no single vision, there can be no consensus in terms of output and action. In turn this both frustrates and heartens her; she is heartened because, in spite of the impossibility of the task they set themselves, they keep on trying. But she also recognises the squidgy thinking, the sort of philosophising that Richard would happily adopt, perhaps even now as he talks to Bradley.

"In the end we have to come back to what we want. Each of us, individually." She pauses. Now is not the time, but she can afford one more nudge. "And you know what I want, Aubrey. Never mind the village, and the shop, the loos, the car park, the ice cream vans. None of that matters; not really."

"I know," he says.

From the volume and the tone she cannot tell exactly where Aubrey is looking, nor where his words are aimed. She suspects somewhere over her shoulder, off into the distance. That would be so typically him.

"I would give it all up tomorrow, you know that. There is only one thing that really matters to me; everything else is incidental. But there comes a point..."

"A point?"

Shirley can tell he is looking hard at her now, even if his face is almost entirely in the dark. She looks up to divine the location of the moon. It is in front of her; her face in what little light there is then.

"Because one day I'll stop pushing and stop asking. Just like one year we won't have this silly meeting to decide nothing at all. And then where will you be with your 'another year gone'? How will you tell the time then?"

"You'll leave?"

She notes the concern.

"I didn't say that. But I might just stop hoping, wanting. You choose the word. Maybe if I do that, then I'll free myself to take on all those things we talked about tonight. Maybe throw myself into the village in a very real way. You know I could do that; and that if I did, it would make a real difference. That's how I'd fill up my life if I stopped waiting for you to make a decision."

"What does Oscar think?"

"Oscar?" She feels her blood rising. "What have we got to do with him? What does Oscar think? He can't even manage to order the right number of loo rolls! He'll think what I tell him to think, and do what I tell him to do. That seems to be how it is with him. He has nothing to do with me - not when it comes to you."

The words trail away as Shirley knows they inevitably must. In spite of Aubrey's passivity, she has loved him for almost too long now. Perhaps it is as Richard once said, a case of opposites attracting. All she knows is that she has a vision of her life going forward, and Aubrey is front and centre in that.

"I'm tired," she says, feeling suddenly defeated, "so I'm going home. As much as I might not want to - or as much as I was hoping I wouldn't - that's what's going to happen." She half-turns. "We may try to run this village by consensus, but I can't run my life that way; at least not the important things. There will come a time, Aubrey, when I will force you to make a decision. And I don't want to do that. I don't want to make you do anything; I want it to come from you. But there will be a time when I'll take it out of your hands. You know that, don't you?"

She waits for him to reply.

"I do," he says.

Shivering suddenly, she turns and heads back towards the shop.

Aubrey watches her retreat, the moonlight not bright enough for much more detail than the outline of her shape, her posture as she walks hinting as to what she might be thinking.

She is a strong woman. He wants to be reminded of his mother, but his memories of her are distant and blurred. He has always admired Shirley for her strength, even before she recognised him, saw him as someone she could spend the rest of her life with. He knows what he wants; he has known it for years, ever since he started working the forge on his own, honing his craft. Part of what he does - the sculptures, the experimentation and nurturing of his talent - has always been for her. He can take solid metal and heat it, bash it, curl it, turn it into something it was never meant to be, but he cannot articulate what he wants, even though he knows what it is.

❖ ❖ ❖

They clear away the detritus of the meeting in silence, taking the plates and remnants of food through the back and into the kitchen. Tommy feeds the glasses into the dishwasher and switches it on. Having done so, he looks along the length of the bar and makes a mental note of the topping up he will need to do in the morning. There will not be much; it has been a quiet evening on that front.

He watches Jenny as she emerges from the kitchen and makes her way back to the tables. She pulls one edge of a tablecloth towards her. Tommy can tell her heart isn't in it.

"Why don't we leave that until the morning," he suggests, knowing that by doing so he is effectively accepting that he'll end up doing it himself, probably before Jenny emerges from the bedroom.

Jenny knows that too, so she lets the corner of the cloth drop back to the table and leaves it as it fell.

"Drink?" Tommy asks. "A nightcap. We deserve it."

He doesn't wait for her to respond, but turns to locate a small glass and then drops a shot of Jim Beam into it from one of the optics. He takes a cube from the blue plastic ice bucket and adds it to his glass. By the time he is finished, Jenny is sitting on a stool separated from him by the width of the highly polished wooden bar. Placing the glass down in front of him, he repeats the same series of motions though this time substituting vodka for bourbon and adding a slice of lime at the end. He slides the glass in front of Jenny then addresses his own once more.

"Cheers," he says. Not expecting a reply, he is not disappointed.

"Do we?" she asks.

"Do we what?"

"Deserve it."

"Why not?" he asks, slightly thrown by her question. "After all we hosted the thing didn't we? And we laid on the food."

She picks up her glass and allows silence to descend. She has often thought that silence in a pub has a strange quality to it; not a good or healthy one, but rather something that is vaguely surreal given the nature of public houses when they are open. She glances around, her eye caught by the digital jukebox which sits on the threshold of the games area. She tries to recall if anyone played any music while they were having their meeting, but can only recall the sound of voices.

"Don't you think pubs are strange places when there's no noise?" she asks, looking at Tommy almost as if she has just recognised his presence. "And a bit strange during the day too, come to think of it."

Tommy scans the semi-darkened room as if by doing so he will be able to locate something that will help him with his answer. Finding nothing, he is forced to call on his experience.

"I wouldn't say so. Mind you, I've always grown up in and around pubs, so maybe it's different for me."

Jenny recalls how she met Tommy at his parent's pub in Colchester. He had been different then, she always tells herself. And having done so, inevitably recognises that she had been different too. For no specific reason other than Tommy's presence, she had come to feel there was a kind of romance in the trade. It had been a romance that Tommy had shared, of course, and for a while they fed infectiously off each other, concocting a dream about running their own place; a dream his parents did nothing to tarnish. They could have warned them about the practicality of it; the long hours, the difficulty finding time to take holidays, the fact that having no distance between where you lived and where you worked could make it feel like a trap sometimes.

The gloss had begun to wear off not long after they had managed to secure their first place together on the outskirts of London. And perhaps it was not just the gloss of being in charge. At her instigation, more than once they had discussed throwing in the towel, but belonging to a pub was the only life Tommy knew. After London, Maunston Quay - and the prospect of a radical scenery change - had buoyed her for a while, and she allowed him to rekindle the dream. But in the end a scenery change was all it proved to be. For some time now, Jenny has felt as if she has been cast adrift and is waiting for something to happen. Or she is waiting for herself to do something, to instigate change. Once she would have asked her elder brother for advice, but now he was gone for good she had no-one to turn to. And in any event, it was difficult to seek change when you didn't really know what you wanted, only what you didn't want.

"You didn't say much this evening," he observed.

"Really? Well there wasn't much that needed to be said was there?"

"What do you mean, Jen?"

"It was the same old conversation, the same old ideas. You could have videoed the first ever meeting we had here - how long ago is it now? - and just get it out once a year and replay it. Would save people the trouble."

Tommy knew her well enough to understand the undercurrents to her silence. He thought he knew her better than she realised, saw further into her than she gave him credit for; but there was no advantage to be gained in trying to make any of this plain.

"I don't think that's fair," he said, trying to remain on solid ground. "There were some new things, I thought. Or different angles on some of the old ideas. After all, how many new things can we do in a place like Maunston? How many would be relevant?"

"None and none," she suggested, a slight note of bitterness in her voice, "no matter what that new woman says."

There is a new tone here that Tommy can't fail to notice.

"Anna? I thought she made one or two useful suggestions. It was good having a different perspective."

"Well you weren't the only one who was all over her."

"All over her?" Tommy is thrown by the phrase. "I'm not sure what you mean. I don't think anyone was 'all over her'. What makes you say that?"

"Nothing, Tommy. Absolutely nothing."

Jenny picks up her glass and drains it in one, the spirit biting the back of her throat.

Chapter 6

Time passes. For Anna it does so in a relaxed, almost lethargic way. Even though the nights are still cold, she takes to leaving her bedroom window open at night more for the purring of the sea and its caressing of the sand than for ventilation. It is a sound that marks time in its own way. Before she knows it, she has been in Maunston Quay for four weeks.

If she had needed a routine to help with her forgetting and fore-telling, then she has fallen into a simple one without thinking; a routine revolving around walking, writing, and taking her time with daily, rudimentary things. As the days pass, it becomes a pattern that looks forwards more than backwards. In the kitchen of her cottage she had found three recipe books and made an agreement with herself to cook one thing from each every week. Having never really liked cooking, it is a discipline proving practical in terms of education as much as anything else. Hunting down the more exotic ingredients she is unable to find on Oscar and Shirley's shelves gives her a reason for the occasional trip into the next town on the train. She has even thought of entertaining.

She is seen almost daily by Lewis, most often if their paths should cross when she is out walking. Sometimes she is seen by Bradley too - usually at one end or the other of her comings and goings, especially when he has the door to his boathouse open. More than once, standing on the pier and looking inland, she has watched him at work, a figure occupying a private bubble and bent to the maintenance of a hull or the winches of his sailboat. He looks well for his sixty-one years. If she has taken to tarrying longer and longer in the village shop it is because she enjoys passing the time with the warring siblings, secretly relishing their little play-acted dramas of baiting and faux discontent. The church has not seen her re-cross its threshold yet, the closest she has come when she walked to the forge one day. Watching Aubrey at work - and being impressed by the elegance of his creations - she confessed to Shirley that she could appreciate what she saw in him. A brave observation made solely woman-to-woman of course. 'The Anchor' has enjoyed her patronage only twice since the village meeting, both times to accompany Lewis and Bradley for a quiet evening drink. She has found Tommy to be a pleasant man at home in his environment - and Jenny to be a strangely cold and frosty woman clearly out of hers. She has seen Richard little, often only from a nodding distance.

In part she feels a little like a goldfish in a bowl, exposed for all and sundry to peer in on her and make judgements and observations. But she also strives to live outside of herself, so that she too is able to cast her own vote and make her own assessment. She has nearly filled a second notebook with writing: scraps of description, the starts of a number of stories, unvarnished poems, and dribbles of halting self-assessment. Although she had been unsure what, if anything, would come of this scribbling, she is finding the process cathartic, a way of working things through as if by subterfuge, tricking herself into having conversations she does not wish to have, confronting - in part, at least - the things that need to be confronted.

As she sits in the window of her lounge, looking out across the sand to the sea, she remembers Richard's words from their first meeting: "Listen to the silence. You will find questions, and you will find answers". And although there were many more questions at first, she is slowly realising that new ones are arising less frequently now, and she can sense answers beginning to form. She believes some of these will reveal themselves in her notebooks, as if she is writing in a kind of code which, through re-reading, will suddenly unveil exactly what she needs to know. It is almost as if she is setting out cryptic tests, puzzles to be solved. Flicking through her second book, she realises there are lots of half-finished pieces about the sea. Whilst this should be no surprise of course, their tone takes her back to her childhood, and through that - and childhood memory - to a kind of simplicity, a paring away of the complex and superfluous.

If she had expected to ruminate a great deal about Ryan and Tom through her writing, she has not done so. They are there by inference and allusion only, not analysis. She finds the sea reminds her of her son, though she does not know why. Perhaps she is trying to fill the gap which has been created, to satisfy the void born from being unable to watch him grow up, unable to see him on a beach, playing in the waves. Perhaps the feeling she gets from it - a soothing yet abstract feeling - is somehow a surrogate for the joy she would have had in building sandcastles with him and helping decorate them with stones and shells. But these invented narratives of reminder - for they cannot be memories - although still frequent, are gradually becoming less pained. She has tried to give her emotion a name, but cannot. The one thing she is certain of, however, is that she is remembering Ryan more fondly, and less often. She finds herself filtering out the unpleasant, the uncertain; relegating their last months together to some almost inaccessible place. Neither he nor Tom appear once in her second notebook, however. If that might have one time felt like an omission, now it just seems right.

❉ ❉ ❉

The view from the top of Simon's Crag is, Anna knows, unremarkable. As she sits on the rock which provides its informal seat, the sea stretches grey and vast before her. It is a relatively calm day, strangely so. There was a slight fret first thing but this has mostly dissipated, though by what means she is unable to say. The wind - what little there is, even up here - seems too inadequate to have blown it away, and the sun has yet to make an appearance. But gone it has, and now the sea, in its somewhat surreal grey flatness, stretches out before her. Her notebook rests, unopened, in her lap.

She had climbed the crag path feeling certain that this morning would be a good morning for writing; as if almost unbeknownst to her some blockage had been cleared overnight and her creativity was about to be unleashed unbridled. Even though the feeling may have been real enough, once she had stood on the crag and scanned the now familiar view in all directions from the cottages - past the station, the church tower beyond the trees, towards the jumble that signified the next tract of land down the coast - she soon was soon captivated again by the sea itself. At that point the nagging premonition of 'another sea poem' crept stealthily upon her, and so she sat and waited, tumbling a few random words and phrases through her mind to see if any of them gained traction. Even if the time since she had sat down had been unproductive, it was not unwelcome. Indeed, it never seems unwelcome. Sitting and simply looking and thinking is a luxury she has come to value, and as the days pass she prizes it more and more.

Catching movement in her peripheral vision, she glances down to the beach and sees a figure walking slowly towards the headland, their eyes turned towards the sea just as hers had been. Lewis. She watches him as he reaches the end of the jetty then mounts the four steps before walking slowly towards its far end. The sea touches the sand about half way along, and she watches him as he pauses to look down at where the two realms interact. Even from here she can tell it is a non-confrontational relationship this morning. After a few seconds, he continues towards the end of the jetty where he stands and simply looks. It is a posture she has come to know both in him and in herself, there being bizarre comfort in the solitude it represents and in the consequent sense of being an insignificant thing in a vast world.

After a few moments, he turns and in doing so looks up. Anna knows it will have been the flash of red from her coat that will have caught his eye. There is the briefest of pauses and then he raises an arm to wave. Compelled, she waves back briefly, then watches as he retraces his steps to regain the beach. Once on the sand, he turns towards the headland and, with a step that seems slightly more purposeful than before, begins to head in her direction. Compelled again, she stands and begins her descent along the path. At the fork she has a choice: if she keeps left, she will return directly to the cottages - and in doing so almost certainly miss Lewis. Going right and taking the steeper path down toward the beach means they will meet, probably somewhere near the rocks. Whether it is knowing that going left might suggest she was deliberately avoiding him - or whether it is something else - she can do nothing but veer to the right and head downwards.

If he watches her as she makes her descent, Anna is unable to say, her concentration given over to the narrow twisting path. She knows now where the most slippery spots are and where she might pause. That she chooses not to is driven by a desire that they should meet on the beach and not at some inconvenient point on the headland path; the flexibility of having space around her is subconsciously important.

She arrives at sea level just as Lewis has reached the other side of the rocks that mark the boundary between beach and headland. Seeing her so close - and knowing there is no point in him going over the rocks to only have to retrace his steps - he waits.

"Morning." His voices bridges the few feet between them.

"Just a sec," she says, intent on the last few rocks. The fret has left them deceptively slippery and, in spite of a special effort of concentration, she still manages to lose her footing slightly on the final slab, a boulder around two feet high, buried into the sand like an abandoned wall.

Lewis, close enough to react, takes two rapid steps forward and extends his arm just in time to allow Anna to grab his hand and reestablish her footing. It is only after she has jumped down onto the beach that they let each other go, an action that is mutual and coincident.

"Strange weather this morning," she offers, smiling, still feeling the warmth of his fingers on her palm.

"The mist, you mean?" Anna nods in reply. "We get that sometimes, more often than not in the spring. It's usually a sign that there's some fine weather on the way."

"From up there it looked more autumnal somehow," she suggests, falling in step beside him as they start to walk, retracing Lewis's recent footprints as if they were a trail.

"We get the fret in the autumn too, but most often with a little less wind. Sometimes almost none. This is definitely a spring day; can't you feel it in the breeze - what there is of it? You'll see, the sun will be out by lunchtime."

They walk on for a few paces in silence.

"Managed to write anything?" Lewis asks, nodding to the notebook she holds in her left hand.

Anna follows his eyes even though she knows what he means.

"No, nothing I'm afraid. Often I travel more in hope than expectation."

"I know what you mean," Lewis laughs. "It's the same with my painting."

"I'd forgotten about your painting," she confesses.

"Be careful; it's painting in the same way Eddie the Eagle used to ski jump," he suggests.

"Badly?"

"Too many bruises," Lewis suggests. Anna laughs. "And after a while it becomes a bit of a struggle to find something new, a different subject."

She allows a small pause to intrude.

"Then you know how it is, don't you? Treading that fine line between wanting to do something new, but being faced with the same old tricks. The stress of trying to decide if it's better to repeat yourself or wait until something new comes along."

"Yes, indeed," Lewis says. "I used to struggle more with that than I seem to these days. I could never decide which was the right way to go. If I waited for inspiration, it might take days or weeks; if I didn't, I'd often end up with something as derivative as the last thing I did. And usually worse."

"Does it matter?"

"That it's bad?"

Anna laughs at the way Lewis feigns a combination of mock surprise and disgust, as if he has been mortally wounded by her insult.

"No," she clarifies, "I mean, does it matter which you choose?"

"I guess that depends who you are." They are within a few feet of the pier now, and Lewis stops. "Look around. Tell me what you see."

"What?" Anna laughs.

"Humour me. Tell me what you see."

"Ok," she turns as she speaks. "The sea; the pier; the beach; the rocks and headland; our cottages; the road; the dunes."

"Of course," he says, "nothing unexpected, is there? But now take the pier. Look at it from here, or from the top of the first step, or from outside the cottages. It's the same jetty, but it appears a little different depending on where you're standing."

"Yes, obviously."

"My point," he says, struggling a little, "is that what you actually see depends on your perspective, on where you stand. It's never just one pier. Not really. I mean, when I first came here I painted all those things you just listed, and then when I thought 'what next?' I had no answer. I thought I'd painted everything there was to paint. But then I tried things from a different perspective. The pier from here, or over there, for example. They look very different. I came to realise that there isn't really one pier at all."

"Very profound, Professor," Anna says, the playful tone still in her voice, "and your point is?"

"My point is that it all depends on how you look at things. That there are multiple perspectives, and never just one. And then when I played with different styles of painting, or maybe watercolour versus oils, all those views multiplied again. So it wasn't just one pier after all." He pauses. "Am I making sense?"

Anna places her free hand on his arm and squeezes slightly, just to demonstrate that she's playing with him.

"Of course."

"So," he says, still trying to answer her last question, "I guess my point is that the supply of material is, I don't know, inexhaustible. It may not be just 'another bloody sea poem' or another 'damned seascape', because we can make it different every time."

"Is that what you try and do?" she asks.

"When I remember to, yes."

Lewis laughs more to himself she thinks, and they begin to walk again still following the trail he had recently laid down.

"You're right, of course," she offers, "I know that. Perhaps it's not so easy with writing; I mean, not so immediate as with drawing or painting."

"You tell me," Lewis says, "I get stuck on limericks!"

They both laugh then allow silence to accompany them for a few strides.

"But it's more than that, isn't it?" she says, the playful tone gone from her voice.

"More than what?"

"More than about just painting and writing. I mean the multiple perspectives on things; on how we look at them."

"Such as?"

"Oh, I don't know. Life maybe."

"Life!"

Anna laughs both at Lewis's response and at the profound but hollow-sounding note she has introduced.

"You know; everything. What we do, what we have done. What we think about certain things; how we go about our 'stuff'. There is never one single view on anything, is there? There can't be. That meeting in the pub the last week. Everyone was talking about the same things, but always from a different perspective; their own perspective."

"And?"

"And? And I think we do that too, internally; I mean when we think about ourselves, our lives, our past. I wonder if we adopt a certain stance about something and then that becomes the truth, the only one we ever see or recognise or give credence to." When Lewis doesn't respond, Anna carries on. "Or is it my turn to not make any sense?"

"No, you're making perfect sense," says Lewis, immediately able to identify more than one situation where her theory could almost certainly apply to him. "Maybe we forget that. Maybe we get comfortable with one version of reality or history or whatever; our own first version. And maybe we treat that with undue reverence, as if it's the only possible answer or explanation. Or outcome, even. When it isn't; not really. I think you can see that in people, people we know."

They stop, having now walked the entire length of the beach.

"I didn't mean to divert you from your walk," Anna says apologetically, realising they have now completely retraced Lewis's earlier route and feeling responsible for having forced them to do so.

"I can't imagine a better way of being diverted," he says, smiling. "How about a coffee? I've got an unopened packet of florentines waiting to be shared with someone."

"Florentines! Not only is that surprisingly sophisticated," she replies, the lighter tone back, "but it's the perfect way into a girl's heart!"

***

"Has anyone mentioned the party to you yet?"

She watches Lewis's back as he speaks, attentive to the cafetière into which he spoons ground coffee. In his slightest of pauses between the second and third measures, she realises how infrequently he probably entertains. If Bradley is ever there, she imagines them drinking tea - or beer.

"Not too strong," she says, trying to be helpful.

He returns the measuring spoon to the caddy and closes the lid.

"In the pub, next Tuesday."

'What's the occasion?" she asks. "No-one's said anything to me and I've not seen any posters or anything."

"Oh, it's not a party like that," he turns, smiling, glancing at the kettle which is just about to boil. "There's no 'event' as such. It's Tommy's birthday, that's all. And it's not really a party, to be honest. More a tradition, I suppose. We like to recognise their birthdays, that's all. Tom and Jerry. Help boost the coffers, if you like. Just to show how much we appreciate them and what they do."

"And because you can't imagine the village without a pub?"

"What a horrible thought!"

He lifts the kettle and pours boiling water onto the coffee.

"Would you mind grabbing the milk?" he asks, nodding towards the fridge. "I'll take this and the mugs through."

When he leaves, Anna tries to absorb the kitchen. Its tidiness surprises her. There is a degree of clutter, but one she feels is at an acceptable level. Where the surfaces are clear, they appear clean; the only thing that isn't is Lewis's breakfast crockery sitting by the sink. On the front of the fridge there are three magnets depicting Van Gogh paintings, but these hold nothing. As she opens the door, she recognises being allowed to do so is a statement of confidence from Lewis. Like the rest of the kitchen, the half-full fridge is neatly arranged. Pulling the milk carton from the inside of the door, she cannot help but cast her eyes over the shelves; mainly healthy, the odd indulgence. She has always believed that you can tell a lot about a person - and perhaps especially about a man - from their level of domesticity. Closing the door, she makes her way into the front room.

Lewis is sitting in an armchair partly bent over a small table where the coffee things sit. He is depressing the cafetière's plunger as she enters. Alongside the mugs sits a small white plate with four florentines on it. Anna puts the milk down on the table and walks to the window.

"It's the same view, I'm afraid," Lewis says, fake apology in his voice.

"Yes," she says, then remembers something, "but then not if what you said on the beach is true."

"What's that?"

"The thing about different perspectives. Yes, it's the same view, but the angles are very slightly different."

"Touché." He casts his eyes around the room as she walks back towards the vacant settee. "And the cottage is exactly the same. Well, almost."

"The same layout," she concedes, "mind you, I defy anyone to get lost between the kitchen and here!"

Lewis offers her the plate and she takes one of the florentines.

"Decadent rather than sophisticated," he suggests.

"Perhaps a little of both." There is a pause as she takes a bite. "But perfectly acceptable either way."

A short silence descends as Lewis pours the coffee and then tops up the mugs with milk. It feels ceremonial, somehow.

"Do you think I should go?" Anna asks.

"Go where?" Lewis replies, unable to disguise the merest hint of alarm in his voice.

"To Tommy's party," she replies, apparently not noticing the fractured tone.

"Of course. Why not?"

"Because I don't think Jenny likes me very much," she says slowly, as if weighing her words carefully.

Lewis passes her a mug.

"She just takes time to warm to people," he says.

"Is that all it is? I wonder." Anna allows the doubt to swim a little between them for a moment. "I would like her to like me, if that's possible. I mean, everyone else is so nice and welcoming. It would be good if Jenny were the same."

"Does it matter?" Lewis asks. He registers the look of surprise on her face. "I mean we can't like everyone, can we? And not everyone can like us."

"No, you're right. But I was hoping there might be a connection."

"Any reason?"

Having taken a sip of coffee, Anna just shakes her head.

For his part, Lewis knows all too well why Jenny might have taken against Anna. He hasn't said anything about the strange relationship he has with her, and for a moment wonders whether he ought to. He decides to let it pass. If Jenny's reticence was in relation to something about which Anna were already aware - either through direct knowledge or inference - she would surely have mentioned it. Or might mention it still. For the moment he decides to keep his own counsel.

"Your place is different to mine."

They have both relaxed into their second cups of coffee - to wash down the second florentine - and Anna has found a posture in such good accord with Lewis's worn old sofa that she feels almost as if it is hugging her.

"How so?" Lewis asks. "I thought we'd already established that the two were identical. Actually, it's that all three are identical; Bradley's is the same as this."

"Except for that monstrosity of a shed of his!"

Lewis laughs at her sudden playful vehemence.

"Don't you mean his 'boathouse'?" Anna shakes her head slightly in reply. Lewis pushes on. "But what do you mean 'different'?"

"I don't know. The feel of it I suppose."

"That's hardly surprising when you think of it. I mean I've lived in mine for some time and yours is - well, no easy way to say it - just a holiday cottage. No offence intended."

"None taken," she laughs, "though I have to say that it feels less like a holiday cottage than it did a few weeks ago."

Lewis finds himself wanting to ask her what it feels like now, but stops himself. He resorts to "So if it's not that, what is it?"

"Well, yours feels like a home - which I know is a bit like what you said," she adds quickly, "but it's more than something superficial like that. Perhaps it's the sense of being lived in. Or that it's owned even. I mean, have you ever met the Johnsons?"

"Once or twice, that's all." He stops, encouraging her to go on.

"Anyway, it's homely and lived in and owned - all that - but it also feels relaxed, at peace with itself. Almost as if it's the right building in the right place. Does that sound daft?"

"Probably not," he admits, "but then I'd be biased, wouldn't I?"

"Of course." She pauses. "And if you think about it, I guess it's not really about the cottage at all. It's more about you."

"Being 'homely and lived in'?!" he jokes.

"Behave!" She wags a finger at him. "No, the part about being at peace and in the right place. I had a sense of it in the kitchen too."

"Has my fridge been whispering about me behind my back?" he asks, smiling.

"Oh yes! But I'm trying to be serious," she pleads, "and to pay you a compliment of some flavour." He bows his head in acknowledgement. "Or am I way off the mark?"

Lewis shakes his head but says nothing, thinking about how he should reply. Anna scans the room again, her eyes alighting on the two framed photographs sitting on the bookcase. In one Lewis is arm-in-arm with a woman outside a stately home; they are both smiling. In the other, three men in fatigues lean against a desert-camouflaged tank. Lewis is one of them. She can relate to both in her own way, based on her own past.

She gets a sense of Lewis looking at her, and glances back to him with the sudden feeling that she has been caught prying.

"Oh," she says, putting her hand to her mouth momentarily, "I'm sorry, I didn't mean…"

She doesn't know what she didn't mean, but Lewis's smile tells her not to worry before his words do.

"It's fine. And you're right, I suppose - though it isn't the kind of thing you can see for yourself, is it? I mean, I know how I feel, but can't possibly know how I seem to others."

"That's part of the challenge, isn't it? The dilemma I guess most of us face one way or another." She allows a short pause before deciding to press on, intrigued now. "Who is she, the woman in the photograph?"

Lewis replaces his mug on the table, choosing not to follow her gaze to the bookcase. He knows the photograph well enough; he has it etched somewhere indelible.

"That's Emma," he says. In spite of his voice being even and calm, Anna gets a sense that he may struggle to keep it that way. "It was taken outside Chatsworth or somewhere like that; I was never very good with stately piles. Much more her thing. Nearly five years ago now, I suppose. The year before she died."

Anna wants to say she's sorry but cannot bring herself to do so, feeling it would be too cheap and too rapid a sentiment. And she doesn't want Lewis to stop.

"We'd been married about six years by then, though we'd known each other far longer than that. That had been a funny holiday. We'd been preoccupied the whole time with trying to make a decision about having a baby. Emma was thirty five; she had been telling me with increasing frequency about her ticking body-clock. But even though she said that, I don't think she'd quite sold herself on the idea."

"What about you?"

"Me?" He seemed to weigh himself up as independently as he possibly could. "I'm not sure I had a particularly strong view. I just wanted us to be happy, so whatever Emma decided was going to be fine with me."

"And did you - decide, I mean?"

"No, not really. And I suppose it was just as well, considering. The world would have looked a very different place if we'd had a baby and then she suddenly hadn't been there."

He allows the image to mature between them.

"What happened?" Anna asks, confident that they know each well enough now; after all, she has shared her own story.

"It was a stupid accident," he says, looking away from her towards the window. "She had been out jogging one morning. Crossing a road either she didn't see the car or the car didn't see her. The driver said she suddenly ran into the road from behind a parked van." He pauses. "I don't know. We never did find out. I met the guy a little later - once everyone was convinced I wasn't going to kill him!"

"Did you want to?"

"The thought had crossed my mind... And I'm sure at one point I could have. But anyway, we met - I can't recall who arranged it, but I was chaperoned. He was a perfectly normal chap in many ways, a bit like me. He just happened to be in the wrong place at the wrong time. He was distraught; I mean really distraught. When we met it seemed that I spent more time consoling him than the other way round. But perhaps I'd already come to terms with it. Or at least started to come to terms with it." Lewis looks back at Anna. "Once everything settled down, I felt suddenly hollow, as if the purpose had gone from my life. So I decided that I needed to rediscover myself. Or what was left of me. I told myself that's what Emma would have wanted. So I started wandering - though in a perfectly controlled and safe kind of way. I'd had enough danger to last a lifetime! And that's when I came across Maunston Quay. And having found Maunston, I discovered this place on the market, cheap. It was impulsive, but somehow I had the impression that it offered me something. A fresh start, I suppose." He waits for her to interject, but she refrains. "So if you say that I seem relaxed and in the place I need to be, well then I guess that must be right."

"You must miss her terribly."

His eyes betray the surprise he feels at Anna having said this.

"Of course, every day. But not in the way I did a couple of years ago. Or even last year. She's with me always, I suppose; but not in the sense of someone who would get in the way, if that makes sense. It's funny, but I feel as if we're friends again; as if she's on my side."

Anna brushes something from her eyes.

"So you see," Lewis steps into a gap that was about to form, "there's a large part of me that can appreciate why you're here. Oh, I know our situations are very different, at least in terms of historical events; but as to why we're here, what we're looking for… You're preaching to the converted!"

"And have you found something? Answered your questions?" Anna asks. "After all, you've a significant head start on me."

Lewis smiles.

"I think I'm pretty close," he says. "Some boxes ticked, if you like; not too many left. And none left to open - if you'll let me mix my metaphors!"

"Mix away!"

Lewis stands and holds out his hand for Anna's mug which she passes to him.

"Any more coffee?"

"I don't think so," she says, then "You're not trying to get rid of me, are you?"

"Of course not! I just thought I'd take these things out. You can stay as long as you like."

She watches him retreat to the kitchen carrying the empty plate, the mugs, and the cafetière. After a few seconds she can hear them being deposited by the sink, then there is a brief running of a tap before he returns.

"Who are the guys by the tank?" she asks as he reenters the room.

This time Lewis follows her gaze to the bookcase. He picks up the photograph and brings it over to her. As she takes it from him, he sits on the arm of the sofa and leans towards her, his finger pointing to the figures in front of her.

"The one in the middle, that's obviously me," he says lightly enough. "I was obviously a lot younger and fitter then."

"When was it taken?"

"About ten years ago now. In Afghanistan. And the big thing I'm leaning on, that's a tank."

She gently punches his thigh.

"Really? I would never have guessed. And the other two? The good-looking ones, who are they?"

"The ugly one on my left, that's Bridger; and the really ugly one on my right, is Stoner. Of course those aren't quite their real names; we all had nicknames of sorts. In the case of these two, they weren't very imaginative. Stoner came from Francis McDonald Stone. Some people called him Mac, though he hated that. Bridger's real name was Bridges. Also known as Mrs Bridges for some bizarre reason that I never fathomed out."

"He doesn't even look like a Mrs Bridges," Anna protests. "And what did they call you?"

"Me? It varied really."

When he shows no immediate signs of elaborating, she nudges him.

"Come on, you can't leave it there!"

"Jerry. They called me Jerry sometimes - because of Jerry Lewis."

"I can see the resemblance," she says, playfully. "And at other times?"

"Weirdly, Bognor. Because Lewes is a place down in Sussex and Bognor's nearby and has amusing connotations, I suppose. The one I'm least proud of is … Fairy."

She bursts out laughing.

"Fairy!"

"It's because of my surname," he sighs with mock disgruntlement, as if he has grown tired of needing to make the explanation.

"Which is?"

"Airey. A - I - R - E - Y. Hence..."

"Airey Fairy!" Anna's laughter makes him smile.

"Indeed. And I can't tell you how often I've heard that one." He pauses before dragging her back. "Anyway, now you know. Stoner was the radio guy; a whizz with anything electronic."

"And Bridger?"

Lewis rises and then returns to his seat.

"Bridger was one of the mine specialists. A slightly crazy bunch, the lot of them. I suppose you had to be to do what they did day-in, day-out."

She notes the change of tone in his voice. For a fraction of a second she weighs the next question, sensing it may prove a difficult one to answer. From some of the things Ryan had said to her before he died, she is aware how fragile military friendships can be; not because they are not strong - far from it - but because other things can get in the way.

"Where are they now?"

"Now?" He leans forward to take the photo back from her, and only speaks when he is holding it. "Stoner's still in the army - I think. We lost touch when I returned home before him and was demobbed. I expect he's no longer on active service but probably training new recruits. Catterick, or somewhere like that."

"And Mr Bridges?" For some reason Anna senses that she suddenly cannot use his nickname.

"Bridger's not anywhere anymore. He didn't make it out, I'm afraid; became a casualty, a government statistic…"

"I'm sorry," she says, feeling that she can use the phrase now not because she is expressing sympathy but because she is apologising for herself. "I had no idea. I didn't mean to make you talk about something so horrible."

Lewis smiles weakly.

"No, it's actually okay. One of my little boxes that I've now got a tick in. I used not to be able to talk about it, not for a long time. But gradually, you know… And it's only since I've been here, funnily enough. And all thanks to Bradley."

"Bradley?"

"As an ex-military man himself he could sense - no, maybe see - that something wasn't right with me; something to do with my service. He knew because he'd been there too. Northern Ireland in his case. Anyway, over time, as I began to feel more and more that I could trust him, it became easier to talk. Then one evening we got terribly drunk together and literally swapped war stories. In the morning I felt like shit - but also as if a terrible burden had been lifted."

"Good old Bradley," she says, trying to support Lewis's own smile.

He hopes for something further from her. Anything would do, really. But when nothing comes, he knows he needs to go on. He knows it will be a test for him, and proof of something - maybe for both of them.

"You want me to tell you what happened?"

She nods.

"I'd like to know, not because I'm secretly into things I shouldn't be, but - I don't know - if it helps you. Or me, maybe."

Anna knows it is a limp justification, but once uttered, she can only leave it with him. Having suddenly found herself towards the edge of the sofa, she eases herself back into its cushions. From somewhere she notices the tick of a clock for the first time, and behind her, outside, hears a hint of the sea.

"It had been a relatively routine patrol - as much as anything was routine out there, I suppose. Three vehicles, various personnel. I was in the third with Stoner and a couple of sappers. Bridger had been in the first. Because he was trained for tell-tale signs of things like mines and IEDs he always went in front. It was a sweep of four or five villages. We went round them twice, maybe three times a week. There was hardly anyone left in them any more; a few women and old men, some kids. That was about it. You always saw someone about, the odd bod whatever time of day. It was getting towards dusk when we came to the last village, just a few miles out of camp. Although we were all keeping our eyes peeled, being in the last vehicle we couldn't actually see that much half of the time because of the dust. Anyway, we suddenly crunched to a halt. Up ahead Bridger and his number two had got out of their jeep and were heading towards one of the buildings. I say buildings, but they were little more than rough huts really. I'm not sure what made them suspicious. Later we heard that there had appeared to be very few people about, and those that were seemed to be staying well clear of the first hut."

"Was that unusual?"

"A little. Often there'd be kids running up to the jeeps when they saw us coming, especially if the villages were friendly or there'd been some kind of aid drop the previous day. Often we'd support medics going in to places; that always went down well. Anyway, something had piqued our guys' interest. They scanned the road and it was clean. But then they headed to this hut. It wasn't that disciplined, I suppose." Lewis pauses just for a fraction. "They must have triggered something. There was an almighty bang, then a vast cloud of dust and sand, then nothing. As soon as I could, I jumped down from the jeep with the rest of the guys. Some of them were shouting but I couldn't hear a thing; the explosion had rendered me deaf for a few minutes. It was surreal seeing these guys running around shouting yet hearing nothing, almost as if I was in a Hollywood movie of some kind. After a few minutes the dust settled and we fanned out to sweep the village. I was one of the first to get to what was left of the hut; one of the first to see what was left of Bridger. My hearing was beginning to fade back in at that point, so once I'd finished throwing up I heard Stoner on the radio back to base. We were told to put the village into lock-down until backup arrived. There wasn't much to lock-down to be honest, but we just assumed the standard containing spread, taking as much cover as possible, and not going in any of the other buildings."

"What happened to the people there; the people who lived in the village, I mean?"

"They vanished. Holed up in the huts they knew were safe. Later we got them out; the interpreter tried to find out what had happened, see if they knew who'd set the trap. They were as scared as we were, I think."

Anna watches Lewis's face as he pauses in his story; watches as he takes in the photograph. He is dry-eyed which surprises her a little, but then she wonders if he is all cried out as far as Bridger is concerned. He seems calm, in control.

"What about you?" she asks.

"Me?"

She nods.

"Afterwards."

He looks up and smiles thinly.

"Afterwards? Afterwards we went back to base, got checked over, debriefed. My hearing was almost fully recovered, but not quite. My mind, however, was far from that. I'd seen nothing up to that point, not really. The aftermath of things maybe, the odd burned out jeep, stories mainly; but I'd never been involved first-hand, part of the target. No-one knows how they're going to cope with something like that - you should talk to Bradley; he's got stories that'll make your hair curl." He tries to laugh at a joke equally thin to match his smile. "Although my hearing recovered, I never did. The images of what I'd seen didn't leave me for days, weeks. Maybe not until I came here in some bizarre way. I got sent home soon after. Soon after that I left the army. Luckily I was coming up to the end of my commitment; seven years. I'd intended to carry on, but I couldn't. And I had Emma waiting for me too. I had something to live for..."

As he speaks, Lewis notices a shadow briefly cross Anna's face, and he regrets those last few words. He finds himself wishing he could take them back, rephrase them. Although he never knew him, he conjures up an image of a man in uniform who could have been Ryan Woolley; a man who had decided he didn't have anyone at home to live for any more. Lewis wishes that Ryan had felt about Anna as he felt about Emma, and knows that, if he had, the two of them - abandoned, orphaned - would not be sitting here in a seaside cottage reliving the most difficult things in their lives.

"I'm sorry," he says, then stands up. Anna is looking at the table, but he knows she has tears in her eyes. He picks up the photograph then walks to the bookcase where he puts it back where it was.

"I'll put the kettle on again", he says without turning, then walks out of the room knowing Anna's eyes will still be focussed on the table.

Chapter 7

Is there a limit on how much we can know, or on how much we should wish to know? It is a question which tests both Lewis and Anna for the remainder of the day, and for different reasons. Instinctively, they both know they can do nothing about the past, and because of that in some sense it should not matter; but that it is tied to them forever and defines who they are is undeniable. Compromise may also be uppermost in their minds. In spite of their individual histories shaping how they live their lives today, how much should they mould or dilute their aspirations for the future as a consequence of the journeys they have taken thus far?

Anna returns to her cottage soon after their second pot of coffee and busies herself with inconsequential things. It had been consumed quickly, accompanied by mere chatter. Back on her own turf, she focuses on domesticity: cleans the bathroom, vacuums the carpets, puts washing on. Although all necessary chores, she does not need to occupy herself with them for at least a couple of days; but occupy herself she does, perhaps in the hope that the mundane will prevent her thinking too much. That it fails to do so comes as no surprise, of course. She tidies away cleaned breakfast things from the drainer and goes through her food cupboards making a small list of where she needs to top-up. As she does so, she thinks of Lewis's kitchen, the unwashed crockery by the sink, his fridge, the food in it. She feels having seen all that has helped her to anchor him, to find a slot in her consciousness that he can inhabit more comfortably.

More than kitchen ritual and domesticity, however, his photographs are the real insights. As she left his cottage, she took one final glance at both, absorbing them as if they were way-markers by which she could navigate. Whether she sees it or not, to a degree they are also mirrors; after all, they might just have easily been pictures of her with Ryan, or Ryan with two of his colleagues in Iraq or wherever it was he went. Clearly they are not, and nor does she possess such parallel images - or at least not one of Ryan standing alongside a tank. And if she did, would she choose to display them in her own albeit temporary cottage? She doubts it, aware that not doing so says as much about her as Lewis's own display does about him.

For his part, once he has seen Anna off, Lewis returns to his armchair. He had stood at his front door ostensibly looking out to sea, but allowed his eyes to follow her until she disappeared from view. In reflecting on her visit as he inevitably does, he reflects first upon himself. Other than Bradley, she is the first person to whom he has told at least part of his Afghan history, and perhaps the worst part at that. Having faced - and feared - the inevitability of doing so for some considerable time, he is grateful to find the experience less traumatic than it might have been. He knows he has Bradley to thank in significant measure for that. Inevitably, he is also conscious of a tangential connection to Anna via Ryan; a link which meant he was divulging his story to someone who was already in possession of an intimate understanding which could only ensure their sympathy. He tries to imagine having the same conversation with Jenny, and knows it would be impossible, largely because she would only be involved in it to further her own agenda. Jenny has yet to set foot in the cottage, never mind having seen his photographs.

If Lewis feels comfortable with Anna, he declines to give his feelings a name. Even though he has not known her long there is something intangible that has allowed him to elevate her to the rank of friend. In spite of all his positive feelings towards those with whom he shares Maunston Quay, thus far he regards only Bradley as a friend. Others may come close in time - Richard perhaps, or Shirley - but he no longer gives friendship away on a whim. He thinks of Stoner and Bridger. They were his friends, one of them ripped from him just when they needed each other the most. Part of the pain he had felt then - pain he has not yet shared with Anna - was the loss of a friend, the severing of a relationship that had become important to him. If he guards himself too closely, if he puts up protective walls to prevent people getting in, then he does so only from the perspective of self-preservation, not because he doesn't want, need or value friendship. Yet even so, here is this new person who has somehow strolled across no-man's-land and breached his defences. Uncertain if that is a good thing or not, he glances towards the photograph of Emma just as he hears the vacuum cleaner start up next door. If she has any insight as to whether or not Lewis has dropped his guard too readily, she gives him no indication.

And so they submit to their quiet routines once more. When their paths cross at Oscar and Shirley's the following day no word is shared in relation to their conversation over coffee. It is evident that they are both aware of it - how can they not be? - and perhaps each permits the slightest sign toward the other in recognition of that fact. It rests between them not as something to bar the way, but rather as a secret which, above all else, acts as a bond.

On his way back to the cottage, shopping in hand, Lewis sees Bradley working at his bench through the open boathouse doors. A few paces further on, his voice calls him back.

"Whistling now, is it?"

"What?" says Lewis turning on the spot, front door key poised.

"You were whistling," says Bradley, appearing from his cavern.

"I never whistle," says Lewis with a laugh.

"No you don't," Bradley agrees, then disappears again to return to his work.

Lewis smiles, shakes his head and opens the door.

Coming downstairs at precisely that moment, Anna hears Lewis's front door close - and hears his footsteps along the hall accompanied by the hint of an usual sound that seems vaguely melodic.

❀ ❀ ❀

There are none of the trappings of a conventional party. No music, no flags or bunting, no over-sized hastily put together posters. But the bar is slightly busier than usual as Anna, Lewis and Bradley enter. They notice immediately the enlarged clientele, the increased volume of chatter. Behind the bar, Tommy - having made an effort to dress a little smarter this evening - looks uncomfortable and helpless.

"He's wearing a tie," Lewis says to Bradley, bypassing Anna.

"That'll be Jenny," Bradley replies, a knowing tone in his voice.

"Who are all these people?" Anna asks. Having located Richard, Shirley, Oscar and Aubrey in the crowd, she counts at least twelve others she does not know. It feels, somewhat bizarrely, as if Maunston Quay has grown during the day to become some other place.

"They only come out when there's free beer," Bradley suggests. "Or a full moon."

"There's free beer?" Above Anna's laugh, Lewis loads his voice with as much incredulity as he can muster. Bradley's glance gives him his answer. He looks at Anna. "What would you like?"

As Lewis moves to the bar to get the drinks, Bradley is diverted by a shout to his right. Anna is left alone momentarily on the fringes of things. She scans the bar wondering if she should find them a table, only to realise that no-one is sitting down. It is, currently at least, one of those events where you would only sit down if you wanted to stand out.

Behind the bar, Jenny patrols up and down looking officious and animated. She has her hostess's hat on, and alternates between drawing attention to Tommy, laughing at jokes, pulling pints, and directing a third person who is helping serve - not that Tommy seems to be doing much of that himself. On the public side of the bar, there are perhaps twenty five people gathered together in little knots. The people she knows seem to have infiltrated them, one to each group, as if part of some grand scheme to inform, promote, dictate or subvert. If you wanted to get a single and consistent message out to people in an impactful way, this would be how to do it. You could create truths this way.

"A penny for your thoughts?"

Richard has detached himself from the nearest cabal and arrived at her side unnoticed. Anna glances down at the glass in his hand, a half-finished pint of Guinness.

"I don't usually," he says, following her eyes, "but as it's Tommy's birthday…"

"Evening off," she suggests, helpfully.

"Yes, why not?"

They both look towards the bar where Lewis is now being served.

"Who's that serving Lewis?" Anna asks, then "In fact, who are all these people?"

Richard laughs.

"We keep them locked up in the crypt and only let them out for special occasions."

"That's what Bradley said."

"Really?"

"No; I'm only joking."

He looks relieved, then returns to her question.

"The young lady behind the bar is Maeve. She actually lives outside the village but comes in from time to time to help Tommy out. She's still at college, so the extra money helps her out. Nice girl. Wants to be a vet."

"And will she?"

"Will she what?"

"Become a vet?"

"I very much doubt it," Richard says, the appropriate tone of regret in his voice. "Not quite bright enough if I'm honest. Don't get me wrong, I'd love to see her succeed, but I suspect she'll end up doing something else."

"Don't we all?" Anna says, letting her guard slip for an instant. "Or did you always want to be a man of the cloth, Richard?"

He shakes his head, smiling.

"Didn't make it into my initial top ten, I'm afraid. But, as you can see, I'm not a train driver, brain surgeon or footballer, so…"

Lewis arrives with Anna's gin and tonic; his own pint is already a quarter empty.

"I was really thirsty," he says, seeing her surprise.

"What about you?" Richard asks him.

"Me what?" replies Lewis.

"What did you want to be when you were growing up? Not a vet like young Maeve, I'm sure."

"Animals and I don't really get along," Lewis confesses. "I suppose I wanted what every boy wants; to play cricket for England, to be a rock star. Usual stuff."

"Cricket not football?" Anna asks, Richard's own juvenile career shopping list still in her mind.

"I was never quick enough. Okay over the length of a cricket pitch, but not a football field. And I had no stamina either."

"A rather miserable specimen then," Richard tries, "somewhat like myself."

It is meant as a joke and they all laugh dutifully.

"And you, Anna? What did you want to do when you grew up?"

"Neither football nor cricket." She smiles. "But probably the usual girly things - though to be perfectly honest, I can't remember any ambition on that front."

"Listen to us," Lewis interjects, "talking as if it's all over; as if there's no more future. Why isn't the question still valid, that's what I want to know. What do you *still* want to do? Shouldn't that be it? Aren't we still entitled to dream?"

"Well said, Lewis," Richard applauds, "quite right too. As you say, perhaps the question should be 'what do you *still* want to do or become?', eh?"

"And isn't this the perfect occasion to ask?" Anna says.

"How so?"

"Well, it's Tommy's birthday. What if it were our birthdays, fifteen years from now? Looking back, how would the future Lewis or Richard appear? What would they have achieved over those fifteen years? And I think we can rule out professional football or cricket!"

❋ ❋ ❋

"I've said it more than once, you could do it, Bradley; you have the skill."

Bradley looks at Aubrey and shakes his head.

"Skill's one thing, but vision's something else. Just because I can maintain a couple of rusty old boats, that doesn't mean I can do what you do. I've no idea how you can see those forms and shapes and create them out of nothing. I'm a straight line and instructions man."

"I think you belittle yourself," says Oscar. "Those boats of yours were pretty much wrecks when you picked them up."

"I needed a project," Bradley says.

"Yes, fair enough. But don't you think you also needed vision and creativity to get them into their current - and very serviceable - state?"

"Not really, Oscar - though it's nice of you to say so," Bradley jousts. "As I say, all I needed was an instruction book and a few straight lines."

Now it is Aubrey's turn to shake his head.

"Some of that metal work on the deck, how you refurbished the cleats, the winches; just perfect."

"That's as may be," says Bradley, smiling, "- and thanks, by the way - but there's a world of difference between something functional like that and your birds."

"How many did you say the guy wanted to take?" Oscar asks, reverting to the original thread of their discussion.

"Five now, and then probably another five a month during the summer, if they sold. More if they sold really well."

"But that's just great, Aubrey," says Bradley. "What's the mark-up?"

"I don't know," Aubrey replies a little disingenuously. "He'll probably sell them for between twenty and fifty quid, depending on size, and I'll get half. That's the deal."

"There are just raw materials and time on your side," Oscar observes, "so that's almost pure profit."

"Maybe so," says Aubrey, clearly unconvinced, "apart from the cost of running the forge."

"But it doesn't take you too long to turn them out, does it?"

"Long enough," says Aubrey taking a sip from his beer, noticing as he does so that Oscar and Bradley are almost empty. "My shout is it?"

❃ ❃ ❃

"How many tonics do we have?" Jenny asks, seeing Maeve serve another G&T.

"At least two dozen," Maeve replies, attempting to ignore the fact this is the second time Jenny has asked the same question in the last few minutes.

"Good. Just keep an eye on them."

Maeve knows her job well enough. As she begins to pull another pint of bitter she catches Tommy's eye. He smiles knowingly and Maeve wants to raise her eyebrows as if to imply something she shouldn't - luckily she is just mature enough not to. In any event, she's sure he knows well enough.

"Tommy," Jenny's voice drags him away to where she is now talking to Shirley. Petra and Janice, the sisters who share the house closest to the forge, are there too.

Tommy smiles at them as Jenny places her hand on his arm.

"They want to know your secret," she says.

"Secret?"

"How you manage to look so young."

"Young?"

"Jenny says you're fifty-six, and I wouldn't have had you a day over forty-eight," says Janice, trying to be obliging.

"Is that what she says?" Tommy shoots his wife a look which causes Shirley to laugh.

"Have I said something wrong?" Janice looks suddenly concerned and begins to redden.

"Jenny's just having a little joke, Janice, that's all," says Shirley, trying to reassure her. "There's a very good reason why Tommy doesn't look fifty-six..."

"Oh!" says Petra, suddenly picking up the thread. "Because he isn't?"

"Because he isn't," confirms Tommy. "In fact he's not fifty-anything!"

Jenny bursts out laughing pleased at her little joke. She leans forwards and pecks Tommy on the cheek. He smiles as he must, knowing that in many ways this evening isn't really about him at all. Jenny, looking more glamorous that she has for a long time, is clearly out to make an impression, and Tommy is convinced that her efforts will not have gone unnoticed. He winks at Janice trying to assure her she is forgiven, even if he finds her assessment of his age a little harsh. Does he really look that much older than he is?

As he turns away, he sees something in Shirley's demeanour that reminds him - if he needed reminding - that she is a wily old bird too.

❊ ❊ ❊

"Is that so wrong?" Anna asks in manner that would tell anyone who happened to drop in on the conversation at this precise moment that the exchange was a light-hearted one.

"I'm not saying it's wrong," says Lewis, feeling as if he has been outmanoeuvred. "Richard, back me up here!"

"Leave me out of this," he smiles, "I have no wish to get caught up in any kind of 'domestic'. In fact," he adds, "I just need to go and see Janice and Petra."

Lewis watches him withdraw, unsure how tactical it was.

"All I'm saying," Anna is pushing on, "is that you don't need to have some kind of grand plan. That's all. And I'm not saying that you personally should have one, or need one. In fact…"

Lewis looks back at her just as she pauses. He sees something akin to doubt cross her face, as if the 'fact' she was about to state was not going to be that at all; as if she had just caught herself up in time.

Which she had, of course. She was about to say that she didn't care one way or another whether Lewis had a plan for the rest of his life or not - and recognising those were the words she was about to utter, she realised that, as a new friend, she did care. They had moved on from the question of 'what you wanted to be' - past tense - to 'what you want to be' - future tense, and her own lack of clarity or ambition had drawn a little heat from both men. Even Richard, who she would have imagined as being more laissez faire that most, seemed to be on Lewis's side.

"In fact?" Lewis prompts, keen to understand where Anna was going with her argument - or where she had decided not to go.

"Hello." Tommy's arrival saves Anna the challenge of resolving a dilemma.

"Happy birthday!"

"Thanks, Anna. It's all a bit of nonsense really," he confesses. "I don't actually care one bit, but Jenny likes to make a fuss; thinks it's good for business."

"Well you seem to be doing okay," Lewis suggests.

Tommy surveys the bar quickly, another four people having just arrived.

"Yes," he says, "not a bad turnout I suppose. We'll probably do more tonight than in a normal week - on the booze side, at least."

"She does seem," Anna pauses, "a little bit 'pumped up'."

They glance towards Jenny who is still smiling and serving and pestering Maeve.

"She's in her element really," Tommy says. "It's this part of the business that she's made for, I suppose. Most of the time it's just a bit slow for her. Nights like this bring out the best in her - from a landlady perspective anyway. I think she's reminded of how things were before we moved here; maybe how she'd like them to be."

"You should do more of them then," Anna suggests.

"The poor bloke can't have any more birthdays," says Lewis, a little aghast. "He isn't the Queen!"

They laugh at the joke.

"That wasn't what I meant, and you know it," Anna admonishes him. "What I meant was to find reasons to get people out; more events, if you like."

"Such as?" Lewis asks, beating Tommy to the draw.

"Such as… Well, what about a monthly quiz night? That might bring people out. Personal pride and all that - even if it were only the locals."

"I'd want to be on Maisie's team," Lewis says with a degree of certainty that surprises Anna.

"Maisie?"

Lewis looks round.

"Just over there talking to Aubrey. Red hair, up in a bun."

Anna locates her.

"I've not met her yet. Why would you want to be on her team?"

"Because she's really bright," Lewis says. "She works at the library in town, which, I have to say, is just so far beneath her. She could have been anything she wanted; I really think that." Anna sees Tommy nod in agreement. "But she's never had the drive."

"And she loves what she does," Tommy adds. "But what else, in addition to a quiz night?"

"Oh, I don't know. Maybe a themed evening, with food perhaps. Like a Pacific Islands night; you could do a special on cocktails, that would surely be worth something. Or how about a 'Superstars' evening."

"Superstars?" Lewis echoes, a little incredulous.

"Teams of locals taking each other on in various pub events: darts, pool, cards, dominoes. You know, like that old TV show where all sorts of famous sportsmen would compete against each other."

"There could be a trophy," Tommy says, immediately and evidently liking the idea, "'The Anchor Gold Cup'. We could play for it once a quarter, say."

Anna looks at Lewis to see if he endorses her idea. He says nothing but is smiling broadly.

"What?" she says, feigning a degree of playful aggression in her voice.

"Nothing," he laughs, "just nothing."

"There is," she says, feeling a little knocked off balance. "I can see there's something, Lewis."

He laughs again.

"I'll tell you later."

* * *

"I spoke to the Thompsons," Shirley says, having sought Anna out and dragged her away from a little group that included Janice and her brother.

"And?" Anna's voice is quieter now than when she had protested at the way Shirley had corralled her, simultaneously declaring that if Oscar were talking it couldn't possibly be anything worth listening to. He had simply raised his eyebrows, weary at being the butt of the same old joke. Anna had wanted to be seen trying to defend him.

"And, she said that they've no plans to come and visit at the moment, or to let it to any friends or anything like that. So if you want it for a little longer, that's fine with them."

"Did they say how long?"

"They asked me that, actually," Shirley glances away from Anna and scans the rest of the bar as if doing so might answer the question that was uppermost in her mind, "and I said I didn't know. Do you?"

"Not really." Anna knows her reply is a little weak.

"Anyway, they suggested why not have the place on a kind of rolling basis, week-by-week, you know?"

"That sounds perfect," Anna smiles.

"I told them I thought it might be." Shirley leaves the comment almost in mid-air, as if it's lingering there awaiting a companion clause to join it. "We thought a two-week notice period on either side would be the most practical. Is that alright with you?"

"Perfect," says Anna.

"Oh, and I was able to negotiate the rent down a little for you - on the basis that you were a good tenant, long-term and all that. And how easy was it going to be for them to find someone else if you left? All that kind of thing."

"Really?" Anna is unable to keep the surprise from her voice. "How much?"

"A third off. I thought that was only fair."

Anna leans forward and gives Shirley a hug, something that clearly takes her by surprise.

"Let me buy you a drink," Anna says, once she has released the now smiling shopkeeper, "it's the least I can do."

"Thank you, dear," says Shirley, trying hard not to sound like someone's mother but knowing she is failing completely, "and then I'll introduce you to Maisie."

❊ ❊ ❊

"Well we've missed it for this year, and I don't think there's anything similar in the autumn," says Petra, standing in a group that includes Richard, Oscar and Jenny, who has relieved herself of bar duty for the first time.

"That's a shame," Jenny says, "the village looked really nice the last year we did it."

"The problem is that we always think of it too late," Oscar points out. "Even if it had come up at that meeting we had a couple of weeks ago it would have been too late then."

"If we wanted to do it - for next year, for example - we'd have to be thinking about it now," Richard concurs. "I expect you need to get entries in for things like 'Villages in Bloom' well in advance; certainly this year for next year's competition."

"Well maybe we should," says Jenny, her face still carrying a flush from being busy behind the bar - that and a indeterminate number of sips of wine she has had over the previous couple of hours. "Your garden was the absolute star last time, Petra."

"Well, we love our garden," Petra says, smiling at the praise, "though Janice does most of the heavy lifting these days." Petra is a small woman and the notion of her doing any lifting at all might seem strange to some. "But most people tried really hard, I thought. I remember the judges were particularly impressed with the areas around the green and the church."

"You didn't let us down there, Richard," offers Oscar awkwardly, plainly out of his comfort zone.

"We had lots of help, didn't we?" says Richard. "I think most people chipped in one way or another. And those clematis were simply splendid."

"It was a good year for clematis, as I recall," says Janice.

❀❀❀

"Lewis tells me that you work in the library in town," Anna says. She has taken an immediate liking to Maisie who seems a bright and vivacious character. She finds herself searching for attributes she may have possessed when she was Maisie's age, even if doing so can only demonstrate the kind of damage seven or eight years can do.

"Yes. I simply love it," Maisie replies, unable to hide her enthusiasm. "I hadn't planned to be working there. Actually, I hadn't planned anything at all really, and I simply fell into it, I suppose. It was something to do while I worked out my grand plan."

"Did you have one - a plan I mean?"

"Vaguely, I suppose. The normal sort of thing; off to University, then find a suitable job afterwards."

"What stopped you?" Anna asks, trying to gauge Maisie's age. "I mean, I assume something did."

"Yes, you might say that." Maisie's laugh is light and genuine. "I suppose I stopped me. You see, I could never work out what I wanted to study - which is a bit of a stumbling block, isn't it? I wanted to apply, I really did. I actually had my sights set on a University somewhere near a coast: Brighton, or Southampton - or even St. Andrew's. I've never wanted to live away from the sea, so that would have been wonderful. I might even have met a Prince!"

Anna laughs at how honest and open Maisie is.

"I think they might have run out of Princes at St. Andrew's by the time you would have got there."

"You never know," says Maisie. "Anyway, I couldn't decide between History or Literature or Philosophy. So I stopped trying. I thought if I took a year or so out it might clear my mind. That was nearly six years ago now. Gosh, how time flies!"

Anna nods in agreement, even if she has become a little unsure exactly how fast - or slow - time seems to pass in Maunston Quay.

"I'll be Head Librarian in a few years unless something happens to change that."

"And that's all right?" Anna asks.

"Just now it would be perfect." Maisie pauses. "But what about you? Lewis says you're sort of taking some time out yourself."

"He said that?"

Maisie blushes slightly, fearing she may have betrayed a confidence. Anna puts a hand on her arm.

"It's fine. And he's right, I guess. Just working out what I want to do next, really. I mean it won't be St Andrews or Sussex University or anything like that, but I need to have some kind of plan I suppose - the men have made that perfectly clear!"

"The men?" says Maisie, confused.

"A little earlier Richard, Lewis and I were discussing ambition and the need to have some kind of goal. I think they may be more structured than I am. I pretended to disagree a little, just for the fun of it, but they're right really."

"So do you have one?"

"Right now just a very short-term one: to unwind here and enjoy a little 'me time'."

"I think that's so important," says Maisie. "You might get lucky, like I have, and find the 'me time' leads into something that's just perfect for you."

"You won't go to university now?" Anna asks, not prepared to consider serendipity as a planning approach.

"I doubt it, somehow. Perhaps I might try the OU a little bit later on if I find I'm feeling academically unfulfilled. But I'll only do that when I know what I want to study. I'm still finding things out, of course."

"Such as?"

"Oh, I don't know. When you're helping people out - especially those who are using the library as a place to work or study themselves - you can get drawn into things. They become interesting for you too. You can actually find out a lot about people just by talking to them. And I've had a few doing research into their family histories."

"Hoping to find they're related to royalty?" Anna suggests.

"Maybe," says Maisie, laughing. "Most often they're interested in something specific. One guy was convinced that he had an ancestor who sailed with Captain Cook."

"And did he?"

"We don't think so. I'm afraid he may have found his way to Australia via a less savoury and glamorous route! But it was fun helping him out. I managed to get a handle on all sorts of sources for people; genealogy is interesting - but probably not a recognised OU subject!"

❋ ❋ ❋

"I know I should apologise," Bradley says, partly to fill a gap in the conversation, partly not.

"For what?" Richard asks, his attention drawn away from watching Jenny as her gaze follows Lewis meandering back from the Gents.

"The other evening. After that meeting we had here."

Richard feigns trying to remember for a moment.

"I can't recall anything you need to apologise for, Milton."

Bradley checks the object of Richard's recent attention before looking back at him.

"I was a little harsh, I think, suggesting that you were - I don't know - 'recruiting' Anna."

Involuntarily they simultaneously scan the bar to see where she is, to ensure she is out of earshot.

"She seems to have settled in rather well, don't you think?" Richard says, deliberately ignoring the thrust of Bradley's comment. "Almost as if she's been here longer than - what is it? - maybe five or six weeks."

"Aye," Bradley replies, incongruously dredging up an image of a Scottish Major from his Belfast days. "She'll do well enough," he says as if passing some kind of judgement.

An awkward pause descends.

"Look, Milton," says Richard, alleviating the other's disquiet, "I know that you struggle with me." Seeing Bradley is about to immediately interrupt, Richard quickly pushes on. "Not me - I hope! - but what I represent. I understand your difficulty, or objection, or whatever the right word is. And I think I understand where that has come from, what's behind it. Red rag to a bull, and all that. And that's fine, Bradley, it really is. I'm not that naive to assume I can convert everyone, nor that it's my job to do so. If it were, you'd have driven me to distraction a long time ago!"

Their laughter defuses any tension that might have been building between them.

"I know that, Richard. And I know that you know it too. I just wanted to let you know that I recognised I was out of line, that's all."

"Apology accepted," Richard smiles. "It was entirely unnecessary, but thank you, anyway." He pauses. "And to respond to your point, yes, I do think think she'll do well enough - however long she stays. Shirley says it may be a little while yet. At least until she's sorted herself out."

"Sorted herself out?"

"You have some idea of her background, if not from Anna herself then from Lewis?"

"A little from Lewis," Bradley confesses.

Richard nods.

"Then you'll have some sense of her being a little lost. Like most of us, I have to say. Anything we can do to help her I'm sure will be welcome. From my perspective, I'm keen to help her as a person first, then as a Vicar second - but only if that's what she wishes. Does that make sense?"

"It does; of course, it does." Bradley glances again to where Anna and Maisie are in conversation. "I think that's the same for all of us. At least I hope so."

✳ ✳ ✳

"This is all very mysterious," says Maisie as she follows Lewis to just beyond the periphery of the crowd. He has come to a halt on the threshold of the conservatory section of the bar and is glancing back to see who has noticed their move away. "What kind of favour is it you need me to do for you?"

"You've met Anna?" he says, coming straight to the point.

"Briefly, yes. She seems really nice. I liked her."

"I like her too," Lewis says smiling. "Did she tell you why she was here - in Maunston, I mean?"

Maisie laughs.

"Why? Sounds very cloak and dagger!"

"It isn't, really," he replies smiling, then waits for her answer. "Well?"

"She said she was just here to unwind. I think that's the word she used. To have a little 'me time' she said."

"Did she say why?"

"Lewis! What is this, the Spanish Inquisition?" In spite of the lightness of her reply, a note of concern has crept into Maisie's voice.

"I know, I'm sorry," Lewis says, trying to reassure her. "Anna's told me all about her husband and her son. I know she's had a difficult time and that she's trying to sort her life out. She's been very open about that. Not only with me, but with Richard too. And I'm really keen to see that she finds what she's looking for, you know? I'd really like her to be happy again."

"And you think she may have told me something else in those three minutes we had together; something that might help?" Maisie's brief concern has now given way to confusion.

"I'm not sure, but I doubt it."

Lewis pauses again and looks back into the main body of the party. He can see Anna at the far end of the bar talking with Janice and Petra. No-one appears to be looking their way.

"It's just that I think there may be something else," he says, trying to speak quietly and evenly. "I just wonder if she has something she's not telling us, and that if I knew - if we knew - we might be able to help her a bit better. That's all."

"Isn't that up to her to say one way or the other?" Maisie asks the logical question, as Lewis knew she would. "Have you asked her if there's anything else; anything more you can do to help her?"

Lewis shakes his head.

"I haven't, no. And I haven't because - I don't know - I guess I don't want to pry or to be so obvious."

"Obvious?"

"I don't want her to feel like she's a special case, or someone who needs help. Do you see? She's had a rough time of things, and I don't want her to feel that I'm harping back to that, making her think of it too much, or appear to be pushy or nosy. I just want to help. As much as I can. That's all."

He delivers his last few phrases with increasing slowness, trying to judge their effect on Maisie as he does so. She has stopped smiling, and he is uncertain if that is a good thing or not.

"And why tell me all this?" Maisie asks. "How can I help, I've only just met her? What favour do you need from me?"

Lewis sighs, involuntarily. Maisie's brow furrows. He suddenly realises how difficult this is; how he is about to cross some kind of line - not in a malevolent or negative way, but in the sense that he feels he is making some kind of statement of his own. He knows he should be satisfied with what Anna herself has told him.

"I was wondering if you could - as a favour to me, and to help Anna really - just find out about how her husband died."

"How he died?" Maisie's surprise is evident.

"Ryan. He was in the Army or Marines or something. You have access to all those records and things at the library. I was thinking that if I knew the truth - or at least a little more of it - then I might be able to better understand. And help. As an ex-Army man myself, you know. I've seen enough in my time…"

Lewis allows his words to tail away. He is being a little disingenuous, but hopes Maisie can't see that. Yes, knowing more about how Ryan died may help him to understand Anna's situation better, may allow him to help her find closure. But there is something else too; something he has not been able to put his finger on. Instinct tells him there is just a little more, and he wants to know if that is true. He tells himself that he wants to know for Anna's sake and not his own, but the boundaries are less clear than he had imagined they would be.

"That's it?" asks Maisie, after a pause. "Let me get this right. You just want me to see if I can find out anything about her husband's death, just in case knowing a little more will let you help her out a bit better?" He nods. Maisie waits a moment. "You know I shouldn't, don't you?" Another nod, another pause. "Let me think about it. And you can buy me a drink as a down payment, just in case I say yes."

Lewis smiles, hoping his relief isn't too palpable. It is relief arising from making it through to the end of the conversation reasonably unscathed. He also believes that, having sown the seed and piqued her interest, Maisie will be unable to not act.

❖ ❖ ❖

"Why don't you come round for some tea?"

Richard looks at Anna as if he has misheard, though only because he is wary of the word 'tea', its flexibility of meaning.

"Tea?"

"Yes," she smiles, missing the subtlety. "You know, the hot brown stuff you put milk in."

"And sugar if you're really uncouth."

"Exactly! I may even try and bake a cake - but if I do, I'll take no responsibility for any unfortunate consequences should you try some."

"I'm prepared to take the risk," he says, making a show of having considered his answer for a moment. "I may take precautions, of course."

"Precautions?"

"You know, an extra prayer before I set off."

She laughs.

"Is there a patron saint of baking?" she asks.

"I don't know, why?"

"Because if there is I might try a prayer or two of my own!"

The joke amuses him and he laughs loudly enough to turn one or two heads.

"That was very indiscrete of me wasn't it?" he says.

"Too much communion wine, Richard?" she asks playfully.

"No," he wags a finger at her, "those are just scurrilous rumours put about by people who are trying to undermine me!"

"Your secret's safe with me," she promises. Out of the corner of her eye she notices Lewis and Maisie heading a little away from the bar. As she scans the room, she sees Petra and Janice glancing her way.

"Is it time for a talk?" Richard asks with some import, his composure reestablished, the true meaning of his words interlaced between them.

"Just a chat," she suggests, with a degree of certainty that is not lost on him, "don't get your hopes up."

"Either way, I'll look forward to it. When were you thinking?"

"Is tomorrow afternoon any good? Strike while the iron's hot and all that."

"Yes," Richard replies slightly hesitantly, never having been particularly good at the spontaneous, "if it's good for you."

Anna senses an underlying question.

"Of course, if you think I need a little more time practicing my baking just to make sure I don't poison you…"

"Oh, don't poison poor Richard!" says a new voice suddenly. "I don't know what we'd do without him, do you Petra?"

Richard smiles on cue.

"Anna, let me introduce you…"

❊ ❊ ❊

"Here we are again," says Oscar, raising his spirit glass in response to Tommy's own, clinking them together with a sound that speaks to both the quality of the glass and the pleasure in the whiskey. "Doesn't seem like a year, does it?"

Tommy, having taken a sip while Oscar was speaking, swills the malt briefly in his mouth before downing it, the warmth on his throat coinciding with a slight shake of the head.

"It doesn't," he says, as soon as he able to speak again, "just like the year before. I think we probably stood here twelve months ago and made exactly the same observation."

"Well, it wouldn't be surprising would it, seeing as how time seems to go faster and faster?" Oscar's tone is heavy with commiseration, as if he were practicing for a wake. "How does the last one one rank then, out of ten?"

It is a little game they have been playing for the last few years. They each have their individual goals, commercial numbers they would have liked to achieved for the year just past - but have never once achieved them. The score is supposed to represent more than that, but by instinct they both start by thinking about their respective bank accounts.

"Six, I suppose," says Tommy with some resignation, knowing that he has again fallen short of his aspirational target. He longs to be able to say 'eight', but there are too many things outside of his control to deliver that level of satisfaction. "Or maybe a bit less."

Oscar nods knowingly.

❈ ❈ ❈

"Look at them," Shirley says, tucked up at the other end of the bar with Jenny, "like a couple of old I don't know what."

"I do," says Jenny, "I know exactly what they are, I just don't know what the word is."

The absurdity of her statement makes them both laugh.

"I'm sure we could come up with a few suggestions," Shirley offers.

"And few of them complimentary."

"You think we might actually one day consider suggesting something complimentary?" says Shirley, shocked. "That can only be the wine talking, Jen."

"You're probably right. I apologise unreservedly."

"Apology accepted."

"Top up?" Jenny asks, reaching for an open bottle on the shelf behind her. "I feel like being more charitable!"

❊ ❊ ❊

Lewis laughs. It is a loud, explosive laugh; the sort of laugh that would register high on a Beaufort scale for laughter, were there such a thing. The fact that he does so with his head thrown back very slightly only serves to project the sound higher into the air and further around the bar, as if it were a ripple on a pond, the result of someone having dropped an over-sized stone into its still waters.

Immediately in front of him, Anna is laughing too, her hand placed lightly on Lewis's chest, her head bent forwards as if she is sharing her part of their joke with the floor; as if between them they are trying to dissipate humour to all parts of 'The Anchor'. They are both red-faced; Lewis, one suspects, from the force behind his laugh; Anna in embarrassment perhaps, because it is something that she has said which has generated this sudden tsunami of sound.

If it had been their intent to ensure that at least some fragments of their mirth were bequeathed to all, then they have succeed; around the bar people look their way or pause in what they themselves were saying, not only as a result of the interruption, but because that specific moment seems to carry the weight of something more significant than their own words.

❊ ❊ ❊

Bradley, prompted by a sudden sound to look their way, sees in his friend a show of relaxation which, after three years of comradeship, he has only occasionally glimpsed. He recognises at least part of the laugh itself, and can, in an instant, recall those few moments when he has heard it in their cottages, usually accompanied by a little whiskey and almost always as a form of release from the gravity of the subjects about which they have been speaking. In addition to the seriousness of their parallel experiences, when they talk about their army lives they have a treasure trove of the ridiculous upon which to draw, often laughing at the innocent misfortune of others - like when Bradley's old platoon commander managed to get himself locked in a jeep and couldn't get out. Such stories are the safety valves that allow them to explore the unpleasant, to exorcise the gruesome, and once these are brokered, laughter follows.

But that laughter is not, Bradley knows, entirely like Lewis's at this precise moment. He smiles to himself, then feels the smile becoming public - and he doesn't care. There is a sense that a seal has been broken and in a good way, as if a restraint has been removed. If he were a different person, he might translate it as being akin to a curse's lifting; but Bradley does not believe in curses. Or luck, good or bad. He has never found it efficacious or practical to do so. If you were to ask him what he did believe in, he would recite a very limited list indeed. Laughter may not be on that list, but it would be nearby for sure.

"Where was I?" Bradley says, turning his attention back to the topic in hand.

❋ ❋ ❋

Richard hears the laugh and thinks immediately of a peel of bells - though he is unsure exactly why. Laughter always makes him smile, and he does so unselfconsciously. It is, for him, proof of joy; and proof of joy is testament to more than just that. He sees Lewis with his head thrown back and cannot help but recognise how rarely people laugh in such an unconstrained way. And then, almost simultaneously, he suddenly finds himself saddened in equal measure. He cannot help but wonder, in that instant, how often people are truly happy - how often *he* is truly happy. Different things work for different people, and he consoles himself that his own interpretation of joy is allied to a significantly more restrained display, and is probably triggered at a modest and humble level. At least, he hopes so.

But Richard also sees Anna, the way she is leaning against Lewis, her own laughter undoubtedly there but drowned out. And though he can only see the merest sliver of her face, he gets a sense of her colour, the shape of her features. Hardly knowing her, he knows enough about her past and her present preoccupations to sense that this is somehow an important moment for her. In his own mind he has her defined as a largely undemonstrative individual, someone who is certainly self-aware. Because of this, her contribution to such a sudden - and loud! - outburst of mirth is a significant measure of her being relaxed, not only with Lewis but, he trusts, with them all. It represents motion, at least of moving forwards if not yet of moving on.

As he returns to the conversation in which he was primarily a listening party, he remembers they are having tea tomorrow, and finds himself looking forward to it anew.

❖ ❖ ❖

Shirley sees Lewis and thinks of Aubrey. Instinctively she knows a laugh such as Lewis's at that moment is a rarity, not only for him, but for everyone. Its unbidden and naive intrusion upon them all, reminds Shirley how much she actually likes him. That he is not her type is a given she has never questioned. Others might make light of a partner being eleven years older, might swat away both internal and external objections in the name of love, but Shirley is not one of them. She has always believed in the order of things - 'a place for everything, and everything in it's place' - and it is a mantra that suits her. She believes that Lewis is in the right place, has a found a home that fits him, and she has hopes that Anna - so obviously in on the joke! - will do so at some point soon.

If you were to challenge Shirley with the accusation that such thoughts were romantic, she would bat the charge away with cold dismissiveness. She has never considered herself fallible in that way, and would never concede that wishing the best for other people ever strayed into that territory. Nor would she regard her affection for Aubrey as 'romantic'; it is, in her terms, 'fit and proper'. In the recent past other epithets might have been more readily and less charitably applied: frustration or resignation, perhaps - and all on her side. She wonders, as she stands for a moment on the edge of things and raises a glass to her lips, whether she has ever heard Aubrey laugh as Lewis does now. She finds herself trying to remember the last time she heard him laugh at all. Finding a memory to provide an echo of his laugh proves strangely difficult. Telling herself that she wouldn't want a man who constantly laughed as Lewis just has, she looks away and scans the room to locate the man from the forge. She discovers he too has been diverted by Lewis, and as she looks at him, he turns his eyes in her direction and fixes them there for a moment.

❀ ❀ ❀

Tommy regards laughter and noise as two of the most reliable measures a man in his position has of proving the success - not only of evenings such as this - but of his entire profession. As he glances Lewis's way - his eyes momentarily diverted from the pint of beer he is pouring - he is grateful. It is the kind of laugh (too rarely heard, he concedes) that lifts a bar, that can act as a catalyst. His trained ear has noted the gradual increase in background volume as the evening has worn on, bolstered by the occasional influx of newcomers and the inelastic relationship between alcohol consumption and volubility. A laugh like Lewis's or difficulty in hearing nearby conversations prove a successful evening.

As he turns back to the rapidly filling glass cradled in his left hand, Tommy tries to decide whether he likes Lewis or not. There are many things about him that he appreciates, of course, and he knows his wife all too well, and has never been blind to the way she gravitates towards Lewis. He has rationalised her behaviour away as being a naive but harmless weakness, convinced that she lacks the courage to carry out any implicit threat. That Lewis seems to keep her at arm's length in a friendly but detached way is, from Tommy's perspective, his greatest attribute. But Tommy also knows there are rewards people are prepared to accept as payment for crossing a line. This is his only true reservation given he has no idea how close to Lewis's own threshold Jenny is capable of inducing him.

❀❀❀

Aubrey, trying hard to follow a somewhat labyrinthine conversation in which Petra and Janice seem intent on out-doing each other, finds himself strangely shocked by the sudden burst of sound for which Lewis is responsible. He is also a little disquieted by its source, never having considered Lewis to be a man capable of exploding publicly in such an exuberant and unrestrained way. Aubrey knows himself to be made of different stuff. Whilst acknowledging he is neither flamboyant nor extrovert, nevertheless he does not regard himself as dull and uninteresting but rather more positively as solid, dependable. It is why, he reasons, working the forge came so naturally to him. He cannot imagine a man who laughed too much or too loudly being steady enough of hand to do what he does.

Seeing Anna brace herself against him is, in Aubrey's eyes at least one item of credit in Lewis's favour. Aubrey admires the predicable and reliable. It is one of the reasons why he holds Shirley in such high regard - and why, he believes, she reciprocates the feeling. He tries to manufacture an image where he has replaced Lewis and Shirley is Anna, a moment in which it is he who is laughing and Shirley, bent double likewise, is leaning against him. It is vision he is incapable of completing; not because he lacks the imagination to do so, but because of its simple impossibility.

Aubrey wonders if Shirley has noted the interruption, and as he does so his gaze is drawn away from Lewis and Anna to where, from across the other side of the bar, Shirley is staring straight at him.

❀❀❀

Jenny is just emerging back into the bar when she hears a sudden outburst, a sound she finds difficult to place. She knows it to be laughter of course, but without more evidence she struggles to define its source.

The first thing she notices is the number of heads all turned in the same direction: Bradley, Oscar, Shirley, Aubrey - even Tommy. By following their gaze she sees Lewis in side profile. That it is he whose sudden laugh has exploded so loudly takes her by surprise; it seems a laugh that belongs to someone else, as if he has borrowed it to try it out. She is not sure it suits him, yet feels herself beginning to smile just the same.

It is a smile, however, that does not progress beyond the embryonic when she realises that Anna is standing immediately in front of him, and that she has her hand on his chest as if, what, pushing him away perhaps? And yet it is not Anna's hand that disturbs her most of all, that very real physical contact, but rather the notion that she may have the capability to make Lewis act in such a way. How can that be possible?

She has been playing her own hand very carefully over recent months, almost imagining herself to be an angler with a prize catch on the end of her line. It is an image borrowed from a father who loved to fish; one of a number to which she fondly returns from time to time. She believes that she has been getting close to landing her catch, as if his thrashing has diminished, as if he is beginning to tire, unable to put up much more of a fight. But now this. A laugh that sees him jack-knife in the water to almost rip the rod from her hands. And why? Because of Anna; because someone else is threatening to land him first.

That is how Jenny sees things in that instant; in the moment before moving; before telling Maeve to get the last crate of tonics through from the back and stack them under the counter; before seeking out her birthday husband, who never laughs as Lewis has just laughed; and before being seen to do her duty once again on this his special day, even if her head has begun to spin just a little. It is a glimpse through time, somehow of both past and present, and, Jenny fears, perhaps of the future too.

Chapter 8

She keeps her photographs in the bottom of a chest of drawers. From originally being something of a default location, a place where one put 'stuff' in transit to its proper home, the lowest drawer became, for various reasons, the ideal one. The small, dark blue A5 album in which the photographs are contained sits among the few of her clothes that she rarely wears: a pale blue turtleneck that proved to be the wrong shade; a patterned cardigan whose large floral motif might one day come back into fashion. The word 'Photos' on the cover is embossed in cheap silver lettering which is beginning to chip at the edges. Bizarrely the 's' seems more vulnerable than the rest of the letters, and she is convinced that one day the legend will simply say 'Photo' to all but the knowing eye.

And in a way this is entirely appropriate. There is really only one photograph in her little collection that she keeps returning to: the one showing her sitting alongside a soldier on a low wall near his barracks after some medal ceremony or other. As she looks at it now, she is amazed at how young they both look; as if they had life perfectly under control, under their respective thumbs. As if nothing could happen that would divert them from their chosen paths - not that she had a 'path' as such then, not if she was honest with herself. She now realised that up until the day that photograph was taken, and for a few short years afterwards, she had been a person who just meandered; there hadn't really been the need to commit herself to anything. In any event, she wasn't the committing kind. But that would come soon enough; certainly sooner than those young sparkling eyes staring into the camera could ever have imagined.

She was wearing a white blouse and pencil blue skirt. It had been a supremely sunny day. She had loved that blue skirt with an illogical passion. It was a garment that offered a yardstick for her self-image, her sense of worth perhaps: all the while she could fit into her pencil blue skirt, she was doing just fine. How long had it been since she had donated it to the charity shop? Although it had still some life left in it - and although she still loved it - one day she had simply given up trying to fit into it any longer. She had thought of buying another, a larger size, prompted by the confidence that she had looked good in it. And she had. But by the time she gave up on it, it had become a symbol of a past into which she similarly no longer fitted; a past life that wasn't her size either.

Looking at the photograph now and thinking back, she knows that she was - in those sunny, youthful days - never truly conscious of image. Not really. She was just Jenny. As she grew older and life began to intrude upon her once bright disposition, and as she fell into a profession more by luck than judgement, she became aware of the need to be able to control her persona. Notwithstanding whether her luck had been good or bad, she came to understand that 'Jenny the Landlady' needed to be a certain person if she was going to be successful - and success became important to her, especially after she lost her bright solder boy. It was a loss she never really understood, lacking as it did the detail of time and place. In some ways it seemed to be the logical culmination of a period when he drifted from her, the gradual losing of touch blamed on tours of duty and the 'need to know'.

Tommy Christie needed her to be successful too, and for a while she was swept along by his hopes and dreams. They filled a void in her life that she failed to recognise was there. Lots of people lost love ones in the forces, especially in times of war; why should she be any different? Why should the lost Corporal Maskelyne - just a brother after all! - be any more debilitating than the lost of a husband? She had met women who had lost life partners, and had been unable to tell the difference between her and them.

So the pubs - and Tommy's dreams - became her escape. She tried hard. She worked on 'Jenny the Landlady', and for a time it seemed to be enough, filling the gap. Whether she knew it or not, this public persona was beginning to drift ever further from who she really was. She began to create a new kind of void, one of her own making. The public Jenny Christie became the Jenny she shared with Tommy and everyone else; the private, old Jenny Maskelyne, gradually withering away, consigned to the bottom drawer.

Maunston Quay had demanded all that. It took her perhaps just two or three months to realise that 'The Anchor' probably represented, for her at least, the final death-knell of the old dream. Tommy had - more by chance than anything else - fallen into a rural life that was his idea of heaven. He had assumed he wanted one thing when all along he had simply needed Maunston Quay. As a result, Jenny recognised the Landlady persona she had been manufacturing was partially out of place and redundant, meaning the fabric - not to say fabrication - upon which she had been living her life was invalid; it had become a lie. When she tried to be the old city-centre 'Jenny the Landlady', she found she clashed with everything; she grated against the pub, against Tommy, against their clientele. A little bit like her pencil blue skirt, it was an old Jenny who no longer fitted. When she consciously discarded it, it left her with virtually nothing.

It had been a Sunday morning some three years earlier. The night before, she had made one last attempt to shoe-horn her old self into a Maunston Quay life - and she had failed again. After lunch, Tommy had asked what was wrong. First thing that morning she had been walking the beach when she suddenly found herself able to articulate her problem, and in doing so felt emptier than she ever had. She had stood on the pier and cried into the sea. As she sits now, many failed months later, flicking through her blue album, she remembers that morning as she always does. It had been a cold and misty start to the day; an inauspicious day. And yet a fitting one; fitting to allow a woman to stand on a pier and cry in mourning over her past. Had she at any point cried for her future? Undoubtedly. But Jenny knows she had not done so on that day. It had been a day for talking to herself, for striving to find that old fighting spirit; the spirit that had seen her through when her world had come crashing down; the spirit that had tied her to Tommy's dreams and made her determined to be successful. She had known there was a glimmer of fight left in her somewhere. She had known she needed to find a new Jenny.

She remembers drying her eyes and walking from the jetty back to the sand and towards the dunes. She remembers seeing a small van arriving outside the far cottage. She had paused for a moment to observe a man get out and stand staring at the sea. Had she thought that there was another lost soul? As she sits on her bed, she smiles to herself at the notion that she just might have. It is a romantic thought. Crossing the tracks and heading back to the pub, she could have had no idea that same man might just be her potential salvation.

The following morning, with all the will and calculation she could muster, Jenny began to walk the painful road of regeneration. She would fashion yet another new Jenny, this time one to fit 'The Anchor'; and she would nurture once again the true Jenny - the vital, self-contained, bereft, private Jenny she needed to be to see her through the trial, the challenge it would inevitably be. As she closes the album and replaces it beneath the outmoded jumper, it is as if she is at the end of a confessional. She knows when she goes downstairs to clean the bar or sort the bottles, she will be that other, public person. It hurts her that this version has become mean-spirited and a little abrasive, but it was the only guise she found she could fashion which allowed her to coexist with 'The Anchor' - and, if she is honest, with Tommy.

As she looks in the mirror she sees a third Jenny, the newest and most genuine one. It is more hopeful and - dare she say it? - more youthful. A Jenny for whom some ideals remain intact. It is the Jenny that she has started to build because she has to, not only for herself, but - she fervently believes - for Lewis too. This new Jenny is the person in whom all her hopes are vested; the only one who sees a future. And as she looks at herself - and thus at all the Jennys, past and present - a cloud spreads across her face. It is the shadow spread by the presence and threat of Anna Woolley.

Whether seeing Lewis's photographs a few days previously has acted as a latent trigger, Anna is unable to say; nevertheless she finds herself, the day after Tommy's party, sitting on her sofa with her laptop, gradually sifting through her own. As soon as she gained the skills and knowledge required, Anna has tried to ensure that the physical photographs she possesses are also stored digitally. She has done so for convenience, for the ability to do as she is doing now; to be able to browse as many or as few as she wants, to go as far back in time as she wishes, and all without the need for searching in or seeking out dusty boxes kept in inaccessible places.

It is a strategy with a subtle downside; in her case this manifests itself in the fear of loss. Her somewhat ethereal, physically insubstantial collection is, she knows, subject to the threat of corruption at any point, the sudden inability to access one or more of these precious images. She worries about how profound the impotence will feel should one day her computer respond to a request with 'file not found' or 'unable to open file'. To compensate, she has separate copies of all her photographs stored on two independent hard drives and a third copy somewhere 'in the cloud', which she has been assured is safe and secure. As she sits pressing keyboard arrow keys to scan through pictures of holidays, landscapes and failed attempts at being 'arty', Anna is conscious, now more than ever, that this virtual and subtly intangible album is her only remaining link to Ryan and Tom, the best but last things she can call on to bring back memories or rekindle past emotions.

That she now feels a sense of distance to both of them is an emotion less new than it once was - and one which is increasingly undeniable. Trying to connect with the pixelated image of little Tom, a few days old, has become something of a challenge. Not long after he died, the struggle had been one of controlling emotions, of fighting to manage how she felt. Now it is a struggle to rekindle those same emotions, not suppress them. She doubts this internal contest should be an unwanted surprise; after all, wasn't it one of the reasons she came to Maunston Quay, to rebalance herself? And is it not inevitable that any rebalancing must require the establishment of a different relationship with her past? In her entire life she has never needed to mourn and let go as she does now, and has no frame of reference for doing so. On that basis, she can do little other than assume a gradual loss of the immediacy of feeling is part of the process and, presumably, a healthy one at that. She knows she will never forget - how could she?! It is how she remembers that seems to be changing.

Glancing up for a moment to the window and the sea beyond, she thinks she understands a little of how Lewis has already made that journey; how he has managed to get beyond the immediacy of pain and begun to reestablish his relationships with Emma and Bridger and Stoner. He has a newer narrative into which they fit and he knows his place within it too, as if there is a fresh equilibrium, a new 'now' where he is happy. Anna wonders if that is what grief is actually all about; coming to terms with loss, yes, but also settling on how the past will be accommodated in the future. If, when looking at Tom lying asleep in his white baby-grow, she does not feel the heartbreak she once did, that does not mean she failed to love him then nor loves him any less now. It has become a different kind of love, one that has negotiated modified terms with her. Perhaps, in consequence, she mourns the loss of that emotion as much as she mourns the physical loss of her son. And perhaps that is a precursor to - even a prerequisite for - her moving on.

She has wondered more than once - as she does again now - whether she should select some of the newer digital-only photographs and turn them into physical things, have them printed and framed. Not only would such an undertaking provide her with an additional layer of security over the loss of the image, it would enable her to keep both of them closer; they would always be there, reminding her, in the same way as images of Emma, Stoner and Bridger do for Lewis. But, if anything, that recent afternoon with Lewis has proven to her that she is not like him.

Whilst a public and persistent display of memory works for Lewis, she knows - even now as she shuts down her computer - such mementoes are not for her. Realising, instinctively, this is a question she will never ask herself again - "should I print out copies?" - she wonders why that might be, and what is it that suddenly allows her to be so decisive? Perhaps it has nothing to do with her, in a way. Perhaps it is a reflection on the nature of those final relationships with the males in her life: drifting away from - and out of love with? - one, and never having the chance to get close enough to know the other. If that is the case, Anna knows photographs in frames would never be on show for her, but rather for others; they would be things that spoke to other people, not to her. As she stands, she glances to where the frames might sit; perhaps one at either end of the mantlepiece. To outsiders who saw them, their message would be clear enough: here is a woman who has loved and lost - and loved and lost in a tragic way. And while the tragedy is undeniable, Anna is profoundly certain that she does not wish anything to speak for her other than herself; if she is to move forwards, move on, then she has to do so on her own terms, not those framed by inanimate photographs. And all of that means being in control of her past.

What will she say, she wonders, if Lewis asks to see pictures of Ryan and little Tom? It is, after all, not such a far-fetched idea that they might one day (and soon, who knows?) convene in her cottage, drinking her tea and coffee, and reminisce there. Will she open her laptop and call up the relevant files? Or will she make an excuse, dismiss his request? It seems suddenly important to her that she should be prepared.

A knock at the door forces her from this reverie. She looks at the relatively unadorned mantlepiece to check the time. It is three o'clock. In a sudden rush she remembers a conversation from 'The Anchor', and is enveloped again in the residual smell from her morning's baking.

"You didn't forget I was coming," Richard asks almost as soon as he is across the threshold.

"No, of course not," she replies. "I baked."

"I thought I could smell something tempting," he confesses, "and, if I'm honest, did so hoping some of whatever it might be is destined to come my way."

"Madeira cake or apple pie."

"Perfect!"

"I should say 'and'," she corrects herself. "You are more than welcome to try both - though after tasting one you might not want to risk the other."

"I'm sure that is going to prove completely untrue." Richard smiles. "Can I help with anything?"

"No, it's fine. Just take a pew in the front room and I'll bring the things through. Tea rather than coffee?" She throws her question back towards him half-turned on her way to the kitchen.

If Richard notes the inadvertent ecclesiastical reference he chooses to ignore it.

"Tea. Of course."

Rather than immediately sit, Richard scans the room. Anna's is not a cottage he has been in often, and for a moment he tries to cross reference what now he sees with a memory buried somewhere in his subconscious. He recalls it being somewhat spartan and lacking soul, undoubtedly as a result of it being a transitory place, somewhere people passed briefly through rather than shed any of their skins there. He senses a few touches which suggest Anna leaving a mark however tentative or superficial, though is unsure whether this is just fanciful thinking on his part.

"Here we are."

He is still standing when she returns with a large tray adorned with tea pot, milk jug, plates filled with cake and pie, and two cups. The latter seem large enough to pass for mugs and not a little out of place.

"Are those mugs new?"

"Yes. I was shopping in town the other day and took a shine to them. Bright aren't they?"

"Very colourful. Cheerful, I'd say," he watches as she begins to pour, then takes his seat. "That's nice."

"Nice?"

"Having something here that belongs to you. I think that's a good thing."

There as a pause as Anna finishes pouring the tea, putting slices of both cake and pie on the plate she hands him.

"Why did you think I'd forgotten?"

"Sorry?" Richard is distracted both by the generous portions he has been given and the conundrum of which to eat first.

"When you came in. You asked if I'd forgotten. What gave you that idea?"

"Ah," he says understanding, his dilemma not quite resolved. "You seemed a little 'far away', that's all. Distracted. I didn't want to intrude if you were busy or anything."

"No. Of course. Well, you can see I hadn't forgotten," she says with a laugh. Richard, in not responding, encourages her to finish what it is she needs to say. Or what he wants her to say. It is a little trick he has; she has noticed it before. "I was just going through some old photographs, that's all. You know how it is."

"In my own way, I suppose. Though being a single man, I suspect my past attachments are a little more shallow than your own."

Pausing to tackle a slice of cake with her fork, she refrains from replying, seeing if she can use his trick against him, confident it will work.

"And?" he asks, vaguely.

"And?"

"Your reminiscences; are they any different now to when you came to the church that day? I know not a lot of time has passed, not in the grand scheme and all that, but how are things? I assume you invited me round because you wanted a catch-up of some kind?"

"And not just to be neighbourly?" she counters. "Or to poison you with my cooking?"

Richard, having settled on the pie first, is about to take his first mouthful.

"Those things too perhaps," he says smiling, "though I'll let you know how successful your poisoning has been in a few minutes."

Anna waits, watching him eat, keen to gauge his reaction irrespective of what he might say; she has always believed that's where honesty lay.

"Excellent," he smiles, "not too sweet, not too tart. And it tastes of apple too."

She knows he has thrown the last comment in as a tease, but lets it go.

"Different, I think you could say," she returns to his original question. "My reaction to the past. You're right that it's not been very long - just a few weeks - but long enough to have made a difference."

"Good or bad?" he enquires, another forkful poised.

Anna relaxes a little, confident now that at least her pie has passed muster.

"Good I suppose, though I don't really know. I mean, it's not the kind of thing you have to go through every day of the week. I suspect there's a deal to be done."

"A deal?" Her metaphor throws him.

"Between me and my past; with Ryan and Tom. In terms of how I should remember them, or how they should occupy me. Whatever the right phrase is."

"You talked about balance before."

"Did I?"

He nods.

"That you wanted to find some sort of equilibrium again. Reconciling your past must be a large element in that, especially in your case."

"Must it?"

"I think so, don't you? If you've got loose ends flapping around, how can you possibly look forward with sufficient confidence?" When she fails to reply, Richard recognises his error. "I'm sorry, I don't mean to be flippant. The 'flapping around' comment... But you know what I mean?"

She nods, finishing a morsel of her cake which, in terms of edibility, she feels will be equally acceptable.

"Having something unresolved. That's what you mean, isn't it? Which is what I mean too, I suppose. And now I know what resolution looks like at least, even if I don't quite feel it yet."

"How so?"

"Lewis," she says, assuming Richard will be able to make the connection immediately.

"Now you've lost me."

"His past. With Emma. And his friends in the army - especially the one who was killed. You know about them, of course."

Richard, having finished another chunk of pie, puts his plate down on the little table between them.

"It took him a while. Not with Emma so much, I don't think. Somehow there was more to resolve in the case of his army friend. It required a different kind of answering, I suppose; after all, the situation asked a completely different set of questions. Milton helped enormously."

"I like him," Anna says.

"Lewis?"

"Bradley," she clarifies. "He strikes me as a man's man for sure, but there's an integrity about him." Richard smiles. "Is that funny? Or wrong?"

"Not at all. Milton and I have had our run-ins in the past. The church - or religion, really - doesn't sit well with him. I'm pretty sure it's because of what he saw when he was soldiering in Northern Ireland; where he lays the blame. I'm the closest there is around here to a representative of the ideas and beliefs he sees as responsible for all that death and mayhem. Mea culpa, and all that. But I know it's not personal - and for all that, he's a man I'd always want on my side."

"First name on the team-sheet?" she suggests.

"Something like that!"

Neither of them seems that anxious to break the silence that slides between them. Richard fills the void by picking up his plate and polishing off his apple pie. Anna, dissecting her cake with small, absent-minded stabs, is less focussed on her eating now.

"So," he ventures, as if trying to insert them back into a dialogue out of which they have inadvertently fallen.

"So," Anna echoes. "The pie was acceptable then?"

"More than that; but I'll take a break before round two," Richard says, nodding towards the Madeira. He watches her for a moment. "You're getting there then?"

It is a vague suggestion and one that he hates; the looseness of it does neither of them any favours.

"Yes, I think so."

"Which is good." He pauses. "And I have to ask, of course, if only in a professional capacity..." He lets the prompt remain there for a moment, to give her chance to consider what she knows he must ask. "Your not being on speaking terms. Our previous conversation. Is there a resumption of the dialogue?"

Anna smiles.

"In your professional capacity?"

"And as a friend, I'd like to think."

"Well then," now it is her turn to wait just a moment. "I don't think there's dialogue - at least not in the way I suspect you mean. How shall I put it? I feel as if it's more like a truce now; the cessation of hostilities at least." Richard laughs a little. "Once or twice - usually when I'm sitting up on Simon's Crag, actually - I feel as if I'm opening up a little. But it's more like a monologue than anything else."

"A monologue?"

"Not in the sense that I'm talking out loud to myself; that would be crazy! But as if I'm holding up my side of the conversation."

"God's not responding?"

Anna notices how Richard's face has taken on the aspect of one who is tending his flock. She shakes her head.

"Either because I'm not listening, or because He knows it's not His turn yet."

He laughs at the notion.

"Maybe you're just too bossy," he suggests. Anna laughs.

"Maybe so. But anyway, I feel like I'm half-way there - compared to where I was."

"But you're uncertain if you want the whole deal? You don't know yet if you want to listen?"

She nods.

"Not yet - or not at all. Is that so bad of me?"

"Perfectly natural, I would say. Entirely understandable. And, if I may suggest, perfectly practical too. Deep down you know that if you do want to open your heart again, God will be there."

Richard waits, expecting Anna to reply, certain there is more to be said. It feels as if this is one of those 'loose ends flapping around' Anna has to rein in. Then, with something of a jolt, Richard senses that there is something else, something new.

"But that's not all, is it?"

"Not all?"

"Pie and cake, a chat about photographs, and an update on the status of your relationship with Our Father. I sense something else. A new uncertainty. Or am I so far wide of the mark?"

Anna smiles, returning her own plate to the table and starting to pour second cups of tea.

"No, not wide of the mark at all."

"Shall I guess?"

"Can you?" she asks, a slight note of alarm in her voice.

"Possibly," Richard says, trying to sound as uncertain as he can.

Anna passes him his tea as she resolves internally what it is she wants to say.

"I suppose I'm concerned about being selfish or disloyal. Or mercenary even."

The last notion clearly surprises him.

"But you're talking about Ryan, I assume? And moving on?"

"I suppose so. But it feels less like moving on and more like leaving him behind; drawing a line under our past. As if it didn't matter. Maybe I'm worried about feeling guilty. Or maybe I already feel guilty. I don't want to think that what we shared was unimportant. Obviously it wasn't. But..."

"But you feel like you might be - at some point in the future - making him irrelevant, or stabbing him in the back?"

"I don't know. Probably."

"Don't you think that's normal given your circumstances? Or if not normal, at least understandable?"

She nods at Richard's suggestion.

"Perhaps look at it another way," he continues.

"How so?"

"This may be a little awkward," he begins, shifting himself on the sofa as if he was making that discomfort real in a physical sense. "If Ryan hadn't died, would you still be with him today?"

"Of course!" The shock in her voice is all too evident.

"I'm sorry, I didn't mean to startle you - but this could be important, Anna." He pauses, then pushes on. "And in a year's time? If nothing had changed; if Ryan had continued down the path he had chosen, if he hadn't died, do you think you and he would have still been together then? Or in two years, or three? Without young Tom as the glue to keep you together?"

"What are you saying, Richard?"

He tries one of his professional, understanding smiles.

"From what you said to me before, I had the impression that you and Ryan were already drifting apart when he died. Perhaps bonds had already been broken. If that is the case, then I'm just suggesting you take that into consideration before you beat yourself up too much. I can understand your not wishing to feel disloyal to the Ryan you met and fell in love with, but is that the Ryan you last lived with? Is that really the Ryan you are leaving behind?"

"I don't know," she replies after moments that feel like minutes.

"All I'm saying is, you can't allow yourself to be shackled to something that's - I don't know - no longer real. If you do, then how can you ever escape? How can any of us, come to that?"

She says nothing.

"Keep Ryan close, by all means, but make sure that you do so in a practical and honest way, and not to fit some kind of idealised version of him because you think that's what's expected of you."

"But that doesn't sound right somehow," she says. "I mean, it sounds logical and reasonable. It sounds like I'm doing a deal with myself, but one that fits me solely."

"Who else should it fit and be right for if not you?! You said yourself there was a deal to be done - with your past, with Ryan, with your future. But if it's a deal, then essentially it's a deal with yourself; an internal one. Perhaps being logical and reasonable - and maybe a little bit selfish - is part of it." He waits a moment, trying to decipher the expression on her face. "Are you surprised that I've suggested such a 'mercenary' approach?" He tries to say it lightly enough. She nods. "Perhaps there's a bit more of the friend than the vicar in me then."

The quiet is that follows is punctuated by the closing of a front door.

"Take Lewis," Richard says, picking up on the cue.

"Lewis?"

"In a way his relationship with Emma, how she 'fits' into his future, is much more challenging. After all, if nothing had changed I'm sure he would say that they'd still be together now. Even so, I think - no, I know - that he is now perfectly able to reconcile a future with someone else alongside his memory of her. I don't believe that she will be an impediment in any way, simply because Lewis knows that she wouldn't want to be. I think he feels he has arrived at a place within himself where he is comfortable with the notion - *his* notion, mind - that Emma would endorse his moving on. He's allowing himself to see her giving him her blessing, if you like. To almost insist upon it. The permission - for want of a better word - isn't hers, it's actually *his*. But you aren't in a position to let yourself give Ryan that opportunity, simply because of how things had become between you. You have to ask yourself if the Ryan you last saw would actually have cared enough. I know I'm being harsh, but if that's what you are looking for, Anna, if you think that by holding on to some misplaced form of loyalty you will be free to move forward, to enjoy another relationship, then - in my humble opinion - I think you are wrong. All that can possibly do is shackle you."

After a moment: "I have to let Ryan go?"

"Yes - but not in a bad way. Lewis - using him as an example, you understand - is being realistic and pragmatic too; but he's starting from a different position, so although his situation or approach might feel or seem a little different, the outcome should be the same. It has to be. Does that make any sense?"

She cradles her cup, staring into it, wanting to see steam rising from it so that her eyes can trace its passage through the air. But it is too late for that, the liquid too cool. She welcomes the residual warmth she can feel through the mug, then raises it to her lips. The tea is just hot enough. There is a point where, when tea becomes too cool, somehow it ceases to be tea and becomes something else; an unpleasant liquid that demands a different name and not just a common adjective. For a moment, she transposes Richard's words onto this panoply of sensations and, in the temperature of the tea, creates a vague metaphor for her relationship with Ryan. She knows there is a difference between hot and cold there too.

Hearing Richard turn his attention to his plate once again, Anna looks up and beyond him to the window where, outside, the world spins on almost entirely oblivious of her.

❊ ❊ ❊

"Afternoon Richard."

Bradley's greeting assails him just as he is closing Anna's front door. Looking to his right, it appears the boatman's departure from his own cottage is entirely coincident.

"Milton," says the Vicar walking towards where the other man is now standing. "It's been a fine day, considering."

Instinctively Bradley looks out across the sand to the sea.

"Indeed. It was a little still this morning. We had some fret for a while, until the wind picked up at least."

"Did you get out?" asks Richard, falling into step with the other man as they head toward the village.

"Had no need to, which is probably just as well."

It is a vaguely cryptic comment Richard lets pass.

"How's she doing?" Bradley asks with a glance back over the Vicar's shoulder, his question cutting to the marrow of things, knowing that Richard will be able to supply all the necessary but unstated context.

"Very well, I think. Don't you?"

"Not sure I'm in a position to say. And it's none of my business, anyway."

"Maybe not, but she certainly holds you in high-enough regard."

"Me?" Bradley seems genuinely surprised. "What have I done?"

"Nothing specific I suspect. Or perhaps nothing that you'd immediately recognise as helping. But you know how it can be sometimes; a word here, a piece of advice there. Often incidental things seem irrelevant to us but can be terribly important to others."

"Ah well," says Bradley, uncertain if he should dismiss the comment or be flattered. He struggles to recall anything but the most rudimentary of help offered to his neighbour, but can find nothing.

"And before you ask," Richard goes on, "it was Anna's invitation - for tea - and I wasn't trying to drum up business."

Bradley's lack of reply confirms to Richard that his remark was well-aimed and noted.

"But I'll tell you one thing," Richard continues.

"Which is?"

"She makes a lovely apple pie!"

They both laugh; short breathless laughs sufficient to see them to the crossing at which, although the gates are open, Bradley still pauses to look down the tracks.

"Can't be too careful," he says, striding up to join Richard who had simply sailed across.

"Do you think she'll stay?" Bradley asks.

"Because of her apple pie?"

"You know what I mean."

Richard can tell by the mock frustration in Bradley's tone that he's being serious and that his enquiry is not one of a man simply passing the time.

"I don't know."

"If you were a betting man, Richard - and I know you're not - where would you put your money?"

It was a question that Richard had asked himself more than once as he sat talking with her just a few minutes previously. He had been unable to settle on an answer then and was unable to do so still.

"Honestly, I think it's fifty-fifty just now. She clearly likes it here, but I think we all know she never landed in Maunston with the intention of staying."

"It was just chance?"

"Well, that's what she says isn't it?" Richard replies thoughtfully. "And, after all, we have a precedent for people arriving here and never going away."

"Lewis?"

Richard nods. They allow the word to hang in the air between them, knowing that more could be said on the history of that individual.

"But, I don't know," Richard begins.

"Don't know what?"

"Oh, I just get the impression that there might be something else."

"To keep her here?"

"No; that brought her here in the first place." He pauses. "But maybe I'm just imagining things."

They remain silent until they reach 'The Anchor', their footsteps on the road their only accompaniment.

"So," prompts Bradley again, "do you think she'll stay?"

Richard slows to a halt, forcing Bradley to do so too. He glances towards the pub.

"There are other factors in play, aren't there? Things that contribute to her decision. The impact of the circumstantial."

Bradley, following Richard's gaze and his train of thought, suddenly laughs.

"You're not serious?!"

"Serious? Why shouldn't I be?"

"Because I can only think of one person who will influence whether she stays or goes, and I reckon in that individual's case there are no other contributing factors."

"Not even Jenny?" Richard asks, his question as sparse as some of Bradley's own.

"Especially not Jenny," says Bradley, the certainty in his voice undeniable. "Lewis has no inclination in that direction."

"You're certain?"

"If he had any ambition there don't you think they'd be long gone by now?"

Richard nods and they resume their walk, heading vaguely towards the neutral territory of the centre of the green.

"You're probably right."

"And the main reason - at least as far as I can see," Bradley carries on, unusually expansive, "is that he likes Maunston Quay too much."

"Maunston?"

"For what the place has given him. His peace, if you like. Oh, I know that sounds all airy fairy," Bradley continues, "especially coming from me, but I know what I've seen and I know what I've heard - what he's told me. I don't think he'd give this - us - up for Jenny. Not in a million years."

"So is the question whether he'd give it up for anyone?"

Bradley shakes his head.

"I think the question is whether anyone would take them as a bundle. Lewis and Maunston are already a couple. Buy one get one free, as it were."

The image makes Richard laugh. He puts his hand on the other's arm, briefly.

"It's a peculiar use of the notion, but I concede you may well be right. Those are the other two points of the triangle." He comes to a halt, nodding towards the church as if confirming his destination and knowing that's one place Bradley won't be heading. "Of course we might be completely wrong."

"Wrong?"

"About Lewis."

"And about Anna?" Bradley clarifies.

"Indeed. It might just be wishful thinking on the part of a couple of sad old loners, hoping to see their friends happy."

"Depends on your definition of 'sad', 'old' and 'loner'," Bradley suggests with a smile. "And you might be right, but..."

"But?" Richard picks up on the pause.

"You don't think we're wrong about Lewis?"

Richard shakes his head.

"I don't. The only question, I think, is what he sees - or whether he sees anything at all."

"I caught him whistling the other day," Bradley offers.

"Whistling?"

"I know. He never does. My question to you - and to him - is whether or not he understands *why* he was whistling."

❋ ❋ ❋

When he wakes, residual echoes tell Lewis this time the nightmare was different. Instead of the three of them leaning against the tank in the desert, they do so somewhere in an English forest. At the end of the dream they are still together; there is laughter and the driving on a woodland trail, the plunging through glades and across rapidly flowing streams replacing the horrors of the explosion and its aftermath. The only screams are the unusually faint one coming from the straining of machinery. It is this difference in sound Lewis recalls before anything else, as if the English pastoral is competing with and defeating the roar of the tank's massive diesel engine - that and the absence of a detonation and the eerie silence which followed it. Bizarrely it is the silence that haunts him even in his dreams. But this time, in Stoner and Bridger's laughter, he finds there is suddenly a tomorrow; no more Groundhog Day.

He surveys his room from the security of his pillow, trying to focus on each component as if he is coming across it for the first time. The curtains, a kind of blue pinstripe, are backlit by the sun which, still low enough, assaults them from across the surface of the sea. He tries to give the blue a name, thinking about the watercolours in his artist's box, but gives up, confident that there is no single tube that matches it. He also suspects that he would struggle to blend it, no matter how hard he tried or the length of time he took. But he knows it does not matter. For now, 'blue' seems good enough. Wandering around the room with his eyes, he alights on objects that he would normally regard from a more conventional angle: the side-on view of the detritus on his chest of drawers he would normally look down on; the loose pile of clothes on the small chair in the far corner from which he can only just make out one shoulder of the shirt he wore the previous day. In its own way it is a refreshing exercise. He wonders if it might be useful to remember it the next time he feels the compulsion to paint something.

Prompted, he has a vague recollection of something he said to Anna about the way changing the perspective on familiar scenes and objects can give them a new lease of life. Looking at his bedside lamp - first with one eye, then the other, then both - he is surprised to find he may have been correct. Given the apparent potency and accuracy of the notion, he wonders if she might have taken his advice - and what doing so may have yielded. He makes a mental note to ask her about her writing. Perhaps now she might let him see something. Maybe they could 'trade', a morsel of his for a morsel of hers. The symmetry of the idea appeals to him.

Thirty minutes later he is showered and dressed - choosing a blue t-shirt rather than the semi-retired shirt from the back of the chair - and stands, coffee in hand at his lounge window, looking out across the sand. It is an habitual pose at this time in the morning. Post-breakfast - today it was two croissants - it seems an appropriate way to consume his second coffee and contemplate the day. Lewis recalls how once such pauses were to be dreaded; working out how to fill them most often felt like torture. Even though he knew that nightfall could only bring a fitful sleep and the prospect of being hurled back into Afghanistan again, he often found himself longing for it; at least it meant he didn't have to think; at least when it was dark he was passive, merely a subject who was only required to react. Initiating, deciding, that had been the issue. Perhaps it was all related to the fateful patrol, he didn't know - and, for many, many weeks, he deliberately tried not to understand.

Walking had helped. It had been an easy, limited commitment. "What shall I do after breakfast?" he would ask himself, and "walk" became his de facto answer. For a while the walks grew longer and longer; the greater the time they took, the further away was the next decision point: "what do I do now?". As his walking routine took hold, so he began to invent others to fill his day. The less time deciding the better. Questions he had feared most of all were those he asked himself about the war - most often the unanswerable one as to why hadn't he prevented his friend from walking into that booby-trapped building.

Bradley had helped. Contrary to any outward appearance, Lewis knew now that his friend was the least organised person in the village. It was probably one reason why his schemes relating to fishing or tourist trips never came to fruition. As he came to know him - and as they came to trust each other and share their histories - Lewis discovered that Bradley and routine were uncomfortable bedfellows. One day an impromptu conversation might last five minutes; another might begin just after tea and not surrender until after midnight.

Painting had helped his rehabilitation too. Choosing to paint was easy - a little like choosing to walk; but choosing what to paint or draw was a different matter. At first he stuck to the safe and obvious, but later on, once all the local resources were exhausted, he had to think some more. Perhaps that was where his idea about changing perspectives had originated. In any event, after a while - months rather than weeks - the early morning, second-coffee contemplation became less of a trial than before. Gradually he allowed himself to consider options other than walking; he loosened the reins on his routine; it became acceptable to do so. He started to read more, he took the train occasionally, once a month he went for a drive somewhere new. And then, one day, from an unpacked box relegated to the cupboard under the stairs, he retrieved the photographs of Emma and Bridger and Stoner, and put them on his bookcase. It was a triumph of sorts; a measure of how far he had come. The first time Bradley had noticed them he simply nodded in their general direction. It was probably as close to explicit approval as he came. The nights were still difficult of course, though gradually less so. This morning things were different again.

Lewis looked across to the bookcase. Stoner and Bridger would have enjoyed their wild driving in the countryside. He knew it would have become competitive almost immediately; they would have mapped out a course and taken turns at timed runs. Being a universally acknowledged driver of the most appalling calibre, they would have given him two runs. It wouldn't have made any difference, Bridger would still have won. Even though it had been an unreal experience, Lewis was glad he had shared something new with them, because that was how it felt. The reality of it was perhaps the greatest relief - and the greatest surprise. It was a promise of something else.

From her perch beside them, Emma looks at him as she has always done, smiling, open, devoid of any agenda or subterfuge. Some mornings Lewis can feel her talking to him, though, as with the really bad nights, such occurrences are becoming less frequent.

This morning she says nothing, her posture unchanged, never ageing but seeming to be increasingly wise as the days go by. Lewis knows this latter attribution is fanciful too, the result of him bestowing his own growing wisdom onto her, and using her image to play it back to him. He finds it easier to accept that way. As he stands now, eyes fixed on her, he expects something, especially after the night just passed. But she keeps her counsel. Perhaps, he thinks, as he retunes his gaze to the sand and the sea, there is nothing to be said after all.

At that moment a flash of red breezes past his window. Lewis, feels himself straighten, downs the remains of his coffee, and goes looking for his walking boots.

❀ ❀ ❀

"You look pleased with yourself this morning."

She has paused half way up Simon's Crag, her progress halted by his call.

"Do I?" he says, breathing hard from the effort to catch her up.

"Not quite cat-and-cream territory," she smiles, "but not that far off. What's up?"

"Up?" he echoes as he reaches her side, suggesting with a motion of his right hand that she is free to resume the ascent. "Nothing that I know of."

"You look like you've won the lottery!"

"That good?! Afraid not. Mind you, if I had I'm not sure how broad my smile would be."

"Why's that?" she asks, having begun to move again.

"Because I don't do it."

"You don't believe in luck?"

"I wouldn't say that - just possibly not that kind of luck," he replies, slightly thrown by the broadening out of his statement, as if someone has jumped to the conclusion of a mathematical proof and missed out a couple of the middle steps.

"Is it the nature of the prize that taints the luck?" she asks, slightly mischievously.

"You mean the getting of something for nothing?" He waits for her to respond, but she is preoccupied with her footing just at this moment, so he answers his own question. "Maybe. Or perhaps I like to think you make your own kind of luck." Having said it, Lewis is not sure he believes it.

Coming to the level section at the top of the bluff, Anna slows down to allow him to catch her up properly.

"Of course in a way it isn't something for nothing," she says.

"What isn't?"

"The lottery. You have to pay. And choose - the numbers I mean."

"Yes, but the reward - if you get lucky - far outweighs either of those contributions, doesn't it? And anyway, I think people forget about those who lose, which is the vast majority of course."

"I can't believe you've never played it," she says. Lewis notes the tone of certainty in her voice.

"A long time ago, perhaps," he says, unable to deny it, "but not these days. I don't think I like the randomness of it any more."

They have reached the large stones at the top of the crag. Ensuring she leaves sufficient space at her side, Anna sits on the widest, facing the sea.

"I'm not so sure," she says as he sits beside her.

"So sure about what?"

She keeps her eyes fixed on the horizon as if she were scanning for something.

"Don't you think there has to be luck of some kind?" she asks, translating what Lewis said into something slightly at its periphery.

"Why so?"

"Oh, to cater for those things outside of your control. The actions of other people, those elements over which you can have no possible influence - I don't just mean the selection of numbered balls that drop from an elaborate gaming machine, but freaks of nature perhaps, or accidents."

"Fate?" he suggests. He allows his own eyes to scan along the edge of the sand from the far end of the bay, trying to recreate the sense of shifted perspective he had rediscovered as he lay in bed. Doing so triggers him into remembering his idea of asking to see some of her writing.

"Maybe," she acquiesces somewhat reluctantly, "but it's a word I've never really liked, 'fate'. It has too many connotations of fairy stories for my liking."

"Or Hollywood?"

As she glances at him, Lewis can sense the beginnings of a smile tracing itself across her lips, but he strives to keep his eyes fixed on the pier steps - and not because he finds them intrinsically interesting at that precise moment.

"Where would we be without Tom Hanks and Meg Ryan?" she asks. He senses the full smile breaking out.

"Ah, the 'Rom Com'," he says, rising. "I'm not sure if that supports or disproves my argument."

"To be honest," she says, standing beside him, "I'm not sure you had one!"

And then with a laugh she has turned and is retracing her steps. Lewis follows, certain she will veer to the right in a moment and lead them down to the beach.

"I was wondering," he says.

"Yes?"

They had descended to the beach in silence, clambering carefully over the rocks still damp from that morning's receding tide. There had been no further discussion of fate or chance, and Lewis, confident the subject had been exhausted, has decided to act on his earlier idea.

"Whether you might show me some of the things that you'd written. I mean, I was wondering if I could read something?"

Although there is nothing in her demeanour to suggest either surprise or alarm - no change in the pace at which she walks, no sudden lateral movement to ensure she is walking further from him - Lewis thinks he notices in her voice a little of both. Or perhaps it is neither. Perhaps she has always expected him to ask and has simply been thrown by his doing so now, as if the timing is somehow inappropriate.

"Read?" she echoes. "Something I've written? Seriously?"

She offers a little laugh that is plainly masking uncertainty.

"A kind of trade," he smiles as he glances at her, trying to keep the tone light to reassure her. "I'll happily let you trudge through a couple of my sketch books in return if you like - though I daresay you won't want to torture yourself for too long."

"There you go!" she says, a little triumph evident in the note she strikes. "Always, when people know their work is okay - whatever it may be - they're happy to be self-deprecating and self-demeaning. You've done it before."

"Have I?" Lewis is genuinely surprised. "Well, perhaps that's because it's true. I swear I'm not trying to be clever or anything like that. I'm not sure I have it in me."

"Hmmm." Anna makes a deliberate show of not entirely believing his last statement.

As they walk on a few paces in silence, Lewis grows fearful that he may have trespassed.

"You really want to see what I've written?"

"I do," he says, trying to sound earnest whilst not seeming to pressurise or be over-enthusiastic, "that is if there are things you'd be happy for me to read."

"Too many poems about the sea," she says, "if that doesn't put you off?"

"Would looking at endless - and endlessly drab - sketches of the beach, the headland and the pier frighten you off? If you're happy to take the risk, then so am I."

The proposition rests between them for a moment.

"Of course, all those things you said about your paintings - about it being a torture to look at them - I can say that about my writing too. And in spades. You've been here for years honing your skills!"

"Trying and failing, I think you might find..." He waits for a moment and then presses for a decision. "Well?"

Anna stops and looks at him. Her voice, when she next speaks, has a business-like tone about it that surprises him.

"When?"

"Oh, how about this afternoon. I'll supply the tea if you bring the Madeira."

"Ha!" Her exclamation makes him laugh. "You wait until I see that Richard!"

"Don't hold it against him. He was very complimentary."

"Alright, I'll bring cake." She thinks for a moment. "How much do you want to see then? What's an equivalent trade for putting me through the turmoil of a couple of your dreadful sketchbooks?"

Lewis tries to look hurt, which only makes her laugh.

"I leave that up to you," he says. "Entirely."

"Hmmm," she says again. Then she holds out her hand, seeking to seal the deal. "Three o'clock? But only if you promise to play nicely."

"Three o'clock," he nods as he makes the shaking of her hand a theatrical event. "And I promise."

❋ ❋ ❋

Sitting on a sofa with her back to the window, the spread of Lewis's small lounge before her, it is not lost on Anna how the roles are reversed in comparison with Richard's visit two days previously. Knowing the cake is hers - a common thread which joins the two events - is of little consequence; she is still the guest. She feels nervous. It is, she tells herself, a stupid emotion; what has she got to be nervous about? She glances to the bookcase. Emma smiles towards her. Anna hopes there might be some reassurance there.

In her lap she cradles two notebooks. It had been a difficult decision knowing what to bring, trying to decide what she was prepared to show Lewis. Ideally she would have selected just a few individual pieces, but not having yet committed them to her laptop, the opportunity to print a choice few was denied her. It had to be the whole book or nothing. In what she can only regard as feeble mitigation, she has managed to insert a few little coloured slips of paper at relevant points; protruding above the top of a page, these are, she has already informed him, suggestions as to where he might want to read, and she has tried to make it plain that venturing off-piste might be frowned upon. It was the best she could do, but knows she is at the mercy of his discretion. Is that something she doubts? She does not think so. Yet even as she sits there, she begins to convince herself that Lewis is, at that very moment, upstairs rifling through his own artistic endeavours, and will soon return with a few individual pieces, the result of him being able to refine his offering through a brief filtering process.

There will be no risk-running if he can help it. Isn't that what she would do if she were in his position?

When she discovers she is wrong - Lewis emerging not with a sheaf of chosen things, but rather two apparently entire A3 books - she cannot help but smile. She hopes that her relief is not too evident.

"Well, it seemed only fair," Lewis says, glancing down to the books he is holding. "You weren't able to be as selective as I'm sure you'd wish, and so I thought it was probably only right that I should be in the same boat - though I haven't, I confess, had time to highlight any suggestions. I'm afraid you'll just have to slog your way through."

"Will I survive?" she asks, happy to be playful now she is beginning to relax.

"Barely. There are some things in here that I'd rather you didn't see, and that one day I'm sure I will consign to the flames... All I ask is that you don't laugh. Laughter, as powerful a force for good as it is, can also be something of an assassin."

"Of course," she says, ripples of excitement now beginning to wash over her. "No laughter, absolutely. And no false praise either."

"False praise?"

"You know; when someone says 'Oh, that's nice, dear' just because they think they ought to say something. For me, that's worse than saying that something's rubbish."

"Fine by me," Lewis says, "no faint praise. We should say what we mean. Only praise what we truly think is praiseworthy." Expecting agreement, Anna's silence surprises him. He can see she is thinking. "What?"

"You know, if we stick to those rules, we run a very real risk of saying absolutely nothing for the next fifteen minutes?"

Lewis laughs at the thought.

"How embarrassing would that be?! Maybe if no-one has said anything for - what? - five minutes, we should relax the rules on faint praise."

"Never!" She makes a show of defiance. "We should stand or fall by our efforts. If you're not man enough to take it..."

"Fighting talk!" he says. "Maybe we should get a bell and a referee."

The notion of having gone from nervous participants to aggressive combatants makes Anna laugh too. She feels her grasp on her books loosen.

"Cake before or after?' Lewis asks.

"After," she replies, "as a reward."

"Fine."

Lewis sits opposite her and offers his sketchbooks with his left hand, his right ready to take Anna's.

"So," he says.

Turning to the first coloured marker, the thing Lewis notices before he has even read a word is the nature of Anna's handwriting. It has a liquid quality about it, flowing effortlessly as if it were hovering just above the lines of the page. The momentum of the words' journey is maintained by the easy way in which she flows from letters like 't', 'h' and 'y' on to the next. Sometimes the simple flourish which finishes one word leads directly into the next, the spaces between them less pronounced, almost invisible. He finds such a transition encourages his eye to travel with pace.

The first thing she has promoted is a short poem about the sea. He smiles as he reads it, not because of anything intrinsic in the poem itself, but rather in recollection of her warning him there would be lots of sea poems. Having read the final draft, he turns back a page or two and sees earlier versions complete with corrections, crossings out, words added to the side or above and below lines. He tries to imagine her on the expedition from first idea to finished article, attempting to understand how her mind has worked through the manipulation of the text. After reading a second poem - also about the sea - and then tracing that one's genesis in a similar fashion, a picture begins to form of the way in which she works; first the broad structure, then honing the images, and finally the trimming back, cutting out any word that seems superfluous. It gives her poems an almost stark quality, but one which works well with their subject.

He is conscious that his own work offers Anna no such insight. Where sketches are in pencil and he has resorted to the occasional - and sometimes liberal! - use of an eraser, such clues are almost inevitably lost, as if he were a criminal erasing finger prints from a crime scene. Where she might find something to decipher is only where he has attempted multiple views of the same subject, though here he fears opportunity for subtle interpretation may also be defeated by consistently bludgeoning the viewer over the head with yet another picture of the pier.

The third marker in Anna's notebook offers a short piece of prose, a description of Simons' Crag. He reads it twice.

"I really like this," he says impulsively and without looking up.

"What's that?" she asks, raising her own gaze, her finger poised to turn another page.

"This description of the crag. Dated a little over a month ago. It must have been not long after you arrived here."

"Yes, I think so."

"And you've updated it recently," he says. "I think I can tell where you added something."

She is about to return to Lewis's book when he suddenly starts reading aloud.

" 'As you approach its crest, the crag begins to level out gradually, little by little teasing you with the sea beyond. And then, just as you think this trick will carry on interminably, there are the large boulders that adorn the top, and beyond them nothing but sea. It is a view that is both reward and disappointment, as if something is saying "here is everything!" while another voice whispers "is this all there is?". Depending on the day, the sea is sometimes a kind of metallic, industrial blue; but most days it is a flat, monotone grey. Irrespective of colour, it seems never the same on any two days, as if its fluidity is a metaphor for something else, of possibilities perhaps.

'If I had initially seen it as a desolate, empty view, that is changing. The blues are beginning to shine through, and even the flood of grey - as I come to understand and appreciate it - has hidden tones, qualities that somehow speak of promise. As I watch a container ship far out toward the horizon, I wonder what it must be like to be on that ship looking back to this point. I suppose the crag is indistinguishable and so I must be invisible. Yet all are important, each in their own place and with their own perspective on things.' "

He had tried to read it sympathetically, perhaps more with her voice in mind than his own, but is uncertain how faithful he has been. For a few seconds Anna says nothing.

"You like that?" she asks eventually.

"Very much."

"Because it was accurate?"

He contemplates her question for a moment.

"You know, I never even considered accuracy. I suppose it is, the way the climb sort of peters out and then you just see the sea. But it was the feeling I liked most of all. It reminded me of the first few times I walked up the crag; that sense of space and promise and desolation. And both smallness and vastness at the same time."

"Desolation?" She picks up on the word.

"Maybe that's too strong. But the solitude of the place can be negative sometimes; at least it was for me. Not every time of course. I think what you see is a reflection of your mood. A bit like the colours you talk about."

"Because there's nothing much there, we have to invest something of ourselves in it - in that precise moment - in order to make sense of it... At least that's what I tried to capture I think."

Lewis smiles, trying to decipher what he can see in her eyes, as if he is searching the sea for the blue, trying to catch her mood, promise versus desolation. She says nothing, returning to her own study.

The sketch now in front of her seems to be one of a series; close-up perspectives on fragments of the jetty. Skipping through the opening few pages of Lewis's first book, she has witnessed an occasional struggle with perspective and scale in his interpretation of the crag, the bay as a whole. Having never been any kind of artist herself, she wonders if it is harder to master these when there is relatively little detail to lean on when composing a picture, too few elements to guide the eye. If she is honest, she knows that the first few pages are not very good - not that she could do any better. Fortunately this current sequence has intercepted what was in danger of becoming a growing disappointment.

Anna imagines where he must have stood - or sat - to draw the images upon which she now focusses. She tries to picture him in some small portable chair, wrapped up against the chill, struggling perhaps with the breeze which is tugging at the edges of the paper. Perhaps because of that, the drawing has a rugged, unfinished quality, and she wonders if it is this which makes it dynamic.

"Why did you draw these?" she asks.

"Which?"

She tilts the book towards him.

"These little studies of the jetty."

"Oh, I don't know. To try something different, I suppose. They were experiments of sorts."

"But they're really good," she says, keen to counter an undercurrent of defeat she picks up in his voice.

"Really?"

"Really."

"But they were just quick things. Nothing important." He sounds slightly off-guard. "I hardly put any effort into them."

"Perhaps that's what I like about them," she says. "I can see they're quick sketches, but the lines and marks are vital - I think the speed at which you drew them gives them that quality - and they have a certain honesty about them. Very dynamic. I like that."

"Better than the others?" Lewis asks, dubiously.

"Oh, yes." She pauses just for the merest instant, concerned she has been too definitive. "From what I've seen so far, at least. I think with some of the others - the more formal landscapes, if you like - I get the impression that you were trying to draw and paint what you thought you ought to draw and paint, or perhaps what you might be expected to present to someone else. As if you weren't doing them for yourself; does that make sense? They were attempts at being conventional. But these are completely different. Because of that speed and freedom - and almost a lack of care - you've actually captured what you saw. And because you've focussed on specific little sections of the pier each time, they have an almost abstract quality. Maybe that's what I like most; the newness of them; the unexpected."

Lewis feels suddenly a little lost. He leans forward and takes his book from her, examining the sketches where the page is open.

"I don't know what to say. I mean, thank you. But I'm surprised. I thought they were insignificant compared to the other things, the ones I'd spent more time over."

"Maybe that's what makes them so fresh, the fact that you didn't spend the time."

"It's funny," he hands the book back.

"What's funny?"

"What you see and don't see. How important it can be to have other people's perspectives on what you've done, or feel, or have taken for granted."

Having taken the book back, Anna places it beside her on the sofa. She is relieved to have found something she likes.

"Now I think we deserve our reward, don't you? Not that we've finished, of course, but just in recognition that we're managing to undertake a delicate little exercise with such skill!"

"And sensitivity," he suggests.

"Shall I cut the cake?"

"And I'll put the kettle on again."

Twenty minutes later, Anna is sitting drinking her tea, looking at Lewis, his two sketchbooks closed by her side. Lewis is still reading. She is concerned that she has finished her review too quickly, and that perhaps she has not been praiseworthy enough. But she knows she has adhered to their rules and only spoken when she felt she needed to. Towards the end of the second book she discovered his revisiting the traditional landscape theme and, with some relief, found these much improved on his earlier attempts. Perhaps it was practice or a greater familiarity with the surroundings; perhaps the increased accuracy and fluency was a reflection of something else. Whatever the reason, she was pleased to be able to be positive about them.

As she watches him, Lewis closes the notebook he is holding and then places it on the small coffee table and on top of its companion. He feels it has been a trial of sorts. Inadvertently or otherwise, he knows they have measured themselves against each other in terms of both creative output and critical appraisal. He smiles, relieved it is over; pleased they have passed the test.

"I like that series of Haiku," he says, picking up his mug. "They're quite recent, aren't they?"

"Reasonably," Anna replies. "In a way they're experimental, a little bit like those quick sketches of the pier. I was trying to focus on just one image, one fragment. I'm glad you like them."

"They seemed - I don't know - somehow more mature, even though they are tiny little things."

She smiles but says nothing, and Lewis knows that now is the time to stop. "Quit while you're ahead", he says to himself.

❀ ❀ ❀

When the phone rings, it is nearly six o'clock. Lewis is in his kitchen cleaning up their tea things, his mind trying to replay as much of the afternoon as possible. As he let Anna out, it seemed - as he rewinds it now - as if they have done something undefinable yet important; they are linked through a bond they did not share four hours earlier. Bonds are important to him, he knows that. He has come to realise he needs them perhaps more than he thought.

"Lewis?"

"Hello Maisie," Lewis replies, his left hand still holding a damp tea-towel. "How are you?"

"I'm fine."

There is a slight pause.

"What can I do for you?" Lewis asks, filling the gap.

"I have a question for you," says Maisie. Lewis notes hesitancy in her voice.

"Fire away."

"It's about Anna."

"Anna?"

"Yes." Maisie gathers herself. "You know you asked me to - I don't know - do a little digging?"

"Oh yes; our conversation in the pub. I'd almost forgotten that," he says with a laugh.

"I just wanted to know if you still want me to do that; you know, to see if I can uncover anything that might help her. Or help you help her."

For a moment Lewis is thrown. In recalling the request and the background to his making it, he is struck by how he now feels, as if they have moved beyond where doubt had laid in wait. His instinct is to say 'no', but he does not.

"Why?"

There is no reply.

"Why Maisie?"

"Because I think I've come up with something, that's all. I don't want to say until I'm sure."

"Is it - ", Lewis searches for an appropriate word, but settles on the simplest: "is it bad?"

"Bad?" Maisie plays it back to him; the word sounds flat and meaningless. "No, I don't think it's bad. I mean, she's not an axe murderer or anything - at least not that I've uncovered thus far."

"That's a relief," Lewis laughs, "because I've just had tea with her. She might have done for me!"

Maisie's own laugh bounces down the line.

"No, nothing like that. But it might be significant, that's all."

"What does significant mean?"

"Maybe that's the wrong word too." A pause. "As I say, it isn't negative in any way. And I don't think it makes any difference, really. Just something you'll need to know, I suppose."

Lewis struggles with what Maisie is trying to convey. Being cryptic - or interpreting the cryptic - has never been one of his strong suits.

"Will it be detrimental to Anna in any way - I mean, me knowing whatever it is you're talking about? Because if it is, I don't think I would want that."

"No," she says, a little more certain. "Not bad for her. Not negative in any way. More a surprise than anything else."

"Well," he says, then stops for a moment. He looks at his hand holding the tea towel and stares at the blue checked cloth as if it's the first time in his life he's seen it. "Now that you've said there's something, I have to know don't I? I mean, I don't see how I could possibly just forget what you've told me."

"Yes. Sorry."

"And if you're saying that it's not a negative thing, and that it won't be detrimental to Anna, then I think I'd like to know."

"Okay."

"Perhaps," he says, trying to corral the conversation and get it back to some kind of acceptable structure and outcome, "the million dollar question is, if you're right and you tell me this thing, whatever it is, does it give me - or us, come to that - a better chance of helping her come to terms with her past and move on?"

No sound comes from the telephone earpiece for a few seconds, and Lewis wonders if they have been disconnected.

"Maisie?"

"Yes, sorry," she says. "Just thinking... Look, I'm pretty sure that it isn't bad and that it will help. Overall."

"And do you think I need to know whatever it is you're talking about?"

"I do, yes."

"Well then," Lewis says, trying to sound definitive and calm. "When you're ready, just let me know. Okay?"

"Alright. I have just one more thing to check. Probably tomorrow."

When he puts the phone down, Lewis is struck by the proximity of Maisie's discovery. As he walks back into the kitchen, he looks at the plate Anna had used, the cup from which she had drunk, and hopes - with a sudden fervour that surprises him - that she has not done so for the last time.

Chapter 9

After an unusually fitful night during which sleep proved to be a reluctant bedfellow, Lewis has awoken with the realisation that he has labelled whatever it is Maisie is now bound to tell him as 'Anna's Secret'. On the whole, he has nothing against secrets; indeed, in his former profession more often than not secrets were essential - and essential that they be kept. Lives depended on them. If he has softened his stance since then, regarding them more as 'guidelines' rather than 'rules', he has done so consciously, knowing a little latitude is a better fit to the everyday. It is somewhat surprising to him, therefore, that by default he regards this whatever-it-is as a 'secret', and also that he should do so adopting the full force of his army-driven understanding of the word.

Perhaps if this feeling was merely superficial, that might be all well and good; but there is something else that troubles Lewis further. He feels inexplicably and - he is certain - unjustifiably concerned that Anna should have a secret at all, even ignoring the fact she has no obligation to share it with him at all.

He knows he has no right to expect profound trust and confidentiality, but such logic does little to dispel his consequent mood which he can only describe as 'gruff'. If it were possible to get out of bed on the wrong side and, in doing so, allow such a mistake to taint the remainder of the day, then that is how he feels even now. It had been how he was when he came down for breakfast and how he remains, sitting outside his cottage on one of the public benches, looking out to sea. He had hoped, vaguely and with no true conviction, by taking his second coffee outside, something in the landscape - if not the wind itself - would 'blow the cobwebs away'. Resorting to such specious and fanciful nonsense is, he knows, merely a measure of how off-balance he has become overnight.

His mood is not reflected in the weather which, more devoid of cloud than it has been for a while, feels like the approaching edge of summer. Part of Lewis would have forsaken this promise of warmth for a more stormy outlook, even if it would have kept him inside; being constrained by such inclemency may have better reflected his mood. But if that is being a little melodramatic, he forgives himself, having in consequence found an additional and newly burgeoning personal question that has nothing to do with Anna: does he have any secrets left himself? This is not an uncertainty he awoke with, but one which seems to have crept up on him whilst his guard was down, as if he has been silently concocting it throughout the process of making his breakfast and brewing his coffee; he might just as well have been spreading the question over his consciousness with a butter knife, or stirring it with his spoon. As he sits looking out across the sand, it is a fully-fledged conundrum.

If he is annoyed with himself, it is for no other reason than having to face the discomfort of needing to provide an answer. Instinctively, he believes this will prove benign, having assumed - as soon as the problematic thought dawned on him - all of his secrets had been exposed, most of them via the marvellously compliant Bradley with whom many remain secret still. Of those he has now shared with Anna, the majority were only echoes of the former. Under such circumstances surely those twice-shared can be secrets no longer, ticked off like items on a shopping list as one wanders through a store. But now his concern is whether or not he has any secrets he has been keeping from himself. Might he suddenly uncover one or two recalcitrant items? It is a new uncertainty, and one which, through bitter experience, Lewis knows he must not allow to linger. He looks out to sea as if, in some obscure way, the answer might lie there.

He knows, of course, he is looking in the wrong direction entirely. The keys he seeks are not camouflaged in the gently breaking sea but behind him, contained within the silver frames that hold his two most precious photographs. In that instant, his grumpy attitude transforms itself into one of weariness. The thought of retracing his steps - to revisit that which he had hoped he was somehow finished with - seems to draw the life from him. At least his being grumpy has some energy about it, even if it wasn't positive; but now he feels he has nothing left to do but to throw himself onto the mercy of the day.

"Penny for your thoughts?"

Bradley's voice rouses Lewis from his reverie.

"Sorry," he replies automatically.

"You were miles away," Bradley says, sitting alongside him. "You obviously didn't hear me."

"No," Lewis tries a laugh. "Miles away, as you say."

When nothing further is offered, Bradley takes his cue.

"Something up?"

"Up?"

"Bothering you? You seem a bit preoccupied - which is unfortunate given the splendidness of the morning."

"Yes," Lewis looks back to the sea, "it looks like it's going to be a good one." Trying to change the subject, he glances back to his friend and then beyond where the doors to the boathouse are clearly open. "Are you going out?"

"Just for a short while, I think," Bradley says. "Care to join me? Nothing strenuous; motor all the way probably."

Lewis shakes his head.

"Sometimes I think you should have been in the Navy, not the Army."

"The Navy?!" The thought clearly horrifies Bradley. "Why do you say that?"

"Because you love the sea," Lewis suggests, even though doing so seems patently unnecessary.

"Ah, there you're wrong," Bradley smiles. "I don't care much for the sea at all. But I care for what it gives me: space, quiet, solitude. And you know how that feels don't you?"

"I do," Lewis confirms.

When Lewis says nothing further, Bradley feels the need to try again.

"So. Anything up?"

"Because I was miles away?"

Bradley nods.

"Not back in the hell-hole, by any chance?"

"Nothing like that," Lewis says, trying to reassure himself as much as Bradley. "At least I don't think that's where I was heading."

"Good. How about somewhere closer to home?" Bradley inclines his head towards the cottage that separates theirs. Lewis's smile in response is not as open or assured as Bradley might have wished it to be.

"Perhaps a little," Lewis says cautiously, as if the uncertainty in his words will betray some other lack of clarity, "but then only as a kind of catalyst."

Not in the mood for riddles, and not wishing to lose the calm of the morning, Bradley stands. Lewis's words prevent his immediately moving away.

"Have you ever thought you'd forgotten something, Brad? May have forgotten something? I don't mean like leaving the cooker on or the front door open, but something important, significant?"

"All the time it seems these days - but, no, nothing significant. Why?"

"Oh something and nothing really."

Seeing Lewis is set on avoiding elaboration, Bradley begins to retreat but then stops.

"Oh, by the way, Tommy wants to have a bit of a follow-up on that village meeting we had a little while back."

"To confirm that we've done nothing?"

"'To square the circle' was how he put it to me. Daft phrase I always thought, that one. Anyway, I assume you'll come along for the sheer entertainment value if nothing else."

"When is it?"

"He doesn't know yet, but probably in the next week or so. I told him I didn't think you'd be going anywhere." His last words are spoken partly over his shoulder as he moves again towards his boathouse. And then another thought brings him up short. "Oh, and would you tell Anna if you see her before I do."

"Anna?"

"Yes. Tommy seemed keen she was there seeing as how she was one of the few who made any sense last time." And with that, Bradley disappears into his boathouse.

Lewis stands up. He is confident he will see Anna soon, but at this precise moment isn't entirely sure under what circumstances.

A little while later, Lewis is trying to busy himself with inconsequential activity when the phone rings. He had returned to his cottage, responding to the call of the photographs in his lounge. Standing before them, he had waited, as if doing so would allow one or other to speak to him. They said nothing. Yet neither did they deny that there was something to be said, something to be found. Unenlightened, he had called a halt to the brief and fruitless exercise and started to 'tidy'. It is a euphemism for time-wasting, but focus seems the last thing he is capable of at that precise moment. He has finished in the kitchen and is contemplating a walk up Simon's Crag when the harsh, electronic sound interrupts him.

"Hello."

"Lewis?"

"Who else, Maisie?"

He hears her short laugh.

"It's funny how we do that, isn't it? I mean, still say the name of the person when it could hardly be anyone else on the other end of the line."

"Maybe the next time someone calls I'll try 'The Archbishop of Canterbury here' and see what reaction I get!"

She laughs again. Then nothing.

"So?" Lewis prompts.

"Yes." She hesitates. "Do you have a few minutes?"

"For you, of course." He tries to sound relaxed and not at all impatient, but isn't sure he pulls it off.

"How much do you know about Jenny's brother?" Maisie asks.

"Jenny's brother?" he replies, completely sideswiped.

"Yes."

"Well, nothing really. I mean, I know she had a brother. He was in the forces I think, but she lost touch with him a few years ago."

"Did you know he'd died?"

"I think so. In fact I'm sure she mentioned it once. But it was difficult territory - for both of us. She understands a little of my background. Knowing it was a delicate and sensitive area, it was a subject I think we both felt best dropped. We've never picked it up. And I don't think we will." Lewis allows a short pause before he nervously asks the obvious question. "Why?"

"Because Jenny's brother's name is Ryan Maskelyne. And Ryan was Anna's husband."

Lewis allows the words to register and then, finding them ridiculous, can not help but laugh.

"No way! Anna's surname is Woolley, Maisie. I'm afraid you've made a mistake, there."

"No, Lewis," Maisie's voice is calm, even, and certain now, "Anna's *maiden* name is Woolley. Anna's married name is Maskelyne. I'm pretty sure no-one knows - no-one - but she's Jenny's sister-in-law."

Lewis has never been able to fathom a Rubik's Cube, even though he knows there is a method for doing so; once someone had even tried to talk him through it. Bizarrely, this is what he imagines now, as if Maisie's words have presented him with a puzzle that needs solving. His thoughts - like the colours on a cube - spin around in front of him.

"You're sure?" he asks, trying to dispel the blurring shades. "Absolutely sure?"

"As I can be," Maisie says somewhat apologetically. Without waiting for Lewis to respond, she pushes on, having prepared herself in advance. "It could be nothing, Lewis, couldn't it? Just one of those wild, fantastical coincidences that happens once in a blue moon. After all, what was the chance she'd end up renting a cottage between two guys who'd have army experience, and who could relate to what she had been through but from the other side? That has to be a coincidence, doesn't it? You can't put something like that into 'find-me-a-cottage' search engines, can you?"

As Lewis listens, Maisie's words come to him slowly and individually, as if he has been able to elongate time. Even though it is somehow not enough, he hears each one clearly and interprets and understands them perfectly.

"I'm sure that's right - I mean about the cottage thing. Pure coincidence. But to end up in the same village as Jenny?"

"I tried it."

"Tried what?"

"I tried a search," Maisie says, "a bit like the kind of search Anna might have used. You know, coastal property, quiet, small, long-let, available - all those kinds of parameters."

"And?"

"And you'd be surprised how many come up. It would have been even more if Anna was looking earlier in the year. My list was certainly a few dozen. You could refine it if you had a rough idea where you wanted to be… I mean, rule out Scotland, for example, and loads disappear."

"So maybe she had a smallish list to choose from; that's what you're saying?"

"Yes, but not so small that she'd had no choice." Maisie picks up on the thought quickly. "Under those circumstances - maybe one out of twenty or thirty - then ending up here could have been just luck, really."

"Or fate," suggests Lewis, dipping into a past conversation with Anna.

"But what if her search criteria had been more specific?" Maisie asks rhetorically. "What if she'd been specifically looking to be as close to Jenny as possible? Ending up in the cottage next to you wouldn't then have been such a huge coincidence after all. Search for Maunston Quay and she may have been offered a shortlist of one."

Then a thought strikes him. "But why doesn't Jenny know who she is? How come Jenny doesn't recognise her, or her name? Why is that? And why hasn't she embraced her like some long lost soul mate?"

"I asked myself that too," Maisie confesses.

"And?"

"The only conclusion I could come to was that she simply doesn't know."

"Doesn't know?!" Lewis is unable not to sound incredulous.

"Maybe they had issues, Ryan and Jenny. Maybe he never told her he was married." Maisie pauses for a fraction. "Do you know when she last saw her brother, when they were last in touch?"

Lewis tries to dredge his memory for something concrete and finds only mud.

"I don't. I know it was a while ago. A long while ago. But could it be that long?"

"Maybe something happened between them? From what I was able to gather, Ryan's postings changed a few years ago, and then he started to spend more and more time overseas. Especially in the year before he was killed. Perhaps it's as simple as them losing touch."

"You think so?" Lewis is unconvinced by her suggestion. "There are so many 'maybes', Maisie."

They are both quiet for a few seconds.

"Look," Lewis says, forcing himself to sound a little more upbeat, "thanks. For digging, I mean."

"It's nothing, really," says Maisie. "What are you going to do?"

"Do?" The thought of having to 'do' anything surprises him, like a sudden blast of a chill wind on a warm day. He shivers. "I don't know. Nothing? Something?"

"Are you going to ask her?"

"Jenny?"

"No, Lewis," says Maisie, as softly as she can. "Anna."

Lewis lets the question hang, already knowing the answer.

❊ ❊ ❊

Anna sits at her small kitchen table, flicking somewhat listlessly through one of the three notebooks that lie before her. Somehow Lewis had been able to see things in her words - or even beyond them - and she is seeking the clues he had spotted, trying to recognise the triggers, the keys that open locks. She is sure there are things hidden away in there, even from her - or perhaps especially from her. She feels as if they are party to secrets she is keeping from herself, shadows hidden in an elaborate morass of words. She wants to feel benign towards them - certainly more than she does at this precise minute - but finds herself unable to do so. Although the text is hers, from her mind and her pen, it feels like a traitor, as if the words have turned on her, as if she is begging them to reveal what they know yet they remain stubbornly dumb.

Perhaps she shouldn't be surprised; after all, don't they say that if you are too close to something then you can't truly see it, not in its entirety? It is a notion to which she tries to subscribe but something in her simply doesn't buy it. Accepting such a principle feels a little like a cop out, an easy - if flimsy - excuse that gives her permission to accept the static, the status quo. But move on she must. She knows that. She has known it from the moment she stepped off the train, walked through the door to the cottage. She has known it from the instant she first met Lewis - and the moment she first saw Jenny. Would it have been easier to have acted then? In as much as she has been struck by the former's openness, she has been put off by the latter's distance and hostility; even dismayed by it. What had she done - there and then, or in those first few days - to warrant such a welcome? But that wasn't a secret. She saw only too well the root cause of Jenny's frozen demeanour even if it had been born - then at least - from a false assumption.

It had been unexpected, this new feeling she had for Lewis. It had not been sought, nor encouraged; she had not tempted it or manufactured it. One day it was just there. She tries to pinpoint the moment, as if in doing so she might more readily explain it and understand how it aligns with everything else. She is most concerned about how it fits in with 'moving on'. She had planned to stay a short while only; long enough to tie up loose ends, to put Ryan to rest once and for all. It is not only what she needs, but what she feels he needs. And now, instinctively, she knows it is what Jenny needs too. Had she fooled herself into thinking it would be easy, flitting in, making her peace, and then simply flying away? Perhaps. But even that notion begged questions at which she had only teased: fly away to where and for what purpose? Stepping off the train, her plan had been simple, single-threaded - and one which did not need an answer to the then unasked question 'what next?'. She believes that Lewis has seem some of that. He had made observations about her writing she thought were perceptive; once or twice he had veered towards the nub of things, even to the extent that she found herself fearful that he might, almost by accident, reveal everything, even those things she did not know herself. And so she now has questions, more than before, and no real answers.

She stands up, leaving the notebooks open, and walks to the window, looking out at the little walled back garden. It is no more than a yard really, but there it is, just what it is supposed to be. She admires it for its simpleness and fulfilment of purpose; she envies its lack of ambition. It is, of course, fanciful to graft human emotion onto a few square yards of turf and paving, onto whitewashed walls, the small apple tree, a few pots beginning to burgeon with spring and early summer flowers. She thinks of her books on the table and wonders if there might be something there, a poem perhaps. What was it Lewis had said about looking at things through a different lens, at a different angle? And she imagines his hands - hands that have been accustomed to guns and ammunition and the full spectrum of soldiery - and tries to see them as they hold a pencil or a brush, caressing the paper beneath them.

It is an incongruous image in many ways, but it is proof of something; of his own moving on, perhaps. And she wonders if he thinks of her and, if so, how he does. Again she tries to find that moment, the instant when things changed, and tries to imagine if they have changed for him too. And she is suddenly afraid of what might happen when he finds out all he does not know; that she has secrets she has been keeping from him. What will that do to this trust they have built, silently, almost stealthily, between them?

She shivers involuntarily. And then there is a knock at the door.

"Hi."

Even though he is smiling, Anna can't help but register a false note, like a chord misplayed because of an errant finger on a keyboard.

And she has never heard Lewis say 'Hi' before.

"Hello," she says, trying not to show that his one short word - and how he delivered it - has immediately put her on edge. She knows it is nonsense, that she has simply been nudged off balance by her recent thoughts, but she is suddenly nervous and doesn't want him to recognise it.

"Got a minute?" he asks, trying to remain casual but sensing trepidation leaking from every pore. He hopes it is not obvious.

"Tea? I was just going to make one," she lies.

"Please."

Having waited for permission, he steps over the threshold as she turns and begins to retreat toward the kitchen, as if her moving away is what gives him leave to enter.

"There's no cake though," she says over her shoulder, "some greedy guts managed to finish it all off!"

Knowing she is referring to him, Lewis endeavours to smile, just in case she turns to check he got the joke. She doesn't.

Anna busies herself in the kitchen, choosing to wait for the kettle to boil rather than go back into the lounge. She adjusts the cups and spoons more than once as if doing so will either speed up or slow down the boiling. She is unsure which she wishes for the most.

Having sat down, Lewis stands up again. The sound of the crockery in the kitchen, cutlery rattling in the saucers more than once, resonate as a bell might. It sounds like tolling, or counting; a count down, perhaps. He wonders if he should have come, knowing he must. He wonders if he should have taken some time just to think. Yet here he is, blundering in through the door without checking for booby-traps.

By the time she returns they have both calmed somewhat. Lewis, as he resumes his seat, looks up, smiling, giving no indication that he has stood and sat three times already. And Anna, confidently depositing the tray on the small coffee table, knows she will never confess that initially she put salt in the sugar bowl even knowing full well that neither of them takes sugar.

"So," Anna says, knowing that one of them needs to break the silence before it grows into something unmanageable, "to what do I owe this unexpected pleasure?"

Lewis offers a quiet smile, obscurely grateful that she has forced his hand. He tries to keep it in play as he suddenly regrets his lack of rehearsal. Knowing it is too late for that now - and knowing it would be beyond cowardly to back out - he edges forwards on the sofa.

"To be honest, I'm not quite sure where to start," he says. It is a tentative beginning.

"Oh dear," Anna says, her face falling just a little.

"What's wrong?"

"It sounds ominous." She shivers involuntarily, a movement not lost on him.

"It isn't meant to be," he says, trying to sound reassuring.

"The last time someone said something like that to me - about not knowing where to start - was when they broke the news about

Ryan." She glances away, and then back at him. "How else were they supposed to start, I suppose; but it's the kind of phrase that always takes you that way, threatening."

"That's the last thing I'd ever want to be," he tries smiling again, and fails. "Though actually it is about Ryan. In a way."

"Ryan?" There is no way she can mask her surprise. Having begun to invent potential reasons to explain his presence, she is confused as to how Lewis can be wanting to talk about her ex-husband. Her mind races forwards, trying to concoct scenarios in which to wrap Lewis's words. Perhaps just as she reaches the very edge of an idea, words of her own trip out unbidden. "What about him?"

"Well not him so much. Not really." Lewis finds himself at the end of a cul de sac with nowhere to go.

"Then who?"

In his mind's eye, Lewis sees himself turn to face the open end of the road. He imagines forcing himself into an upright stance, chest out, shoulders back. Time to be a brave little soldier as his mother once said - and as others had many times since then.

"I just want you to know that whatever I can do to help, all you need to do is ask. Anything. Right now it's the only thing that matters to me."

She is staring at him now, an intensity suggesting she has the power to burrow through his eyes and get to the heart of things. Lewis thinks about the eyes being the soul's windows. He hopes his are being truthful, that what she can see is what he really feels.

"Lewis," she says slowly, a slight vibrato in her voice, "now you really are scaring me."

"I'm sorry," he says, leaning further forwards from the edge of his seat, trying to get as close as he can without alarming her any further. "It's just that I've found out - no, not that. It's come to my attention. Shit, that's not right either."

"Lewis!" It is an almost silent, breathless shout.

"Anna, I know who Ryan was. And so, I suppose, who you are. I know about the connection. With Jenny."

The movement of her left hand to her mouth is involuntary, as if to limit a sudden intake of breath. She is conscious of it a moment later, and lowers the hand to her lap where it joins her right. The slight flush in her cheek comes, not from the discovery, but from the embarrassment at this involuntary slice of melodrama. But it is over in a second, her mind processing what Lewis has just said and trying to encompass it in the whole landscape of her past, her few weeks in Maunston Quay, her foggy and uncertain future. It is then that relief engulfs her; relief that she has not needed to broach the subject, to be the one who has to reveal her secret. She is released by the fact that Lewis knows, and that her last-but-one secret is discovered. From somewhere a voice whispers "what now?" into her ears, and the fret which hovers about her seems suddenly and impossibly dense. If the sigh that escapes her says all of that, she wonders how much he can interpret. The word 'fret' fails to leave her. She is struck by how apposite it is.

"I see," she says, somewhat inappropriately. She knows she should ask him how he knows, but the relief that he now possesses her secret trumps everything.

Lewis waits, as if watching a coin spinning mid toss, uncertain how it will land. He wants to wager 'heads' or 'tails' yet cannot do so for fear of losing.

"I'm sorry."

Her words surprise him. They are words he had imagined saying himself, for surely he is the one who has transgressed, the one who is in the wrong; it is a feeling he has been unable to shake since that first conversation with Maisie.

"*You're* sorry? I don't understand. Why should you be sorry?"

"Because I should have told you and I'm sorry I didn't." She feels her body relax, tension released. "I meant to tell you. More than once, in fact. Recently. Once when we were walking. And then the other day, when we were doing that writing-painting thing. But I couldn't. I was - " she wants to say scared, but knows that is the wrong word, "not brave enough." She tries a weak smile. "So, even though I didn't tell you myself, I'm glad you know. Truly."

More than anything else Lewis wants to hug her now; to pull her close, to wrap her in his arms and tell her everything will be all right. But he can't. Not yet.

"Do you want to tell me now?" If there is hope in his voice he longs for it to carry to her untarnished.

"If you want to hear it."

He nods and waits.

"I didn't know Ryan had a sister. Not at first, anyway. He never mentioned her. At all." Lewis senses her pausing, as if she is internally verifying the chronology of her story. "I always thought he was an only child. Or at least that's what he led me to believe."

"How did you find out?"

"When his father died. He refused to go to the funeral, which I thought was odd. And then I saw some papers, legal things he had to sign, and there was Jenny's name. At first I thought he might have been married once before; it was the same surname, after all. At that point he had to tell me." A pause. "It was hard for him, especially at first. There was a lot of anger. It seemed to be all directed at her, but later I could see much of it was actually aimed at himself. They'd had a falling out, he told me that much. It had been maybe a couple of years before he met me. I think it might have been about Tommy or the life Jenny was choosing for herself. He was never that explicit really. They'd put this wall up between them, you see. A big, high wall. I don't know who started it - it was probably mutual - but it was evident he wasn't going to be the one to try and tear it down." Another pause. "Has Jenny ever said anything?"

"Nothing," says Lewis, shaking his head. "I knew she had a brother killed in combat somewhere, but I never pressed her. It was none of my business."

She lets his words settle, then moves on.

"And then he started to get these postings, and I saw less and less of him. When he died and the Army contacted me, I asked them who else he had registered as next of kin. They said there was only me. Even then - even after I knew all about Jenny - he still didn't acknowledge her. Later, when we buried him, I couldn't help but think there was someone missing; as if there was this space at his funeral, a space that should have been filled by his sister."

"You didn't think to contact her yourself?"

"Not then I'm ashamed to say. But I was in something of a state myself at that point, what with little Tom not long gone too... I was on autopilot; a bit like a zombie, I suppose. I stumbled through, one day after another, never quite sure if I was glad the day was beginning or glad it was ending. But then you know what that's like too, don't you?"

They exchange smiles filled with sympathy and empathy in equal measure, signals like weak lamps reflected in a foggy mirror.

"It was months later I suppose - once I'd come to my senses a bit more - that I thought I'd try and find Jenny. There was something that needed to be resolved, closed. I realised not only did I owe it to Ryan, but I owed it to Jenny too. And to myself, I suppose; but me least of all. I guess I knew I couldn't carry that kind of thing around with me for ever. I'd told the Army about her and asked them to let her know - and asked them not to mention me. Perhaps I thought that would be enough to acquit me. It was an excuse at the time, but I told them I'd contact her in my own way, even though I had assumed I wouldn't. They were very understanding."

"They can be," Lewis says. "It surprises people. They think everyone's a hard-nosed macho soldier, but there are some real people in the Army too."

"Present company excepted," she suggests.

He laughs, relieved that she is trying a joke.

"Major Carmichael his name was. Lovely man." Another pause. "Anyway, I eventually found having the Army do my dirty work wasn't enough; I decided that I needed to close the loop with Jenny myself. Simply having her told by someone else began to gnaw at me. I thought I'd closed the chapter, if you like, but I hadn't, not really."

She leans forwards and pours herself another cup of tea. Lewis shakes his head when she looks his way and just waits. She finishes putting in the milk, stirs unnecessarily, then leaves the cup on the table.

"I didn't know where to start, of course. I tried going through Ryan's things - what few I had - to see if I could find any mention of her. I just needed a phone number, an address, something. But there was nothing. She might just as well have never existed. And then Major Carmichael came to mind. I still had his details so I contacted him. Luckily he remembered me, but better than that, he remembered what I'd said about contacting Jenny later myself."

"Elephants," Lewis suggests, obscurely. "Some of the officers have memories you wouldn't believe. Maybe it's a requirement for promotion or something. I never met an officer who didn't have the recall of a genius."

"Which was lucky for me, I guess. He gave me the address of a pub in London, but when I contacted them they told me Jenny had moved on - but they didn't know where. That stumped me for a little while and then I thought to try the brewery. Eventually - after a few calls and a few bald lies - I found out about 'The Anchor' and Maunston Quay."

Anna pauses and glances down at the table as if seeing the freshly poured tea for the first time. Trying to disguise her surprise, she lifts it from the table and drinks, small, repetitive sips. Lewis waits. When she returns it to the table, the mug is half empty.

"I'd made up my mind that I wanted to meet her in person. I didn't have to, of course. I still could have tried to walk away and left it; or perhaps written some kind of letter. Or even done something anonymously, I suppose. But I didn't want to do that. Not then."

"And now?" Lewis asks, articulating the question that she had prompted.

"The only question was how," she continues, ignoring his interruption. "I thought if I could work my way into it gradually rather than barging in, that might be the thing to do. You know, get the lie of the land. Reconnaissance; isn't that what you Army guys call it?"

"Something like that," he smiles.

"So I started to search. The internet makes it so easy these days. When I found this place was available, I couldn't believe my luck."

"Fate?" he asks, unable to resist being playful.

She smiles.

"If you like. Anyway, it seemed like the reviews left by people were few and far between, and it seemed totally unbooked forever. I knew that probably meant the cottage was rubbish and the place was rubbish, but that didn't matter. It was in Maunston Quay and near 'The Anchor', and that was all that counted. I could come here, stay a week - two at most - close the loop like I'd planned and then move on."

Lewis is suddenly struck by the unspoken sentences that seem to pack the silences between her words; the questions that hang unarticulated and invisible. That they are there is undeniable, and as he looks at Anna he knows instinctively that she sees them too.

"That was your plan..." he prompts.

"It was a plan of sorts, yes. But when I got off the train and stood by the dunes and looked down at the cottages..."

"Yes?"

"I don't know. I was scared, I suppose. I thought that I'd done the wrong thing. That it was all a huge mistake. I wondered if I could live without the reconcilliation after all. Part of me wanted to change platforms and get a train back. Not to home, just back. Away."

"I saw you."

She had been looking over his shoulder and out of the window as he had spoken. His words jolted her back, her eyes locking his.

"You saw me?!"

"I was in the car, waiting at the gates for the train to go through. You were wearing your red coat. You looked - well, a little lost I suppose."

She shakes her head and smiles.

"I didn't see you. I don't even remember there being a car there."

"But you did stay. You did walk across the dunes and to the cottage. To here." She nods at his words. "Why?"

"Why?" There is a pause as she releases his gaze and returns to look at the window. "I don't know. Maybe it was the sea. There was something about it, perhaps. And I hadn't been to the coast for so long. It suddenly seemed like an opportunity. I didn't know what for, but it was different, and different was good. Either that or..."

Lewis mouths the word 'fate' once more and she bursts out laughing. It is a moment that releases a tension which had been building unbeknownst to them, engrossed as they both were in her story.

"So I pretended to make out I was on some kind of retreat. But I never lied. When we first met and I told you why I was here, about my past, none of that was untrue. I didn't lie to you, Lewis."

"I know," he says softly.

"I may not have realised some of it myself until I'd actually said those things aloud, but that's a different thing isn't it? Perhaps Maunston was already working it's magic somehow. Within a couple of days I think I'd already begun to feel as if things had shifted somehow. As if I had shifted. Maybe it was the sea, the sand, the walking."

"It does that to you," Lewis says, "just ask Bradley. Just ask me. Or Tommy or Richard come to that. It weaves a simple kind of spell, I think. Enchantment, a trance; something hypnotic, especially the sea."

She laughs.

"You make it sound too much like Walt Disney!"

"Touché!"

Anna glances down at the half empty mug but leaves it where it sits, a prop she no longer needs. Outside there is a sudden break in the cloud and a shaft of sunlight pierces the window. It is enough to make Lewis turn and look that way.

"And then I met Jenny," she says to his back. He returns his focus to her. She studies his eyes for a moment as if gauging a measure of something intangible, then carries on. "When the evening in the pub came up - you know, the meeting about the village - I couldn't believe my luck. It was a way of meeting her without commitment or fanfare. It would give me the chance to judge, to decide how best to approach her. As an opportunity, it seemed perfect."

"But…" Lewis feels the word coming, but prompts for it anyway, needing Anna to see this through. It is nothing like an exorcism, but he feels if she can make it to the end of the story, to bring it up-to-date, to the here-and-now, then there will be nothing left to separate them. His mouth is suddenly dry, his eyes suddenly not.

"Yoo." She pauses, a little tremor back in her voice. "Is it possible to say how disappointed I was? I had hoped - I don't know - for something else. For a person who reminded me of the good Ryan, a person I could like. I had hoped for a connection of some sort; probably selfishly, because it would have made my job so much easier."

"And what you found," he offers, striving to smooth the way for her, "was an impolite, hostile individual who seemed rude and impossible."

"Lewis!" She is shocked more by the tone in his voice than the words themselves.

"Well, am I wrong?" he says, unable to disguise a minor chord of challenge, knowing he cannot be denied.

She shakes her head.

"I was so disappointed. It was almost as if she hated me before I'd even walked through the door. There was no effort; not a smile, a kind word, nothing. I'd never come across such focussed lack of engagement. I tried to make a contribution to the meeting, partly to buy some time to see if she would soften, and partly to try and take my mind off it. I don't think it really worked."

"Well the contribution did," he smiles, "though I know that's scant consolation."

"And then there was Tommy's birthday thing. I thought that might give me a second chance. Part of me still wanted to find our first encounter had been a one-off. If the context was more relaxed would that make it easier, better, whatever?"

They say nothing for a few moments.

"That was a wonderful evening - at least I thought so." He feels as if he stepping out onto a frozen lake, not knowing how thick the ice is.

Anna looks up at the window, sunlight still flooding in.

"Shall we go for a walk?" she asks.

❊ ❊ ❊

"Of course you know why she was so hostile towards you?"

They had left the house, briefly debating the need for coats, and walked down to the sand. The sun had warmed the morning considerably and the early clouds had largely absconded. Bradley, who happens to be glancing out from his bedroom window at the precise moment Lewis speaks, watches as they walk slowly towards the pier, their two footprint trails just far enough apart to suggest that there could have been someone invisible walking between them. It is an odd notion, but one that does not leave him. His eyes follow them as they traverse another ten yards or so, then he turns away and goes downstairs.

After leaving her cottage, they had said nothing, Lewis's words now breaking into the extended silence that has followed them all the way to the jetty steps which, without hesitation, Anna begins to climb. As she is in front of him, when he speaks Lewis can only see her back. She waits for him just beyond the top step.

"Yes, I think so."

Her words act as a trigger for them to stroll on, their footfall in tune, tapping out a slow rhythm.

Lewis senses her uncertainty. There are questions he has to answer too. This unburdening is not all on Anna's side. Head down, watching their feet, he realises that today - once he had initiated this chain of events - could never just be about her.

"I think Jenny's a very unhappy woman," he suggests, trying to adopt a sympathetic view as if balancing a complex equation.

"Unhappy?"

"Maybe more unfulfilled then. Or disappointed. It has nothing to do with Ryan as far as I can tell, but having something unresolved that's so important and personal, so many unanswered questions, well, it can't help can it?"

"With Tommy? Is that where her issue is?"

"Partly," Lewis takes a moment to try and choose his words. "I know they're not doing so well right now - but I don't think it's anything to do with him either."

"He seems a perfectly nice man," Anna suggests.

"That's how I've always found him, considering."

"Considering?"

They are half way along the pier now and Lewis looks up to scan the horizon. If he is expecting to see something there he does not say.

"She doesn't like Maunston Quay," he says. "Running 'The Anchor' and living here may be Tommy's dream but it isn't Jenny's. I think she resents him for their coming here. That's part of the problem."

"And the other part?" asks Anna, taking her turn to act as prompter.

"And the other part is that she wants to escape. She knows Tommy won't leave but she wants to get away. And she's too scared to do it on her own. So she's looking for a way out. And, I suppose, that's where I come in."

Lewis pauses, expecting Anna to make a comment, a remark of some kind. But she says nothing, knowing he must go on, just as she had been forced to carry on when they were in the cottage. There are conclusions to be reached before anything else matters.

"For some reason - and don't ask me why - she latched on to me a while ago. It seems a long time ago, anyway. As if I might be her ticket out of here. She's been trying to… I'm not sure I know the right words, but she's been trying to get me to take her away from here."

"On her terms?" Anna asks. The words sound strange; it is a question Lewis realises he has never articulated himself.

"On any terms," he replies, knowing full well their import. "On any terms," he says again, for emphasis, as if doing so underlines something he needs Anna to realise. "But unfortunately for her, I've never really been interested. I'm not different from Tommy in a way; I don't think I want to leave here either." He glances towards Anna at this point and finds it is her turn to be intent on the boards upon which they walk.

They have reached the end of the pier. Without hesitation, Anna lowers herself down and, dangling her feet over the edge, sits squarely facing the sea. Lewis has no choice but to sit alongside her.

"I've tried to be kind, friendly; I've tried to make it clear that I'm not the solution to her problem. I don't want to hurt her, of course; and I don't want any bad blood. But it hasn't seemed to have worked so far."

"It rarely does," says Anna, looking towards him and smiling.

"Rarely?" Lewis sounds confused.

"In my experience - from people I know, you understand - there is no easy way out of such a trap. People like Jenny, considering her situation, her motivation and how much she has invested in this dream of hers, can only be shaken from it but some kind of jolt. Usually you can't get a jolt from someone being kind and considerate."

"You're saying I have to hurt her feelings?"

Anna glances down to the boards and where Lewis's left hand is resting, supporting him as he sits there. She places her right hand over his and squeezes it gently.

"You already have," she says.

Felling the warmth of her palm on the back of his hand, Lewis looks down to where their hands rest together.

"Yes, I suppose I have."

She squeezes his hand again and then lets it go.

"The odds were stacked against me even before I met her weren't they?" Anna asks, now tracing the horizon herself.

"I think so. People gossip. She'd heard about you, inevitably. People had seen you about, occasionally seen us walking together. You were my neighbour, right there next door to me. She would have got it into her head that you were a rival, illogical though that may have been at the time." Lewis, having chosen those last three words with care, glances at Anna's face to see if they have registered. "And so when you finally appeared in person - and in my company, to boot - she'd already made up her mind. You didn't stand a chance."

Their brief silence is caressed by the lapping of the water at the pier's uprights, soothed by the slow drag of the waves on the sand behind them. Overhead a gull suddenly cries, and they look up in unison, watching it as it wheels away above them.

"And do I now?" she asks in between the gull's cries.

"Do you what?"

"Stand a chance."

Lewis considers the prospect, but there can only be one answer.

"I don't think so. I can't see how she'll relent."

Anna eyes have retuned to the sea. She waits a moment.

"I didn't mean with Jenny."

If Bradley were to look out of his window at this precise moment he would see two figures sitting at the end of the pier. They are closer now than at any point during their walk. He would see one of them, the man, lean towards the other and place his arm gently about the woman's shoulders and ease her towards him. He would sense, if not exactly see, the woman suddenly relax, allowing her head to fall against the top of the man's chest. And then there is no further movement, other than the constant repetition of the sea and a lone gull soaring overhead.

"More than anyone in a very long time."

These are the words that Bradley would fail to hear, accompanied by a brief glance between them that says so much more.

"I'm glad," Anna says, the climax of her sudden relief, her complete unburdening, manifested by tears she is unable to staunch. They make her laugh. It is a different kind of laugh, one Lewis is hearing for the first time.

He allows his right hand to find her face, his fingers gently brushing the tears away; it is an action that makes her laugh a little more.

"Stupid me," she says, lightly, easing her head from his chest. "But I wasn't sure."

"Of me?" Lewis asks, his left arm still about her.

"I guess so. Or of me either. If I'm honest." She allows her free hand to take up the task of wiping her tears away, setting her eyes toward the sea as if the volume of water there will shame them into becoming still. "I'm sorry," she says.

"What for?"

"I'm not very good at this. I haven't done something like this in a long time."

Lewis laughs softly.

"That makes two of us." He pauses. "And I wasn't sure either. But I hoped; for a little while now I suppose."

"Since when?"

"When?"

"When did you...have an inkling? About me." Her voice is suddenly younger, less secure. Lewis finds himself wishing he had known her five years earlier.

"I don't know."

"It was in 'The Anchor'," she says. "Ironically."

"'The Anchor'?"

"When there was that joke and you laughed like I'd never heard you laugh before."

Lewis lifts her left hand from her lap and places it on his chest.

"And you put your hand just there, and even though I was laughing I could feel a surge of something flood through me."

It is just now that Bradley emerges from his cottage and pauses at his front door. In the distance he can see Lewis and Anna sitting at the end of the pier. He sees Lewis pull her close. He sees them kiss. Bradley smiles, looks up at the now empty sky, and starts to whistle.

❋❋❋

"There's only one thing left to do," Lewis says as they are crossing the sand back towards the cottages. This time their footprints are too close together to admit anything between them.

"Really?" Anna says, trying to appear a little surprised. "I thought your intentions were entirely honourable, Sir!"

Lewis laughs briefly and pulls her to a halt. He revels in the fact that he can now draw her close to him and kiss her softly.

"That's very naughty," he says in mock admonishment.

"You were the one…"

"No," he says, allowing the smile to fade from his face. "Jenny. We have to tell Jenny."

Anna, knowing he is right, is relieved he has said 'we'; it is a measure of something important, proof that she is no longer alone. Suddenly she is struck by how solitary she had become, and feeling his arms about her brings on her tears again.

"Hey, hey," Lewis says, feeling her sob. He lifts her face with his hand, smiling reassuringly. "I didn't mean to upset you so soon."

She shakes her head.

"No, it's not that. And you're right of course. It's just that I didn't realise how much I'd missed being part of a 'we'. I don't think I understood until now, at this precise moment, how alone I had become. You block those kind of feelings out, just to give yourself a chance of getting through the day."

"You do," says Lewis. "It hadn't occurred to me in that way yet; I guess I'm still in shock."

"In shock?"

"You see how nervous I was?" he says quietly. "But you're right; you do cut yourself off, especially from other people. I don't think we have the capacity to think of others when we're so wounded ourselves."

"And now here you are," she says, allowing a note of pride to creep into her voice, "already thinking of someone else."

They start walking again.

"But you do agree with me, don't you? We cannot be happy knowing that Jenny doesn't have the whole truth."

Anna says nothing for a moment.

"Yes, I agree. Completely. And I think I can do it now, no matter what kind of welcome she gives me."

Lewis stops as they reach the road.

"Let me," he says.

"Tell Jenny?" There is immediate gratitude in her voice that she is unable to suppress.

Lewis nods.

"Before we do anything else. Let me tell her. For you. It will be easier. She'll listen to me - probably. There are too many barriers in the way for her to pay attention to anything you say. I have to be the one - if you'll let me."

She squeezes his hand and looks up the road toward the crossing gates, knowing the village lies beyond.

"You realise that you'll be telling her more than that; more than something that's just about Ryan. She'll know, even if you're not explicit; she'll know the thing she feared or thought was true is exactly that."

He nods again, then leans forward and kisses her cheek.

"Another reason why it has to be me." He eases his hand from her grip and takes a first step away. "I may be a little while."

"It sounds like you're going into battle." He laughs in response. "Or maybe you're Captain Oates!"

"But hopefully I'll make it back alive!"

Anna watches him walk away.

"I'll try and bake something nice for lunch," she calls after him. He half turns and waves, but does not stop walking.

She is unsure if she can apply words to what she feels as he ascends the slight incline in the road and then angles towards the station. After a while he waves without looking round, confident that she will still be there, watching him. Moments later he has disappeared, freeing her.

As she moves, she realises Bradley is standing in his doorway and that he has been following Lewis too.

"What a splendid morning," he says, looking back at her and smiling brightly. "You know, I don't think I can recall such a pleasant morning."

Anna walks over to where he stands and gives him a hug.

"Thank you," she says.

"Thank me? What have I done?!"

She laughs at his surprise, and squeezes his arm.

"Thank you for being Lewis's friend, for helping him through things when he needed it."

Bradley shakes his head.

"I was just minding the shop," he said, "until you came along." Seeing Anna is in danger of bursting into tears again, Bradley hurries on. "Well, get on with you then, if you're going to cook something for the man's lunch. He'll probably be scarred and bruised when he returns."

"Will he be all right?" she asks after a brief laugh.

"Lewis? He'll be fine. He's been in fiercer fire-fights in his time." Bradley looks up the road, almost as if he can see Lewis now crossing the track and taking the shallow arc in the road that leads to the pub.

❋ ❋ ❋

"You know we're not allowed to serve you yet," says Tommy with a laugh as he sees Lewis appear through the open door and walk towards the bar where he is busy checking the optics.

"Then you shouldn't leave your doors wide open, Tommy," says Lewis, sharing the joke, "otherwise it just encourages hardened drinkers like me to stray."

"If you're an example of a hardened drinker then we're all in trouble!"

Lewis watches Tommy as he laughs at his own joke, turning back to the display where he finishes mounting a fresh bottle of rum into its stand.

"You know, these things can be a really good indicator of how well we're doing."

"How so?" Lewis asks.

"By how often I have to change them," Tommy explains. "You'd be surprised. Whiskey at least once a week; maybe twice if things are going well. Gin and Vodka almost as much - though gin's really coming on strong now."

"And rum?"

Tommy shakes his head.

"Not as popular as it used to be. Once a month, maybe." Tommy pauses as he turns back to face his mid-morning guest. "If you need a quick one, Lewis, just say. I was only joking."

"No - but thanks." Lewis, momentary tempted, knows he has no subtle way of making his request. "I came by to see Jenny. Is she around?"

Tommy's face darkens a shade.

"Just out the back, I think. Shall I get her?"

"Please." At least on his walk up from the cottages Lewis has had the chance to map out a strategy this time. "And come back with her, Tommy. It's probably best that you're here."

Tommy shoots him a quizzical look.

"Very cryptic," he says, the dark look now replaced by a frown of puzzlement.

Left alone, Lewis scans the bar.

It is not, he knows, a bad pub. He has been in worse. Often. When you're in the Army, postings can mean you have very little choice where you take your ease. Even so, Lewis knows 'The Anchor' lacks a certain something, a spark that would edge it closer to being a really nice pub. He feels there is a idea buried somewhere that might make all the difference to the two of them if only it could be unearthed.

He has just taken a stool against the bar when Jenny appears, Tommy in her wake.

"Hello stranger," she says brightly, "what's up?"

She glances towards Tommy as if giving Lewis a signal, knowing she could dismiss Tommy with ease if he wanted her to.

"Tommy's fine just there," Lewis says, surprising himself by being explicit, "I think he needs to hear what I have to say too."

This time it's Jenny's face which hosts the worried look. She leans against her side of the bar in an almost involuntary preparatory movement. Lewis wonders what she fears most; what, in that instant between him speaking and now, she may have concocted as being the worst possible thing he might have to say. He knows his new and surprising and wonderful reality is a candidate.

And he knows that cannot be what comes first.

"I have some news for you, Jenny," he starts slowly.

"News? For me?" She shoots a glance and a nervous smile towards Tommy, her frown asking him if he knows. Tommy shrugs. Looking back at Lewis, she laughs falsely. "Maybe we've won the lottery."

"Unfortunately not," Lewis says. "That's not one of my sidelines I'm afraid." There is a pause no-one fills as they wait for him. "It's actually about Ryan."

This time Lewis's words make her sag a little, the surprise hitting her like a fist to the midriff. Tommy makes to move forward, but her hand halts him. She allows the bar to support her a little more securely.

"Ryan?"

"Yes. Sorry I was a little abrupt, but there's no easy way to broach the subject." Lewis knows he has lied. Debating his options on the walk up, he is sure there are more gentle introductions available to him, but he wants to keep the interview short and the frills to a minimum. There is also the hope that if Jenny is off her guard, she may look upon the news more favourably, more as rescue than abandonment.

"What news? Have you been speaking to someone in the Army? One of your old officers?" There is a hint of hope in her voice, though hope for what Lewis isn't quite sure.

"No, I haven't." Again the smallest wait. "I do have a little more detail about what happened to him, though I'm guessing that's probably no more than you know already."

Jenny looks confused, and this time her demeanour is enough to see Tommy at her side, his hand resting on the one she has placed on the counter-top. She doesn't protest.

"I have the facts; the when and where. Not the why or how, but that doesn't seem to matter any more," she says.

"It's about earlier; before then." Lewis gives her time to process this, to realign herself to a life she has already lived and given up on. "I know there was a time before he died when things weren't good between you and Ryan, when you were estranged." It is an odd word, and it falls unnaturally from his lips; yet, like so many words, it is appropriate, apt. And they were estranged, as strangers for so long.

"I don't know," she says somewhat emptily. "I don't care about then."

The air in the bar seems suddenly heavy; Lewis feels the burden of his task increase.

"But you do care," Tommy offers, squeezing her hand. The gesture is not lost on Lewis. Tommy looks directly at him. "Jenny tortures herself sometimes about what happened to him, what happened to them. I know she does."

"Tommy..."

"It's true, Love, I know. There *is* a gap there, Lewis, and it's been gnawing away at her for so long now." He pauses to place his free arm around Jenny. "So if you've found something out that helps to fill the gap, please tell us. I know it may be hard, but we need to know."

Lewis notes Tommy's use of 'we', of the joining of the two of them together to make it a shared burden, a shared trial. It is perhaps the first time Lewis has ever been able to regard them as a couple. There is an echo of what they may have been once upon a time.

"Jen?" Tommy says, looking at her as softly as he can. Her eyes are fixed on Lewis, but it is obvious that her focus is somewhere else.

She nods. It is a small nod, a fearful nod. It is a nod that gives Lewis permission.

"A few years ago - probably a year or so after you last spoke to him I'm guessing - Ryan married." He waits, determined to play the facts out one at a time, to make sure that they are absorbed, understood.

"Married?" Jenny echoes.

Lewis nods and waits for his next cue.

"I didn't realise. I never knew," she says. "I didn't think he was the marrying kind. I thought he was too hard for that; married to the Army perhaps, isn't that what they say?"

"For some people it can be a bit like that," Lewis says, trying to smooth the way. "And then, a little less than two years ago - so probably about a year before he died - he had a son. A little boy."

Jenny's intake of breath is almost a gasp. The shock is evident. There is a brief lull, then Jenny's face softens a little.

"I would never have seen him as a Dad," she says, glancing at Tommy for a split second. "He was always - I don't know - so rough. A little boy, you say. What was he called?"

"Tom."

There is a little laugh. Tommy begins to smile. Lewis needs to recapture the moment.

"But," he says, enough warning in his voice to interrupt any relaxation, "I'm afraid the little boy died."

"No," this time Jenny does gasp, her hand gripping Tommy's rather than the bar.

"He had been born poorly," Lewis continues, "and never recovered. He was just a few months old when he died. And then a few months after that, Ryan ..."

Lewis lets the phrase complete itself in the silence. He doesn't want to be calculating, but he knows he has to deliver the hardest news of all at the moment when Jenny will be most receptive to it. Having taken on this burden, he knows he has to do the very best he can for Anna. He needs to tip the scales far enough to allow them to swing just a little in her favour.

"Wow," says Tommy quietly, his voice a combination of shock and sympathy.

"But," says Jenny, her voice revealing just the beginning of a quiver, "how dreadful. How awful that must have been for his poor wife; to lose her little boy and then her husband. Just like that. In so short a time." She pauses, lifting her free hand to brush it across her face. "I can't imaging what that must have been like."

"And there's one last thing," Lewis says, trying to speak as quietly as he can while still being certain they can hear him.

"There's more?" Tommy asks. "Surely not."

"It's about his wife," says Lewis as evenly as he can. Both Jenny and Tommy are rapt now. He holds them for a second longer than he thought he dared. "It's Anna. Anna Woolley was Ryan's wife."

He wants to elaborate, to go further; he wants to plead her case, to emphasise how hard life has been for her, how she just needs a chance to be able to have a future. He wants to tell them that he hopes he has a part to play in that future. He wants to plead with

Jenny to be gracious, to imagine what it must have been like; he knows he would go down on bended knee to beg her to do so.

But he does none of those things. He forces himself to wait, to focus on Jenny's face, to try and decipher the tumult of emotion he sees encapsulated there.

❊ ❊ ❊

"You don't have to knock now you know!" Anna shouts from the kitchen on hearing rapping on the front door.

She finishes drying her hands, surveys the work surfaces to satisfy herself that all is tidy after her baking preparation, glances into the hot oven to check the cake, then hangs up the tea towel. Even though she is apprehensive about what Lewis may have to report, as she walks through the lounge towards the front door she can't restrain the smile spreading across her face.

"Didn't you hear..." she has half-opened the door when her words fade as rapidly as the smile.

"Can I come in?" Jenny asks, striving to appear calm and untroubled, her tone almost business-like.

Anna hopes her own face does not betray her quite as much.

"Jenny. Yes. Of course. Sorry."

It is a staccato beginning. Anna stands to one side. Once Jenny is past, she leans out of the front door in the hope that Lewis is there, but she can see no-one. She quickly checks the pier and the beach. Empty.

By the time she closes the door and returns to the lounge, Jenny is standing by the fireplace.

"Please; sit down." Anna watches her guest take the sofa nearest the window - the one Lewis chose earlier in the day - and then sits opposite.

There is a short, uncomfortable pause.

"You weren't expecting to see me?" Jenny asks, her voice strained as if some invisible pressure was being applied to her vocal chords.

"No," Anna says, then corrects herself. "Yes, I mean. But perhaps not now."

"You know Lewis has been to see me?"

It is a strangely blunt, factual question. Maybe, Anna thinks, it is better that way.

"Yes. He wanted to…" unsure of the correct phrase to use, she is forced into cliché, "break the news."

"You didn't want to tell me yourself?"

"I did. Of course I did."

"Then why didn't you?"

Anna wonders how she can possibly avoid inserting emotion into the dialogue at this point; if it proved to be destabilising, she fears where it might lead.

"I planned to. But I thought it might make sense to - I don't know - get to know you a bit first. To see how…"

"You had a chance," Jenny jumps in.

"I'm sorry?"

"Probably more than one. You could have told me at that stupid meeting we had in the pub. Or at Tommy's party." Jenny pauses. It feels a little like a joust; a joust where she has the upper hand. "Why didn't you?"

Given how far they have come individually - and how far they still have to go - Anna knows that there is no point avoiding the truth. Not any more.

"You seemed…upset. Preoccupied."

"Preoccupied?" Jenny questions.

Anna knows it was a stupid word to use.

"I didn't feel welcome," Anna says. There is a sudden degree of relief in her now that she has been forced to contribute to the peeling away of their conversation's veneer.

Jenny waits, weighing how she should respond; feeling slightly off balance, she hopes Anna will say something else to give her more time to counter. Nothing is forthcoming.

"Maybe you weren't," Jenny admits, her voice slightly quieter. She looks away from Anna and allows her gaze to float around the room as if there might be a clue that can help her.

Anna notices Jenny's gaze suddenly freeze. She doesn't need to check to know where she is looking. On a set of drawers near the entrance to the kitchen, in a small silver frame, is a picture of Ryan cradling their baby. In the end she had chosen to retrieve it and set it out, partly because of Lewis and his relationship with Emma.

"You might not have been unwelcome," Jenny says, her eyes still fixed on the photograph. They return to Anna in the pause that follows. She corrects herself. "You would not have been - if I had known."

Anna looks down for a moment, examining her hands.

"Perhaps I just wasn't brave enough," she suggests looking up again. "And maybe I simply didn't know what to do. Or say. Or how to do or say it."

There is another silence overwhelmed by the weight of things that fill it - a weight hardly lightened by the little fellow-feeling currently forthcoming.

"Would you like some tea?" It is an almost inevitable offer, one of ceasefire, of soldiers singing carols across the trenches.

Jenny nods and Anna leaves her for a moment. The kettle is still warm and it takes her almost no time to make their drinks. She chooses individual mugs rather than make a pot, it seeming sensible to impose some kind of time limit on things. When she returns she gets the sense that the ceasefire is holding.

She has just placed the mugs on the table and resumed her seat when Jenny speaks again.

"It must have been hard. To lose both of them like that."

Anna nods. Although it is painful - and what she is about to embark upon feels instinctively so much more difficult than talking to Lewis - she is glad that they have found less hostile territory. Or something better than that. Neutral territory perhaps.

"It was. Though I never really realised how difficult until later. There wasn't much time after we lost little Tommy before there was another maelstrom. I ought to say that I felt a little like an emotional punch-bag or something clever like that, but I don't think I felt anything at all. Not really."

"I can't imagine," Jenny says. "Did he look like you?"

"Sorry?"

"Your little boy. Did he look like you?"

Anna thinks about retrieving the photograph but decides not to interrupt the fragile flow. She wonders why Jenny has not asked if he looked like Ryan.

"I don't know. I mean people always say stupid things like that, don't they? But in the end babies look just like babies. Apparently he had my eyes, for what that's worth. But the shape of his head, the spacing of his features, they weren't mine."

She refrains from using Ryan's name, as if sensing that it needs to be Jenny who does that first. She doesn't know why. Perhaps part of her feels that, of the two of them, somehow Jenny has the greater claim.

"We had been hopeful that he would get better," Anna continues. "The doctors had tried to give us hope - but on the other hand told us not to. I guess they didn't really know."

"Perhaps they were trying to be kind," Jenny suggests.

Anna nods. "Perhaps." Then picks up her tea. She waits.

"When did you decide to come here?" Jenny asks. "Lewis said it was a little while later."

"A few months. I was in some kind of numb trance for a while; on autopilot, just floating through the days - but not in a good way. Then one day something simple triggered it - I don't know what - and it all came flooding out. I cried it seemed for days. It was a release, the beginning of grieving, I suppose; call it what you like. It was only after that I eventually began to start piecing things together, to think for myself again. I knew I had to force myself to do something."

"To come here," Jenny says, gathering up her own mug.

"Not at first. In the beginning the notion was just to get away. And then I had the idea of coming to find you." She pauses. "I'm sure Lewis told you a little about how I found Maunston Quay. How I found you."

"A little," she confirms. "Enough." They both sip their teas for a moment. "But did you come here for you or for me?"

Anna is about to seek clarification, if only to buy time, but she finds she knows what Jenny's question really means.

"For both of us, I hope. For me because I needed to break away from my old life, and anywhere but where I lived would probably have met that need. But when I decided to find out where you lived - find Maunston Quay - then it seemed right somehow. For me because it would allow me to close a difficult chapter in my life. But I thought of you too. I guessed that you might need some kind of closure too. That's what they call it, isn't it; 'closure'?"

"What made you think I needed anything," Jenny asks, unable to keep the barb from returning to her voice. "What did Ryan tell you about me?"

"Nothing really." Anna knows she cannot avoid the truth, that it would be unfair to do so. "Nothing. I didn't realise he had a sister until later. Until after your father died."

Jenny is unable to keep the shock of Ryan's deception from her face. She needs two hands to steady the mug and then return it to the table. Her hands shake a little. Anna knows she needs comforting - and knows she is in no position to assume that responsibility.

"Because he invited so few people to our weeding - just some of his Army colleagues - I assumed he had no family. He'd always been a little coy about your parents, but never led me to believe he was anything but an only child. When your father died I saw something with your name on it. I asked who you were. I thought you might have been another, earlier wife. He had to tell me then."

Anna waits for Jenny to respond, but she just drops her head and says nothing. Anna knows they must finish this trial together.

"What happened, Jenny?" she asks. "Why was he so angry? He never told me, no matter how much I asked him. And I wanted to know. Even then I knew I wanted to meet you."

A shadow flits across the room and Anna knows someone has just walked by outside. She rises and goes to the window where she glimpses Bradley's back as he heads towards his cottage.

"We had an argument." Jenny's voice, aimed towards somewhere between the kitchen and her knees, arrives a little muffled and softened. If there is trembling there - and Anna knows there must be - it has been filtered out by the room and the things in it, as if everything is suddenly on their side. "It was a stupid argument." Anna turns to face Jenny, staring at the back of her head. Other than that, she does not move. "He was frustrated with me. He had just been promoted; his life in the Army was going well. He could see a future all mapped out. He was enthusiastic, ambitious, full of life." Jenny pauses without moving. "I hope you saw some of that in him, at least. Anyway, I suppose he wanted the same for me, I don't know. He was frustrated with me though, with the life I was choosing to lead. He always said that I was better than a barmaid. It was the word he used when he wanted to upset me. I told him I was more than that; I tried to make out I was a business woman.

And he'd just laughed. He had never liked Tommy; not really. The day he really let fly - there was no stopping him. I was so shocked. He thought Tommy was beneath me, that I was letting myself down, settling for second-best not only in what I was doing but who I was doing it with. There must have been something that triggered it, that last day. It was the worst I'd seen him, the most vitriolic. And I was in the mood to fight back. It got out of hand. Nasty. We said some things - about what we were doing, about each other - that we never should have. He stormed out. I assumed he would come back at some point, that we would apologise and it would all be fine. But then there was something about our argument this time... It felt final in a way. But I never imagined that it would be; that I'd never see him again."

Seeing Jenny begin to shake is Anna's cue. She takes three steps towards the back of the sofa and places a hand on one of her shoulders. It is a touch rewarded by another as Jenny covers it with a hand of her own, and then she cries, openly. Anna stands and waits. She is aware, obtusely, of a smell coming from the kitchen. It is the smell of a cake that has been in the oven for too long. 'Let it burn' she thinks to herself; she knows she can make another. But this moment, this coincidence of feeling between her and Jenny is unique and precious. It is one of the reasons she came to Maunston Quay.

Chapter 10

No matter how often she hears it, there is something about the rhythm of the hammer's sound, the unleashing of controlled force transferred from arm to anvil, that stirs many things in her. It draws her towards the forge like a homing beacon; a pattern that allows her to recreate the feeling of Aubrey's heart beating against her chest. It is an encapsulation of life, of living; as if only in those moments is she a whole and complete being.

But now, unexpectedly, it has become something else. Ever since she had first seen Lewis and Anna walking arm-in-arm across the green, it has become the tattoo of time, like some giant clock ticking, counting down towards a silence she has no desire to experience. When the sensation first assailed her, she had wanted it to stop so badly that she stayed away from the forge when she knew Aubrey would be working. It was only for three days, but it was an abstinence which prevented her from satisfying other feelings too. Confronted by the gnawing angst such separation has caused her, Shirley knows a scale has been tipped. Needing to hear the sound and not wanting to hear it are mutually exclusive; it is a torment - sudden and unexpected - she needs to overcome.

As she walks toward the hammering once again, the day's warmth encouraging her to feel that finally Spring is really here, she does so with unusual purpose. It is a day, she knows, that has always been coming; a day which, the longer she has put it off, the more she has been able to blur and dissolve it into soft focus as if it were merely a child's fairy story, a fable, something unreal. But Lewis and Anna have, unwittingly, changed all that. Her disquiet returned again today as soon as they left the shop and she watched them walk away. In that moment, she had felt something over her shoulder and turned to look, assuming it would be Oscar. But there had been no-one there - no-one, perhaps, except the Big Bad Wolf or the Wicked Queen, or the Old Witch stirring her cauldron and preparing her brew. Shirley had shivered, removed her apron, shouted towards wherever Oscar may have been, and walked out of the shop into the sunshine.

Aubrey is standing behind the anvil when he sees her approaching. Something has made him look up just as he has paused to consider the line and form of his latest piece. His big order is nearly complete, one or two more of the smaller birds and he can deliver it. He would like to shield his eyes to better watch her approach, but with his hammer in his right hand and the tongs that hold the hot metal swallow in the other, he is unable to do so. Even so, he can tell there is something in her direct and purposeful stride that is unusual.

Rather than pause on the threshold as she usually does, Shirley marches straight into the forge and, taking advantage of Aubrey's hands being full - and knowing he would never relax his grip on either the hammer or the tongs in any uncontrolled fashion - she puts her hands to the sides of his face and bends it towards her. She kisses him softly, his mouth opening to find her tongue. She tastes him. It is a taste that surprises her always; it defies adjectives. There is nothing rough or artisanal about it. If anything, she thinks he tastes like a poet.

The kiss stops the drumming which brought her there, and she moves her mouth away and looks into his eyes. Saying nothing, she allows her hands to trace down from his face to his broad chest where they pause for a moment. She stares at them as if they belong to someone else, then watches as they track down the muscles of his arms to his hands, dirty with labour. She rests them there, squeezes slightly, then moves silently away and into the house. Shirley has delivered her message.

When Aubrey finds her a few minutes later, she is already in bed, waiting.

❊❊❊

In the stillness of the bedroom, the only beating of which Shirley is now aware is that of her heart, blood pumping through her veins, its pace beginning to slow. There is no hammering from the anvil now, replaced by the tempo of Aubrey's heart, the only thing she can hear it as she rests her head on his chest.

She had watched him remove his t-shirt, soiled from his morning at the forge, and refused his suggestion that he shower first. Her need to defeat the beat of time was too great. And now she feels victorious; victorious and determined that her triumph should not be a temporary or shallow one.

"Have you seen Lewis and Anna?" she asks, her voice trailing along the surface of the duvet and toward the end of the bed where their legs remain gently entwined.

"No," Aubrey says, simply, "I've been too busy."

""I'm pleased," she says, "for Lewis especially."

"But I've heard," he continues, as if she had not spoken.

"Heard? From who?"

"Richard. He came by yesterday. He told me. Said he'd seen them."

"Did he say anything?"

"About them?"

Shirley nods slightly. Aubrey feels her head move against his sternum.

"Not much. A bit like you, he was happy for them. I think more for her in his case."

"Well, she's had it rough too," Shirley agrees.

They remain silent for a moment.

"What did he want?" she asks.

"Who?"

"Richard."

"Nothing," says Aubrey in a fashion which, if you did not know him, could be interpreted as either evasion or truth. "He was just passing the time."

"Being neighbourly," Shirley suggests, and this time it is Aubrey who nods.

There is a quarter peel from the bells of the church clock and then silence. Shirley is suddenly struck by how quiet it is. Not only is the forge eerily still, but the sound of her blood - their blood - has calmed too. If it were possible, she would freeze this moment and keep it safe, as one she could always return to, as if it were what 'happy' should feel like. She thinks again of Lewis and Anna, and wonders if it is like this for them too.

And then from somewhere reality intrudes, not into the scene itself but into her thoughts. She knows this is only a transient intrusion, but in recognising it she remembers why she has come here this afternoon; why she is lying here in Aubrey's arms.

"Aubrey," she says quietly, still looking towards their feet, watching as he shifts a leg and three toes appear beyond the edge of the duvet. He says nothing, but she knows he is listening. It is minuscule, but she senses a slight tightening in the arm he has draped about her; that and a slackening in his fingers. "I need to know, Aubrey. I need to be sure. About us, I mean; about our future. That we have a future - a proper one - together." Pausing for an interruption that she knows will not come, she prepares to move on. He knows her well enough to know she hasn't yet finished. "All this is wonderful, but it's not perfect. I know there's no-one else - that there can't be anyone else - but I need to see that commitment. Call me a stupid, shallow woman if you want to, but I can't help myself."

She feels his arm gather her closer.

"Is it because of Lewis?" he asks eventually.

"What do you mean?"

"Seeing him, with Anna. Has that triggered something?"

"I don't think so," Shirley says, somewhat hesitantly. "Or maybe it has. I don't know. But whatever, I feel that now's the time, Aubrey. This has been coming, you know it has. You know what I've wanted for a long time - you've known it for almost as long as I've wanted it. Wanted you. And, for whatever reason, I feel as if the waiting needs to be over; that it's got to stop. I want to be with you, here, all the time. I don't want to just come over for the afternoon, or the evening. I want to be here when you wake up in the morning, when you get ready for the forge; I want to be here when you come in hot and aching from working too hard, ready with a drink, some food, whatever you need. And before you say anything, this isn't about getting away from Oscar or the shop; this isn't running away, this is running *to*."

She suddenly realises that she has begun crying, and senses her tears falling into the hairs of Aubrey's chest. She rarely cries, but she doesn't mind. She is not even sure whether her tears are those of joy or sadness. And in a way it doesn't matter, it only matters that they are there.

Aubrey moves his free hand to brush her cheek and then gently strokes her hair.

"I know," he says.

And from the way he says it, the way he is caressing her hair, Shirley is sure that he does know. She feels the depth of his understanding in those two little words. And yet she knows there is another little word as yet unspoken. It is a 'but'; the question of alternatives. If Aubrey were to ask her about options or compromise, she doesn't know how she would respond; she has been compromising for too long already. Once upon a time she would have been in a position to deliver an ultimatum more credibly, before she was in too deep; but not any longer. She is beyond the point where she can see any alternative and knows trying to pretend otherwise would be a bluff Aubrey would immediately see through, like a poker player sitting on a King-high and knowing their adversary is holding a fistful of Aces. Now it has become a simple game of heads or tails.

To his credit, Aubrey doesn't even try to raise the stakes. "I know," he says again. She turns her head for a moment to glance in the general direction of his face, needing more than that. Yet what can he say? He knows there is no point in replaying his old arguments from the past; they may still be valid, but like an elbow on an old jacket, they are wearing thin. He is not even sure if he believes them himself any more.

"What do *you* want, Aubrey," she asks, changing tack. "I feel like I'm always telling you what I want, forcing you to respond to that. But what do you want?"

"Don't you know?" he asks.

And there, she realises is her problem. She only thinks she understands what Aubrey wants, but he believes she knows for certain. He has the utmost confidence in her, while in contrast she needs proof from him. It may be nothing more than splitting hairs, but it gnaws at her, this imbalance. Everything she has been trying to communicate to Aubrey is related to that, to where they stand on the narrow line that divides knowing from assuming, that splits confidence from uncertainty.

She smiles to herself. It is a wistful smile. She should be glad Aubrey has confidence in her. She knows it is a rare and precious thing. Perhaps she has seen that too earlier today, burgeoning between Lewis and Anna as they take their first fragile steps together. Such steps begin with assumptions and trust; knowing comes later. And even if Aubrey knows - and she really believes he might - the equation is still not yet solved. What she is asking for, she realises, is the thing that will allow her to stand the same side of the line as he, to know as he knows.

"Yes," she says, the silence having gone on too long, "I think I do. It's just that…"

Finding the words to encapsulate all she has been thinking is, she sees, impossible. But she wants not to let him down, to try, and in trying make it easier for him.

"Just what?" he says, still stroking her hair.

"I just want to be certain. More certain, I mean."

And that is what Aubrey cannot understand. How can she not be certain? How, if she feels about him as he feels about her, can she need any more confirmation? What else is there? Yet even as he asks himself that question, he knows the answer. He has always known the answer. And as unnecessary as he feels it may be for him, the more vital it seems to be for her.

He tilts his body forward and kisses the top of her head.

"You know I love you," he says as he releases his hold on her and slides himself to the side of the bed. "You do know that?"

"Yes," she says, moving herself upwards so that her head is resting on his pillow. "Yes, I do know that."

He smiles and stands up. She watches as he moves away from the bed and towards the bathroom. Welcome though it is - and not as unusual as it would once have been - his statement does not satisfy her; it is perhaps a placeholder, little more.

And to be fair to Aubrey, as he turns on the shower and waits for the hot water to come through, he knows it too.

❋ ❋ ❋

When the church clock strikes four, Aubrey is stepping into the shower. In the church, Richard is undertaking the monthly dusting of his office with his usual lack of enthusiasm. In the shop, Oscar, frustrated that Shirley has been away for too long, is checking a list in readiness for their dry goods supplier who will be dropping-off their weekly order in the morning. In 'The Anchor', Tommy is busying himself cleaning tables in the conservatory and checking that the menus on each are still serviceable and not too creased or stained. In a way, each man is preoccupied by routine and the need to ensure that things are as they should be: clean or dust-free, well-stocked or presentable.

In his own way, Lewis is following a similar theme. He is bent over the open door of his washing machine to retrieve his weekly load of 'coloureds' when he hears the knock at the door. He stands, draping the damp socks he holds in his hands over the bottom rail of a drying rack. He knows that it cannot be Anna; she has recently begged leave of him to attack a pile of ironing that, she said, 'has been waiting an age for her attention'. And she no longer knocks in any case. He has arranged to go to the pub for a pint with Bradley later, but it is far too early for him to call. History tells him that there are only a limited number of people it could be; cold callers and Jehovah's Witnesses rarely make it to Maunston Quay, unless they have managed to get themselves lost whilst seeking out more fertile ground.

Having recognised all that, Lewis still manages to be surprised when he finds Jenny on his doorstep.

"Jenny," he says unnecessarily.

"Can I?" she asks.

He steps aside to let her in. Fully briefed by Anna about their encounter two days previously, Lewis has managed to resolve a number of things internally - though if pushed to say exactly what those things are, he would be hard pressed to do so. He had expressed himself both pleased and relieved that their meeting - brought about by Jenny's surprise visit - seemed to have gone well. "As well as it could possibly have - in the end", was how Anna had put it. Lewis had never considered what might come next; perhaps he harboured an assumption that a thawing would follow, after which - well, after which he hadn't been entirely sure. Just as he was now entirely unsure as he sat opposite Jenny in his own lounge.

She is casting her eyes around the room - a room in which she had never set foot since Lewis's occupation of it, in spite of an oft-hinted desire that it should be otherwise. The visit being overdue - at least from her perspective - she looks about as if taking the room's measure and, in doing so, also the measure of the man. That her eyes rest for a moment on the photographs on the bookcase is not lost on him.

"Sorry to arrive unannounced," she offers.

Lewis tries a laugh.

"I was just rescuing some damp laundry from the machine, so it's not an unwelcome interruption."

"There's always something, isn't there?" she suggests, less in the manner of philosophical theory than small-talk.

Lewis lets it go and waits.

"You know, of course, that I went next door?" Jenny pauses. "To see Anna." She allows the words to fall out of her mouth more of their own volition than at her instigation. Lewis notes the way she says 'Anna' almost as if it is a word from a foreign language, one that Jenny is struggling to get to grips with.

"Yes," he nods. "She told me."

"About it all? What we talked about?"

"A summary, only. And from her perspective, obviously; what she thought about it, how she felt."

"Which was what?" Jenny returns her eyes to Lewis having finished taking in the room.

"That it was," he pauses, slightly disconcerted by her sudden stare, "a good start. A beginning. A breaking of the ice, if you like." He waits for some acknowledgement, then "Is that fair?"

"There was a lot to talk about," Jenny avoids the question. "In the end. A lot of ground to cover. Gaps to fill in."

"History can be like that, can't it?"

"Like what?"

"Oh, not everyone has the whole story, the complete picture. You need more than one person to see things in the round."

"Is that what you think?" Jenny asks, almost implying that the idea is not his, as if he may have stolen it. "Have you ever only had half the story?"

Lewis laughs again, this time a little involuntarily.

"All my life. And in all walks of life," he confirms, on safer ground now. "Whether it's just me, or something that men are cursed with, I don't know. I often think that we never quite see the full picture."

At this Jenny smiles. It is a slightly melancholy smile, layered with many different stories and experiences.

"Based on my experience with Tommy, I'd say it was a man thing." She pauses again. "And also with you."

"Me?"

"Don't worry," she says, trying to dissipate the criticism she realises she has allowed to slip into her voice. "It *is* a man thing. Often you can't see the thing that's right in front of your faces - or don't have the gumption to actually look around whatever's there to see what's on the other side."

"So we're all cursed then?" Lewis suggests, keen to pick up on the almost conciliatory tone Jenny seems to have struck.

"You less than most" is what she says - and Lewis does not fail to miss what she has left out. "Tommy is hopeless," she offers, "Ryan was worse than that. Or at least that's how I remember him. Maybe how we all remember him, I don't know." There is a slight delay, as if a tape has slipped from its spool and Jenny is trying to rewind it. "But I didn't come to talk about Ryan. Not directly."

"You talked about him with Anna?"

Jenny ignores him again.

"I came to talk about you, Lewis." She notes his surprise and twists the knife. "About us."

"'Us'?"

She laughs. It is a somewhat hollow and meaningless sound.

"There you go, looking at things all wrong again. I know what you're thinking. 'What "us"? There is no "us".' And you're right, of course. But there could have been. There could have been, Lewis. You know that don't you? I know you do."

Lewis, sensing her waiting for some kind of response, offers the slightest nod, suddenly nervous about saying anything at all; afraid of what he thinks he can see, and concerned about what he can't.

"At least there could have been for a little while. Don't ask me when, or why, or why not. It doesn't matter now, does it? You have 'moved on', I believe the phrase is. And that's why I'm here. To make it official."

"Official?"

Jenny shakes her head as she leans forward from where she is sitting to place a hand on Lewis's knee. She allows it to rest there for a moment. Lewis looks at it, both surprised and relieved that he feels unthreatened by her action.

"I'm letting you go, Lewis. Of course I don't need to do I? I mean, after all there isn't really anything to let go of - as well you know." She pauses. "Call it a gift of some kind if you want to, me giving you up. Ending what I'm sure you've seen as some kind of bizarre pursuit. You don't need to deny it," she says, just in case he were about to interrupt. "Whether it was or wasn't hardly matters any more, does it? Not really. It's not important. And before you say anything, I'm not doing it for me; I'm doing it for you, because you need to hear it, to know it. So that you're not scared of me any more. I don't want you to be scared of me."

He has never realised until now that was exactly what he had been, scared. Whether it was being scared of Jenny as a person or what she represented, he is unable to say. He had assumed he had merely been nervous or unwilling; at best unready, not a risk-taker. But now that she has framed it for him, he thinks he can see it for what it was. But when was the last time he had been scared? Those were different and difficult circumstances surely? In the desert, for sure; when Emma died, for certain. But since then? Moving to Maunston Quay had been frightening in its own way without doubt, but that had been benign trepidation. As he tries to weigh Jenny's words, to assimilate them and translate them into something that has relevance and meaning for him, he thinks of Anna, and wonders why he has never been scared of her. Why, when they were sitting at the end of the jetty, putting his arm about her felt the most natural thing in the world. If there were a fog about him it is beginning to clear as Jenny continues.

"I'm lying, of course. At least in part. It isn't just for you, this nonsense about letting you go. It's for me too. Maybe more so, who can say? Perhaps I just need to hear myself saying the words; perhaps doing so releases me from this stupid bondage I have myself entangled in." She pauses, but not to elaborate.. "Is that fanciful? I don't care. But it's of my own making, of course, and because of that I need to be the one to cut myself loose. It isn't something someone else can do for me - not effectively anyway. And if I am going to 'move on' too - though to where I'm not quite sure yet; backwards probably - then it has to be me that does it. Do you see that?"

It is a rhetorical question, Lewis knows that; but having spoken so little, he feels the need to contribute something.

"Yes."

Jenny laughs again, though this time there is a degree of genuine amusement in her voice.

"Of course you don't! Though it is sweet of you to say you do. But do you know why? It's not about freeing you, but freeing me too.

It's freeing me so that I can carry on liking you. Can you imagine what it would be like to see you, happy, with someone else, if I hadn't released you? Can you? Torture. And under those circumstances how could I be happy for you? How could I see you in the pub and not feel resentment or anger or something? So I have to let you go. It has to be my decision, my choice - no matter what you say or do." She pauses and allows her eyes to wander the room again. "You might be surprised by this, but I quite like Anna."

"Really?" Lewis is unable to help himself. Luckily - and for the third time - Jenny ignores him.

"Of course it helps that she was married to Ryan. The link is important. It endows her with something I suppose, at least in my eyes; the fact that he loved her." She allows a thought to settle. "Well. Maybe I was going too far too soon. Maybe I should have said that I think I will be able to like her. Is that better? And one of the other reasons that might be true is because you like her Lewis - so perhaps she has a head start there as well. And so, if you are going to be around a little while longer - both of you, that is - then it seems right and proper that I give you a chance. The two of you. All of us." She looks back at him. "Maybe I should just shut up now. After all, isn't it about time you said something?"

For some reason Lewis stands and walks behind where Jenny is sitting to stand at the window. Outside everything is as it always has been. Inside - right here and now - he feels as if his life is returning, journeying back towards something it once was. And he knows he has to be grateful, grateful to everyone who is making that possible.

"Thank you," he says, still staring at the sea.

When there is no response, he twists slightly to be able to look back into the room. Jenny is now perched at an angle on the edge of her chair looking his way. There is an expression on her face that Lewis has never seen before; one he is unable to decipher. But it is far from hostile.

"I mean," he pauses trying to find better words, but cannot, "thank you."

"What for?"

She is smiling as she asks the question. Lewis is certain that she knows why, and recognises that this is part of the deal, his acknowledgement, his rite of passage. He has to balance his side of the equation.

"For wanting to like me. For wanting to like Anna. For making it easier."

"For making it possible," she suggests.

Lewis nods, a single inclination of the head that recognises the strange supremacy of her position. He will not accept that she has released him; how can he? He has never felt bound by her in that way. He is gratified that she has articulated what he felt, that the hold she had over him was one of fear - and he is pleased to know it is a feeling that never need haunt him again.

"I can't say what comes next," he continues, glancing at the photographs of Emma and Stoner and Bridger. "None of us can, of course. But it is good to have something to look forward to. An opportunity. A chance, if you like."

"Even if it ends up not going where you want it to?"

There is an echo of disappointment in her voice, of failure; the tragedy of wanting, yet remaining unfulfilled. Lewis wonders if she is thinking of him, or of her life with Tommy. Or of the past she missed sharing with Ryan because of a stupid argument. Maybe Jenny is right. A woman might know, be able to interpret the clues, read the signs. Perhaps that was what, in the end, helped Anna to build the bridge between them. He finds himself smiling.

"Something funny?" Jenny asks.

He shakes his head.

"No, not really. Just a little awe or amazement - whatever the right word is."

"About?"

"About how things turn out sometimes. Not the bad, but the fact that good can follow bad. Eventually."

Jenny glances at the bookcase again.

"You still miss her dreadfully, don't you?"

He is surprised at how perceptive she is. And then finds himself amazed at the entire interview, how she has behaved, handled herself. The Jenny before him now is one he has never seen before; either that or seen but never recognised.

He takes a step towards her and places his hand on her shoulder. She covers it with one of her own, and then, a moment later, stands.

"I should let you get back to sorting out your laundry before it starts to crease or smell or something."

He laughs.

"And that would never do, would it?"

❋❋❋

In all the years he has been living at Maunston Quay, Lewis has never put a single toe into the sea. The closest he has come is transferring from Bradley's boat when it has been loosely moored at the jetty, the occasional splash from an errant wave hitting the side of the vessel and sending renegade drops of salt water in his general direction. But now, as he sits half way along the jetty on the side facing Simon's Crag, looking down at the water lapping gently beneath him, he feels the time has come. He is unsure as to why he thinks the gesture is important, nor why now is the right time. The water will be cold, icy. Indeed, Lewis assumes that the water will always be cold here, fed by nothing but North Sea currents, chilled for a large part of the year by easterly winds. The sun is out, yes, and his fleece lies discarded at his side after a brief but vigorous walk up and down the crag, but he knows it is not truly hot, his own warmth generated more from the inside out.

He glances up towards the cottages and then lifts his right leg up onto the wooden planks. After removing the attendant shoe and sock, he repeats the operation with his left and then stands. Picking up his fleece with one hand and his shoes with the other (socks tucked neatly inside them), he makes his way back to the steps then down onto the sand. About six feet before the edge of the water, he reaches up and places all the things he is carrying back onto the jetty, then turns his attention to the rolling up of his trouser legs. It feels ceremonial.

Pausing to stare at his now exposed ankles and feet, he is struck by the absurdity of what he is about to do. And yet, paradoxically, it seems an action that is long overdue - and one where it is too late to change his mind. He steps forward one pace and looks back at the footprints he has just made, prints that are quickly absorbed by the damp sand. Two further paces ahead, the water laps benignly against the beach, today a rhythm more akin to a calm inland lake than the frontier of the North Sea. The edge of the tide.

When the water hits his toes, he gasps involuntarily, immediately convinced that no word exists in the English language that can possibly describe how cold the sea is. And yet there should be, surely. For an island nation, shouldn't the English have as many words for the sea and how to describe it as the Eskimos do snow? Gritting his teeth, he edges forwards another foot and stops. The next slow wave passes over his feet to caress his ankle. It feels more slap than kiss, but one he is prepared to endure. He thinks if he waits long enough he will not notice the cold; the sea may even begin to feel warm. And so he glances up towards the horizon, checking to see if there is any activity which might divert his attention from a searing cold that is now verging on pain.

Satisfied, a few seconds later Lewis retreats, stepping back the three paces to where he stood initially and from where he can easily retrieve his clothes, never taking his eyes from the sea. "Well then", he says to himself. He is unsure if his small experiment has been a success, partly because he was never certain what he was trying to achieve; and yet, obtusely, he does feel as if an exchange of some kind has taken place, as if in submitting himself to the sea he has been able to close out a chapter or find the last stubborn clue in a crossword puzzle.

As he makes his way barefoot back towards his cottage, Lewis feels the sand becoming gradually dryer, and with dryness comes marginally greater warmth. Pausing at the steps up to the road he looks back to see what kind of a trail he has left behind. Closer to the sea, and where they still remain, his footprints are more distinct, definite; but here where the going is a little harder, the drier sand offers little more than scuff marks as testament to his excursion. He wants to interpret them somehow. Perhaps he might try a painting one day. He is sure 'footsteps in the sand' is a little trite, but if they are his footprints and it's Maunston's sand…

Ten minutes later, his feet washed and adorned with clean socks and his favourite slippers, Lewis is sitting on the sofa, 'The Observer' from the previous weekend open on the cushions alongside him. It is a small ritual that sees him collect the paper from Shirley and Oscar's on a Sunday morning and then take the whole week to make his leisurely way through it. His news can be a week old. An affectation born from habit; doing so has become one of many repeated patterns he has adopted since his arrival at Maunston Quay. In the early days such routines had acted as his transport allowing safe passage from dawn to dusk. Later they were just the things he did, and some - like the newspaper - became fixed into how he chose to to live his life. The Sunday paper, a pint with Bradley on a Tuesday evening, the long walk on a Sunday. But now he is beginning to feel the solid ground he has built for himself begin to shift, and Anna is the earthquake.

It is a good thing, he knows that. Better than a good thing. Yet like the cold of the sea, he is unable to find the right words to describe how nerve-wracking the prospect is. More than once he has thought of himself as a castaway of sorts; a fancy that living in the cottage and staring out into the sea day-in, day-out, allowed him to perpetuate. And perhaps like a castaway he has begun to tame his environment, to get it to work for him, to bend it to the way he wants to live. It has imposed conditions on him too, he knows that. For all the soft caresses of Maunston, she can still be a harsh mistress, and occasionally the pressure she places on him and the restrictions she enforces are hard to bear. Most often such trials manifest themselves in a sense of loneliness, and even though these episodes have receded, there are still moments.

He glances at the photograph of Emma and recalls Jenny's words. Of course he misses her. But they - and he still feels it is a 'they' - have learned how to cope. Yet now there is Anna, and with Anna - he has suddenly realised - there is something to be afraid of again. Having invested in nothing but himself for five years or so, and having built a life that is independently his, he looks at Emma and tries to remember what it was like to be a half of something. He has learned to be an individual whole again, but knows he is on the verge of a journey back to a state he can only recall through fond remembrance. And Lewis recognises the need to sacrifice part of himself - the part he has so successfully subdued in recent years - if he and Anna are to 'work', whatever that might mean. If he was unaware he had been afraid of Jenny, now Lewis is painfully aware of the new fear assaulting him. It is fear of failure - the failure of a self-contained 'whole' comprehensively unable to revert back to being a loving and successful 'half' again. And there is the fear of loss too; that, at some point along the way, having found Anna, he might then lose her. It is a terror which, unbidden, has him question how he truly feels. It is demanding to know if it is worth the risk, if he wouldn't be safer to remain as a castaway. He wonders if he really wants or needs to be rescued.

Perhaps he knows the answer well enough: that there is too much potential, too much promise not to take the risk. The sensation of someone having placed their hand in yours, the brush of their lips against your skin, the warmth to be extracted from a hug; all these are things denied him for far too long. Or luxuries he has denied himself. He has become an emotionally poor man, denuded of those things that give a spark to life and a meaning to existence. He suddenly remembers talking with Bridger once, a quiet moment as they waited for the sun to rise sufficiently to permit them to go out on patrol again. It was a part of the day that scared Bridger the most - not because of the thought of the patrol and the dangers it must possess, but because he knew that this could be his last sunrise, the last time he might think of his family back home, and what death might steal from him. It was not his life he was worried about, he had said, but losing the ability to feel love. A strange confession for an Army grunt armed to the teeth and prepared to kill if necessary. Lewis had not really understood what he had meant until now. If he were here now, Bridger would simply point out that he had the chance to feel love again, and that was what made life worth living.

Lewis checks his watch. If he were to relate his dilemma to Bradley, who he is due to see in less than an hour, he is certain the advice would be the same. He knows Bradley's perspective is a different one and the experiences that have come to form it are to some degree removed from Bridger's; but Lewis is certain that their counsel would be the same. Resting his hand on the newspaper almost as if some greater wisdom might seep through the print and into him via his skin, he realises that there is probably no-one he knows who would warn him against taking the plunge. Not even Jenny. Indeed, he knows that in many respects the die is already cast. Anna has placed her wager on that dormant part of him; it is a gamble as much on her own self as it is on him. They are, of course, living parallel lives; Lewis can see that. If he is thinking these things, having these doubts, then surely she must be too? But if so, he gets no sense of it. She has seemed calmly certain over the last two or three days, as if there were no risk involved at all. Perhaps that is all part and parcel of being a woman - and his own inability to understand it (as Jenny might argue) simply a result of his being a man.

❊ ❊ ❊

"Walk?" Lewis asked.

Anna had checked her watch.

"Do we have time? What time does the meeting start?"

"We've time for a short one."

She had been the first to retrieve her boots and now stands outside Lewis's cottage looking up towards Simon's Crag. She wonders if that is where he intends to go, though cannot dismiss the notion that it doesn't really matter. There was a tone underlying the way he'd asked the question that told her he was not going to be denied and that for some reason getting out of the house was, at this precise moment, important to him. Already she can decipher some of the things Lewis says, not in the words he uses but in the way he relays them. As she waits she vows to see if she is able to catch how *she* says things, to judge if there is a reaction from Lewis based on something other than her words. Yet even though it was a normal enough suggestion, she finds herself slightly on edge. 'Walk'. It is a simple and innocent enough word, but just then it carried a veneer that was new to her and one which she has not yet learned to penetrate.

"How was Bradley last night?" she asks as Lewis emerges from his front door.

"Same as ever," Lewis says as he takes her hand and they begin to walk along the road. "Sanguine, philosophical, undemonstrative. All the things you would normally expect from him."

"Warm, funny, and not a little charming?" she suggests.

"Hey!" Lewis tugs her arm and forces her closer to him. "Just watch it, miss!"

She laughs.

"Well isn't he those things?"

"I couldn't possibly comment."

They make their way up to the edge of the dunes and then onto one of the sandy paths that weave between the tufty slabs of hardy grass and gorse that punctuate there; Lewis walks in front, the path - such as it is - too narrow for the two of them to travel side-by-side. Usually, either individually or when they have walked this way together, they keep to the beach, but today Lewis steers them along the crown of the dunes until the path runs out. He pauses where it ends and waits the moment needed to allow Anna to catch up. They can either turn right and down onto the strand proper or left and strike inland, either following a rough track that mimics the shape of the out-of-reach shoreline further west or cut towards the fields and a path that takes them over the railway line and eventually leads them in a wide arc back into the village proper.

He takes her hand again and heads left.

"I thought we'd take the scenic route."

"Won't we be late?" she asks.

"It takes somewhere between thirty-five and forty minutes," he says, checking the watch on his free arm. "That is, if we don't get distracted."

She laughs.

"And do you intend to get distracted?"

"Well," he says, turning just enough so that he can kiss her lightly on her forehead, "I don't have a history of it, but there have been some strange things happening recently!"

"Unprecedented," Anna suggests, smiling.

"Totally and undeniably unprecedented."

Apart from the sounds of their feet brushing through the long grass and the occasional comment about the landscape, they walk on in silence. After a few minutes they see a buzzard wheeling above a copse of trees a little way in the distance and pause to watch it.

"There didn't used to be many around a few years ago," Lewis observes, "at least not when I first came here; not that I can remember anyway."

Shielding her eyes, Anna traces her gaze across the sky as she follows the bird's glide.

"It's amazing how they can be so graceful."

"And efficient," Lewis suggests, his eyes fixed on the bird too, "being able to climb and soar like that with so little effort. It seems a paradox that it uses all its effort to remain still." Then right on cue the bird starts flapping it's wings vigorously to remain stationary in the air, holding its position both vertically and horizontally. "There!" he says, a little triumphant tone in his voice.

"Right on cue!"

Anna looks up at Lewis who remains rapt, intent on the bird. She examines his still face, its lack of motion allowing her to see it in a way she has not previously, as if suddenly privy to normally hidden insights. It occurs to her that when she looks at other people's faces they are almost always on the move; the mouth because they are talking, the eyes because they are watching, scanning. Heads turn as people look and speak; there is always motion. Always. Except for fleeting moments like this, here and now. For a moment she feels as if she might be an anthropologist, examining a subject - and then the moment is gone.

Lewis, sensing her gaze upon him, turns to look at her.

"What?" he asks, seeing a look on her face that seems a mix of speculation and concern.

"I was just wondering," she starts, then stops.

"Wondering what?" Lewis squeezes her hand gently.

"I was wondering if you were a bit like that buzzard," she says.

Lewis laughs softly; a little nervously if he is honest.

"Why? Because I have been waiting for my prey?!"

She releases his hand and slides her arm around his waist, looking away to where the bird had been hovering. The sky is now empty.

"No, of course not."

"Well? You have to tell me now; you can't keep that a secret from me. We have no secrets." Lewis knows this last statement is a risk, but he has said it before he thinks about it. The notion is suddenly out in the open and he cannot recall it. He wonders if he would want to, were he able. And in wondering if it is true, he realises he wants it to be, desperately.

"It suddenly occurred to me that you might have been spending all your energy keeping still," she says quietly, eyes still fixed on the distance, scanning the tree-line for the bird.

"And you don't mean by not moving, do you?" Lewis asks, conscious of a more subtle undertone. "I haven't moved physically, of course - well, not for a little while anyway. And that has taken almost no effort at all!" He tries to lighten his tone, but can tell, even before he speaks, that she is being serious. It is a tone he had been keen to strike at some point, but she has beaten him to it.

"No," she confirms, answering his question. "And anyway, I wonder if Maunston has the ability to induce a benign kind of paralysis of sorts."

"You mean of not wanting to move away?"

She nods.

"First Bradley, then you - not to mention Tommy or Oscar or Richard."

"Do you feel it too?" he asks.

She nods again, then tries to absorb herself further within him.

"Though *you* might have something to do with that."

It is a cue, Lewis knows that; the chance for him to shift the agenda to what is bothering him. But he knows Anna is not yet finished.

"So if it isn't the lack of physical movement that's taken all my energy, what is it?" he prompts. "What lack of movement makes me like a buzzard?"

"I don't know. The emotional, maybe." She lets the idea hang between them, partly to see if he is going to respond and partly because she is not sure how to continue. Lewis says nothing. "As if it has taken all your energy to remain detached, aloof almost; as if all the effort has gone into building a wall around yourself. For protection."

She wonders if she has gone too far.

Lewis bends down and kisses her, softly, briefly.

"Well it was obviously a rubbish wall if you were able to simply walk through it!"

"You know what I mean," she protests. "Or am I being unfair, way off the mark?"

It is Lewis's turn to look over the fields towards the copse.

"Unfair? I don't think so. And maybe you're right. But if so, it wasn't deliberate. Or conscious. Maybe that's the better word. If I needed to settle, maybe it was more than simply in terms of the place. Maybe I needed the distance Maunston gives me - gave me - and the wall, as you call it, was more like a moat."

"To protect you from the past?" she asks, looking up at him now.

"To protect me from the future, probably." He pauses. "Perhaps that was what scared me about Jenny. Maybe I was frightened that I was staring into a future, and I wasn't ready for a future because the ghosts hadn't settled."

"I'm sorry," Anna says. There is the thinnest sliver of regret in her voice.

"What for?"

"Threatening you with a future."

Lewis stares into her eyes. He knows in part she is joking, but he can see there is a nervousness about her, a vulnerability that is in danger of wiping away all her confidence. It is as if she has been told that the premise upon which she has laid a wager might be nothing but smoke and mirrors. It is the question Lewis has been asking himself but cloaked in different garb.

"You haven't threatened me with anything," he says as softly as he can. "You have given me a glimpse of possibilities, of how life might be. Again. Yes, there are echoes of the past, of course there are. You have reminded me of how I used to be, the person I once was."

There is something in his manner that prevents her from taking his words at face value.

"Are you saying that may not be a good thing?"

He smiles.

"No. Quite the opposite. I'm saying that's a wonderful thing."

"I can hear a 'but' there, camouflaged in your voice Lewis."

"Really?"

"I think so." She waits a moment. "I hope it's not me."

Lewis laughs and suddenly wraps both his arms around her and lifts her off the ground, turning as he does so. Anna lets out a little shriek of surprise.

"How could it possibly be you?" he says having delivered her back to earth. "You are the most wonderful thing that has happened to me in - I don't know how long."

"Since your 'bromance' with Bradley probably!" She laughs.

"That's a disgraceful thing to say!" he laughs, and then in a mock hurt voice, "We're just good friends."

He turns and they begin to walk on, the path wide enough here for them to remain close, his arm about her.

"It isn't you at all," he says, carrying on with the thread. "If there is a 'but' then it's with me, with the questions I suddenly have to ask myself."

"Such as?"

"Am I ready? Am I brave enough?"

"Brave enough?"

It is Lewis's turn to nod.

"Maybe like that buzzard. If I've been spending all my time and energy keeping still, am I ready to move, to dive, to speed through the air again? If there's a 'but' then it's hidden in there somewhere."

Anna says nothing, knowing it's a question she cannot answer for him as much as she might want to be able to.

"Can I ask you something?" Lewis says.

"Of course."

"How do you feel? I mean, what about you and standing still, or moving on; of suddenly being propelled forward towards a future you probably hadn't planned or seen coming? Does it frighten you too, just a little bit?"

Anna stops walking, forcing Lewis to do so perhaps a stride in front of her. He turns. She takes both her hands in his.

"We're so similar, you and I. Perhaps that helps to make things easier, for me at least." She smiles, but only for a moment. "Do I have a 'but' lurking somewhere? Probably, but it hasn't come knocking and I'm not going looking for it either. Am I nervous? If I were to think about it, yes. And probably a little bit scared, or frightened even. Do I worry, about myself, about you? I could do, but I don't want to. What's the point?" She shakes his hands gently, as if she were trying to release something that was locked up within him. "Of course none of this was planned; how could it have been? How could I have known that in coming here for one reason I have suddenly, somehow, found something completely different; something special? Something that could be really special. I don't want to analyse it or worry about it. If I have learned one thing it's that if you have something precious then you should grab it, hold on to it, because it could be taken away from you - from any of us - at any time. If you are asking me if I'm afraid of that, then I have another question for you. Would you rather not try, not take the risk, and never know? Would you prefer to be safe and alone rather than sharing and caring and being cared for? Do I want what I've had in the past that was wonderful - even the chance of having that again? If you have to ask me those questions..."

She allows the sentence to die, to be picked up by the breeze and dispersed through the grasses and the wild flowers beginning to bud.

"No," Lewis says, "I don't want to ask. I don't need to ask. I trust you already; how could I not?"

"But am I nervous, and frightened, and unsure? Am I worried where this - us - might lead me? Am I afraid that it will all get stolen away from me again one day? Yes to all of those things, Lewis. Of course, yes. And of course it must be yes for you too, because of your past - and all that time you've spent going nowhere. But I don't want to be nervous or frightened, so I simply won't allow myself to be. I want to go to the pub with you, hand in hand; I want to go back home later - because it feels a little like home - and I want to make love to you. And I want to wake up in the morning next to you with a new day ahead of me, of us, with the prospect of being able to do whatever we like. And right now I want that today and tomorrow and for as many days as I can see ahead. And that's what keeps the 'but' away for me. I want to soar and dive again, Lewis. I hadn't realised that's what I wanted until I met you, and now I know. And look, now you've made me cry, you selfish brute!"

And Anna is indeed crying. Lewis frees his hands and holds them up to her face where he brushes her tears away with his fingers. And before he knows it, he finds that he is crying too, which makes Anna laugh suddenly and brightly. And as they embrace, a buzzard rises above the tree-line and soars away into the blue.

❅ ❅ ❅

"Finally!" Tommy's voice vaults through the bar from where he's sitting as all heads turn at the sound of the front door being opened with unusual vigour.

"So there you are," says Bradley somewhat less demonstrably, unable to keep a smile from his lips.

It is evident that Lewis and Anna have been running, and it would be reasonable to assume that their extreme haste has been brought about by leaving the cottages late. Lewis laughs, waves and heads to the bar where Jenny happens to be waiting, while Anna smiles and walks immediately towards the table. Perhaps they will tell the truth a little later on, though Lewis already feels their having at least one secret is no bad thing - especially when it is an unimportant one, in the grand scheme of things. Anna suggesting they race across the green to the pub was, if anything, juvenile in the extreme; a youthfulness only matched by Lewis's offer to give her five seconds head start.

Still breathing heavily as he reaches the bar, he is still wondering how he managed to miscalculate so badly; so poorly, in fact, that it was only in the final stride he succeeded in overtaking Anna who had proved herself to be much faster on her feet than he had anticipated.

"Worried about being late?" Jenny asks, unable to suppress a smile.

"Not really," says Lewis, pretending to be less out-of-breath than he actually is. "Just late."

Jenny nods.

"The usual?"

"Please."

"What kept you?" asks Bradley as Anna takes her seat next to him, she having already said hello to Richard and Tommy.

"Nothing, really," she says, trying not to laugh. "Let's just call it a miscalculation."

"A miscalculation is it?" says Richard, looking back towards the bar where Lewis is already making short work of his first pint. "Well at least it seems to have been a happy one."

"You haven't missed anything," Tommy offers, evidently trying to restore a degree of decorum, "we were just about to start without you."

Anna looks round the bar.

"No Shirley or Oscar?"

"They've cried off," says Tommy, unable to hide his disappointment.

"I'm led to believe," Richard says, cutting in, "they have a crisis which requires both their attention."

"A crisis?" Anna's demeanour changes at the word.

"Oh, nothing too dramatic," Richard smiles. "At least I don't think so. Or I assume not. Probably just a poor choice of word on my part."

Lewis and Jenny arrive at the table, Lewis carrying what's left of his pint, Jenny with Anna's gin and tonic. She places it on the table in front of Anna and offers a small, private smile, almost as if she has no desire to let the others see she has weakened, changed her spots. But it is a signal not lost on Richard, nor on Lewis who manages to catch her eye before she resumes her seat next to Tommy.

"Right then," Tommy says in his best chairman voice, "let's get started, shall we?" He waits for them to dutifully turn their attention towards him before he carries on. "So, this is a follow-on from the meeting we held, what a month ago now."

Jenny interrupts to provide the date. The odd glance is exchanged around the table.

"I know you all assumed I wasn't paying attention at the time," she protests, feigning hurt. "But I was - and I made notes afterwards." She picks up a piece of paper that had been laying on the table in front of her and waves it in their general direction.

Richard applauds in a way which is clearly appreciative rather than condescending.

"Yes, thanks love," Tommy says, vaguely thrown by an unmistakably positive wave of feeling towards his wife. "I don't think there were any specific actions we agreed at the time - " he glances to Jenny who shakes her head - "though one or two of you might subsequently have chosen to show some initiative." His voice betrays the certainty that no-one will have. "So in that case, this is really a chance for us to see if we've had any further thoughts since then. If anyone has had any more ideas."

As Tommy pauses and scans around the table, glances are exchanged between the participants, each one expressing something unstated.

"From what I can remember," it is Anna who speaks first. All eyes turn in her direction. "From what I can remember, I had a sense that we might have decided - in a round-about way - to focus on next year rather than this." She glances at Lewis seeking his support, but it is Richard who speaks next.

"I think that's right. I mean, that's what I recall too; and I think it's the right approach. We've so little time to prepare for this summer."

"And so much time to prepare for next."

If they had been less able to control themselves, one or two of those who heard Jenny make that third contribution might have been forgiven for emitting a gasp of surprise. That there is none is probably just as well, but Jenny is not so insensitive as to miss the impact her simple statement has made.

"Indeed," says Richard, picking up the thread. "I think the ladies have it to a tee. Surely it makes sense for us to plan ahead in something of a more structured way. One of the reasons we always struggle is because we never give ourselves enough time."

"And now we have," says Lewis. "Now we can plan ahead."

His immediate glance toward Anna is also noted by their friends, though none of them would have any idea as to the conversation in the field on the way over, their debate about what the future might hold, about faith and fear. He looks up and smiles at Bradley who, he knows, has been watching the two of them steadily throughout. Bradley offers the very slightest of nods. If anyone comes close to understanding, Lewis is pretty sure that it's Bradley.

"Is that agreed," says Richard hopefully, "can we focus on next year? What do you think, Tommy?"

Whether Tommy has been able to read the subtexts in the conversation thus far, comprehend the messages in body language, or the meaning of a glance or smile is open to debate, but he understands the words well enough. For him they carry weight, potential, the promise of another year. All Tommy really wants is certainty of some kind. He has wondered recently if that is all he has ever wanted. He glances at Jenny who at that precise moment has her eyes focussed on Anna. He can tell she has registered what Richard said, and he knows she is preparing to respond to him, to speak for both of them. Tommy sees them looking at him, but more than anything else he wants Jenny to speak next.

❈ ❈ ❈

"I must confess I was a trifle surprised," Richard admits a little later, sitting with Lewis apart from the others who are still gathered at the bar.

"At?"

Richard reassures himself that no-one is in earshot before responding.

"Jenny."

"Ah."

"I don't think I've ever seen her quite as engaged at these meetings of ours; always aloof, disinterested. But not tonight it seems."

Lewis recognises Richard's barely disguised hook and chooses to dodge the bait for the moment.

"Yes, it did seem a little - out of character."

"And so positive about next year - relatively speaking, that is." Richard pauses, again scanning for eavesdroppers. Finding none, he lowers his voice nonetheless. "And why is that, do you think?"

Lewis laughs quietly.

"Why ask me, Richard? Why not ask the lady herself?"

"Because, my dear friend, I think you know the answer, that's why."

"Well maybe I do," Lewis offers, "but only part of the story I assure you. That and some guesswork."

"It has to do with you, of course. And Anna."

Now it is Lewis's turn to ensure they are still at a safe distance. He sees Anna glance their way and smile, but she shows no sign of intruding.

"I suppose so. Now that things are - shall we say, 'in the open'?" He checks to see if Richard is going to respond immediately. "You heard of course."

"That Anna's late husband was Jenny's brother?" Lewis nods. "Of course. Something like that, well, it travels quickly. Especially when it is the lady herself who tells you."

"Anna?"

Richard pauses, allows his eyes to focus on the glass that he lifts from the table.

"No. Jenny."

"Jenny!"

Now it is Richard's turn to laugh.

"Indeed. And that was my reaction too. She actually came to see me; sought me out in the church, of all places."

"Of all places," says Lewis with a smile.

"You know what I mean!" Richard protests then drains his glass. "I think she had not long found out. I know you told her, but she didn't come and see me until she had spoken to Anna. Indeed, I get the impression she came to see me right after that." At that moment they hear concerted laughter and look up in unison to see Anna and Jenny side-by-side laughing with Bradley who, it seems likely, has just offered something a little risqué.

"How was she?" Lewis asks, not changing the direction of his gaze.

"Upset. Confused. You choose the word. Lost, I thought. More than anything else perhaps, lost. We talked for over an hour. Or she talked and I listened. She cried a little too. Grief and guilt; guilt and grief." Richard pauses. "I know I shouldn't be telling you this, but you are - involved. You have, I know, their best interests at heart."

"Their?"

"Both Anna and Jenny," Richard clarifies. "Now tell me you don't."

"Well," says Lewis, knowing full well that Richard has the answer already, "it seems whatever you said did the trick."

"It wasn't what I said, not in the end. I don't believe I made any significant contribution at all. It was what *she* said that counted." He pauses again. "Now, as that's all you'll be getting out of me, be a good parishioner and get your parched vicar another shandy!"

❀❀❀

"Are you frustrated, Tommy?"

Bradley's direct question clearly surprises the publican who has just refilled their glasses before they return to the table for the second half of the meeting.

"Frustrated? Why should I be frustrated any more than anyone else?"

"I didn't mean to imply that your angst exceeded the rest of ours - though how you might measure it, I don't know." Bradley tries to strike a tone to keep his enquiry light. "It was just at the beginning there. Not what you said, but the way you said it. Reminded me of the last meeting. And the time before that too, if I'm honest."

"Well," says Tommy, picking up his whiskey and soda, "if I have been frustrated you can hardly blame me. Or blame any of us, come to that. Though I think I'm safe in saying that Shirley takes the biscuit in that department."

"Being frustrated?"

Tommy nods and moves toward the end of the bar.

"Mind you," Bradley suggests, "she might have been pleasantly surprised with how it's gone this evening."

"Do you think so?"

"Don't you think the tone is a little more upbeat, forward-thinking. If I wasn't a cynical old bugger I'd almost say it was positive."

Tommy laughs.

"Steady on! Don't want to hex the whole bloody thing by being too optimistic."

"But you do agree with me," Bradley watches Tommy incline his head in the affirmative, "and that Anna and Jenny have been quietly chivvying us along."

Pausing to turn and close the bar flap behind him, Tommy turns back to Bradley.

"Again I can't disagree with you." He thinks a moment. "Anna would be a welcome addition if she were to stay around for a while."

Bradley glances toward the table where the remainder of the group are clearly debating some point from earlier in the evening.

"You don't think she will?"

"What do I know?" Tommy's smile is almost imperceptible. "I get most of my opinions from Jenny; isn't that how marriage is supposed to work?"

"You're asking the wrong chap about that, and you know it. You and Lewis are our resident experts where that's concerned."

"Then heaven help us if Lewis and I are your benchmarks!" They both laugh but do not yet resume their walk to the table. "But from what Jenny says - well, she thinks there's a chance Anna might stay."

"Only a chance?" Bradley cannot conceal his surprise.

"She says that it isn't up to her. Anna I mean."

"Oh?"

"She says it's all down to Lewis; to what he thinks and wants."

Bradley focuses on his friend for a moment before turning back to Tommy.

"Well from where I'm standing I have to say that I haven't seen him as happy in a very long while. If ever. Why would he want that to change, to revert back to how things were a couple of months ago?"

"You tell me," says Tommy as he levers himself away from the bar and takes the first step back toward the table. "Remember, I'm not an expert either."

❊ ❊ ❊

"So is everyone fired up?"

Richard laughs as he delivers his question. The lights outside the pub soften the fabric of the building and the entrance to the car park. Across the village green, the church, standing in a sepia highlight cast from a single streetlamp, looks inviting and romantic. It is an image of which Richard never tires.

"Well it was a little different, wasn't it?"

"Just as I was saying to Tommy at half-time," Bradley endorses Lewis's comment.

"What do you mean, different?" Anna asks, her arm wrapped through the crook of Lewis's elbow, keeping him close.

"Strangely positive, I suppose," Lewis elaborates, "not that there's anything strange about being positive, if you see what I mean. But rather that it's a little unusual for us."

"Unusual?" Bradley laughs. "Remarkable, I'd say. In fact, I'd go even further. Recognising that I'm taking the parallel a little out of context, I'd say it was a bloody miracle!"

Richard smiles, clearly not having been offended - nor surprised - by Bradley's assertion.

"While that may be going a tad far, I do think Milton's right; it was 'promising'. We've never managed - in all my years here anyway -

to leave one of these sessions thinking that, just maybe, this time it will be different; perhaps we will actually do something, achieve something."

"And that's a good thing?" Anna asks.

"Good?" Bradley and Lewis echo together.

"I'm just testing," she says, "playing Devil's advocate if you like."

"Entirely appropriate after my miracle reference," Bradley suggests.

They all laugh.

"I mean, yes it was positive and up-beat, and yes I do get the sense that there was a willingness to change, to try, to risk. But how will people feel tomorrow or the day after that? Do people really want to change - that's all I'm asking."

"You don't think they do?" Lewis wonders.

"It's not for me to say," Anna replies, "after all, you know these people far better than I do. You've lived here a while; I'm just a newbie. Don't people like things the way they are? Aren't they comfortable? In the cold light of day, is doing something to disturb their equilibrium really what they want?"

There is a silence. Lewis feels Anna shiver suddenly and loosens her arm from his so that he can pull her closer to him.

"I think it's a different question. I think the real question is do the people here want the equilibrium they've got?"

"What do you mean, Lewis?" Richard asks.

"Is Tommy happy with his turnover or footfall or profit - call it what you will. Is he happy with how 'The Anchor' is today? Is Shirley satisfied with the money the store takes, or would she like some more custom, maybe a reason to extend out the back a little like she's always talked about? Would Aubrey like to have some meaningful passing trade coming from more visitors to the village?"

"Would I like to have more people hiring my boat or wanting to be taken out?" Bradley suggests.

"Exactly," says Lewis, feeling vindicated. "I think people realise that there might be a better equilibrium - and I think that maybe they're ready to take that chance."

"Well," says Richard, after a short pause, "my equilibrium is telling me I ought to be getting off to bed. I have to go to a conference in town tomorrow; we're being graced with our Bishop's presence."

"Graced by His Grace," Anna suggests.

Richard laughs, bids them goodnight and then turns toward his picture postcard church.

"Nightcap?" Bradley asks after they have walked in silence for a while and have reached the station.

"Not tonight Bradley," says Anna, "but thanks. All that being constructive and positive has taken it out of me."

"Well, best not make a habit of it then."

❋ ❋ ❋

"That was quite a day," Lewis says, his arms around Anna, staring into her eyes. Without the light on, there is a surreal air with his living room lit only by the moon through the window, a moon seeming suddenly full and bright.

"But a good day?" Anna asks, stretching to kiss him; a short, soft kiss, full of meaning.

"Oh I think so," Lewis smiles, "though I confess I was feeling a little concerned earlier on."

"Walk," says Anna.

"What?"

"The way you said 'walk'. It was clear you had something on your mind. You said it with such purpose. It was so definite; a tone that said it was not to be messed with."

"Ah," Lewis waits a moment. "That was just me being silly."

"No it wasn't," she says. "It was you being nervous, unsure, worried, scared - all of those things."

"Probably. But weren't you?"

"Well I'm glad you got the tense right."

"What do you mean?" He furrows his brow.

"If you had said 'aren't you sure' *then* I would have been worried."

He allows him a moment to compute what she has said.

"But were you" he asks, "unsure, worried, scared - all those things you said?"

"Did you think I was?"

"Never for a moment," he answers as honestly as he can, "and for a bit that sort of freaked me out a little too." Anna laughs. He carries on. "But it doesn't now, because I'm not."

She eases herself away from him a moment so that she can see clearly into his eyes.

"Truly?"

"Truly. Scout's honour." He bends to kiss her again. This time the kiss lasts a little longer. "Especially as I'm beginning to like the way this new equilibrium is shaping up."

"Well," she says, taking him by the hand, "I think I'm liking it too. Very much."

Chapter 11

"Why don't you take the afternoon off?"

Shirley freezes mid-movement, her hands occupied with two packets of digestive biscuits which are destined to fill a rather obvious gap on the middle shelf. She glances to her right to where Oscar stands similarly holding McVities' finest. She hadn't noticed him pick them from the opened box resting on the floor between them.

"What?"

"You've been working really hard lately. All that stock taking. You deserve it." Oscar is struggling to sound caring. His effort is, he knows, in danger of sounding more like parody than anything else.

"Have you been over to the pub?" She laughs, a short, punchy laugh, then places the packets she is carrying in their rightful place. She holds out her hands for those Oscar is cradling.

"I have not," he says definitively, sounding hurt. "How can you think that?"

"Well," she says, the word laden with years of knowing her brother. "Let me have those." She tries to take the biscuits from him but Oscar refuses to let go. "You'll make me drop them!" she threatens.

"Then let go, Shirley. Let me do it. I mean it. Take your bloody apron off for once and..."

"And what?" she asks, brusquely.

"I don't know. Get some fresh air. Go for a walk. The beach, maybe. Or something. Just this once, as I'm offering, do yourself a favour."

If there is such a thing as an 'old fashioned look', Shirley delivers one now. She closes it with another short laugh, and then, muttering to herself, makes a show of untying her apron and holding out in front of her. She suspects Oscar is trying to make up for the argument that had kept them both from attending the village meeting earlier in the week, a inconvenience which had annoyed her more than him. If she was honest with herself, she would know that there was no particular reason for Oscar alone to be contrite given that fault for the row had lay in equal measure on both sides, and no matter what he might say about her working hard, if his reasoning centres around their disagreement then it is simply and unsurprisingly flawed. In the round, however, it is too good an offer to turn down, and though she huffs and puffs at its acceptance, she is not ungrateful to have a couple of unexpected hours to herself especially as she knows what she will do with them.

"There," she says, "now it's off. Is that all right? Am I dismissed? How much free time have I got Oscar, before I'm back on duty?"

Oscar glances toward the clock that adorns the wall behind the counter.

"It's nearly three. We'll close up about five today, shall we? It's hardly busy."

"It's never busy," she interjects, "and we always close at five."

"So don't worry about it," Oscar continues. "I'll see out the rest of the day."

"Well then."

And with that, Shirley throws her apron over one of Oscar's outstretched arms and begins to walk to the door. She pauses as she opens it.

"This isn't a joke?" she asks. "You're not going to suddenly call me back. I mean, you've missed April Fool's, you know that?"

"I'm not that senile," Oscar feigns hurt again, already moving towards the shelf where they keep the biscuits. "Now will you just go!"

Outside, early morning clouds have gradually been burned away, and in full sunlight it is surprisingly warm. Shirley walks across the narrow road outside their shop then pauses on the edge of the green. Though she is no longer romantic, there is something about this particular time of year she finds vaguely inspiring. The promise of the summer and the prospects at which it hints - no matter how nebulous - still manages to thrill her a little, even if far less so than when she had been younger.

As she resumes her walk, she hears a shout. To her left Richard is tending the flower beds by the churchyard gates.

"What a splendid day!" he waves.

"Yes," she replies, waving back but not moderating her pace, "splendid!"

The Vicar waves again then starts to brush his hands on the front of the loose and besmirched jacket he always wears when gardening. There is something odd in the movement, Shirley thinks; it strikes her as guilty somehow. But perhaps she is imagining things. Most often Richard seems to be able to tend his plants when no-one is about, as if it were a secret pastime he was desperate not to be caught undertaking.

Heading across the green, something moves in her peripheral vision and she glances towards the pub. Tommy is outside also taking advantage of the fair weather to wash his car. Seeing her, he too waves, though if he says anything she is too far away to hear it. What she does hear as she reaches the tarmac that has wound around to the other side of the green is the tell-tale ring of Aubrey's anvil, a ring that seems to resonate with as much promise as the brightness of the afternoon.

The sudden sound of the church bell - a single note - stops her in her tracks. Shirley checks her watch. It is not quite three and so there should be no bells yet. The single note confuses her. She looks back towards the church but can see no sign of Richard. Assuming he has accidentally pulled one of the bell ropes - to prevent himself from falling over as he tripped, perhaps - she strives to think nothing more of it, yet as its echo dies away, she realises the hammering from the forge has also stopped. It is suddenly eerily quiet. Not only is there no sign of Richard, but Tommy seems to have abandoned his car washing duties too. Shirley shivers involuntarily; suddenly alone, she feels as if she has been dropped into the middle of some supernatural drama. She tries to recall the name of a series from the television, quickly landing on 'Tales of the Unexpected', and, remembering how implausible she used to find their stories, allows herself the comfort of a light laugh and a private smile.

When she reaches the forge it is evident that Aubrey has been working there recently. The coals are still hot and a pair of tongs and a hammer are resting across the top of the anvil.

"Aubrey," she calls, waiting at the entrance to the forge proper, her fingers tracing the edges of various tools on the bench by which she has paused. There is no reply. Expecting the door to the cottage to open she calls again. When there is no sign of movement, she goes over to try the front door herself but is unable to move it.

"Aubrey," louder this time, "this isn't funny! I know you're in there."

She waits. She has always reacted badly whenever anyone has tried to play a practical joke on her, and feels a degree of pride in knowing none has ever worked, that she has always been able to see through them. But this - if it is some kind of joke - feels different, bizarrely so. If there is a motive, she is unable to see it, and finding it unfathomable, she is unsettled.

Behind her, Shirley is suddenly conscious of a rustle, movement. When she turns, she sees not Aubrey but Richard, Tommy, Jenny, Lewis and Anna walking towards the forge. Even Oscar is there.

"Oscar?" She turns and begins to walk towards them. "Why are you all here? What's wrong? Is there something wrong."

Immediately concerned for Aubrey, she is unable to keep a tremor from her voice, unable to disguise how unsettled she suddenly feels, and rather than be reassured, she is further disturbed by the fact that they are all smiling. Every single one of them. And then, as if it were perfectly rehearsed, all six stop walking. Behind her she hears the cottage door open.

The Aubrey that emerges is not the Aubrey Shirley is expecting to see. Yes, his hair is untidy and his face remains flushed from his exertions - a tone that usually takes an hour to fade and which he invariably blames on the heat of the fire - but this Aubrey is not wearing his working garb but rather his only suit, a white shirt, and a bright red tie she has never seen before. If Aubrey had a twin, Shirley would be convinced that this was the person walking toward her now.

"Aubrey?" she begins, her voice full of confusion, its tone teetering on the dividing line between plea and rebuke.

A small ripple of applause breaks out behind her which, as soon as she turns her head, is silenced even though the smiles remain.

Closer now, Shirley gives this apparition of Aubrey her full attention. Arms behind his back, he is walking stiffly, as if being acted upon by some external force, or finding his clothes impossibly starched. He does not smile, nor does he say anything. After a few paces, he stops, leaving Shirley equidistant from between him and the crowd behind her.

"Would someone please tell me what is going on?" Shirley says, beginning to lose what remains of her composure. "If this is supposed to be funny, some kind of joke, then let me tell you…"

"Hush lass," says Aubrey, firmly but softly. Having never interrupted Shirley in his entire life, the shock of his doing so now has the desired effect. If he is trying a smile, he is failing, finding himself overcome by the situation as much as anyone else. He tries clearing his throat.

"Shirley Ryle," he begins hoarsely, slowly. "How long have I known you? How long have we been friends? Don't tell me, though I'm sure you know." And Shirley could say, but refrains from doing so. "How long have you been coming to see me work at the forge as my friend? And how long have you been coming here as more than my friend? A long time."

Although Aubrey is plainly struggling, he appears to be warming to his task, and from over Shirley's shoulder a quiet "Hear, hear!" escapes from Richard, unable to control himself. Aubrey hears it and for a moment allows his glance to drift over Shirley's shoulder. He nods slightly in recognition, then refocusses.

"A long time. And how long has it been, lass, since you have wanted more than that? A long time. And what about me? What have I wanted? I'm just a lummoxing great bloke who only knows how to heat and bend metal. A simple bloke who wants a simple life. And because of all of that, I've never really understood or been able to contemplate those two things together, what you want and what I am." Aubrey pauses for a moment, and sees that Shirley - even though she is clearly fighting herself - is beginning to cry. "Until now. Don't ask me what did it, or what made me see sense. Just blame me for taking too long. Just blame me for being a blind bugger. But I see it now, Shirley, just like all our friends here see it."

Aubrey pulls his hands from behind her back then cups them together in front of his chest. There is a small red box.

"Will you marry me, lass?"

❀ ❀ ❀

"What do you think of the ring?" Richard asks over the rim of one of the best china cups his bachelor's vicarage has to offer.

Anna, having just replaced her own in its saucer, looks back up at him.

"Isn't it completely beautiful?" she says, enthusiastically. "Who would have thought Aubrey could turn his hand to such intricate work?"

"Not bad for a rustic blacksmith," Richard agrees between sips. "Mind you, it did take him quite a while; the first two or three attempts you wouldn't have wanted to put through the nose of pig!" He laughs at his own inventiveness, but then realises the parallel is not entirely appropriate. "Not that I'm saying…"

"How long had you known?" Anna rescues him.

"About what he was planning?"

She nods.

"Oh, a little while I suppose," the reply is both nonchalant and non-committal. "The hardest thing was keeping it from Shirley. Well, from everybody really. I was so pleased when he told me: 'came to his senses' was the phrase he'd used. And he was determined to make the thing himself, which kept poor Shirley dangling longer than he would have wanted. I think he felt it was getting to a critical point, and then - as if by divine intervention - he comes up with that marvellously fine ring."

"I love the way the different coloured golds intertwine. Did he see that somewhere?"

"Not that I know of; after all, Aubrey's not the kind of man to go browsing in jewellers' windows, is he? I saw some early sketches of his ideas and they looked nothing like that."

"So you *have* known for a long while then!" Anna says.

"Certainly a number of weeks."

"And the bell," she presses, "the teeing us up as it were, giving us the signal; whose idea was that?"

Richard smiles.

"I can't take any credit for that. Once Aubrey was ready, we told Oscar. Aubrey was determined that he wanted his friends there to act as witnesses, to prove to Shirley that he meant what he said. Oscar suggested the date and time, convinced he could get Shirley out of the shop - and knowing where she would go once he had freed her. That was why I was gardening and Tommy was washing his car."

"And why Lewis and I were in the pub - though we didn't know the reason at that stage."

"With the actors in the wings, all we needed was to see Shirley heading for the forge. The bell - Oscar's idea - was primarily to alert Aubrey that she was on her way, but it also gave us our cue."

"It was marvellous though, wasn't it, the look on Shirley's face?"

"And now she's over the shock, I don't think she's stopped smiling since," says Richard who takes a last draught from his tea and puts the cup down. He looks back at Anna who, momentarily, is distracted by the room she is in; the 'best seat in the house' as Richard had earlier described the settee in the vicarage's lounge. "But you aren't here to talk about Shirley and Aubrey. Not really."

"No, not really," she admits, "though it is nice to, don't you think?" She doesn't wait for any reply. "I really wanted to come and say a 'thank you' of my own."

"Thank me?" Richard's surprise is evident and unforced. "What have I done that you've got to thank me for?"

"Oh, I don't know. Just being around, I suppose. For being someone to talk to - especially when I first arrived. Those first few days - weeks even - weren't that easy."

"I could see that. Maybe we all could. But I don't think I did anything apart from listen - and that's included in the job description. It's not as if I had cause to resort to subterfuge and bell ringing!"

Richard's attempt to make light of his role in Anna's affairs is only partially accepted.

"But listening was important, especially when I had no-one I could turn to - physically or spiritually."

"Well, not until you found Lewis," Richard suggests.

Anna inclines her head a little. A wistful smile that verges on the nostalgic plays on her lips, but there is no sadness there.

"Who would have thought," she says open-endedly. "The person who happened to be living in the cottage next door to mine... Almost as if he had been there waiting for me."

"And vice versa," Richard suggests.

Anna frowns.

"What do you mean?"

"Simply that he was waiting for you in order that he could save you - and so that you could save him too. Don't you agree? Though I think the notion of 'saving' is a little melodramatic - but you see what I mean?"

"Fate," she suggests, "which - as you well know - is not something any of us should really believe in. And for a whole variety of reasons!"

Even though it is the slimmest of jokes they both laugh. Richard makes to pour another cup of tea but Anna's hand straying over her cup stops him.

"We aren't mad, are we?" she asks. "I mean, Lewis and I? Not that I've said anything to him, but I worry if it isn't all a little - I don't know - desperate..."

"Does it feel desperate?"

"No," she says, simply. Her smile broadens. "Not in the least. But it's not magical either - I think we're both too old for that! It does feel as if we've been given another chance, though; and that chance feels natural, it feels right." She pauses. "Almost from the very start I found myself able to tell him things that I would never have dreamed of sharing with a stranger. And he with me too, I think. Why do you think that is?"

"Ah," says Richard standing and walking over to the window from which, along the path that separates the two buildings, he can see the entrance to the church, "who can say? I don't think there are ever the words to express something like that. We try, of course, but for me such emotions must always evade capture. We tend to trot out the usual words - like 'love' and 'trust' of course - but they're really only a social veneer; something that gives us a clue but can never truly get at the heart of things."

"I'm surprised, Richard," Anna says, unable to disguise a slight tone of disapproval. "How can you say such a thing?"

He turns to face her, smiling.

"About love - or about the word? I say it not because I don't believe in wonderful things, like the feeling you and Lewis have for each other, but because I myself don't know how to properly express them." He walks towards her and resumes his seat. "I join people in wedlock and see the joy in their faces; I officiate in funerals and observe the grief of the family; I watch people truly uplifted sometimes at a Sunday service because they feel closer to God. And can I describe any of that? Not really. I see it and appreciate it and embrace it, but I can't describe it. Heavens, I can hardly describe my own feelings to myself! But that doesn't make any of them the less worthy or valid. In fact I think it makes them *more* worthy. What you and Lewis feel for each other is beyond words, it has to be. We can call it love if we want to, but what we really should do is to rejoice in the feeling. I see two people who have been through harsh and difficult times; two people who have found each other and in that finding have been reborn, have found again those feelings that they perhaps had thought lost or perhaps feared they would never feel again. I see them smile and laugh and be happy. And I don't want to call that anything or analyse it or label it. I just want to rejoice in it and praise God that it has happened."

Anna allows his words to reverberate inside her, senses them permeating into the very fabric of the room where, she is sure, they will be welcomed and understood.

"And you're right, of course," she says, "now that you've explained what you mean. How can you not be? But it's a struggle, isn't it, when you live in a world that demands the concrete of you all the time."

"Let me ask you a question," Richard says, still smiling, perching himself on the edge of his chair.

"Okay."

"How did you feel yesterday when you watched Aubrey's declaration to Shirley?"

"How did I feel?"

Richard nods.

"I was happy, of course I was. Happy for them. It was - what was the word you used? - joyous. It was wonderful, uplifting, emotional."

"I rest my case," he eases himself back in his chair.

"How so?"

"'Happy', 'wonderful', 'uplifting', 'emotional'. Those were the words you used." he quotes.

"Yes."

"But is that how you felt? Really? Is that what made you cry? Or did you think your heart would burst? Did you want to sing or shout? Did you want to hug them and never let them go? Did you want to do something to ensure they would always feel as they did at that precise moment?" Anna starts to smile. "Because I did," Richard continues, "and I would argue words like 'happy' and 'wonderful' do those kinds of emotions scant justice. I felt God was there. I knew He was. And where are the words for that? If you know, please tell me because I have been searching for them all my life."

* * *

As Tommy wakes from a dream that involved abandoned concert halls and a seemingly never-ending pursuit up and down enormous flights of stairs, he realises the space in the bed next to him is empty. He closes his eyes for a moment to give himself the opportunity to prove that this is not just another chapter in his nightmare. As he opens them again, he is as confident as he can be that he has emerged from his dreamscape and is alone in the bedroom. Feeling his heart still beating quickly from the imagined chase, he lays still for a moment, permitting himself a turn of the head to check the electric clock on his bedside table. The numbers seven, two and three glow back at him. For a moment he wonders if these might be some kind of code, and then admonishes himself for blurring reality with dream.

So he listens for a clue to Jenny's whereabouts, trying to focus on the en suite. It strikes him as a strange and undoubtedly bizarre pursuit to attempt to focus one's hearing. Ears aren't like eyes; they are indiscriminate, they accept whatever they are given. And even though he is trying to attune them to the sound of running water or the creak the floorboard near the sink cannot help but emit, it is the chink of glass he hears first, a sound that emanates from downstairs. He checks the clock again, concerned that he might not yet be able to trust either sight or sound, worried that the bedroom door might suddenly fly open and his pursuers, released from the semi-dark auditorium, have finally found him in a location where running away is impossible.

He discovers Jenny, wearing her roughest jeans and sweatshirt, on her knees behind the bar surrounded by bottles. Apart from a large glass cafetière which is half empty, the surface of the bar is adorned with empty glasses, and even though she is partly obscured from sight as she leans into now empty shelves, wiping them vigorously with a damp cloth, it is she who speaks first.

"There's still some coffee if you want some," she remains focussed on her task and doesn't look round, "though it may be a little cold now. If you want to make some more that would be good."

Tommy pulls a bar stool to the end of the bar where he can see her, and perches himself on it.

"What are you doing, Jen? It's not long after seven."

She pulls away from the shelf, eases herself back onto her haunches and looks vaguely in his direction.

"I know. Sorry. But I was awake. And these bottles have been bothering me."

"Bothering you?"

"Yes," she waves her rubber-gloved hand in the general direction of the bar's surface. "I've been thinking that the mixers should be further to the left, and that we should have the pale ales and things nearer here. I just don't think they're particularly convenient where they are right now. And if the ciders and speciality beers are here then they're more visible; we might sell more of them." She looks at him directly for the first time. "What do you think?"

Tommy glances along the shelving and tries to imagine how the revised layout might look.

"I think you're right. I'm sure that will be better." He pauses. "But I still don't get why you're doing it now, at half seven on a Sunday morning."

He knows it is only half the question he wants to ask, but it's a start.

"Why not?" Jenny replies, leaning back into the shelves, her right hand beginning wiping duties again. "Are you making some more coffee?"

Ten minutes later Tommy returns with a tray containing the refilled cafetière and some croissants he has just warmed in the oven. Jenny has already placed the mixers in their new home and he can instantly see the arrangement will be better. As he waited for the pastries, Tommy had tested himself with the questions he wanted to ask, partly to try them out and see how they sounded, and partly to discover if he already knew the answers. His re-emergence with the tray also sees him slightly more nervous than before: the questions had sounded crass and inappropriate, and he discovered that he knew none of the answers. All the more reason for asking them, he had told himself.

"Here you go," he says as he places the tray in a now vacant space on the bar. "I warmed up some croissants too."

"Hmmm," Jenny says as she straightens up, then stands, "they smell good."

They take a croissant each. Crumbs fall from Tommy's onto the counter and he makes to sweep them up with his hand.

"Don't worry," Jenny says, "I'll need to clean up once I've finished this lot; a few more crumbs won't make any difference."

If he were prone to pinching himself, Tommy would do so now. He finds himself unable to recall the last time he had seen Jenny working with anything that approximated to a purpose. Not only that, but she seems relaxed in doing so. In spite of himself, Tommy wonders if he has edged back into his dream - a second reason for a pinch.

"What?" says Jenny, pulling him back.

"Sorry?"

"You look like you're thinking," she says, "which is never a particularly fruitful labour."

"Thanks a lot," Tommy smiles in spite of himself, glad to find her still acerbic.

"Well, if not exactly thinking, then worried. What's up?" Jenny smiles, knowing the answer. It is a familiar position in which she finds herself, and suddenly she is grateful to be on safe ground again. Perhaps she never realised how adrift she had cast herself until these last few days, and she feels relieved to be 'moored' again.

"Just this," Tommy says once he has finished the last of his croissant and freed his hand to sweep towards the bottles and shelves.

"You don't want me to do it?" Jenny asks, trying to feign innocence.

"No, of course not. I think it's a great idea. The right thing to do."

"But?"

"I'm just a bit confused, Jen, that's all."

"By the way I'm sequencing the bottles?" She teases him, glancing back to her handiwork.

"You know that's not what I mean," Tommy can't help but show a little frustration. He teeters. "That you're doing it at all - never mind that it's early on a Sunday morning. I mean, wouldn't you normally just tell me to do it, and then be the one making the coffee?"

"Is that true?" she asks, her face clouding a little.

"What?"

"That I'd just tell you what to do and expect you to get on with it?"

"It has been known," Tommy replies trying to keep his tone playful.

Jenny's countenance flits between light and dark.

"Well then," she says after a moment's thought, "you should be all the more grateful that I'm doing this. But don't go believing that a leopard can permanently change its spots."

"I don't," Tommy says, "and I'm not sure I'd want to anyway."

"Meaning?"

"I don't know. Maybe if you were like this all the time I'm not sure I could cope."

"That's reassuring," Jenny says, "because I wouldn't want you to get used to it." She laughs. "And you couldn't anyway."

"Couldn't what?"

"Cope."

Tommy pours coffee into the two mugs he has brought out from the kitchen and adds milk. He passes one to Jenny.

"You're probably right of course," he says, knowing he is half-joking - and, more importantly, knowing Jenny knows this too, "but this is a nice surprise."

"Ugh," says Jenny.

"Something wrong with the coffee?"

"No, the coffee's fine. It's that word: 'nice'. It never means anything, does it?" She pauses, sensing it important that they push on through this. "What do you mean, Tommy, 'nice'? Pick another word, just for me."

Not having expected this, Tommy rummages for an alternative.

"Surprising, maybe? Good to see?"

"Okay, but why?" Jenny sees confusion beginning to encroach on Tommy's face. "I need to know, Tommy. I think I need to understand what you really think."

He suddenly feels as he did when he was being pursued through the theatre, a huge flight of stairs before him down which he is about to plunge.

"I'm surprised because I didn't think you cared any more - about the pub, I mean." His qualification is probably unnecessary and comes as much as a surprise to him as it does to Jenny. But Tommy knows it is the qualification that has taken them both slightly aback, and that what he really wants to say is in the unspoken part. He feels as if a coin is spinning in the air.

"Well," Jenny buys a little time, "probably not as much as I should have; and certainly not recently." She wants to choose her words carefully too; to try and answer both the question Tommy has implied and the one he hasn't. If she has been trying to resolve her own feelings over the last few days - unconsciously or not - this is where they will be revealed. "Perhaps I had realised what I was missing. I mean, there was always the hustle and bustle in the city, always something going on; maybe I missed that. Nothing ever changed. Just like those meetings we have here; always the same, every year since we've been here."

"Except for the last one," Tommy suggests.

"Yes, the last one was a little different."

"And do you know why?"

Jenny is suddenly afraid of the answer, of what it might be, and what it might say.

"Tell me," she says, avoiding the responsibility.

"Because of you, Jen."

"Me?"

"You. Because you took an interest, because you made a contribution. You made a difference."

"Hardly."

"But you did," says Tommy warmly, "and people could see that. You might not think any of that matters to people, that it's all nonsense; but it does matter - and to me most of all." She glances away, so Tommy carries on. "Just like these shelves and these bottles. You might not think that's much, not in the grand scheme of things, but it is; it matters to me. And you'll see when people come in later, they'll spot the difference and they'll say something;

and it will be positive too, I'm sure of that. And then it will matter to you."

"You think so?" She shrugs her shoulders, but Tommy can see that it's a half-hearted gesture. "I'm not doing it for them anyway."

"No, I know that. Or at least I think I do. And before you say anything, I'm pretty certain that you're not doing it for me either."

Jenny looks back at him, trying to gauge whether or not he is fishing for a denial, for her to tell him that she's really doing it all for him. But she can sense that he isn't, and that they both know it. She suddenly feels as if she is seeking clues that will lead her back to something she has lost, and in that context Tommy is right; it's all about her. She has never been lost - or at least would never admit to that. If anything, she has allowed herself to become entangled in an ever-tightening web. Unable to see a way out - relying on the possibility of Lewis releasing her - she simply accepted her fate. That she was increasingly unsatisfied with the prospect - and increasingly nervous that Lewis would never prove her shining knight - she allowed fate to take over; after all, if there was no way out, what was the point in anything?

"Do you want a hand?" Tommy asks.

She shakes her head.

"No - but thank you. I need to get this done myself. It was my idea, my initiative; it's important I finish it." She waits a moment. "I know it's a small step, Tommy; probably a small step on an impossibly long road, but I've started so I'll finish. That's what they say, isn't it?"

"I think you started a week or so ago."

About to take some more bottles from the bar to relocate them, Jenny stops, fearful again.

"What do you mean?"

"When you found out about Ryan." Her brother has remained unmentioned, a topic of conversation they have instinctively avoided since Lewis broke the news. Tommy cannot leave him out now; the lifting of that particular veil has been too fundamental. "That was when things started to change, Jen. Knowing something, being certain of something. I can't really imagine it. It must have been like having a nagging question finally answered."

She allows her hands to fall to her sides.

"You may be right," she replies, no longer inclined to play games with him. "It was like the proverbial weight being lifted. I guess I hadn't realised how much not knowing his full story had been pressing down on me, compounded year after year. It was like finally being able to put him to rest. Maybe that's what allowed me to lift my head up, to even contemplate being able to do so."

Tommy allows the pause to build, then sensing that it will remain untroubled, rises to take the tray back into the kitchen.

"Thank you," Jenny says more to his back than him.

Tommy half-turns.

"What for?"

"Putting up with me," she says, simply.

He smiles.

"I can't pretend that it was always easy, but why wouldn't I have 'put up with you'? Isn't that part of the deal?"

She laughs.

"It should be only a small part, and I know I blew it up out of all proportion. *I* would probably have left *me* if the roles had been reversed."

"Well, you nearly did - even if I was never going to."

❖ ❖ ❖

"There is a question you haven't asked me," Anna says, breaking into the moment as if she were a masked raider on a smash-and-grab. They are sitting together on the settee in Lewis's front room watching a re-run of a Nora Ephron film. Of the two of them, Lewis has confessed himself the greater fan of the Hanks-Ryan combination, and for a while they played with the argument as to whether or not that made him the most romantic. "Define romantic" Anna had challenged. In the end, they agreed to differ on the precise definition, but found themselves satisfied that each of them seemed romantic 'enough'.

Lewis, his left arm about her shoulders, glances at her. Anna's gaze seems resolutely focussed on the bunch of daisies Meg Ryan is holding.

"Oh? I'm sure there are lots of questions I haven't asked you yet. Enough to keep me going for some considerable time, I shouldn't wonder."

She looks at him as he says this.

"Maybe you *are* the most romantic," she says, and laughs a little. Then she waits.

"So what's the question I haven't asked you?" Lewis asks dutifully. "It must be more significant than 'what's your favourite flower?' or 'where shall we go on holiday this summer?' otherwise you wouldn't have mentioned it."

"Do you want a little time to think about it, to see if you can figure it out?"

"That," Lewis says with a fake grimace, "sounds like a double-edged sword. If I haven't got it now, then how rubbish will I look if I still haven't got it in ten minutes?"

"Pretty rubbish," Anna confirms still smiling.

"So why don't you just tell me what I should have already asked you, then we can just cut to the chase?"

She looks back at the television just as Hanks is ensuring that the ailing Ryan is comfortably tucked up in bed.

"In a way," she says, not looking back at him, "I can understand why you've not asked. But having said that, I'm still not sure whether I should be flattered or annoyed."

"Annoyed?"

"You haven't heard the question yet," Anna says.

Lewis follows her gaze, knowing he is in a 'no win' situation. For a split second he tries to draw a parallel between himself and Ephron's male lead but can only see such an attempt failing on every level - not least because he isn't a multi-millionaire.

"No, it's no use. I don't see how I can come out of this with an ounce of credibility intact, so you might as well tell me what I should have asked you."

"So you can ask me?" Anna clarifies.

"So I can ask you, yes."

Anna leans forward and picks the remote control from the coffee table and turns off the television.

"Shit!" says Lewis instinctively. "This must be serious."

She eases away from him slightly so that she can turn on the settee to face him almost square on. Although she is still smiling a little, Lewis can tell the time for joking is over. Feeling slightly panicked, he tries to see if he can conure up the missing question in the few nanoseconds before she next speaks. He fails.

"It's very simple, Lewis," she says as placidly as possible, "and I do understand why the question may not even have occurred to you. And if it hasn't, I think I understand why."

"Well?"

She places a hand on one of his.

"You haven't asked me if I'll stay."

Without the background chatter of the television, Lewis can suddenly hear a clock - the kitchen clock. It is almost as if someone has boosted the power in its batteries so that it can run on an 'extra loud' setting.

"If you'll stay?"

"Here. With you. In Maunston Quay."

Lewis allows the words to settle into the quagmire that his consciousness seems to have suddenly become. Had that question ever occurred to him? And if it had - or hadn't - what does he assume the answer to be? Does he know? He knows there is no chasm in front of him and he feels as certain as he can of his footing, and yet he knows appearances can be deceptive. Quicksand always looks solid enough.

"Oh my God." The words escape him before he can do anything about them.

Anna's smile seems a little bolstered.

"OMG indeed," she says, squeezing his hand. "Let me help you out here while you remind yourself how your jaw muscles work so that you can close your mouth again!" Lewis does so. "At this point there are probably only two scenarios. The first is that you thought of the question, but had assumed you knew the answer, so didn't bother to ask. The second is that it never occurred to you in the first place. Am I right?"

"I'm so..."

She quickly saves him.

"In the first case I could be annoyed that you've assumed you know the answer. Or I could be flattered that you think you know me well enough. In the second case I could be annoyed that you've never even thought to ask me; or I could be flattered that you are so sure of your ground and how you feel about me - and how I feel about you - well, why would it even need to cross your mind?"

Lewis feels crestfallen. It is as if he has committed a blunder so fundamental, an error so crass, that everything he has assumed about the future that was beginning to crystallise before him is all at risk.

"Jesus," he says, "I'm so sorry."

At this Anna laughs. It is a loud, relaxed and happy laugh, but if intended to make Lewis feel any better, it fails spectacularly.

"There's no point you seeking divine intervention, my lad!" she says, but then seeing how distraught he is on the verge of becoming, she now employs both her hands to cradle his own. "There's a simple way out of this little conundrum in which you find yourself."

"There is?"

"There is. Just ask me. Please." And then, in order to stop an instant response, she raises one hand to his face and places her fingers on his lips. "But before you do ask me, just think about how you are going to do it. Don't just rush in, not now. Let's pretend that you've had a couple of days to think it over. Let's pretend that this is for real. Let's pretend that everything hangs on this question, and how you ask it will influence my answer." She pauses for half a second. "Because it might; you never know."

And now the intrusive kitchen clock comes to Lewis's rescue. He searches for its sound while his eyes search Anna's face for clues. As he begins to count to twenty - the random number he has chosen - he catches a glimpse of Emma's smile in the photograph just visible over Anna's right shoulder.

Seven. Eight. Nine.

He wonders if seeing Emma again, at that precise moment, is a hint, a clue. Even now he wonders if she is still speaking to him.

Twelve. Thirteen.

Given the two alternatives Anna has given him for his apparent failure, he tries to alight on the one that most likely applies. If he is hoping that might help, he discovers it does not.

Seventeen. Eighteen.

And suddenly there are two seconds to go - and then they are gone.

"Of your two reasons," he begins, striving to find somewhere to start that permits him a modicum of certainty, of credibility, "the one which applies is the second. I hadn't even thought to ask. I'm not sure if that is the lesser of two evils. Or if it matters any more."

Lewis waits, hopeful that Anna will spare him what might rapidly become tortuous. But she does not. The only comfort Lewis is able to take from the image she presents is that she is relaxed, unperturbed. This is not, he knows, the same as unconcerned. Overall, he wonders if she has greater faith in him than he does himself.

"If you had told me that I would end up feeling as I do about the stranger in the red coat who stepped off that train all those weeks ago, I would have told you that you were mad. I have no crystal ball, and if I had I'm pretty sure that it would have been fog-filled that day, just as it would have been for far too long before that. And if I *did* have a crystal ball, I am pretty sure the picture it would have shown me would look very different today." He pauses to try and arrange the random thoughts which are assailing him from all directions. "I wasn't looking for anything, for anyone. I wasn't looking because I guess I thought I'd found something, a state, a way to live that was okay as far as it went. It was a life with limitations for sure, but it felt like the life I somehow deserved. All I deserved." She squeezes his hands again at this. "I had been rescued by Maunston Quay and the funny little life it had gifted me. Maybe I thought that was enough. And then there you were. Unexpected. Brilliantly unexpected. Someone I could relate to; a lost soul in the way that I was lost. Someone I could talk to - and who needed to talk to me. It was like a little spark, you know? As if someone had mended a fuse. Let there be light, and all that. Don't ask me when I started to feel what I feel now. It was gradual, I suppose. Little things. You permeated my skin, little by little. I started to look for you out of the window to try and time my walks to coincide with yours. When there were days I didn't see you, I felt bereft, as if someone had stolen something precious from me. Because that's what you are, precious and wonderful. You have filled up a part of my life that I never truly realised was empty. And I cannot imagine living through those empty days again. I don't know if I would be able to cope."

His voice having become dry all of a sudden, Lewis pauses and swallows. Anna's eyes, moist now, remain steadfastly fixed upon his own.

"And perhaps that is why I hadn't thought to ask you the question. Perhaps it was because I didn't want to hear the answer just in case it wasn't the answer I wanted. In case... Anna. I can't imagine you not here. I simply want to be with you all the time. You have made me whole again. Please don't take that away. Will you stay, here, with me? For a while longer at least. Please."

Staring at her for a moment, for once hoping his face betrays everything he is feeling, he then drops his eyes to where their hands have remained entwined throughout. He allows his right index finger to trace the contours of the back of her hands as if it is surveying there for the first time, mapping out their shape as an explorer might were he preparing to draft a map for future posterity. Something moving in his peripheral vision causes him to look up again. Anna frees her hand to brush a tear from her cheek.

"I have a small secret," she says, quietly. Lewis's finger ceases its exploration and for once he is immediately certain that his face is speaking for him as, seeing its expression, she rushes on. "No, don't think it's a bad thing! It isn't. Or at least I don't think so."

"We have no secrets," Lewis suggests. It is half plea, half statement.

"The truth is, I hadn't even considered the question myself until this afternoon. It was only when it hit me - I mean, that you hadn't asked me - that I began to wonder whether you should have. And if you did, how you would, and what I might say in reply."

"So you have been making assumptions too," Lewis says, seeing a path emerge from her clarification, as if someone has begun to illuminate the way out of a maze. She nods. "And - I hope - the same ones that I have been making, consciously or not?"

Anna releases her hands and almost visibly shakes herself, sitting slightly more upright as if she has just given herself a good dressing down.

"It might help if I answer your question," she suggests, "after all I have rather bullied you into asking it haven't I?"

Sensing he is nearing the exit of the maze, Lewis tests out a smile.

"There is, of course, a short answer," Anna says, "and that answer is 'yes'. Yes, of course I'll stay here with you, Lewis. It has never occurred to me that I would do anything other than that - which is probably why the question never occurred to me either. I'd guessed or hoped or knew that's where you were too. Any doubt as to what was going to happen next never even registered with me. Or at least not until I realised you'd not asked. Part of me thought you may not have asked because you were thinking I was going to go - or that you wanted me to go. That none of this was as real as I'd imagined."

Now it is Lewis's turn to take her hands. He lifts one of them to his lips and kisses it.

"I am happy, Lewis. I never thought I would be again; or at least not so soon. I hadn't been looking for it. It feels a little like a precious trinket one has lost and given up finding; but then, suddenly one day, there it is, at the back of a drawer or under some socks or something."

"You're comparing me to socks?!"

"Don't be silly!" She laughs. "You know what I mean. And if anything was lost, then it wasn't a silly trinket - but it was me, just like you said. And I'm not any more. I came here without a home, or a place to call home. I know you understand what that's like because that's how you were when you came to Maunston. And here we are, history repeating itself - and in so many ways. So yes, I will stay here. Of course I will. After such a pretty speech how could I not?"

Lewis bows his head as if he were modestly taking an encore from an audience.

"Well, I had a long time to prepare for it..."

Relaxing her posture, she leans in to him again, allowing his arms to envelop her.

"You asked if I would stay for a while longer. I don't know how long that is, but I hope it's a long time. I hope it proves to be a long time. I don't want those empty days either. I want my walks to be with you, I want to share my future - and my past - with you." She pauses, not looking at him now. "I want to revel in your kindness, your protection. I want to try and love your vaguely experimental cooking, your too-strong tea, the annoying way you fold down the corners of the books you are reading to keep your place..."

Lewis never discovers how long Anna's list might be. As she starts laughing, he twists her towards him, their laughter and kissing sealing the contract.

❄ ❄ ❄

As it turns out, the Johnsons would have forced Anna's hand in any event. Two days later, in a call to Shirley, they had broken the news of enough summer interest in the cottage at the full holiday rental rate for them to decide to issue notice on their current tenant along with their thanks for her stamina. When Anna reflects on Shirley's visit to break the news, she recalls how they had laughed over the word.

"Stamina was what they called it," Shirley had said with a laugh.

"If only they knew!" Anna had replied between the laughter, though not entirely sure what she meant.

Them making her last week a free one was a gesture which, Anna knew, would have seemed significant on their part; the only true way in which they could actually make their appreciation of her relatively long-term tenancy concrete. She was grateful, of course, though not to the extent that the invisible Johnsons had perhaps imagined she might be.

"Will they come to check the place out before the season?" she had asked, as if there were such a thing.

"I doubt it," had come Shirley's reply, "they usually rely on my judgement. Provided you haven't trashed the place, they'll be fine with me giving them the all clear."

They had laughed again, and Anna made a joke about being a rock star and wondered if she should indulge in a little mayhem just for the sake of it.

Standing in the bedroom, Anna surveys the suitcase that lays open on the bed. As she has packed, it has become evident how threadbare some of her jumpers and jeans have become through persistent wearing since she has been there; that and the repeated exposure to sea and wind. Even though tempted to do so, she had previously been reluctant to add to her wardrobe. But things are different now, and Lewis has already converted his second small bedroom into something of a 'dressing room', keeping the bulk of his clothes in the wardrobe and chest of drawers now congregated there. Doing so has permitted him a less cluttered main bedroom - and, she knows, is an arrangement that can accommodate her small collection of clothes at least twice over. There is a surprise frisson of excitement as she anticipates a little shopping expedition into town. It feels like both a celebration and a triumph.

Their agreement has been a loose one in terms of timing, and although her forthcoming eviction does put an end date on things, she had begun to gather herself together almost as soon as she and

Lewis had discussed their future. If anything, Anna was surprised how relaxed Lewis had been when it came to defining timeframes - and doubly surprised at her own lack of urgency. Had they wanted it that way, she could have moved in within half a day, yet here she was only now finishing her packing nearly a week on.

Something telling her that what was about to happen was as much a symbol as a transaction, Anna found herself wanting to close out this portion of her life in her own way. She was soon to be clearly and domestically part of a couple once again, and so the movement from her cottage to the one next door is more than the simple transportation of goods and chattels just a few feet laterally. Almost catching herself unawares, she found the need to mark the end of her recent life as a singleton in concrete ways; it would give more meaning to her taking up residence next door. There was no list as such, but she knew certain things needed to be recognised as 'the last'. She also knew these needed to be solitary events.

Insisting that her last few nights be spent alone in her cottage, she had risen early enough to be outdoors before Lewis could accompany her. Completion of the last of her favourite walks, found her sitting alone on Simon's Crag. It had been cold, in spite of the weather's gradually warming, and as she sat and stared out to sea she had shivered and told herself she was being silly and irrational - but still she sat, feeling the need to eke out the moment and to make it somehow significant.

Whether it had been or not was a question that had come to her as she had warmed herself with hot tea and a cooked breakfast half an hour later; and it is a question that has resurfaced as she empties the last of her clothes from the drawers which had been their home for so many weeks. She wants to feel her approach has been worthwhile, that the walks, the time spent alone reading or writing has served its purpose. She has looked back - both consciously and less so - more with the mind of a historian than someone who has experienced them first hand, as if in doing so she might arrive at a more meaningful assessment of their worth.

Yet underneath all this is the knowledge that the only thing which matters is the fact that she is moving on, and that moving on means moving out. She knows the thing of paramount importance was not the life she had led there in Maunston Quay, but the life she was about to lead. Even though, in many respects, little would change, Anna could not but help feel that everything was about to. As she leans on the case to force the zip closed, it is as if the sound and the action symbolises something greater than the closing of a bag. In as much as it might, to her fanciful mind, represent a closing on the past, it will soon symbolise the opening of the future, for that same sound will be heard again - tomorrow now - as the bag lays on Lewis's bed and she unzips it.

Pulling it to the floor and resting it by the foot of the bed, Anna makes her way down stairs. As she does so, she can't help but try and remember how all those 'firsts' had felt; the first time she had climbed those same stairs, the first time she had walked through the door, the first time she had filled the kettle and switched it on - which is exactly what she is doing now. It seems a little sad to her as she pulls a mug from the cupboard - the red one she likes the best - and fills it with instant coffee, that in the end it doesn't really matter. She isn't sure if that is relevant or not, a good thing or not. And then she smiles to herself because a good thing has happened - the best - and because from tomorrow it is going to get better still.

❋ ❋ ❋

Having spent a short while reorganising his clothes, Lewis sits on the small upright chair in the corner of the second bedroom and looks into the now empty half of the wardrobe. Most of the furniture had come with the cottage and through relocating it he now discovers that the wardrobe's back is comprised of particularly knotty pine slats. If that has any relevance beyond its age, quality or value, he lets it pass, his main preoccupation being to try and imagine the back no longer visible, the view blocked by whatever clothes Anna has hanging there. It is a small leap into the future.

She has already told him that she has almost nothing with her at present - "just imagine how little fills a medium-sized suitcase" she had said - nevertheless he has tried to condense his own clothes as much as possible with the aim of freeing up half of all the available space. It was a challenge only to a limited extent given he possesses a hardly expansive collection of garments himself, but he feels it is important to start off in the right way; that was his driving force. At some point he can foresee her needing to add to what she initially installs, and wonders if they will drive to her old home and salvage more from there. Imagining that, the wardrobe fills before his eyes, and in doing so forces him beyond that first leap of time onto the threshold of a second. What happens when all the space is filled? Not just all the hanging or the space in these drawers, but on the shelves downstairs and in the kitchen cupboards. At some point there will come another question not unlike the one they weaved their way around a few days days previously. Suddenly the wardrobe becomes a symbol of something else.

It comes upon him with a shiver of surprise. Who would have thought staring at strips of pine could take you on such a journey? But once the question has surfaced he knows it must be tackled, not in any definitive sense but in order to do the spadework at least. Lewis realises that, having never considered moving on in the sense of emotional transference from Emma to someone else, he will have tackled the prospect of physical departure from Maunston Quay even less. It was never a consideration in relation to Jenny because the premise upon which the move would have been based was hopelessly flawed. But this is different. Anna's moving in with him is simple, natural, a logical step that is easy to execute. But what happens when they have filled the house, not just with themselves but with all their 'stuff'? There will be no simple options at that point.

Having done the damage by recognising the dilemma, the back of the wardrobe fails to offer any clues in terms of its solving, and so he stands, closes the door and makes his way back downstairs.

Planting himself in the centre of the lounge, he looks carefully around it, not attending to the things that are there but seeking out the gaps and spaces, the nooks and crannies, for where things might go. He tries to imagine Anna's things in those spaces in the same away as he has with her clothes upstairs, attempting to gauge the capacity of the cottage to take her in, and in doing so, to measure the extent of time they may have there together. For it is not space but time that is uppermost in his thoughts now.

He is assuming they will fit well together - the two of them and his cottage - like fingers in a glove, and if he had any doubts before (and he is sufficiently self-aware not to deny that he did), then these are now banished. It is, therefore, more a question of 'where next?'. Anna may suggest they return to the house she has left behind, though given the attachments it must hold for her, he cannot see that as anything but a last resort; indeed, she has already talked loosely of selling it. He has no alternative himself, having sold the house he and Emma shared years ago in order to fund the purchase of the cottage. So moving on again - and he has already convinced himself that at some point they must - morphs to become not only a question of time but suddenly one of distance too. It becomes a question of his relationship - no, their relationship - with Maunston Quay.

Thrown by something this complex - sideswiped by it almost - Lewis sits in his favourite chair and looks out toward the beach and the sea. It is a timely reminder of why he loves the cottage so much, and why he has become wedded to the place. Maunston Quay - the real Maunston Quay - is, for him, right here; it is this small stand of cottages, the incline up to Simon's Crag, the short flat beach, the dunes, and the pier itself that links everything to the sea. Beyond the railway line is Maunston Quay, the village represented by the name, but he realises that for him this is no more than an adjunct. If they managed to find a place near the green or a little further afield close to where Maisie lives, would that still feel like Maunston? He doubts it. And if the sand and the sea were paramount in this relationship, what would it be like if he found somewhere else - large enough for them both and their future - on a different stretch of the coastline? How would that feel? He tries to lift himself a few miles up or down the coast to where he knows there are similar stretches. "Can I imagine myself there?" he asks himself rhetorically, because he knows the answer already.

He catches himself up. "Can I imagine us there?" he asks again, chastising himself for the natural habit he has lived with for years and out of which he must now grow. "Us" he says to himself again, rolling the word around in his mind, allowing it to settle. And even though it is a usurper of sorts, it and the recalibration it must of necessity force upon him is more than welcome. "Can I imagine *us* there?" And he cannot, for in his mind it is not just he who is wedded to this strange little place. However much he might like to find the answer it is, he knows, a question that he cannot answer for both of them; indeed, he suspects he would struggle to answer it for himself alone. He will leave it then; park it somewhere safe, under wraps as it were, until it is time for it to be brought out into the light again.

Lewis smiles to himself. "Who am I kidding?!" he thinks, as certain as he can be that it will be Anna who will recognise the time has come and be first to broach the subject. "How do you feel about Maunston Quay?" she will ask one day, and he will be cast adrift once more.

❀ ❀ ❀

As the train approaches the station from the east, the driver sees the signal set to yellow before he takes the gentle curve to reveal the level crossing and the short platform beyond at whose far end the signal is set yellow too. With no instruction from the Guard to do otherwise, the train will ease through the gates and the station, and then pick up speed once more. Passing over the road at just twenty miles an hour, the driver looks out to the right. Beyond the road and the dunes he can make out the sea, the flash of a small and inconspicuous huddle of cottages, and the promontory beyond. The sign on the platform is as neatly painted as ever. In all his years on this route, he can recollect only stopping a handful of times since it became a request stop, and from where he sits now, staring ahead once more to check the signal is still in his favour, he wonders why they bother at all. Clicking the throttle up two notches to start gathering momentum, he tries to recall if his wife - a relatively local girl - has ever passed comment on the place, but he can recall none. In a few seconds the train is through. He imagines the crossing gates opening behind him and doubts anyone ever passes through them, after all where would they go?

Perhaps later this year, once the summer is in full swing, the train might stop just once or twice more than usual, a car held at the gates awaiting its passing. Of course he is mistaken in his general assumptions about Maunston Quay; assumptions born from prejudice and a lack of understanding or sympathy, perhaps. Mistaken because, although it is a small place - in some quarters only marginally worthy of the title of 'village' - it is one still capable of exciting and enclosing the same universal passions as larger towns and cities; the same hopes and dreams, anger and desire. Such is the persistent fate of people, wherever they may be. And he is mistaken because a year or two from now, there will be a few more people who choose to come to Maunston than before. Not that many to be fair, but more. And they will be drawn by the promise of a small and secluded beach, private boat trips - angling even! - and the local public house which has somehow managed to find itself a new chef who is beginning to make a name for himself. It is a place for him to nurture his dreams too.

There are rumours of a small car park to be built adjoining the station. Nothing grand, but, in spite of its modesty, sufficient to attract the odd passer-by or day-tripper. And when one of the houses on the outskirts of the village - previously occupied by a local librarian who has found love and moved away to Birmingham - is sold for a sum that will take away the breath of even the most hardened and sanguine local, a stir is created that leads to husbands and wives sharing meaningful glances across their morning Cornflakes and silently asking 'what if?'. It will never be as grand or as well-known as its near neighbours, but Maunston Quay will, eventually, find its way onto the map - even though it has always been there.

Stop there in a small number of years and you will see cars parked around the village green, see the village shop recently sold to a national chain and doing brisk business, and watch the curious tourists following the signs which point them to the local forge. Many will come away with something as a souvenir, perhaps having enjoyed an impromptu al fresco tea and homemade cake from the artisan's wife who seems happy and content, and gives the impression she has lived there all her life. The new vicar is friendly enough, but a trifle younger than you might have expected, recently drafted in after the sudden and tragic demise of the previous incumbent suddenly taken by cancer. If you listen to the stories, you would believe the whole place was in mourning for months after his passing.

Well, perhaps it might be so in a place such as this.

But then people tend not to come and go that much, do they? Even though the train - when it does stop - drops off and picks up visitors, you might be forgiven for thinking those who live there, who are part of the fabric, never move on. But question that in 'The Anchor' and the landlord will remind you of the librarian, and those who sold up soon after her to cash in on what they had seen as a windfall property market. If he mentions such things, his wife will remark somewhat ruefully that those who left had never really understood the place, for if they had they would never have left. At this point, she and the publican would exchange a look you would be unable to fathom, and so you will laugh, just to humour her, and move away to your table and await the chef's signature dish which you had seen lauded on-line. He too will be moving on soon enough, you might think - and in that particular case you will probably be right.

Although it would mean nothing to you - and thus it almost certainly would never be mentioned - a family called the Johnsons have begun to be seen on a regular basis, taking advantage of their little holiday let, one of the three cottages overlooking the beach. If you enquired - at the pub or the shop or the forge - you would be told that it is occupied almost year round now. If it were the old Boatman from next door who was telling you this, he might do so with something of a wistful and inscrutable look in his eye; but there is something about him which prevents you from enquiring further, not least because his somewhat bent gait and brusque manner scares the children. Catch him later in the pub, however, and he seems a different man, as if there were two of him, identical twins, one with the job of work and the other free to enjoy himself. It is amazing how someone so taciturn can become so jolly; at least that is what your wife might think, looking at him nervously over the top of her Niçoise salad.

And what of the third of the cottages, you might ask, the one closest to Simon's Crag? It is clearly locked up, and if you spent a day on the beach, you would see no-one coming or going. Yet stand at the window and peer in and it looks just as a cottage should; cosy and comfortable, filled with books and pictures, photographs and ornaments. It is a cottage that looks lived in and loved. Occasionally you might see the Smith's wife unlocking the front door and popping in, but she goes in and out empty handed, giving no clue as to the nature of her visit. Under certain circumstances - perhaps if you had been out on his boat during the day and had plied the old boatman with a pint or two in the evening - he might tell you of his neighbours. And if he did, he would do so with a fond smile. "Away," he might say. Or "travelling", if he was feeling expansive. It would be almost as if he had told you nothing at all - yet in the way he said it, and in the words he chose *not* to use, you might sense there was meaning interwoven there and a story worthy of the telling.

Acknowledgements

In producing a second edition of this book, I am indebted to my friend Tom Furniss for suggesting a number of revisions.

Cover image: A wooden jetty in fog over Brofjorden at Holländaröd, Sweden. Photograph taken on 12th March 2018 by W. Carter. The image is located on www.commons.wikimedia.org and has been released free of copyright.